MY

ON A FIELD OF THE DEAD . . .

Dan saw someone moving across the battlefield, carrying canteens, stopping here and there to give aid and solace. It was too dark to make out the features, but there was something about the figure that arrested Dan's attention. He gasped, and stared at the familiar way the man carried himself.

"Burke?" Dan called in a hesitant voice.

"My God, Dan, is that you?"

The two men moved toward each other, there in the dark, in the middle of the wounded and the dead, on a field of battle in which half a nation had tried, desperately, to kill the other half . . .

*St. Martin's Paperbacks Titles
by Robert Vaughan*

YESTERDAY'S REVEILLE
TEXAS GLORY
BLOOD ON THE PLAINS

BLOOD
on the
PLAINS

Robert Vaughan

St. Martin's Paperbacks

BLOOD ON THE PLAINS

Copyright © 1997 by Robert Vaughan.

All rights reserved. No part of this book may be used or reproduced in any manner whatsoever without written permission except in the case of brief quotations embodied in critical articles or reviews. For information address St. Martin's Press, 175 Fifth Avenue, New York, N.Y. 10010.

ISBN: 0-312-95872-2

Printed in the United States of America

St. Martin's Paperbacks edition/January 1997

10 9 8 7 6 5 4 3 2 1

$$\star\star\star$$

One

Emma Murphy carried a lighted candle into her bedroom. Her husband, Patrick, was snoring loudly. Their two sons, Timothy, fifteen, and Michael, fourteen, were asleep just down the hall. Mrs. Murphy's workday had begun early this morning before her family awoke, and it was just now ending, long after the rest of her family had gone to bed.

Still shy after sixteen years of marriage, Mrs. Murphy blew out the candle and used the cover of darkness as she got undressed and slipped into her nightgown. She climbed into bed beside Patrick, thankful that his body heat had already taken the early spring chill out of the bedsheets. Without waking, Patrick accommodated his body to his wife's presence, and within a few moments Mrs. Murphy's snores joined with the others of the household.

A group of horsemen, eerily illuminated by the flickering torches many of them were carrying, appeared on the crest of the hill that overlooked the Murphy farmstead. The leader of the group looked down on the little collection of neat buildings.

"Whose farm is this, Oliver?"

The rider by his side consulted a piece of paper he was carrying. "Patrick Murphy lives here, Pa. He's pro-slavery."

"Don't look like he's got any slaves, though," one of the other riders said.

"How do you know he doesn't have any?" the leader asked.

"Well, look around, Reverend Brown. Do you see any slaves' quarters?"

"Means nothing," John Brown replied gruffly. "He could be keeping slaves in the barn, or making them sleep out on the ground like animals. Concern for the comfort of their fellow creatures means nothing to people like him."

"Do you know Murphy, Pa?" Oliver asked.

"I don't need to know him. I know his kind," Brown snorted contemptuously.

John Brown was fifty-six, lean, sinewy, and ramrod straight. His face was hawklike, with a sharp nose and a pointed chin. His eyes were gunmetal gray, though tonight, in the flickering light of the torches, they were demonic red.

"Is everyone here?"

Oliver, one of the two sons who rode with him, stood in his stirrups and counted the horsemen who had come up to join them.

"We're all here, Pa."

"Very well, then, let's get to work. We've the Lord's business to tend to," John Brown ordered.

The night riders, who were known as Jayhawkers, rode quickly down the hill to the Murphy farm. Without any further specific directions, a couple of the riders broke away from the rest of the pack and headed toward the barn. One of them tossed a torch inside the barn, where it landed on dry hay. The other threw his torch up onto the dry-shake singles of the roof. Within moments the barn was on fire.

"Shall we bang on the door, Reverend?" one of the riders asked.

"Just have patience," John Brown replied, sitting still in his saddle. "They'll come running out soon enough, like maggots from under a rotting log."

For nearly two minutes John Brown, his sons, and twenty other Jayhawkers sat silently, staring at the house, their hate-twisted features glowing in the flickering flames of the burning barn.

As the popping, snapping fire grew in heat and intensity, the horses and cows trapped inside the barn realized their danger and began screaming in terror. The Jayhawkers patted the necks of their own mounts reassuringly, for their animals were very nervous at being that close to the blaze and had begun to prance about.

They waited.

Then, from inside the house, they heard a young voice call the alarm.

"Pa! Ma! Wake up! Wake up! The barn's on fire!"

Timothy's shouted alarm awakened Emma, and she poked her husband awake. When he opened his eyes, he didn't have to ask what was wrong, for by now the light from the burning barn lit up the bedroom as bright as day.

"What in the world! How did that happen? Emma, get the buckets! Timothy, Michael, turn out, boys! We've got to save the animals!"

The three Murphys dashed out through the front door in their long underwear, not bothering to take time to get dressed. They tumbled off the front porch, then were brought to an immediate stop by the sight of more than a score of men, backlighted by the burning barn and looking as if they were ghost riders from hell.

"What the . . . who are you?" Murphy asked.

"Are you Patrick Murphy?" John Brown thundered in a booming voice. He and several others dismounted.

"Yes."

"Mr. Murphy, you and your two sons have thirty seconds to make your peace with your Maker before we dispatch you to eternity."

"What?"

"Pa?" Michael asked, his fourteen-year-old voice breaking in fear.

"Hear the Word of the Lord!" John Brown said. "For thou hath done evil in the sight of the Lord thy God, provoking him to anger!"

Emma Murphy arrived on the front porch at that moment, carrying three buckets. When she saw the frightening array of men around her husband and sons, she knew that they were border ruffians, though she didn't know which side they represented or why they were here.

"Oh, my God!" she gasped, covering her mouth with her hand. The wooden buckets fell to the porch with a clatter.

"Hear these words from the Book of Deuteronomy," John Brown said.

"No, you hear *my* words, you son of a bitch! You did this, didn't you? You get the hell off my farm!" Murphy shouted in anger and fear.

Ignoring Murphy, John Brown began quoting Scripture. " 'I call upon heaven and earth to witness against you this day, that ye shall soon utterly perish from off the land; ye shall not prolong your days upon it, but shall be utterly destroyed!' "

Almost imperceptibly, John Brown nodded to one of his followers. "And I am the destroyer!" he concluded.

At Brown's signal, a man stepped forward out of the shadows and, using his sword, thrust Murphy through, then withdrew a bloody blade, which glistened in the light of the burning barn.

Gasping in surprise and pain, Murphy put his hands over the wound, as if by that action he could stem the flow of blood that spilled through his fingers.

"Patrick! No, my God! Patrick!" Emma cried. She jumped from the porch and ran toward him. The man who had stabbed Murphy raised his sword toward her, but John Brown held out his hand to stop him, then shook his head, forbidding her slaughter.

Emma sat on the ground beside her husband's prostrate body and cradled his head on her lap.

"Emma, get the boys and run," Patrick gasped, barely able to speak.

"No! I won't leave you!"

Murphy's two sons stood by in shock, watching their father bleed to death before their eyes. Then, suddenly and without warning, the two men closest to the boys brought the knife edge of their hatchets down on top of the boys' heads, splitting open their skulls like watermelons.

"No! God, no!" Emma screamed, more horrified now than before.

"Who are you, woman, to invoke God's name?" John Brown challenged. He pointed a long bony finger at Emma. "It is a sin against God and man to hold another human being in bondage!"

"What's the matter with you? Are you crazy? We have no slaves! Can't you see that? *We have no slaves!*"

"It doesn't matter whether you own slaves or not. You are known sympathizers to the abhorrent institution, and thus you are equally as guilty as would be he who owneth one hundred."

"Murderers! You are all murderers!" Emma screamed.

"Chief, what about the bodies?" one of the Jayhawkers asked.

John Brown looked at the two dead boys and the dying father.

"Chop them into small pieces and leave them for the hogs," he said disdainfully.

THREE WEEKS LATER, IN WESTERN MISSOURI

The wagon, pulled by a team of mules, lumbered slowly down the road. Horace Pugh was driving the wagon, with his wife, Fonnie, by his side. The wagon was heavily laden with large crates.

"You see those trees up there, Fonnie?" Horace asked, pointing to a prominent thicket of elm trees. "When we get there, we'll be in Kansas. We'll be safe."

Fonnie reached over to put her hand on his. "It truly seems strange, doesn't it?"

"What's that?"

"That here, on this side of the trees, men, women, and children can be held in bondage. While on that side they are free. The air we breathe is the same, the dirt beneath our feet is the same, God in heaven is the same, and yet here, men, women, and children can be held in bondage, while there, slavery is prohibited."

Fonnie turned and tapped on one of the crates. "Take heart, dear friends!" she called. "We are but a quarter of a mile away from Kansas and freedom!"

"Praise be to the Lawd!" a muffled voice replied from inside the crate.

"Fonnie, everyone, quiet! Bushwhackers!" Horace suddenly hissed loudly.

Turning back around in her seat, Fonnie saw what her husband was referring to, for coming toward them from the trees ahead were half a dozen horsemen. The bushwhackers rode toward the wagon at a gallop, then pulled to a stop in front of them. The leader was a small man, who was wearing a flat-brimmed hat adorned with a long sweeping purple feather.

"Who are you?" Horace asked.

"Russell Hinds, at your service," the leader said. "And who might you be?"

"I'm Horace Pugh. This is my wife, Fonnie."

Hinds took off his hat and rubbed the top of his head. " 'Tis a fine day for a ride," he said. "The sun is warm, the wildflowers are blooming."

"Yes," Horace agreed.

Hinds replaced his hat. "You and your missus goin' to Kansas, are you?"

"Yes."

"From the looks of your wagon, you'd be movin' there. Don't know why anyone would want to leave Missouri for the uncivilized wilds of Kansas. Why, that place is just full of Jayhawkers and Satan's angels. Satan's angels is what I calls abolitionists. If I had my way, I'd round up every abolitionist there is, and hang 'em by their scrawny necks until they was dead."

Fonnie moved closer to her husband, fear tightening her grip so that her fingers pressed painfully into his flesh.

"You're not wantin' to move to Kansas so's you can live with that kind, are you? Those angels of Satan?" Hinds put his hat back on.

"We aren't moving," Horace said quickly.

"Oh?" Hinds said. His eyes narrowed, and he nodded toward the boxes. "Then what you got in them boxes?"

Fonnie gasped aloud.

"Nothing," Horace said quickly. He reached over to pat his wife's hand reassuringly. "Just some old used furniture that we're taking into Kansas to sell, that's all."

"Well, maybe me and the boys here is in the market for some used furniture. Open up them boxes and let us have a look-see. No need to send good Missouri furniture over into Kansas. Why, that'd be like castin' pearls before swine."

The bushwhackers laughed.

"You wouldn't be interested, believe me," Horace said.

"Well now, Mr. Pugh, that's the whole point, you see. We *don't* believe you. I think you've got contraband nigras in them boxes, so I'm goin' to ask you to open 'em up.''

Horace shook his head. ''No. I know my rights. Not even a representative of the government can make me open those boxes without a proper warrant, and I have no intention of opening them for the likes of you. Now, if you and your men would just move out of the way, we'll continue our journey.''

Hinds pointed to the boxes, then looked over toward his men. ''Shoot 'em up, boys,'' he growled.

Laughing, the six men with him drew their revolvers and began firing, shot after shot, into the boxes.

''No!'' Fonnie screamed. ''No, stop! Please! Stop!''

Hinds jerked his hand down in a signal, and the men stopped firing. The echoes of the last few shots rolled back from the nearby hills.

Fonnie turned in her seat and, seeing blood coming from both boxes, cried out.

''God in heaven! What have you done?'' She climbed over the seat into the back of the wagon and began trying to open the boxes, sobbing as she did so.

''Fonnie! Fonnie, get back here!'' Horace called to her.

''Help me, Horace! Please help me! We have to tend to them!''

''Well now, lookee there,'' Hinds said with a wild giggle. ''That there furniture these folks is carryin' is bleedin'! Bet none of you boys ever seen furniture bleed before.''

Again the bushwhackers with him giggled.

With a resigned sigh Horace climbed over the seat to help his wife. Within a moment he had both crates open. Each crate held four escaping slaves, for a total of six adults and two children. Two of the men were already dead; the third was dying. Two of the women were badly wounded, as was one of the children. One of the women and one of the children, though shaken, were unhurt. All were silent, except for the unwounded child, who was crying in fear.

''How could you do this?'' Fonnie cried to Hinds. ''How can you call yourself a human being and so cruelly kill other human beings?''

''Don't blame us, lady,'' Hinds said. ''It's your husband's fault. He's the one told us there was nothin' in them boxes but furniture. Why, if'n we had know'd they was contraband in there, we wouldn't've shot 'em. We would've took 'em back for the reward. Hell, they sure ain't worth nothin' to us the way they are now."

Again Hinds nodded, and again his men opened fire. As Fonnie looked on, screaming, Hinds and his men shot and killed every one of the escaping slaves, including the two who had previously been unhurt.

When the last shot was fired, Hinds looked at Horace and Fonnie, who were still standing on the wagon, clutching each other in terror, looking down in horror at the murder victims. Hinds pointed his pistol at them and pulled back the hammer. Horace and Fonnie closed their eyes, waiting for the bullets to tear into their bodies.

They waited for a long moment.

"Well, ain't you goin' to beg me to let you live?" Hinds asked.

Shaking almost uncontrollably, Fonnie whimpered, but she said nothing.

"Beg. I might be merciful," Hinds suggested.

"No, by God," Horace said. "If you're going to shoot us, then shoot us and be damned! We'll not beg your wretched soul for our lives."

Hinds continued to point his pistol at them for a long moment before he finally eased the hammer back down and lowered the weapon. He giggled insanely.

"You know who I am? I am God. I can kill you or let you live . . . whichever I choose. And I choose to let you live. I want you to remember that it was you who caused these here nigras to die. And I want you to tell the rest of your abolitionist friends in the Underground Railroad what will happen if they try and smuggle any more slaves. And I want you to remember Russell Hinds."

"Oh, you need have no fear of that, Mr. Hinds," Horace growled. "I will not forget you."

"Did you hear that, boys? He won't forget me."

"We ought to kill 'em, Russell," one of the riders said.

"No," Hinds replied. "Let 'em live. I want 'em to take the message that Russell Hinds is upholdin' the laws of the state of Missouri."

Hinds nodded to the others, and after they rode away, Horace and Fonnie remained where they were for a long moment, still entwined in each other's arms. Fonnie's quiet sobbing could be heard over the drumming hoofbeats of the retreating horses.

In the distance, a crow called.

ON BOARD A TRAIN BETWEEN PHILADELPHIA AND WASHINGTON

Lieutenants Dan Morris and Burke Phillips were fast friends and had been so since their cadet days at West Point. Now they were responding to orders to proceed from Philadelphia to Washington, where they were to report to John Floyd, the secretary of war. The "where" and "when" of their orders were quite specific. It was the "why" of their orders that gave their journey an air of mystery.

During the train ride to Washington the two young officers made the acquaintance of several civilians who were also on the train. To while away the long hours of the trip, the officers and their new civilian friends gathered at the rear of one of the cars to drink, tell tall tales, and engage in various wagers.

Feeling the effects of the drink, one of the civilians, a man named Andrew Martin, made a two-dollar bet that he could exit the car through a window on the left side of the train and reenter the car through a window on the right. The others took him up on it, and once the pot was collected, Martin went out the window, climbed to the top of the car, crawled across the top, and was at this moment climbing down the opposite side of the car.

The boisterous laughing and conversation came to a complete stop as the adventurer worked to lift the window and climb back in. Even the other passengers in the car, those who weren't involved in the bet, turned in their seats and were watching anxiously as Martin hung precariously to the outside of the car.

The car hit a bad section of track, and it was jostled severely. Martin nearly fell but managed to hang on, thus preserving the bet, which included the provision that no one else could help him or even touch him. Once he was safely back inside, people crowded around him to offer their congratulations.

"You did it!"

"Well done!"

"Bet no one else can do that."

"I can do it," Burke Phillips offered. "Only I'll do it under the car," he added.

"What?" one of the civilians asked, not certain that he understood Burke's proposal.

"I will go out the same window Mr. Martin exited, and I will come back in the same window Mr. Martin entered, but I shall pass *under* the car rather than across the top."

"No one can do that," someone said. "That's a foolish bet, which you wouldn't make if you were sober."

"Drunk or sober, I can do it," Burke insisted in his North Carolina drawl.

"That, I would like to see," one of the others said.

"And you shall. You all shall," Burke said. "If you are willing to bet five dollars each to see it."

"Five dollars? Mr. Martin bet only two."

"Yes, but what I am going to do is harder than what Mr. Martin did."

"There are seven of us. Can you cover thirty-five dollars?"

"There are only six of you who will bet against him," Dan Morris said. "We, of the army, stick together. I shall be betting on Burke, and I will put up half the money."

"Lieutenant Morris, you are a true friend," Burke said.

Dan laughed. "No, Lieutenant Phillips, you are the friend. I put up half the money and I stand to make half the profit, but I don't have to take the risk."

"That's because you are a Yankee, sir, hailing from the staid old state of Vermont, known for producing pragmatic sons." Burke hiccuped halfway through his speech. "Whereas I, on the other hand, am from North Carolina, and our people have always been gamblers and risk takers."

"You're from the North," one of the men said, pointing to Dan; then to Burke: "And you're from the South. But you are friends?"

"We are more like brothers than mere friends," Dan insisted.

"If you really are a friend, you won't let him go through with this ridiculous bet."

"It is obvious, sir, that you do not understand the meaning of true friendship," Dan replied. He finished his own drink, then set down the cup. "For were I to attempt to stop him it would be an insult to his honor. And to a gentleman of the South, honor is everything."

"Why don't we quit talking about it and see if the brave soldier boy here can do it?" Martin suggested, a little piqued that his own moment of glory was so short-lived.

"Here, hold my drink," Burke said as he started for the window. "Don't spill any of it. Wait, I may as well finish it so you can't spill anything."

Burke tossed down the rest of the whiskey, then, smiling, snaked headfirst through the window, holding himself from falling to the track bed by spreading his legs against the window frame.

Everyone rushed to the left side of the car to look out as Burke dangled, head down. At thirty-five miles per hour, the track ballast was flashing by only inches below his head, so fast as to be a blur.

The first trick was to be able to find some way to allow him to get under the car. Burke worked on it for several minutes, all the while precariously close to falling. Finally he managed to secure a hold in the sculpted side paneling of the car, thus allowing him to lower his body and extend it parallel with the track. He held himself that way for a long moment, until he was able to swing himself to a position of purchase in the underframe of the car. Shortly after that, he disappeared from view.

"He's gone!"

"He fell!"

Quickly Dan thrust his own head and shoulders through the window and looked back along the cars toward the end of the train. He could see the track unwinding behind them, and he could see, too, that Burke's body wasn't there, as it surely would have been if he had fallen.

"No, he's still down there," Dan said.

"Well, he'd better stay there for a few minutes," one of the other passengers said.

"Why is that?" Dan asked.

"We'll be coming to the Risco Bridge shortly," the passenger answered. "The bridge trusses are so close to the track that no one can cling to the side of a car. If your friend is trying to come up at that precise moment, he'll get raked off.''

"Why didn't you tell him that?'' Dan asked. "There's no way he'll be able to see a bridge coming from beneath the car!''

"He was the one making the bet. I figured he knew what he was doing.''

"I've got to warn him!'' Dan said.

"How are you going to do that?''

"There's only one way.'' Dan started toward the window. "I have to go down there with him!''

"Remember, if you touch him, the bet is off!'' Martin called to him.

"I won't touch him.''

"How will we know what's going on, when you're both down there?''

"You could accept our word as officers and gentlemen,'' Dan said. He paused and smiled, then added, "Or, you could come down there to keep an eye on us.''

"No, that's all right,'' Martin replied quickly. "You are both officers and gentlemen. We trust you.''

"I thought you might,'' Dan said just before he went out the window.

It wasn't as hard for Dan to get underneath the train as it had been for Burke, because Dan had watched Burke explore until he'd found a way to do it. Now Dan duplicated Burke's method, so that less than a minute after he went out the window, Dan was beneath the car.

The noise underneath was deafening. The wheels were roaring, steel on steel, the car was groaning and creaking with every twist, and the wind was blowing a gale.

"Burke! Burke!''

Burke, who had already reached the other side of the car, was just beginning to start his climb up.

"Dan! What the hell are you doing here?''

"Wait! Don't go up yet! There's a bridge. . . .''

Suddenly the train plunged in between the heavy support timbers. Had Dan's warning come a second later, Burke's head would have smashed into the first timber. So close to each side of the car was the bridge that the concussive effect of its passing beat upon them like the pounding of timpani.

Dan and Burke hung on to the tie rods and underframe beneath the car until the train cleared the bridge. Burke looked back at Dan. "Thanks for the warning," he said, smiling at his friend. "Guess we'd better get back inside now."

Dan watched until first Burke's legs and then his feet disappeared. Then Dan moved across the bottom of the car and stuck his head out the other side. The first thing he did was look forward to make certain there were no more obstructions. Then he looked up just as Burke was crawling in through the window.

"Well, at least one of us made it," Dan growled as he started his own climb back into the car. After he was completely out from underneath, and hanging on to the side of the car, the train entered a very sharp curve to the left. This created a strong centrifugal effect to act against Dan, and only a last desperate grab at the bottom of the window kept him from being completely thrown off the side of the car. For a long moment Dan supported himself with one hand.

Several windows on his side of the car opened as anxious passengers leaned out to get a firsthand look at Dan's ordeal. Burke, now safely inside, leaned out the same window from which Dan was hanging.

"Come on, Dan, you can do it."

"Give me a hand!" Dan shouted up to him.

Burke shook his head. "Can't do it. If I touch you, the bet's off."

"Your bet has nothing to do with me! And you're already inside! Now give me a hand, damn you!"

By now Burke had another drink in his hand, and he took a swallow before he answered. Again he shook his head.

"Figured since you were down there anyway, we may as well get something for it, so I made the bet double or nothing that you could do it, too. Now quit fooling around and come on in here!"

Straining, and slapping at the window, Dan finally managed to get a hold with his other hand. Then, with his grip improved, he started feeling along the side of the car with his feet until his toes found an indentation in the sculpting. Using both hands and kicking upward, he managed to propel himself through the open window, doing so with such force that he wound up facedown on the floor of the car.

The passengers in the car who had not lost money on Dan's effort cheered mightily, and several came over to help him to his feet.

"Here you are, Lieutenant!" one of them said, thrusting a fresh drink into Dan's hand. "You earned yourself a drink! That was quite a show you and your friend put on for us."

Dan looked over at Burke, who was smiling and triumphantly waving a fistful of money at him. Dan couldn't hold on to his anger, and despite himself, he laughed.

"Yes," he said. "After we get out of the army, I think my friend and I are going to go to work for P. T. Barnum."

"Washin'ton! We're comin' into Washin'ton!" the conductor called, passing through the car at that moment. He was a little surprised to see so many people standing toward the rear of the car.

"You folks might want to take your seats, now," the conductor chastised. "When the train starts slowin', it's liable to jerk you off your feet. Wouldn't want none of you to get hurt."

"Let's do sit down, Dan," Burke said. "Trains can be dangerous things, you know."

The laughter that greeted Burke's comment surprised the conductor, and his face mirrored his curiosity, but as he had work to do, he asked no questions.

★★★

Two

CLAY COUNTY, MISSOURI

What pleasant days I have spent here, in this place. There have been many bright, sunny days, with the house filled by guests of my father, buggy rides, walks, dances, happy, kind voices coming from laughing lips, and bright eyes sparkling with pleasure.

But now the place is filled with grief; long days and nights of heartbreak so painful that even God seems too distant to be reached by prayer.

My father is dead.

For the last several days people have gathered in the house, here to "comfort" me, not realizing in their comforting words that I was feeling only a greater pain.

"He was such a good man," they say, using the word "was" in a way that brings home to me the fact that he is no more.

"You poor dear, you are an orphan now." They remind me of this, though in fact I was half an orphan for all my life, my mother having died while giving me birth.

But I held up during the ordeal of the funeral. With Thelma's help, I served tea and cakes and gave such an outward show of calm that no one would have guessed what pain I was actually suffering.

How well my father was on Saturday, when, as I entered his room for the first time that day, he smiled and asked: "How is my beautiful daughter today?"

He talked with everyone in a cheerful and joyful

way, and little did anyone think that, before the morrow, he would be dead.

But, dead he is, and I no longer wish to stay in this house, happy though the memories of this place may be. Instead I feel that it is much better for me to apply myself to accomplishing the task that lies before me, and for that, it is necessary that I move into town. My reward for this will, I am sure, be twofold. It will help me to more quickly accommodate myself to the loss of my father, and it is work that I believe will be pleasing in God's eyes.

Entered in my diary this 15th day of May, in the Year of Our Lord 1859, by Catherine Darrow.

All morning long the buckboard, pulled by a team of matched grays, had rolled up and down the streets and avenues of Independence, Missouri, seeking out houses that were for sale or rent. Emil Cotter, a local real estate broker, was driving the buckboard. Riding in the seat beside him was Catherine Darrow, a beautiful twenty-three-year-old woman with dark hair and amber brown eyes.

Sitting on the flatbed, facing the rear, an ebony man and a cinnamon-colored woman, both in their thirties, watched the street unroll behind them.

"Ever'one was just real sorry to hear about your pa passin' like he did," Cotter said to Catherine. "Professor Darrow was a wonderful man."

"Yes, thank you," Catherine said. "I shall miss him terribly."

"But we feel you done the right thing, sellin' the farm like you did, and decidin' to move into town. A farm is no place for a woman livin' alone."

"My father was the farmer of the family," Catherine said. "And I know I would be unable to do credit to the farm should I attempt to run it. But my father was also an educator, and that, I can do."

"As a member of the school board I was very happy to recommend that we hire you, full-time, as a teacher. And of course there is the added bonus of my being able to do business with you by selling you a house. Speaking of which, this here is the Welsh home you asked to see."

Cotter stopped the buckboard to point out the house, a large, two-story brick home.

"Oh, it's lovely," Catherine said.

"I'll show it to you, but as I said before, I don't think it is at all suitable for you."

"Oh, why not?"

"It has no place for your coloreds."

"Surely you are mistaken. It appears to be quite a large house. There will be plenty of room for them. And I was told it has a cellar. I want a cellar."

"A cellar? Yes, it has a cellar. But what use have you for a cellar?"

"I plan to have a garden, and I intend to can all my fruits and vegetables. I shall need a place for storage."

"But the Allen home, as you may recall, had a pantry, which would serve that need quite well."

Catherine shook her head. "No. My father always insisted that a cellar helped to preserve the freshness of canned foods."

Cotter got down, then walked around to help Catherine. "Well, this house does have a cellar, but I'm sure it is much too dank and dirty for you to examine now."

"It isn't necessary that I examine it. Willie will check it out for me, won't you, Willie?"

"Yes'm, I'se be powerful glad to go down inter dat hole and have a look," Willie said, hopping down from the back of the buckboard and starting toward the house.

"Miz Catherine, if'n it be all right with you, I'se g'wine go with my man and have a look, too."

"Of course it's fine with me, Thelma. After all, if I buy the house, we're all going to live here, and you'll be helping me with the canning."

"Yes'm, I 'specs so," Thelma said.

Willie and Thelma opened the cellar door, then walked down the steps to have a look around, while Cotter took Catherine through the front door to show her the house. Downstairs the house consisted of a huge front room, a slightly less spacious dining room, a small kitchen, and a tiny pantry. Upstairs there was a landing and six bedrooms.

"It's perfect," Catherine said when they came back down the stairs. "If the cellar meets with Willie's approval, I'll buy the house."

Cotter looked at her in surprise. "Do you mean to tell me that you would buy or pass upon this house based purely upon the opinion of your slave?" he asked in disbelief.

"Of course I would. Why shouldn't I? I trust Willie completely."

"Someone told me that your two slaves are married. I mean, actually married."

"They are married."

"By a preacher, and with a license and everything?"

"It's all legal," Catherine said.

Cotter shook his head. "You know, Miss Darrow, that's not very good policy."

"Oh? Do you think it would be better if they lived in sin?"

"I don't figure the Lord looks at colored folks livin' together without bein' married as any more of a sin than a couple of animals livin' together."

"Well, I don't see it that way, Mr. Cotter. And neither did my father, for Willie and Thelma were married while he was still alive."

"Suppose you let a couple of your slaves get married and you decide you'd like to sell them. But suppose one buyer needs a good field hand, while another wants a housemaid, so they are split up when they sell. Bein' married like that, they ain't goin' to want to split up. That can cause trouble."

"Oh, I would never sell Willie or Thelma. Why, that would be like selling a brother and a sister. They are family."

"That's another thing, Miss Darrow. Perhaps it isn't any of my business, but I feel I should caution you about how you treat your slaves. These are troubled times, and anyone who . . ." Cotter paused for a moment, as if looking for the correct word, then he continued, "Who 'mollycoddles' their slaves is quite apt to be looked upon as an abolitionist. Now, you certainly don't want your neighbors to think of you as an abolitionist, do you?"

"Quite frankly, I don't care what my neighbors think of me. And as to how I treat my slaves, why, that's nobody's business but my own. Not even yours, Mr. Cotter," she added with a disarming smile.

"No, I . . . I suppose not," Cotter mumbled, duly chastised by Catherine's retort.

Outside, Willie knocked on the door.

"Come on in, Willie," Catherine called pleasantly.

" 'Scuse me, Miz Catherine, Mist' Cotter. Beg pardon for intrudin'," Willie said deferentially, holding his hat and looking down as he came into the house. Thelma, projecting as much servility, shuffled into the house behind him.

"You aren't intruding at all. So, what do you think? Will the cellar serve our needs?"

"Yes'm, I 'specs it'll do just fine."

Catherine looked over at Cotter. "I'll take the house, Mr. Cotter."

"Are you sure you want to do this, Miss Darrow? There are a couple more houses that you haven't seen yet, either one of which, I believe, would be much more appropriate."

"This house, Mr. Cotter, I want this house. Please prepare the paperwork."

"Very well, I'll have the deed ready tomorrow. If you'd like, I'll give you a ride back to the boardinghouse now."

"Thank you, but I believe we'll stay and look around for a while so I can get an idea of how much work needs to be done."

"How will you get back to the boardinghouse?"

"I shall send Willie to the stable to rent a rig for me. I'll get along fine, please don't worry. And now, Willie, would you see Mr. Cotter to the door?"

"Yes'm. Mist' Cotter, the do' be right over here," Willie said.

"I know where the door is, you black fool," Cotter replied sharply.

"Yes, suh. I'se jes' tryin' to be helpful, is all," Willie said, reacting stoically to Cotter's sharp reply.

Cotter looked at Catherine. "For the life of me, I cannot understand why you would want this particular house, when there are so many other houses that are nicer and more suitable. But if you insist upon this one, I will have the papers ready for you tomorrow. Good day to you, Miss Darrow." He touched the brim of his hat.

"Good day," Catherine replied.

Catherine, Willie, and Thelma waited until the buckboard

was rolling away. Then, when they were completely alone, Willie spoke again.

"The cellar is absolutely perfect for our needs, Miss Catherine," he said. Gone were the slow drawl and shuffling demeanor.

"You agree, Thelma?"

"Oh, yes. There is enough room for individual quarters and a small, but functional hospital," Thelma added. She, too, had lost the heavy dialect.

"Willie, how long do you think it will take us to get it ready?"

"To put in a false wall and some storage shelves, I'd say four or five days. A week at most."

Catherine smiled. "All right, I'll put the word out. We'll be ready within a week."

"You be very careful, Miss Catherine," Thelma cautioned. "It could be dangerous for you."

"I'm more worried about you," Catherine replied. "What if people find out that you both have papers of manumission and are merely playing the role of my slaves? I wouldn't blame you one bit if you both left now."

"We aren't going anywhere," Willie said. "Your father gave us an education, and you gave us our freedom. Now we want to give something back, and what better way to do it than to help you?"

Catherine smiled. "No one ever had dearer friends, or more capable partners. I'm glad you are going to stay with me, for I don't know how I could do it without you."

THE WILLARD HOTEL, WASHINGTON, D.C.

The lobby was high ceilinged and crowded with guests who managed to fill nearly all of the many dark, wine-colored armchairs. The floor was liberally dotted with brass spittoons, kept shining by the half a dozen black porters who stood by, waiting to tend to the slightest need of any of the hotel guests. At either end of the lobby, coal-burning stoves pushed back the early morning spring chill.

Dan and Burke, who were sharing a room on the fourth floor, came down to the lobby together and walked over to the marble counter at the check-in desk. The hotel clerk was examining the registration book, comparing the entries with those of guests who had already checked out. When he looked up he saw, standing across the counter from him, two officers in dress blue uniforms, complete with scarlet sash and ceremonial saber.

"Yes, gentlemen, you are checking out?" the clerk asked.

"No," Dan replied. "My friend and I have an appointment with the secretary of war at ten o'clock this morning. It is our understanding that the War Department will be sending transportation for us."

"And you would like to be notified when it arrives?" the clerk said.

"Yes, if you don't mind," Dan said.

"We'll be having breakfast," Burke added.

"Very good, gentlemen. Please enjoy your breakfast. I'll take care of everything."

Dan and Burke went into the dining room, where they were shown to a table and handed menus.

"Pickled herring, shad roe, cream of wheat," Burke grumbled as he perused the menu. "You would think that, coming back south, I might be able to get a decent breakfast of ham and eggs and grits."

"Would you like ham, eggs, and grits, sir?" the waiter asked.

"Yes, do you have it? I don't see it on the menu."

"I'll take care of it," the waiter promised.

"You're a good man," Burke said, folding his menu and laying it aside.

Dan ordered pickled herring and scrambled eggs.

"What do you think the secretary of war wants with us?" Burke asked when the waiter left.

"Clearly, we are to get a new assignment," Dan answered. He smiled. "It may even mean a promotion."

"I hope so," Burke replied. "And I hope we stay together."

"Oh, I'm certain that we will. Otherwise we wouldn't have both been summoned on the same set of orders."

To the surprise of the two young officers, the carriage, driven by an army private, stopped not in front of the War Department building, but in front of the White House.

"Private," Dan said, leaning forward, "there has been some mistake here. We aren't in Washington City to see the sights. We are here to meet with Mr. John Floyd, secretary of war."

"Sir, my instructions were to deliver you to the White House," the private answered.

A rather large colonel with a full beard stepped toward the carriage. "Lieutenants Morris and Phillips?"

"Yes, sir," Burke answered for both of them.

"This way, please, gentlemen. The president is waiting for you."

Dan and Burke looked at each other in surprise.

"The president?" Dan asked.

"Of the United States?" Burke added.

"President Buchanan, yes. Quickly, gentlemen, one should never keep the president waiting."

The colonel led Dan and Burke in through the portico and down the hall to an oval-shaped sitting room filled with chairs and a couple of sofas. They recognized the president immediately, from the photographs and drawings they had seen of him. Smiling, he came toward them with his hand extended.

"Greetings, gentlemen, thank you for answering Secretary Floyd's invitation to meet with me."

Dan and Burke looked at each other, then chuckled.

"What is it?" the president asked.

"Sir, although we would have proudly answered an 'invitation,' official army orders do carry a little more weight."

President Buchanan laughed out loud. "Yes, well, I hadn't thought of it like that, but I suppose you are right, aren't you? You really didn't have any choice. You had to come when summoned." He extended his hand toward a nearby sofa. "Nevertheless, I am glad you are here. Please, have a seat, gentlemen."

"After you, Mr. President," Burke replied.

Buchanan sat in a chair across from the sofa, then Dan and Burke sat.

"I know you are wondering what business the president of the United States could have with a couple of army lieutenants," Buchanan began, "and I'll get to that in a minute.

But first, I want to know a little something about each of you."

"What would you like to know, sir?" Dan asked.

The president studied Dan for a moment before he spoke. "Let's see, you are the taller of the two . . . dark hair and eyes, you must be Lieutenant Dan Morris," Buchanan said.

Dan nodded affirmatively.

"You are from St. Albans, Vermont, your father publishes a newspaper there, you were an excellent student in school and an accomplished musician. In fact, I believe your mother wanted you to become a professional musician, but you chose to attend West Point instead."

Dan nodded. "Your information is remarkably accurate, Mr. President. I don't think I would have anything to add."

"There is, however, one very important thing my information doesn't give me," President Buchanan said.

"What is that, sir?"

"I would like to know your position on slavery."

Dan blinked, then cleared his throat. "Sir, I, uh, consider that to be a political question, and as a military man I . . ."

Buchanan held up his hand to stop Dan. "I realize I am asking a lot of you," he said. "And if you do not wish to share that with me, I will not insist that you do so. You can take the next train back to Philadelphia and no one will be the wiser for our conversation. However, if you intend to take the assignment I have for you, it is vital that I know, exactly, where you stand on the slavery issue. And please be very candid. Honesty is important."

"All right, Mr. President, I'll be as honest as I can," Dan said. "I am from New England, and therefore find slavery abhorrent. I believe that slavery must, as it eventually will, be eliminated. I can appreciate the fact, however, that it is an institution that has been some two hundred years in the building and that its sudden dismantlement would wreck the economy of half our nation. Therefore, I believe that reasonable men must find a reasonable solution to the problem by compensating the slave owners for their investment or, at the very least, provide a system whereby the slaves, by the sweat of their own brow, can earn their freedom."

"Thank you, Lieutenant Morris." Buchanan turned to Burke. "Your physical description fits you as well, Lieutenant Phillips. I was told you are about five feet seven inches tall, with a muscular build, sandy hair, and gray eyes. I am quite certain I could've picked you out of a crowd.''

''I'm five feet eight inches tall,'' Burke said resolutely.

Buchanan chuckled. ''Yes, well, the president has no wish to deprive one of his officers of an inch. Five eight it shall be. You are from Fayetteville, North Carolina. Your father is a judge, you are an excellent horseman, considered by many to be the finest horseman in the county.''

''If you'll excuse a bit of vanity, Mr. President, it's not just the county. I consider myself as good as any in the state.''

''And I've no reason to doubt you, Lieutenant,'' Buchanan said. ''Like Lieutenant Morris, you attended West Point, where you had a brilliant academic record. And now, Lieutenant, I must ask you the same question I asked Lieutenant Morris. It is your choice as to whether or not you will answer. But if you do, I must have an honest answer.''

Burke paused for a moment. ''Very well, sir, but I don't think you are going to like what you hear.''

''Please, Lieutenant, the truth,'' Buchanan insisted.

''Even though my family owns no slaves, I am a product of the culture of North Carolina. I know the necessity of maintaining a *perpetual* source of inexpensive and manageable labor. And, I believe that slavery is both ordained and approved of by God, for slaves are mentioned throughout the Bible. Slavery is as old as mankind itself, and it is not, as an institution, inherently evil. It is by the caprice of God that one is born free or born slave, just as one may be born a king or born a pauper. Our peculiar brand of slavery is the most benevolent that has ever existed, for we recognize the spiritual as well as the physical needs of the men and women who are indentured. That is all that is required in the eyes of God.

''I will admit that there are some evil slave owners, just as there are evil men everywhere. But the solution is to eliminate from the institution those who are evil, not to eliminate the institution itself.''

''Thank you, Lieutenant, for your frankness,'' President Buchanan said. ''You two men are from opposite regions of the country, and hold opposite beliefs on the question of slavery, yet you remain very good friends.''

"We are friends, yes, sir,'' Dan said.

"In fact, you are such good friends,'' Buchanan continued, ''that you, Lieutenant Morris, risked your life to crawl under the car of a train in motion, to warn Lieutenant Phillips of the danger of an approaching bridge.''

Dan's and Burke's faces registered shock.

"You *know* about that?'' Dan asked. ''But how could you? It just happened.''

"There was someone in the car watching you, the whole time. His mission was to observe the two of you, then report to me.''

"And what did his report tell you?'' Burke asked. ''Other than what you have already shared with us.''

"It told me that you are both men of courage and daring, and it convinced me that you are perfect for the mission I have in mind for you.''

"Mr. President, that is the second time you have alluded to some sort of mission, but you have omitted telling us what it is,'' Dan said.

"It is not a mere omission. It is by design that I have told you nothing, for your mission is, and must remain, a very closely guarded secret. I can't tell anyone . . . even you, until you agree to undertake it.''

"But how can we agree to take the assignment if we don't know what it is?'' Burke asked.

"You will have to take it on trust,'' Buchanan said.

"What do you think, Dan?'' Burke asked.

Dan shrugged. ''Well,'' he said, ''if you can't trust the president of the United States, who can you trust?''

"You have a point,'' Burke replied. ''All right, Mr. President, we'll take the assignment. Whatever it is.''

"Gentlemen, I thank you, and your country thanks you,'' Buchanan said. ''Now, have you heard, or read, anything about the border war that is going on between Missouri and Kansas?''

Dan nodded. ''Bloody Kansas, yes, I've seen stories in the newspapers.''

"Not just Kansas, but Missouri as well. The incidents on the border have been atrocious, on both sides. Pro-slavery partisans have attacked and murdered abolitionists, abolitionists have murdered pro-slavery partisans. With wholesale arson and looting, the depredations have gone unchecked. I fear, gentlemen, that this may very well be a precursor of what our entire nation will face if the problems that divide us as a people are not resolved.''

"A frightening prospect," Dan said.

"Yes, it is. But, there is also hope. You two prove that. By your own candid statements, you hold diametrically opposite positions on the question of slavery, but you are fast friends."

"Mr. President, you spoke of a mission for us," Burke said. "Other than the fact that we are able to get along with each other, what part do we play in all this?"

"I want the two of you to proceed to the Missouri–Kansas border. Separately," he added. "I don't want anyone out there to know that you are friends, or even that you know each other. You will pass yourselves off as civilians. Lieutenant Morris, I want you to ally yourself with the most active abolitionists in Kansas. Join the group. If possible, exert some ameliorating influence over their activities. And if that isn't possible, then keep us informed of what is going on."

"How do I do that, sir? Keep you informed, I mean?"

"You will be provided with the name of a federal marshal who can be trusted, and who will transmit your reports back." President Buchanan looked over at Burke. "Lieutenant Phillips, I should like you to go to Missouri to join one of the active pro-slavery groups. You, also, will report on their plans and operations."

"To the same U.S. marshal?" Burke asked.

Buchanan shook his head. "No, as you will be in Missouri, you will have your own marshal to report to. The federal marshal you report to will know nothing of Lieutenant Morris, and, of course, the marshal he reports to will know nothing of you. I shouldn't have to remind you gentlemen that under no circumstances are the two of you ever to have contact with each other."

"Mr. President, if I know my geography, that area isn't too crowded. How are we to avoid incidental contact?" Dan asked.

Buchanan stroked his chin, then nodded. "You're right. There may be no way to avoid incidental contact. But keep it incidental. Are there any more questions?''

"Just one, Mr. President," Burke said.

"And what would that be?''

"How soon do we start?''

"I like your attitude, Mr. Phillips. Get yourself outfitted with some civilian clothes today. You will start west on this evening's train. Mr. Morris, your train will leave the Baltimore and Ohio station at six A.M. tomorrow morning. Godspeed, gentlemen, and God bless the United States of America.''

"God bless the United States of America," Dan and Burke replied as one.

THAT EVENING

As the two men, dressed now in mufti, walked toward the waiting train, Dan Morris tugged at his sleeves while Burke Phillips pulled at his collar. They were uncomfortable in civilian clothes, which was understandable, as they had worn nothing but uniforms for the previous six years: four years as cadets at West Point and two years as active officers in the United States Army.

They were in the train shed of the Baltimore & Ohio depot, which echoed with the sounds of bells and heavy, rolling wheels. Half a dozen trains, busily attending to their schedules, arrived or exited on the network of tracks. Smells of wood smoke and steam commingled with aromas of sausages and other foods from the many vendors who moved through the crowded platform, peddling sack lunches to the departing passengers.

The engine already had its steam up, and as the relief valves opened and closed, it sighed and hissed as if it were breathing. Many of its passengers were already on board and could be seen through the lighted windows, moving up and down the aisles of the cars, looking for their seats.

"Well, I guess this is good-bye," Dan said.

"Yes, but not for long. You'll be coming after me tomorrow morning," Burke reminded him.

"I know. But after this, we can't acknowledge each other, even if we meet again," Dan said.

Burke smiled. "Now, how shall it be possible that I

would see your face without passing some remark?''

''A remark of nonsense, no doubt,'' Dan growled.

Burke laughed. ''To be sure, for what sense can be made of one who is as ugly as you?''

That was in itself a joke, for Burke well knew that women found Dan very handsome.

''Seriously, Burke, you know that from henceforth we must remain strangers.''

''Yes, I know. Dan, I hope all this business doesn't . . .'' Burke let the words hang, the sentence unfinished.

''I understand what you are trying to say,'' Dan said. He took Burke's hand in his. ''Suppose we swear a solemn oath between us now, that regardless of what happens out there, you and I will always be friends.''

''Always,'' Burke said, taking Dan's hand.

''All aboard!'' the conductor called.

''Don't miss your train,'' Dan said.

''Don't miss my train,'' Burke repeated. He chuckled as he started toward the mounting step. ''Now, how will I ever make it without your constant supervision?''

Dan watched Burke board the train, then find a seat. He waited for Burke to turn and wave good-bye, but almost immediately thereafter, a pretty woman got on the train, and through the window, Dan could see Burke turning his attention to her.

Dan chuckled, then turned and walked away just as the train started to pull out of the station.

★★★

Three

Dan Morris thought that the first part of his mission, locating and joining one of the active abolitionist groups, would be easy. That wasn't the case, however, for the group he most wanted to join, that headed by John Brown, seemed to be quite elusive. Every time he would think he had a lead, the lead would evaporate, as had, for that matter, John Brown himself. He was beginning to believe that Brown had left the country entirely.

Dan's biggest problem seemed to lie in being accepted as a member of the community. Although nearly everyone in Kansas was a newcomer, Dan was the newest of the new, and thus it was important that he establish himself. This he was able to do, through his skill as an armorer. He took a job with an Olathe, Kansas, gunsmith; this provided him with a visible source of income while enabling him to keep an eye on the flow of guns into the territory.

Dan had just finished repairing a trigger spring when the little bell on the front door rang, signaling that someone was coming into the store. Taking off his work apron, he walked out front to greet the customer. The customer was Hank Byrd, a man whom Dan strongly suspected had ties with John Brown.

"Good morning, Mr. Byrd," Dan said. "What can I do for you?"

"Good morning," Byrd replied. "I'm looking for Ben. Is he in?"

Ben was Benjamin Agee, the store owner.

"I'm afraid not. Mrs. Agee was feeling poorly this morning, so Mr. Agee went home to tend to her. Perhaps I can help.''

"No," Byrd said. "I have some business to discuss, some orders to place, but I think it would be better if I spoke with Ben.''

"I'm certain I could take your order, Mr. Byrd.''

Byrd shook his head. "No, I don't think Reverend Brown wants me to discuss it with anyone but Ben.''

Dan looked up quickly. "Reverend Brown? That would be John Brown?''

Byrd's eyes narrowed suspiciously. "What business be it of yours whether the Reverend Brown I'm talking about is John Brown?''

"It's no business at all," Dan replied. "I've heard the name, but I've never met him.''

"It could be that he's some particular about who he lets meet him," Byrd said.

Dan backed away quickly, so as not to frighten away this potential source of contact. "Well, if I can't help you, Mr. Byrd, I have some work to do in the back of the store.''

Dan had started toward the rear of the shop when, from out on the street, he heard the loud pop of a bullwhip, followed by a cry of pain.

"What's going on out there?" he asked, coming back to the window.

Looking across the street from the gunshop, he saw a black man cringing against the side of the livery barn, while a large, powerfully built white man used his whip against him. Several townspeople were standing around, watching.

The whip whistled out again and popped loudly, and there followed another cry of pain.

"He's going to kill that poor man," Dan said. "Where's the sheriff?''

"You aren't going to get the sheriff to do anything," Byrd said. "The fella with the whip is Angus Malloy.''

Dan looked around at Byrd. "Angus Malloy. Is that name supposed to mean something to me?''

"You've heard of Russell Hinds, the bushwhacker? Folks say he takes his orders from Angus Malloy.''

"And does our sheriff also take his orders from Malloy?''

"No, our sheriff is afraid of him. But if the chief was

here, he would stop it," Byrd insisted. "He'd stop it in a minute."

"The chief?"

"John Brown."

"John Brown," Dan said, scoffing. "As far as I know, there is no such person as John Brown."

The whip whistled and popped again, and again the victim of the whipping cried out in pain.

Dan started out the door.

"Where are you going?"

"I'm going to stop that whipping."

"I'd be careful if I were you. Angus Malloy is not the kind of man you want to anger."

"Neither am I," Dan called back over his shoulder.

Out in the street, Dan could hear Malloy talking.

"You know what I'm going to do to you, Julius?" Malloy was saying in an angry hiss. "I'm going to strip the hide off your back, then I'm going to nail you to my front gate so anyone else who has a notion of freedom can see what it gets 'em."

Malloy threw the whip back over his shoulder, preparing to use it again. The black rawhide strap of the whip snaked into the dirt in front of Dan, and Dan stepped on it just as Malloy tried to whip it back around. The sudden and unexpected resistance to the strap of his whip caused Malloy to jerk around angrily.

"Mister, you get the hell off my whip!" Malloy growled menacingly.

"I've got a better idea," Dan replied. He raised his pistol and pointed it toward Malloy. "You get the hell out of town."

Dan was playing a dangerous game, he knew, but so far he had been unsuccessful in his attempts to establish contact with any of the Jayhawkers. It was his hope that the risk he was taking now would pay off.

"Mister, do you know who I am?" Malloy asked.

"Yeah, I know who you are. You are the low-life, bush-whacking bastard who calls himself Angus Malloy," Dan said quietly, his voice somehow making the words sound even more ominous than if they had been shouted.

Dan heard the townspeople gasp in surprise. Malloy glared at him for a long moment, his temples throbbing in anger. Then he smiled evilly and glanced back toward the black man sagging against the barn, the shoulders and back of his shirt red with his own blood.

"I reckon we'd better go, Julius," Malloy said. "It looks like we aren't . . . welcome . . . in this town." Malloy twisted the word "welcome."

"Julius is welcome," Dan said. "He stays, if he wants to."

Malloy jerked back around toward Dan. "What? The hell he does!" he sputtered. He pointed to Julius. "That nigger belongs to me!"

"Maybe in Missouri. Not in Kansas."

"According to the law, he belongs to me no matter where he is. Haven't you ever heard of the Dred Scott decision? That's the law."

"The only law you've got to worry about now is this pistol and me. And I'm telling you to get out of town."

"Do you think I'm going to ride out of here without my property?"

"You *are* going to ride out of here, mister, and you've got two choices as to how you do it. You can either ride out of here sitting in your saddle . . ." Dan pulled back the hammer on his pistol, and the deadly click of the cylinder rotating into place could be heard in the sudden stillness of the street. "Or you can ride out belly down. Now, which will it be?"

Malloy glared at Dan for just a moment longer, then he went over to his horse. Just before he mounted, he looked back at Dan.

"What's your name?" he asked menacingly.

" 'And I looked, and behold a pale horse: and his name that sat on him was Death,' " Dan said.

"All right, Mr. Death," Malloy said. "I'm going. But we'll meet again."

"I'm counting on it," Dan said.

Malloy turned and rode out of town without so much as a sideward glance, trying, under the circumstances, to maintain as much dignity as he could.

The townspeople applauded Dan, while some, Dan was glad to note, hurried over to tend to Julius. Byrd came up to Dan, smiling broadly.

"That was really something, the way you handled Malloy like that," Byrd said. "Yes, sir, that was really something."

Several others came over to shake Dan's hand and congratulate him.

"What was that you said?" Byrd asked. "Those words about a pale horse and death. Are they from the Bible?"

"The Book of Revelation, chapter six, verse eight," Dan replied.

Byrd laughed. "Damn, that was just like the chief, the way you did that . . . quoting the Bible and all. He's always quoting the Bible, too."

"The chief?"

"John Brown. I told you."

"And I told you I don't believe there is such a person."

"Well then, I'll just have to make a believer out of you, won't I?" Byrd replied.

INDEPENDENCE, MISSOURI

"Burke, Barney Caulder ordered a new wagon wheel and it just came in today. Would you throw it into the back of the buckboard and take it out to him?" Tom Peters asked. Tom owned the livery stable where Burke was working. Burke had taken the job to better fit in with the social fabric of the community he had joined.

"Sure thing, Tom," Burke replied, hanging the harness he had just repaired on a hook on the wall.

"I swear, I don't know why Barney doesn't just buy a new wagon outright," Tom said. "This is the third wheel he's bought this year, and he got a new tongue last year."

"Maybe he is buying a new wagon, he's just not buying it all at the same time," Burke joked as he put the wheel into the back and started to climb onto the seat.

Tom laughed, then asked: "Aren't you forgetting something?"

"Not that I know of."

Tom nodded toward the wall, where Burke had just hung the harness. On a hook next to it hung his pistol belt, holster, and revolver. "What with the Jayhawkers and bushwhackers raising such havoc, you might want to be armed."

"I've got no fight with either one of them," Burke replied. "And if I'm not armed, maybe they'll see that I'm no threat."

"Maybe so," Tom said. "But you should be careful, nevertheless."

"I will be," Burke promised, and clucked to the team. He noticed that Tom had voiced neither support nor condemnation for either the bushwhackers or the Jayhawkers. Such lack of commitment was proving to be the real difficulty in fulfilling the president's mission of joining one of the groups, for most Missourians, like most Kansans, felt an equal degree of disgust for the raiders from both sides, referring to Jayhawkers and bushwhackers alike by the pejorative term "border ruffians."

One Hour Later

Five miles out of town, four riders stopped on a little hill overlooking the Caulder farm, then ground-tied their mounts about thirty yards behind them. They moved to the edge of the hill at a crouch and looked down toward the house.

"Looks like they're eatin'."

"So, what do we do?"

"We start killin'. Get your rifles."

The men returned to their horses and pulled their rifles out of the saddle holsters. Taking a moment to tamp down the ball and powder, they waited until all four rifles were loaded, then they took aim.

"Shoot!" the group's leader said, squeezing the trigger that snapped the hammer down on the primer cap.

The four rifles boomed simultaneously. One hundred yards away the barrage of .51-caliber bullets crashed through the window. Mr. Caulder was hit in the side of the head and died instantly. His eight-year-old daughter was hit in the chest, and his wife was hit in the shoulder. The fourth bullet burst a kerosene lantern sitting on a shelf above the stove. Kerosene began dripping into the stove.

In addition to the eight-year-old girl, there were two more Caulder children: a baby in its crib and a four-year-old girl, who began screaming in terror.

A black housekeeper came running into the kitchen, and when she could see Caulder's brain oozing through the exit wound, she turned and ran, adding her own screams to those of the little girl.

Marcie Caulder saw immediately that she could do nothing for her husband, so she knelt over her eight-year-old daughter.

"Molly!" she called. "Molly!"

Molly's eyes were open but unseeing, for the little girl was also dead.

At that moment the kerosene that had been dripping into the stove caught fire with such explosive force that the stove lids were blown off. Flames leaped from the stove to the wallpaper, which caught fire.

"Tammy," Marcie gasped. "Tammy, run outside, quickly! The house is on fire!"

Responding to her mother's command, Tammy climbed down from her chair and ran out into the yard, where the screaming housekeeper had attracted several other farmhands curious to see what was going on.

"Mama! Mama!" Tammy called.

"What happened? What's goin' on?" one of the field hands asked.

"It be Marse' Caulder! He done got his head blowed half off!" the housekeeper said, pointing with a shaking finger to the house.

At that moment Marcie reached the front door of the house, carrying the baby with her. Smoke was pouring through the door, and Marcie, weak with pain and the loss of blood, staggered onto the porch, then leaned against the porch column.

"Travis! Come take the baby, quickly!" she called.

Travis, who was the oldest of the slaves, hurried onto the porch to take the child and help Marcie down the steps and out into the yard.

"Travis, ought'n we to get buckets and fight the fire?" someone asked.

Travis shook his head sadly. "It's too late," he said. "Buckets ain't goin' to do no good with that fire. It's comin' up through the roof already."

"And me just through puttin' them new shingles on, too," one of the others said.

Travis, the housekeeper, the other slaves, the terrified child, and a dazed Marcie stood in a huddled group and watched as the house burned furiously.

Burke heard the volley of shots, then he saw a puff of smoke drifting over the top of the next hill. A moment later four riders came galloping by, bent low over the necks of their horses.

"What is it? What happened?" Burke called to them as they galloped by.

No one answered his query, nor did they slow down. However, one of them did pull his pistol and snap off a shot in Burke's direction. But because they were going so fast, and because the rider had turned in his saddle to shoot, there was very little danger of Burke's actually being hit. Nevertheless, it did cause him to dive out of the wagon and into the ditch that ran parallel with the road.

The riders were too hunched over for him to be able to get a good look, but he did study the four horses. One was a blood bay, another was a buttermilk. There was a chestnut with white socks on the right forefoot and the left hindfoot. The fourth horse was black with a patch of white on his forehead.

As soon as the riders were over the rise, Burke jumped back into the wagon and whipped his own horses into a gallop. He pulled the team to a halt, standing on the brake lever as the wagon slid to a stop in the Caulder yard. He jumped out and ran over to Mrs. Caulder.

"Where's Mr. Caulder?" he shouted.

"The marse' 'n one o' the little girls still be inside the house!" one of the slaves answered.

Burke started toward the house, but the terrible heat from the roaring flames pushed him back.

"It ain't no use tryin' to go in after 'em," the housekeeper called to him. "They both done be dead!"

Burke looked back at Marcie, who confirmed the housekeeper's words with a nod of her head.

"Are you all right?" Burke asked her.

"Who would do something like this?" she replied in shock. "Who could do such a terrible thing?"

"I 'specs it was some folks from Kansas. They calls themselves redlegs," Travis said.

"Redlegs? You mean Jayhawkers?" Marcie asked. "But why would they attack a peaceful farm like ours? Barney wasn't political. He didn't belong to the regulators."

"When folks gets to warrin' against each other like them Kansas folks and you Missouri folks, I don't reckon a body needs much of a reason," Travis said.

"Mama, if our house is burned all down, where are we going to sleep?" Tammy asked. Where to sleep was a bigger concern to her than what had just happened, because she did not fully understand the concept of death.

"Sleep? I . . . I don't know, darling," Marcie replied. She was still concentrating on the flames and on the fact that the bodies of her husband and daughter were inside.

"The little girl has a point, Mrs. Caulder," Burke said. "Do you know anyone in town you can stay with?"

"In town?" She was still somewhat dazed.

"Yes, we need to get you to a doctor, then find a place for you to stay."

"I don't know, Maybe Catherine can put us up. She used to be our neighbor, and now she lives in that big house all by herself."

"Catherine?"

"She be talkin' 'bout the lady what teaches the chil'run," Travis explained.

"Miss Darrow, yes," Burke said. "That's a good idea. Why don't you get your things and get into the wagon, and I'll take you?"

"Things?" Marcie answered in a small voice. "Why, Mr. Phillips, I don't believe I have any things left."

Someone met them on the road when they were still about a mile from town. The townspeople had seen the smoke, and one of them was coming to investigate its source. Burke explained what happened, then asked the rider to hurry back to town and arrange for the doctor to meet them at Catherine Darrow's house.

It was obvious that the rider told more people than the doctor what happened, for from the moment the wagon reached the edge of town it was surrounded by anxious citizens, concerned about Mrs. Caulder and expressing their shock and sadness over what had happened to her husband and daughter. By the time the wagon stopped in front of

Catherine Darrow's house it had gathered an entourage of nearly one hundred people.

"Where's the doctor?" Burke called as he set the brake.

"He rode out to the McAdams place this afternoon," someone said. "We sent for him, but that's eight miles from here."

"But Mrs. Caulder needs a doctor now!" Burke insisted.

"Don't worry about that. Thelma can tend to her," said a beautiful young woman as she pushed through the crowd to the wagon. "She's as good as any doctor. Willie, please carry Mrs. Caulder into the house."

"Yes, ma'am, Miz Catherine," replied the big black man who had come out to the wagon with Catherine.

"Put her in the front upstairs bedroom," Catherine called as Willie picked up Marcie and carried her easily toward the house. Thelma, carrying the baby, walked alongside.

"Tammy, darling, why don't you come with me?" Catherine suggested, smiling and extending her hand toward the little girl. Obediently the little girl put her tiny hand in Catherine's.

"Am I going to sleep here tonight?" Tammy asked, looking in wonder at the big house and all the people.

"You sure are, darling. You and your mama and your little brother."

"Daddy and Molly aren't here," Tammy said. "They got hurt."

Catherine looked around at Burke.

"We couldn't get them out of the house," Burke explained.

"You are Mr. Phillips, aren't you? You work at the livery?"

"Yes, ma'am," Burke said, touching the brim of his hat.

"Mr. Phillips, I want to thank you for bringing Marcie Caulder and her children into town."

"I just wish I had been there a few minutes earlier," Burke said. "Maybe I could've stopped it."

"Or maybe you would've been killed, too," Catherine said. "And what would that have accomplished?"

Burke stood by the wagon and watched as Catherine led the little girl into her house. It was funny, he thought. He had seen the schoolteacher before, had even spoken to her. But not until this moment had he noticed the gold matrix in her amber brown eyes or how those high cheekbones set off her dimple and that clear complexion.

Burke climbed back into the wagon and drove, slowly, to the livery stable. Not until he started unhitching the team did he notice that the wheel, which was the reason he had gone out to the Caulder farm in the first place, was still in the back of the wagon. He turned the horses into their stalls, pitched in a few forks of hay, and walked back to the wagon to retrieve the wheel. That was when he saw two men standing by the wagon. They had the tough, leathery look that Burke had come to associate with Missourians. One had a full beard, the other a sweeping mustache.

"Burke Phillips?"

"Yes."

"My name is Lonnie Butrum," said the one with the mustache. "This here is Vern Woods. We belong to the Jackson County Regulators."

This was it! This was the contact he had been looking for!

"What can I do for you gents?" Burke asked. He forced himself to show little interest as he picked up the wagon wheel and set it over near the wall.

"Mr. Phillips, we was wonderin' if maybe you got a glimpse of them redlegs today?"

"Maybe I did, maybe I didn't," Burke said cautiously.

" 'Cause if you did, and if you're of a mind to ride with us, me an' Vern was thinkin' on goin' over into Kansas and puttin' things right."

Burke ran a hand through his hair as he studied the two men. "The regulators?"

Lonnie shook his head. "No, just me'n Vern."

Then this wasn't quite it, Burke thought. Two men did not the regulators make. Still, it was a connection.

"I wouldn't be interested in going over there just to burn a farm in retaliation," he said. "But I might be interested in finding the men I saw today."

"Do you think you can do that?"

Burke nodded. "I think I can."

Lonnie smiled. "I told Vern I bet you seen 'em. You'll ride with us, then?"

Burke held up his finger. "Yes, but only to get the Jayhawkers who did this," he insisted. "Not to raze any innocent people."

Lonnie raised his right hand. "That's all we're goin' to do," he said. "My hand to God."

"When do you want to go?" Burke asked.

"Thought we might go right now," Lonnie answered.

"Right now?"

If they left immediately, Burke would have no chance to contact the U.S. marshal and inform him of his plans.

"Some reason you can't?"

"No. No reason at all."

"Then, what do you say we get started?"

"I'll be with you soon as I saddle my horse," Burke said.

Burke told himself that he shouldn't miss this opportunity to make contact with the regulators, even though he wouldn't have time to tell the marshal. But the truth, which nagged at him from the back of his mind, was that he didn't want the marshal involved. He wanted to go after the men who burned the Caulder farm today, not because it was a mission for the president, but because they were evil bastards who should be made to pay for what they did.

SHAWNEE, KANSAS

The bright glow of lights from the little town was visible for a mile before Burke, Lonnie, and Vern got there. As they grew closer they could hear the sounds of reverie from the saloon: loud voices, the high-pitched trill of a woman's laughter, and the tinkling of a piano.

As the three men entered the town, a barking dog darted out to greet them. Vern, who had a good chew of tobacco worked up, spat a wad on the dog's head, causing him to turn and run away.

The main street of the town was without street lamps, though it seemed adequately illuminated by the golden squares of light that splashed through the windows of the houses and buildings that fronted the street. The largest, brightest, and loudest building was the saloon at the far end of the street. At least half a dozen wagons were parked in front of the saloon and more than a dozen horses. Burke saw the four horses he was looking for immediately, though for the moment he said nothing.

"Hey, lookie there!" Vern said a few moments later as they drew closer. "Ain't them there the horses you described?"

"That's them," Burke answered.

"Yeah, but how do we know who was ridin' 'em?" Lonnie asked.

"You ask me, it don't matter who was ridin' 'em," Vern said. "They inside the saloon, ain't they? You figure there's any of our people in there? I say we just burn the whole damn place down."

"Good idea," Lonnie said.

"No!" Burke said quickly.

Lonnie and Vern looked at Burke suspiciously.

"If we do that, the sons of bitches we really want might get away."

"So what do you suggest?"

Burke pulled his horse to one side of the street. "I suggest we just wait out here until they leave."

"Yeah," Vern agreed. "Yeah, we can tell who they are when they get on their horses."

After tying off their horses, the three men sat on the board sidewalk that passed in front of the hardware store, across the street from the saloon.

"How long you figurin' on waitin'?" Lonnie asked.

Burke pulled his legs up in front of him, then wrapped his arms around his knees. "You got anything better to do?" he asked.

"Reckon not," Lonnie replied.

Vern spat another wad of tobacco.

The hours dragged on.

Customers exited the saloon, laughing and calling to each other, but none of them mounted any of the four horses the men had staked out.

The piano player left, and the saloon grew quieter.

More people left, and Vern began snoring. Lonnie chuckled.

"Ol' Vern can go to sleep pert' nigh anywhere," he said. He got up, stretched his arms and legs, then stepped around the corner of the building to take a leak in the darkened shadows. He came back and sat down again. "What the hell are them boys doin' in there?'' he asked.

"Wait a minute, here they come,'' Burke said.

"Vern! Vern!'' Lonnie hissed. "Wake up!''

Vern snorted awake. "What is it?'' he asked in a sleepy voice. "What's goin' on?''

"They're a-comin'!''

There were only two of them.

"What the hell?'' Lonnie asked. "Where's the other two?''

"Either of you ever been over here before?'' Burke asked.

"Yeah, I have,'' Vern answered.

"What's in the rooms upstairs?''

Vern snorted what might have been a laugh. "Them's whores' cribs up there,'' he said. "Never been up there myself, 'cause I don't want nothin' to do with a Kansas whore.''

"I don't think our friends have that problem,'' Burke said. "I just saw a lantern go on in one of the upstairs rooms.''

"Damn, that means two of 'em is goin' to get away from us,'' Lonnie said.

"No, they aren't,'' Burke answered. "You and Vern take care of these two, I'll take care of the ones in the saloon.''

"You're goin' to take care of both of 'em, by yourself?''

"Yeah,'' Burke answered without further elaboration. By now he was already halfway across the street.

"What are me and you goin' to do, Lonnie?'' Vern asked.

"Get your horse, Vern. Like the man said, we're goin' to take care of the two redlegs that left.''

When Burke started to go inside, he was met at the door by the saloon keeper.

"We're just closin', mister,'' the saloon keeper said. He had a towel draped across his shoulder.

"You'll stay open long enough for what I want to do,'' Burke hissed.

"The hell I will! I told you, we're—'' The saloon keeper stopped in midsentence when he saw the pistol appear in Burke's hand. Then he sighed in disgust. "I ain't got no money on me. It's over there in the box. Take it. You can have it."

"I don't want your money."

The saloon keeper looked confused. "You don't? Then what the hell do you want?"

Burke motioned toward the ceiling with his pistol. "I want the two men who are upstairs."

For just a second the look of confusion remained on the saloon keeper's face. Then realization set in, and he broke out into a sweat, noticeably more nervous now than he had been when he'd thought he was being robbed.

"You're . . . you're from Missouri, ain't you? You're a goddamned bushwhacker!"

"You've got no problem with me, mister, as long as you stay out of my way," Burke said. "Besides the whores, is anyone else up there but the two men who were riding the horses that are tied up out front?"

The saloon keeper's eyes narrowed. "No," he said. "Them two is all that's up there."

"Good. Now, you go on over there behind the bar and stay out of trouble," Burke said.

"Yes, sir, mister, yes, sir," the saloon keeper said nervously. "You ain't goin' t' have no trouble outta me."

Burke watched until the saloon keeper was behind the bar, then he started up the stairs.

There was no one on the bottom floor of the saloon except the saloon keeper, and in the silence that filled the empty space, Burke could hear a man's low voice and a woman's husky laughter from the floor above.

With his pistol in his hand, Burke started up the stairs toward the second floor. He took them one at a time, as quietly and as secretively as possible. When he reached the landing, halfway to the top of the stairs, he happened to glance toward one of the socket lanterns, so-called, because they fit into a slot in the wall. In the polished glass globe of the lantern, he saw the reflection of the saloon keeper.

That saved his life.

Burke spun around quickly. The saloon keeper was, at that very moment, raising a shotgun.

"Wait, no—what are you doing?" Burke shouted, holding out his hand. "I mean you no harm!"

The saloon keeper pulled the trigger and the shotgun

roared, just as Burke dropped to one knee. The charge passed harmlessly overhead, taking out part of the railing and crashing into the wall behind him. The shotgun was a double-barreled model, and the saloon keeper now pulled back the hammer to the second barrel.

Burke fired and saw his bullet strike the saloon keeper in the neck. The saloon keeper fell back, discharging the second barrel into the ceiling and falling into the glass- and bottle-laden shelf behind the bar, causing it to tumble down upon him.

"Pete! Pete, what the hell is goin' on down there?" a voice yelled from upstairs.

Burke turned toward the sound of the voice and saw a man standing at the head of the stairs in his underalls.

"You!" the man shouted. "You're the son of a bitch we saw on the road!"

The man had a gun in his hand, and he brought it up and fired just as Burke fired at him. The man at the top of the stairs missed, but Burke's bullet found its mark, and Burke saw a big red hole suddenly appear in the middle of the man's chest. The man dropped his pistol, then fell head-first down the stairs. Burke moved to one side as the man slid by, then quickly Burke ran up to the second floor.

A woman, naked, except for the blanket she was holding in front of her body, was standing in the hallway, her eyes wide with terror.

"Where's the other one?" Burke shouted.

Screaming, the woman ran back into one of the rooms and slammed the door.

Four doors opened onto the upstairs hallway, and Burke moved down the hall, kicking the doors open one by one. Three of the rooms were occupied by women. One was empty. There were no other men.

"Where is he? Where is the other one?" Burke bellowed in rage.

"Please, mister, I don't know what you're talking about!" one of the women whimpered. "There were only two men here. Pete, he runs the place, and Eddie, the man you just shot."

From outside, Burke could hear barking dogs and shouting men.

"What's going on? What's all the shootin' about?"

"It's bushwhackers!" somebody called. "Get your guns, ever'one. We've got some Missouri bastards over here!"

"Ladies," Burke said, touching the brim of his hat. "I do hope that you pardon the intrusion."

He ran back down the stairs, taking them two at a time, and jumped over Eddie's prostrate body at the bottom. After a glance toward the bar, where he saw Pete's grotesquely twisted legs sticking out from beneath the overturned shelves, he pushed through the front door and ran across the street to his horse.

"Does anybody see anyone?" a voice called from the darkness.

"Shoot the bastards!"

"Wait, make sure you know what you're shooting at! It's dark! We don't want to wind up shootin' each other!"

Burke climbed into the saddle, then slapped his legs against the sides of his horse. The horse bolted forward as if shot from a cannon, and he galloped right down the middle of Main Street.

"There he is!" someone shouted. "It's a bushwhacker! Shoot 'im! Shoot 'im!"

Fortunately for Burke, only two or three of the men had their weapons with them and charged, for only a few scattered shots were fired, none of which came close. Burke twisted around in his saddle and fired back at them, scattering those who had ventured out into the street.

He held his horse to a gallop for nearly two miles, then eased back into a trot and finally a walk. A few moments later he heard two other horses coming up behind him, and he quickly got off the road and waited under the shadow of some trees. He recognized Lonnie and Vern before they saw him, and he stepped into the road and called out to them.

"Lonnie, Vern, over here."

"Burke, it's you! Was you hit any?"

"No," Burke replied.

"Whowee! We heer'd all that shootin' a-goin' on, and we was that sure you'd been kilt," Vern said.

"Did you get 'em?" Lonnie asked.

Burke nodded. "And you?"

"We left 'em both lyin' in the road, deader'n shit," Vern said.

"Yeah," Lonnie added with a laugh. "It'll be a long while before any more Jayhawkers come into Missouri from this town."

★ ★ ★

Four

Item in the *Independence Bulletin:*

On July 4th, a gala celebration will take place in our fair community to celebrate our independence from England. It is fitting that our own town should bear the name Independence, for that word has, perhaps, even more meaning to us now than it did when our town fathers christened this community.

The independence that we seek today, however, isn't from some foreign sovereign, but from the federal authorities in Washington who, in exercising their brutal power over the individual states, are, in fact, committing as great a crime against freedom as ever was perpetrated by King George. Our celebration this year is all the more meaningful because of our determination to be free of that yoke of federal oppression.

In addition to the fireworks, foot races, and band concert, there will be a picnic and a basket social. All the young men of the town are looking forward to the opportunity of purchasing a picnic lunch from the lady of their choice, for it will afford them the opportunity not only to spend some time with the female in question, but also to determine who can, and who cannot, prepare a tasty meal, certainly one of the most important considerations in any marriage proposal.

The picnic and basket social will take place immediately after the band concert. Proceeds raised from the auction will be contributed to the widow Caulder, who recently lost a husband, child, and home to Jayhawkers.

Because Lonnie and Vern spread the story of Burke Phillips going in alone to shoot it out with two of the four men who had attacked Barney Caulder's farm, he became something of a hero among those who had southern sympathies. And, in Independence, that was just about everyone. Therefore more than one young woman tried to catch his gaze when the bidding began for the box lunches.

Burke, however, had his own idea as to whose picnic lunch he wanted. He waited until Catherine Darrow's basket was put up for auction, then he bid five dollars, which was five times more than anyone else had bid for any basket. His bid was followed by gasps of surprise.

"My," the auctioneer said. "You must really like fried chicken."

The auctioneer's comment was met with laughter as Catherine looked away in embarrassment. Burke, smiling broadly, paid the five dollars, then picked up the basket and walked over to offer his arm to Catherine. After taking it, she walked with him out to a flat rock that overlooked the Missouri River.

"You needn't have bid so high," Catherine said as she spread the cloth out on the rock. "There are a few who know about my cooking. I think a dollar would have accomplished the task."

"I wanted to make certain that I got your basket," Burke said. He smiled. "And your cooking has nothing to do with it. Besides, the money is going for a good cause. Although nothing can ever repay Mrs. Caulder for what those butchers took away from her."

"Yes, that was a terrible thing," Catherine agreed. "Of course, there have been terrible deeds committed by both sides. The people from Kansas as well as the people from Missouri."

"How can you compare what we have done with the evil that has been done by the Kansans?" Burke replied. "In every case we have merely reacted to what they have done. We don't ride over into Kansas and steal their livestock."

"Is that what you consider slaves to be?" Catherine asked. "Livestock?"

"Well, no," Burke said. "I mean, unlike horses and cattle, Negroes are human, and they have an immortal soul. But they are also property, and when the abolitionists help them escape by the so-called Underground Railroad, they are stealing private property."

"I suppose that is so," Catherine said.

"Well, look at your own case. You own two slaves yourself. How would you like it if someone stole Willie and Thelma from you?"

"I wouldn't want to lose Willie and Thelma. They are two of the dearest friends I have."

Burke laughed.

"What is it? Why are you laughing?"

"I'm laughing at you calling them your friends."

"Do you think Negroes and whites can't be friends?"

"I suppose they can. But, being as they are your slaves, they don't really have much say in it, do they?"

"No," Catherine said. "No, I guess I hadn't thought of it quite like that."

"Burke," Lonnie called from up on the levee. "Burke, come here for a moment."

"If you're asking me to leave a pretty girl to talk to you, it better be good, Lonnie," Burke teased.

"It'll only take a minute," Lonnie promised.

Burke excused himself, then climbed up the levee.

"Got someone I want you to meet," Lonnie said. "He's standin' over there under the tree, with Vern."

Burke walked with Lonnie over to the tree where Vern stood talking to a small man wearing a flat-brimmed hat adorned with a long sweeping purple feather.

"Burke, this here is Russell Hinds. He's the leader of the Jackson County Regulators," Vern said.

Hinds stuck out his hand. "Heard how you handled them redleg bastards over in Olathe," he said. "I could use a good man like you, if'n you'd care to ride with me."

"I'd be honored," Burke said, shaking Hinds's hand. "Anytime you need me, just let me know."

"How about tonight?" Hinds asked.

"Tonight?"

"We got word there's some contraband bein' smuggled in tonight."

"They'll be comin' up the Stony Point Road," Vern said.

"Going where?" Burke asked.

"Well, now that part we don't rightly know. I mean, we know that there's one of them depots on the Underground Railroad right here in Independence, but we don't know who's runnin' it." Hinds smiled. "But that don't really matter none. If'n we can stop the contraband out on the road afore it ever gets to the depot, then the depot ain't goin' to do much, is it?"

"Cain't have a depot without a railroad, and you cain't run a railroad without passengers," Lonnie said, and they all laughed.

"Do I have time to finish my picnic basket?" Burke asked.

Hinds laughed again. "Sure, go ahead. I heard you paid five dollars for that basket. Sure wouldn't want to take you away from that."

"We'll meet down at the livery right after it gets dark," Lonnie said.

"I'll be there," Burke promised.

Catherine was sitting quietly, her knees pulled up in front of her and her arms wrapped around her legs, looking out at the river, when Burke came back down the levee. He dislodged a rock as he came down the little hill, and she looked around, then smiled when she saw him. Burke didn't think he had ever seen anyone more beautiful.

"Hello again," she said.

"You didn't eat all the fried chicken, did you?" Burke asked.

"I didn't eat any of it," Catherine said. "I saved it all for you."

Burke pulled out a drumstick and began eating. "You ever heard of a man named Russell Hinds?" he asked.

"Yes," Catherine said. "He isn't a very pleasant person," she added.

"I just met him. He was introduced to me as the head of the Jackson County Regulators."

"Did you join?"

Burke was silent for a moment. He hadn't been told to keep his membership a secret, but he knew that most did, for he had had a difficult time finding out anything about it when he'd first arrived in Missouri. On the other hand, it wasn't as if he really was a member; he was only doing this in compliance with the assignment given him by President Buchanan, and letting Catherine know that he had joined the regulators might prove beneficial to his mission.

"Yes," he said.

"I see."

"You sound as if you disapprove."

"I told you before, I think such organizations only inflame the passions on both sides of the border."

"You've got it all wrong. We aren't raiding farms, burning houses, and killing people the way the redlegs do. All we're doing is upholding the law. Tonight, for example, we're going to be out on the Stoney Point Road to meet a wagonload of contraband."

"What will you do with them? Will you hurt them?"

"No, we won't hurt them. Why would we hurt them? I told you, they are the same thing as livestock. If we found some stolen horses, do you think we would hurt them?"

"I wouldn't think so."

"Of course we wouldn't. All we would do is take them back to their rightful owners, and that's exactly what we're going to do with the escaped slaves we find tonight."

Catherine smiled and put her hand on his arm. "What you are doing, it can be dangerous, can't it?"

"I suppose."

"Then, please be careful."

Burke smiled back. "Why, Miss Darrow, are you worried about me?"

"Of course," Catherine teased, taking a piece of chicken from the basket. "Who else could I get to pay five dollars for a basket of fried chicken?"

The moon hung as a bright lantern in the midnight sky, painting the rolling fields just out of town in sharply delineated shades of silver and black. Willie was singing as he drove the lumbering wagon down the road: "Swing low, sweet chariot, Comin' fo' to carry me home."

Ahead of him, two riders appeared. They waited in the road as Willie approached them.

"Hold on there, you!" one of the men shouted, holding up his hand.

"Whoa, team, whoa," Willie called, pulling back on the reins and setting the brake. He pushed his hat back on his head and smiled at the two men who had stopped him.

"I'll be damned. What you think of this, Logan? It's a nigra," said the larger of the two men.

"Yes, suh, mastuh, be dey somethin' I can do for you gemp'mens?"

"What's a colored man doin' out here on the road this late at night?" asked the one called Logan.

"You gemp'mans lookin' fo' contraband, ain't you?" Willie said. "Well, suh, I ain' no contraband. I belongs to Miz Catherine Darrow."

"Well, that just shows what you know," Logan said. "The contraband is comin' in on the road from Stoney Point, not from Liberty."

"Hush your mouth, Logan. Don't be tellin' this nigra things he don't need to know."

"Sorry, Emmitt."

Emmitt stroked his chin. "Miz Darrow know you out here, boy?"

"Oh, yes, suh, she sho' do know. Yo' can ride back inter town an' ask her if'n you want."

"What are you doin' out here this late, anyhow?"

"Well, suh, Miz Catherine Darrow, she put up some canned peaches fo' me to take up to Liberty to sell."

"It's after midnight," Logan said. "You expect us to believe you been out here sellin' canned peaches all this time?"

Willie shook his head. "My, oh, my. Didn' have no idea it be that late. Miz Catherine is liable to be some put out wif me fo' comin' home so late like dis. Most especial' since I didn' sell no peaches a'tall."

Emmitt chuckled. "What's the matter? Did you get drunk?"

"No, suh, I didn' do nothin' like that," Willie insisted. "Just couldn' find no one what wanted any peaches to-day."

"More'n likely he didn' even try and sell any. He prob'ly met some young black wench and they did a little sportin'," Logan said, and he and Emmitt laughed.

"After the sportin' you done with that high-yella gal over at the Loomis place, you ain' got no room to talk," Emmitt bantered.

The two riders laughed again.

Willie climbed over the wagon seat, then opened one of the crates, removed a couple of jars, and held them out toward the riders. They glistened in the moonlight.

"Maybe you gemp'mens would like to buy some peaches from me? Miz Catherine's goin' be powerful sorrowful if'n I gets back an' ain't sold none a'tall."

"We don't want any of your peaches," Emmitt said.

"I got some more in this crate. It'll only take me a second to open it up an' show 'em to you." Willie picked up a crowbar and started to open the top of the largest crate in the wagon. The nails creaked and groaned in protest.

"We told you, we don't want any of your damned peaches," Logan growled.

"But, don't you want to even look inter this here crate, to see what a fine crop we got?" Willie asked, poised over the crate with the crowbar.

"No. If we wanted to look inside, we'd ask you. Now, get on out of here. We got better things to do than stand around here palaverin' with a nigra in the middle of the night."

"Yes, suh," Willie said, reclaiming his seat. "But Miz Catherine, she sho' goin' to be put out when I comes back wif as many peaches as I had when I left."

"That's your problem, not our'n."

"Yes, suh, I 'specs so." Willie slapped the reins against the side of the mules, and his team started forward.

"An' if you see anyone tryin' to smuggle nigras over into Kansas, you let us know. You hear?" the larger man shouted after Willie as he left.

"Yes, suh, I be sho' to do that," Willie called back over his shoulder. Then he resumed singing:

> I look over Jordan, and what did I see?
> Comin' fo' to carry me home.
> A band o' angels comin' after me.
> Comin' fo' to carry me home.

When Willie reached town the mule's hoofbeats echoed hollowly on the hard-packed dirt road as the wagon moved slowly down the dark street. Willie looked, closely, at every house they passed without seeing so much as a flicker of light. Even the saloon was dark and quiet.

He turned off the street and drove up the alley that ran behind Catherine's house. Then he turned into Catherine's backyard and pulled up to the side of the house, stopping by the outside entrance to the cellar. After halting the team and setting the brake, he moved back to the cellar door and opened it. The door opened upward, into two halves. One-half of the door protected the cellar steps from the view of anyone who might be out in the street. The other half protected the cellar steps from the view of anyone who might be in the alley, though at this hour of the night, Willie was certain no one would be watching what he was doing anyway.

A flickering candle appeared in the cellar, casting a dim but usable light over the steps that led down inside.

"Hello, Willie," Catherine called up from the bottom of the steps. "Thelma and I have been worried about you. Did you have any trouble?"

"I'm a lot later than normal because I went the long way around. I headed north from Stoney Point, then connected with the Liberty Road. I was stopped by a couple of men, just outside of town."

"You were?" Catherine asked anxiously.

"Don't worry, there wasn't any trouble. You were right, by the way. The main body was over on Stoney Point Road. I think these men were just lookouts." Willie chuckled. "Whatever they were, they didn't seem too interested in buying any peaches."

He climbed up into the back of the wagon and, using the crowbar, opened the crate he had tried to open earlier. The nails creaked as he forced them up.

"Shhh! Willie, open it quietly!" Catherine hissed.

"Sorry," Willie said. He opened the lid slowly and quietly, and when he had it open he smiled and looked inside.

"You folks can come out now," he said.

Hesitantly, and stiffly from their time spent in confined quarters, a black man, woman, and child crawled out.

"Don't let anyone see you. Move quickly, down into the cellar," Willie ordered.

The three contrabands moved through the shadows and into the shelter of the door.

"Watch your step," Catherine said solicitously. "They're steep."

"I sho' thought we was goners back there," the man said when they reached the cellar floor. "I thought you was goin' to open that lid an' give us up."

Willie laughed. "The best way to keep a white man from looking at something you don't want him to look at is to pretend that you *do* want him to look at it."

The black man laughed. "I 'specs so. Whatever you done, it worked, but I don't mind tellin' you, we had done quit breathin' inside that box."

"Good," Willie said with a broad smile. "If you had been breathing, they would've heard you."

"Come back here, quickly," Catherine said. "We have beds for you. You can stay here until you are ready to go on to freedom."

"Will you be takin' us on into Kansas?" the man asked Willie.

"No," Willie answered. "This place is just a depot in the Underground Railroad."

"The Underground Railroad to freedom," the man said almost reverently.

"Freedom," the woman repeated. "Praise de Lawd, we soon goin' to be free."

Catherine put her hand on the little boy, then jerked it back. "This child feels hot. Has he been sick?"

"Yes'm, he begin to take sick sometime today while we was nailed up inside that box," the boy's mother said. "But I tell him don' make no noise, else we'll get cotched by the slave chasers, so he be real good an' quiet."

"Aren't you a brave young man?" Catherine said to the boy.

"Yes'm, I be brave all right," the boy answered.

"Thelma, see what you can do for him," Catherine said, moving the little boy on inside. "We can't let a brave young man like this be sick, now, can we?"

"You come with me," Thelma said soothingly to the little boy. "I'm going to fix you up real good."

"Are we really goin' be free?" the little boy asked.

"Yes, honey," Thelma said, putting her arm around the boy. "You are really going to be free."

The little boy looked up at his mother and smiled. "Did you hear that, Mama? We goin' be free!"

Five

When Dan Morris and Hank Byrd stepped down from the train, they were greeted by a tall, smiling black man who wore a high-crowned hat with a printed card that identified him as the baggage master.

"Welcome, gentlemen, welcome to Harper's Ferry," the man said. "I'm Shephard Hayward, a free man of color, at your service. Has you gots baggage?"

"We have much more than baggage, Mr. Hayward," Byrd said. "We have several boxes of farm implements which we are to deliver to Mr. Brown."

"Do that be Mr. Brown on the Kennedy farm, across the river in Maryland?" Hayward asked.

"Yes."

"My, oh, my, that Mr. Brown sure be someone for bringin' lots o' folks'n farm equipment together for such a small farm. I'm right curious to see what he be raisin' out there."

"You shouldn't be too curious, Mr. Hayward," Byrd said. "It isn't healthy."

"No, sir, no, sir," Hayward replied quickly. "I knows better than to gets too nosey 'bout things that don't concern me none. Will you be needin' a wagon?"

"It was my understanding that Mr. Brown would have a wagon here to meet us," Byrd said.

"Yes, sir. I'll see to the baggage and the boxes for you. You gentlemens can wait in the waiting room."

As Dan and Byrd started toward the waiting room, Dan saw the telegraph office and headed for it. He had managed to get off only one message before they'd left, informing

his contact that he believed he was being taken to meet
with John Brown. But as Byrd had been his constant com-
panion for the entire journey, he had not found another
opportunity to report. As a result, he was now on the Maryland–Virginia border, not too far from the nation's capital,
while the president of the United States, the secretary of
war, and his own personal contact assumed he was still in
Kansas.

"Where are you going?" Byrd asked.

"To the waiting room," Dan replied.

"It's over here."

Byrd was watching him too closely. He wasn't going to
be able to sneak in a message. "Oh."

"Anyway, we don't need to wait. There's Watson now."

"Watson?"

"Watson Brown. He's one of the chief's sons," Byrd
said. "Come on, I'll introduce you to him."

Dan saw a rather slight-looking young man stepping
down from the driver's seat of a farm wagon.

"Hello, Hank," the young man said, coming toward
them. "Did you have a pleasant journey?"

"Yes, thank you, Watson. Watson, this is the man I
wrote to your father about, the man who stood up to Angus
Malloy."

"Good for you, sir, good for you," Watson said, shaking
Dan's hand. "My father was most impressed with Hank's
account of your action. We are very pleased to have you
join us."

They heard the sound of iron-rimmed wheels rolling
across cobblestone, and when they looked around they saw
Hayward coming toward them, pulling a large baggage cart
upon which was loaded not only their luggage, but four
long crates.

"Help me load these boxes onto the wagon," Watson
said, "and we'll be on our way."

"Lord, these are heavy," Dan said. "What are they?"

"They are grub hoes," Watson said, grabbing the other
end of one of the crates. "We have a lot of weeding to
do."

"Yeah," Byrd said with a little laugh. "Weeding."

Fifteen minutes later, and at least a mile and a half out
of town, Watson looked over at Byrd. "Why don't you

open one of the boxes?'' he suggested. "Mr. Morris might be interested in looking at our, uh, *farm equipment.*"

Byrd crawled over the seat into the back of the wagon, then pulled the lid off one of the boxes.

"Take a look," he said.

The box was full of pikes, six-foot-long poles, to the ends of which had been affixed bowie knife blades.

"We have hundreds of these . . . thousands," Watson Brown said confidently.

"What are they for?"

"You haven't told him?" Watson asked.

"No," Byrd said. "I haven't told him anything except that I was bringing him out here to meet your father. I figured whatever information you wanted him to know was up to your father."

"Nonsense. If he is going to be one of our recruits, he certainly should know what we are all about," Watson said. "Mr. Morris, you are about to participate in history. These pikes, and hundreds more like them, are to be given to the Negro slaves who run away from their masters and join my father's army."

"Your father's army?"

"Yes, sir, my father's army. It is his intention to mount a revolution against the slave owners. We believe that all Negroes, whether in bondage or not, will rush to join our banner once they hear that the revolution has begun. Within a very short time we will have a mighty army, numbering in the thousands, with my father at its head."

"Think of it," Byrd said. "A mighty, avenging army composed of slaves who will be fighting for their own freedom! Can such an army be turned back?"

"I don't know. Perhaps a better question is, can such an army be controlled?" Dan asked.

"Controlled? What do you mean, controlled?"

"I mean, once they get started, is there not the danger of wholesale slaughter? What is to keep your army from going on a killing spree?"

"That is a risk we must take."

"And your father is willing to take it?"

"You must understand, Mr. Morris, that my father knows blood will be spilled," Watson explained. "Some bloodletting is absolutely necessary. But he will be able to control them by the force of his own personality.''

"That is asking a lot of the force of one's personality,''
Dan suggested.

"He is a forceful person,'' Watson replied.

"Wait until you meet the chief,'' Byrd added. "He is a
person of great strength.''

"I see you have met one of my sons,'' John Brown said
to Dan shortly after the three men arrived at the Kennedy
farm, which was five miles on the Maryland side of the
Maryland–Virginia line. Dan saw immediately that there
was a great deal of activity going on around the farm, but
none of it had anything to do with farming. Some were
cleaning rifles, others were making paper cartridges, while
still others began unloading the crates of pikes Watson had
brought out with him. "I would like you to meet one of
my other sons who has also joined this crusade.''

Brown waved at a young man who was involved in the
unloading, and the man came over.

"This is my son Oliver.''

"Pleased to meet you, Oliver,'' Dan said, extending his
hand.

"Have you come to join us, Mr. Morris?'' Oliver asked.

"Yes,'' Dan said.

"It's a wonderful plan, don't you think? We'll build a
new nation here, and my father will be its founder, and its
head.''

"God is its head,'' Brown corrected him.

"Yes, sir, but you are his appointed representative on
earth,'' Oliver replied quickly.

"That is true,'' Brown agreed.

"When do we go?'' Byrd asked.

"We go tonight,'' Brown answered.

"Tonight?'' Dan gasped in surprise.

"Yes. We have enough men here now to fulfill our mission. And the longer we wait, the more chance there is for
our plans to be compromised. I believe it is imperative that
we move as quickly as possible.''

Dan felt frustrated. He was supposed to ameliorate the
more radical activities of the abolitionists if he could or, at
the least, give a warning if something drastic was about to
occur. What could be more drastic than the launching of a

civil war? Yet there was absolutely no way to get word out as to what was going on.

"Father, may I tell the others now?" Oliver asked.

"Yes, you may tell them."

"Men! Gather round!" Oliver shouted.

The men, sixteen white and five black, stopped their various labors and walked over to hear what Oliver had to say.

"My father has something to tell you," Oliver said.

"Men," Brown said to the anxious faces, "get on your arms. We proceed to the Ferry."

"Hurrah! Hurrah!" the men shouted, and, smiling, they began shaking hands and slapping each other on the back. And though Dan was feeling a little squeamish over the idea of being caught up in a revolution, he forced himself to spread a wide grin across his face in order to participate in the general excitement of the moment.

It was just after midnight when John Brown's men, walking alongside a wagon, approached the bridge across the Potomac. The wagon contained nearly one thousand pikes, which were to be issued as weapons to the escaped slaves Brown expected to join them.

Dan had asked several questions before they left, trying to ascertain just what Brown's ultimate plans were. It quickly became evident that Brown had no plan whatever, beyond making a show at Harper's Ferry. Even the weapons he had assembled for the escaped slaves showed a lack of understanding of real warfare. How could Brown expect men armed only with knives tied to the end of sticks to go up against a modern army equipped with revolvers, rifles, and cannon? That was, if any slaves actually joined Brown's movement. There had been no recruitment and no preparation of any kind, for which Dan was thankful. He was reasonably certain that the slave revolt Brown was trying to bring about would never happen.

On the other hand, there were nearly a score of heavily armed men heading into Harper's Ferry on this cold, drizzly night, and Dan knew that no good could come of it. He wished he had some way to stop it, but at this point there was nothing he could do about it but observe.

The bridge watchman, a man named William Williams, curious at the approach of so many men at this hour of the night, came out of his little watch house to see what was going on.

"Hello, fellas," he called amiably. "What are all you folks doin' out on a night like this?"

"Take him prisoner," Brown ordered.

"What?" Williams protested as two men grabbed him. "What's going on here?"

"Shut up, you. You are a prisoner of the war of liberty," one of the two men said. They tied his hands behind his back.

"The war of liberty? What the hell war is that? Who are you?"

"You will learn soon enough who I am," Brown replied. "Before this night is done, the entire world will learn who I am."

After crossing the bridge, Brown and his men stood just at the edge of town and looked down the long street that ran parallel to the railroad track. On the left side of the road was the engine house and several buildings of the arsenal. On the right was the rifle factory. The engine house was surrounded by a stone-and-iron picket fence.

"We will take up a position in that building," Brown said, pointing toward the engine house with a long bony finger.

The driver clucked to his horse, and the wagon rolled through the wet, predawn darkness until it, and the men walking alongside, reached the fence that surrounded the arsenal. Brown stepped up to the gate and called out.

Daniel Whelan, the nightwatchman at the arsenal, came to the gate to see who was there and what they wanted. When he reached the gate he saw several men pointing guns at him.

"What is this? Who are you? What do you want?" he sputtered.

"I have come from Kansas," Brown replied. "I intend to free all the slaves in this state. If the citizens interfere with me, I will burn this town and I will have their blood."

"What? Have you gone mad?"

Brown's eyes flashed in the wet, dim light. "Call me mad if you must," he said, "for geniuses have been called mad before me."

"Open the gate," Oliver growled.

"The hell you say," Whelan replied. He turned and started back inside. He was stopped by the sound of half a dozen rifles being cocked.

"Open the gate," Oliver said again, "or we will shoot you dead and force it."

With shaking hands Whelan turned back, then unlocked the gate. He stepped away as Brown and his men began streaming into the arsenal.

"You, and you," Brown said to Williams and Whelan. "Sit down over there and stay out of our way." Brown turned to his men. "All right, those of you who have been given assignments, proceed now to carry them out."

Half a dozen men left the little group and started moving quickly and efficiently through the dark streets of the town. Dan, who had no specific assignment, was posted to a position by a window and told to keep a watchful eye on the outside. Several minutes later the men Brown had sent out returned, each of them bringing one or more prisoners to be used as hostages.

"You," Brown called to one of the prisoners. "You are Colonel Lewis Washington?"

"I am, sir," Washington said, pulling himself up to his full height.

"I am told that you are the grandson of President George Washington."

"You were told wrong, sir. President Washington had no children, thus he had no grandchildren. I am his grand-nephew."

"Colonel Washington, you are now a prisoner in the war of liberty. You are all my prisoners," Brown added.

"What . . . what are you going to do with us?" one of the prisoners asked fearfully.

"It is too dark to write now, but when there is sufficient light I shall require each of you to write a letter to your slave-owning friends, demanding that they send a Negro man apiece, as ransom for your release."

"Why are you doing this, Mr. Brown?" Washington asked. "What do you hope to gain?"

"It is more than mere hope. I am here to free the slaves."

"Pa! Pa, someone is coming," Oliver called. Like Dan, Oliver had taken up a position by one of the windows and was looking outside.

"Who is it?"

"I expect that is Patrick Higgins," William Williams said. "He is coming to relieve me."

"Grab him," Brown ordered with an impatient wave of his hand. "Bring him in here, with the others."

Two of Brown's men went outside and started toward the bridge.

"Halt!" one of them called.

"Willie, lad? Is that you?" a voice called from the darkness.

"Halt, damn you!"

"You ain't Willie!"

"Stop, I say!"

Instead of stopping, Higgins turned and started to run. Both men fired, their rifles flashing in the predawn darkness. Higgins was hit and went down.

"We got 'im!"

Higgins got up, felt his head, then pulled his hand down to look at the blood. The bullet had only creased his skull. He got up and started running again, and because both rifles had been discharged, he was able to make it into a nearby house before they could reload and shoot at him a second time.

Here and there around the town a few lanterns were lit. Dogs started barking, and voices called out.

"What was that?"

"Did someone shoot?"

"What's going on out there?"

Shortly after that the whistle of an approaching train could be heard, and Higgins, who believed that a group of men must be planning to rob the train, hurried back out to the track to stop it. He might not have gotten it stopped had one of Brown's men not shot at the train. The bullet hit the iron window post near the engineer, striking sparks and getting his attention. The engineer braked the train to a stop, just as Higgins ran up to him.

"Back up!" Higgins shouted. "Train robbers ahead! Back up!"

The engineer threw the train into reverse and started backing up the track, out of danger. There the engine sat, wheezing and breathing, as the train crew waited to see what was going to happen next.

Back at the depot Shephard Hayward, the "free man of color," had slept through the gunshots, because he had trained himself, even while asleep, to filter out all but the sound of an approaching train. When he heard it coming he woke up, then trudged out into the cold drizzle to await its arrival so he could tend to his job as baggage master.

"There's someone there!" one of Brown's men said, and he pulled the trigger.

The bullet caught Hayward in the middle of the chest and he fell, then got back up and staggered back into the station office, where Higgins had taken shelter.

"Lawd, Mist' Higgins, help me!" Hayward said, his voice racked with pain. He gasped for breath a few times, then fell again.

Higgins stretched a wide plank across two chairs and laid the badly wounded Hayward on it. Quickly he opened Hayward's shirt, then saw the big, black hole, pumping blood.

"What happen to me?" Hayward asked.

"You've been shot."

"Shot? What for, Mist' Higgins? What for did they shoot me?"

"They shot you because they are evil men, Shephard. They are evil men," Higgins said, wishing he could do something to help Hayward. But it was too late. Hayward gasped a few more times, then stopped breathing.

"Evil men," Higgins said again, though he knew by now that Hayward could no longer hear him.

"Captain Brown," Dan said critically, "so far our effort to free the Negro has succeeded only in killing one who was already free."

"How do you know he's dead?" Oliver asked.

"He was hit in the middle of the chest and he went down, hard," Dan said. "People don't survive that kind of wound."

"Yes, well, it is too bad. But it is inevitable that some blood will flow," Brown replied.

"Even the blood of an innocent, harmless, free man of color?"

"The blood of the innocent will mingle, freely, with the blood of the guilty, for such is the way of cleansing the soul of our nation."

"Amen," a few others said, and Dan, sitting in the dark,

wished with all his soul that he had never accepted President Buchanan's assignment and that he could be anywhere in America but here.

Dan stayed at his post by the window until it grew light. Finally, enough gray, morning light splashed in for him to be able to look around inside the armory at the men with whom he had cast his lot.

The prisoners were drawn together in a solemn, huddled mass on one side of the room. John Brown was sitting on the floor, leaning against the back wall, his greatcoat pulled around him. His thin, hawklike face, gray hair, and the beard he had recently grown made him look, indeed, like an avenging angel.

The other men were in varous positions around the arsenal. Some, like Dan, were manning windows, and some, like Brown, were sitting on the floor.

"You know what we didn't think of?" one of the men said, disturbing the early morning quiet. "We didn't think about bringin' anything to eat. I'm ready for breakfast."

"Yeah, what's there to eat, holed up in here like this?"

"We won't be holed up long, boys," Brown said. "As soon as word spreads to the slaves that the revolution has begun they'll be joining us in the tens, hundreds, thousands! Then, all the bounty of the South will be there for the taking."

"Someone's comin' up to the front gate, Pa," Oliver called.

Brown got up and went through the door to the front gate. "Who are you?" he asked.

Obviously unaware that anything was going on, the man looked at John Brown and then at the others with him. "I'm Daniel Young, master machinist, coming to work," he explained.

"There will be no work today."

Some of the men chuckled.

"Who says there will be no work today?"

"I say so."

"And who, may I ask, are you, and what are you doing here?"

"I am here to give freedom to every slave in Virginia."

"What? In whose name do you derive such authority?"

"In the name of God," Brown replied.

Young ran a hand through his hair and looked around nervously, seeing now that Brown, and the men with him, were heavily armed. He didn't know what was going on, but he was clearly uncomfortable with the situation.

"Very well, sir. If you derive your authority from the Almighty, I must yield, as I derive my right to enter from an earthly power, the United States government." Young started to leave, but just as he did so, he turned back to Brown and held up a finger. "But I must warn you that before this day's sun sets, you and your companions will be corpses."

"We are prepared to pay that price for the liberty of others," Brown replied. "You may go now. I grant you safe passage. I want you to tell the others of our mission."

"Yes," Young said. "I will tell the others."

★ ★ ★

Six

Shortly after Young left, a church bell began to ring.

"What they ringin' the bell for?" someone asked. "This ain't Sunday."

"They're calling a town meeting," Dan said. From his position at the window, he could see several of the town's citizens gathering.

"Lord, we're in for it now," Byrd said. "Chief, maybe we'd better get out of here before it's too late."

"No, no, don't you see? If the townspeople know about us, then so do the slaves. By now word has probably reached every town, hamlet, and farm in Virginia. Before noon there will be one thousand ebony-skinned warriors marching down that road, coming to our rescue."

From somewhere outside a shot was fired, and the bullet crashed through one of the glass windows, then slammed into the brick wall at the rear of the building.

"They're shootin' at us, Pa!" Watson shouted.

"You may return fire," Brown said, and half a dozen men fired back. Dan fired as well, though he made sure that his bullet hit no one. The others weren't as careful, for two of the town's citizens went down under the hail of fire.

The shooting stopped.

"How many are there?" Brown asked.

"Not many, Pa," Oliver replied. "And what ones there are, aren't well armed. Looks like they've got nothin' but a few squirrel rifles and a shotgun or two."

Brown smiled and rubbed his hands together. "Keep a sharp lookout for our army of coloreds. At any moment now, they'll be coming up the road."

They waited.

The morning dragged on, cold and more dreary because of the falling rain.

"Mr. Brown," Colonel Washington said, "as you are the commander of this group, you are responsible for the welfare of your prisoners. We are hungry, sir, and we demand our breakfast."

Brown looked over at Washington with an expression of disgust. "You are in no position to demand anything," he said. He then looked up at Watson, who was standing beside a window. "What do you see out there now?"

"Nothing, Pa," Watson answered. "Just a bunch of people behind the corners of buildings, barrels, fences, things like that."

"Any sign of our army of freedom?"

Watson strained to look beyond the edge of the town. "No, I don't see nothin' like that."

"They'll come," Brown said.

They waited.

At around ten o'clock there was a great deal of commotion outside as the townspeople began shouting to each other and cheering.

"Is that it?" Brown asked excitedly, getting up from his seat on the floor. "Has our army come?"

"I don't think so, Pa," Watson replied.

"Well, what is it?"

Dan looked through his window. "It appears as if they have called out the militia," he said.

"Oliver, take two men out to the bridge and have a look around."

An expression of fear flitted across Oliver's face, but it quickly became evident that he was more frightened of disobeying his father than he was of what he might face outside. He nodded, then looked over at the others.

"Hank, you and . . ." He paused and nodded toward one of the black men. "What's your name?"

"Dangerfield, suh. My name is Dangerfield Newby."

"All right, Dangerfield, you and Hank come with me."

"Get a good look, then come back and tell me everything you see," Brown said, walking as far as the front door with his son. "And keep your head up, proudly."

Dan chuckled.

"What is it, Mr. Morris?" Watson asked. "What are you laughing about?"

"Most people would say 'Keep your head down.' ''

"Most people aren't my father," Watson replied.

Through his window, Dan studied the scene outside. He saw Oliver Brown, Hank Byrd, and Dangerfield Newby start toward the bridge.

Suddenly there was a volley of shots, and Newby went down. Oliver and Byrd turned and started back to the engine house at a dead run.

"What was that? What happened?" Brown asked.

"Newby was shot. Oliver and Hank are comin' back," Watson called from his position.

"The cowards! Why are they coming back?"

From outside, Oliver and Byrd began banging on the door. Their cries could be heard, muffled through the door.

"Let us in! For God's sake, let us in!"

The man nearest the door looked fearfully at Brown. Finally Brown nodded, and the man opened the door. Oliver and Byrd dashed inside, and the door was closed behind them.

Oliver put his hands on a stack of boxes, breathing in large, gasping pants until he got his breath back.

"You left one of your men to the enemy," Brown accused.

"He was dead, Pa," Oliver replied, finally regaining his wind.

"How do you know he was dead?"

Oliver looked at his father for a moment, then held out his arm. It was spattered with blood and little flecks of yellowish gray matter.

"Because I'm wearing his brains on my jacket sleeve," Oliver explained dryly.

"Then he will be the first of his race to die in the noble cause. The others will remember him as a martyr."

"There are no others, Pa. The great army of liberation isn't coming," Oliver said.

"How do you know? You weren't outside long enough to look around," Brown accused. "You were only there long enough to bring dishonor on yourself."

"We were outside long enough for one of us to get killed," Oliver answered. "The coloreds aren't comin',

Pa!'' he said, more forcefully this time. "The only people that's goin' to be comin' up that road are more soldiers!''

"Oliver's right, Pa. Maybe we ought to get out of here,'' Watson suggested.

"It is too late to leave,'' Dan said. He had been studying the positions of the gathering townsmen. "All avenues of retreat are cut off.''

"Mr. William Thompson, would you come here, please?'' Brown called.

Thompson leaned his rifle against the wall, then came over to see what Brown wanted. Brown jerked down a white curtain and tied it to the end of a stick.

"Here,'' he said. "Take this flag of truce out to the enemy and ask for an armistice while we consider terms.''

"Yes, sir,'' Thompson said.

Dan resumed his vigil through the window. He watched as Thompson, holding up the flag, walked toward the end of the railway station. Suddenly three men jumped out, as if from nowhere, and grabbed him.

"I think they just took Mr. Thompson,'' Dan suggested.

"What do you mean? He was my personal emissary, acting under a flag of truce. Surely they recognize a flag of truce between warring governments?'' Brown said.

Dan looked around quickly. Did Brown consider himself the head of state of a government? Was he that delusional?

"What do we do now, Pa?'' Watson asked.

"It is written in the Book of Matthew, chapter twenty-one,'' Brown said. " 'And the husbandmen took his servants and beat one, and killed another, and stoned another. Again, he sent other servants more than the first: and they did unto them, likewise. But, last of all he sent unto them his son, saying, Surely, they will reverence my son.' ''

Brown looked at Watson. "You shall go, Watson, bearing a flag of truce from me.''

"Me?''

"You are my son.''

"Pa,'' Oliver said quietly from his position over by the window, "why didn't you quote the next verse?''

Watson looked at his brother. "What . . . what is the next verse?'' he asked.

" 'But when the husbandmen saw the son, they said

among themselves, This is the heir; come, let us kill him,' "
Oliver said.

"Pa?" Watson said. "Pa, is that true? In the Bible, did
they kill the son?"

Brown didn't answer the question. "I have given you a
job to do," he said sternly. "I expect you to do it."

"I'll go with him," Aaron Stevens said.

"Thank you, Aaron."

"You may carry the flag," Brown said to his son, tearing
off another strip of the curtain and making a second white
flag to replace the one that William Thompson had lost.

Watson and Stevens stopped at the front door, looked at
each other for a moment, then they nodded to the keeper
of the door. He opened it, and, holding the flag and their
hands up, the two men started toward the edge of the depot
platform.

Suddenly several shots rang out. Both Watson and Stevens went down.

"They shot 'em!" Oliver called from his position at the
window. He turned to look back at Brown, who remained
absolutely stoic. "Pa! The bastards shot 'em both!"

"Are they dead?"

"I don't know," Oliver said. He looked through the window again. "Wait, Watson is coming back. He's hurt bad,
Pa. He can barely walk."

"You may let him in," Brown said to the doorkeeper.

Nodding, the doorkeeper opened the door and Watson
staggered in, then fell. His belly was covered with blood.

"Put him over there, out of the way," Brown said by
way of dismissal. He made no effort to speak to or approach
his wounded son.

"You bastards!" Oliver shouted. He fired through the
window, and his shot was answered by a fusillade of shots.

"To the windows, men," Brown said. "Return fire!"

For the next several minutes the shooting continued in
force. Two of the citizens of the town were hit and, Dan
believed, killed. Then, in retribution, the townspeople
brought William Thompson out to the edge of the bridge.

"Hold it, hold your fire!" Oliver said.

"I gave no such order!" Brown shouted up from his
place on the floor. "Why did you instruct the men to stop
shooting?"

"They have Willie out on the bridge, Pa. If we shoot now, we're liable to hit him."

"It is the risk we all agreed to take," Brown replied.

"He's trying to run," Dan reported.

William Thompson had, indeed, broken free. He made it through the railings of the bridge, then stood poised on the edge, as if he were about to dive into the river below. The townsmen opened fire, and Thompson's body was struck by at least half a dozen bullets. Dan saw a little mist of pink spray explode from his body just before he tumbled from the bridge into the river. He hit the water with a splash, then started floating downstream, facedown and motionless.

Suddenly the side door of the engine house opened and three of Brown's men dashed outside. "We're getting out of here!" one of them shouted.

"Come back here! Come back, you cowards!" Brown called to them.

The townspeople saw them as well, for they started shouting to each other.

"Look out! Look out, they're trying to get away!"

The townsmen's shouts were followed by heavy and sustained firing, and Dan saw two of the runners go down. The third threw up his arms and, miraculously, wasn't killed but was taken prisoner.

"What happened to them?" Brown asked.

"Two of them were killed," Dan replied.

"The pity is that all three of the cowards weren't killed."

The day dragged on with periodic outbreaks of gunfire. During the long lulls, Brown's men stared anxiously through the windows as the noose about them was drawn tighter and tighter.

"Any sign of our army of liberation?" Brown asked.

"No, Pa, no sign," Oliver said.

Oliver got down from his box and went over to look down at his brother. Watson's eyes were open and blank.

"How is he?" Brown asked.

"The prophecy has been fulfilled, Pa," Oliver said. "The son has been killed."

"Brown!" someone called from outside. "John Brown! You are John Brown, aren't you?"

Brown got up, then moved over to one of the windows

and called back. "I am John Brown," he replied.

"John Brown, you can see the spot you and your men are in. Our prisoner tells us that you're expectin' an army of slaves to come save you."

"They will come!" Brown insisted.

"No, sir, that's not going to happen, and you know it. Why don't you surrender now? Surrender and you and your men will at least get a fair trial. No need for you all to die in there."

"I have prisoners as well," Brown called back.

"We know you do."

"I won't surrender, but if you will give my men and me safe passage until we are across the river into Maryland, we will release our hostages, unharmed, on the Maryland side."

"No deal!" The refusal was underscored by another round of firing from the outside. The bullets whipped through the open windows and kicked up little chips of brick and masonry as they careened and ricocheted around inside the building.

Finally darkness fell, and for the most part, the shooting stopped. It wasn't entirely silent. As if letting those inside the engine house know they were still there, the darkness was interrupted now and again by the flash of a rifle, followed by the report.

At about two o'clock in the morning, Dan was sitting on the floor with his back against the wall, dozing, when he heard someone grunt in pain, then fall from the top of boxes that had been stacked up by the windows. At the same time, he heard the report of a gunshot from outside. When Dan opened his eyes, he saw that Oliver was the one who had been hit.

"Oliver!" Dan said, moving to him quickly.

"Oh, God," Oliver said. "It hurts! It hurts!"

Oliver had been hit high in the chest, and from the frothing, pink blood, Dan knew the bullet had penetrated a lung.

"Mr. Brown," Dan said, "you'd better come see to your son. He has been shot."

Brown, who was sleeping, opened his eyes but didn't get up.

"Is there anything I can do for him?"

"No, I don't think so."

"Then there is no need for me to come to him," he said.

Morning dawned, the second sunrise Brown and his army had seen since occupying the engine house. Brown got up and stretched. He looked over toward Oliver, who was moaning and whimpering quietly. He walked over to talk to him.

"Am I going to die, Pa?" Oliver asked.

"I expect so," Brown said. "You've been shot through the lung."

"It hurts, Pa. Do we have any laudanum? I need something for the pain."

"We brought none with us," Brown said.

"Pa, give up. Maybe they've got some laudanum in this town. I can't stand the pain."

"Hush, boy. Hush your crying and die like a man. Look at your brother. He didn't go out whimpering." Brown walked away from Oliver, then looked over at Dan, who had resumed his position by the windows. "What do you see out there now?" he asked.

"Marines," Dan answered.

"Marines?"

"The U.S. Marines, led by, it looks like, a couple of army officers. A colonel and a lieutenant."

"Militia, townspeople, marines, army . . . how many would you say are arrayed against us, Mr. Morris?"

"I would say at least two thousand," Dan replied.

"Hear that, boys?" Brown asked proudly. It's taking two thousand of them to get us. Oliver? Oliver, what do you think of that?"

Not hearing a reply from his son, Brown shrugged. "I guess he is dead," he said easily.

"Here comes one of the army officers," Dan said. "He is carrying a flag of truce."

"Let's shoot the son of a bitch!" Byrd said. "That's what they did to our emissaries."

"You are right," Brown said. "Very well, kill him when he is within range."

"No, wait!" Dan called quickly.

"Wait for what?" Brown replied.

"Perhaps they are ready to recognize you now," Dan

suggested, trying desperately to buy time, to prevent the murder of the army officer. "Yesterday they wouldn't even recognize the flag of truce. Today they are operating under one."

"All right, hold your fire," Brown ordered. "Let's see what he wants."

Everyone remained deathly quiet as the officer approached. They could hear his footsteps, then they heard him banging on the door.

"Mr. Brown! Mr. Brown, I am Lieutenant J. E. B. Stuart. I have a message for you from Colonel Robert E. Lee."

"What is your message?" Brown called through the door.

"Colonel Lee begs to inform you, sir, that your situation here is untenable, and he demands your immediate and unconditional surrender."

"Tell your commander, sir," Brown answered, "that I will not surrender. I will, however, negotiate a settlement whereby my entire party is allowed to escape in return for the lives of these hostages."

"I will carry your reply back to Colonel Lee, sir, but I do not believe these to be acceptable terms."

"Then, do what you must, Lieutenant," Brown said.

Lieutenant Stuart withdrew then, and there was a long period of silence. Dan watched through his window as the marines formed into two squads. For the moment he was the only one watching, so he said nothing as the marines came across the street and approached the front door. They began banging on the door with a sledgehammer.

"Ready yourself, men! They are coming in!" Brown called.

Miraculously the door held up under the force of the sledgehammer blows, so the marines grabbed a forty-five-foot-long ladder and used it as a battering ram. This time it took only two attempts before the door gave way.

Brown's men were formed in a semicircle around the door, and they fired, point-blank range, as the marines poured in. One of the marines went down, fatally wounded. But the marines were firing as well, and half a dozen of Brown's raiders went down, including Brown himself, who was badly wounded by a slicing blow from the sword of the marine lieutenant in command of the attacking force.

With Brown down, the fight left the rest of the men and they threw down their weapons, then put up their hands.

The battle was over.

Brown was carried out and laid on the grass outside the engine house.

"Are you John Brown of Kansas?" asked Colonel Robert E. Lee.

"I am he," Brown answered painfully.

"What were you and your men doing here, Brown? What did you hope to accomplish?" Lee asked.

"To free the slaves from bondage."

Lee shook his head sadly, then looked at his lieutenant. "Take them away," he said.

Dan Morris was taken prisoner with the others, but the secretary of war ordered him freed the moment he learned of Dan's circumstances. Dan provided the court with a written statement of everything that happened and every word that was spoken, to the best of his memory, from the moment he met Brown at the Kennedy farm until Brown and his men were captured.

John Brown, Hank Byrd, and Brown's accomplices—Cook, Coppock, Copeland, Green, Stevens, and Hazlitt—were all tried and condemned to die. On the morning John Brown was to be executed, Dan asked for and received permission to visit him in his cell. He showed up in full military uniform.

"Judas," Brown said. "You lack only the kiss by which I have been betrayed."

"It is not I who is the betrayer, John Brown, but you," Dan replied. "By the blood you shed you have done great harm to the idea of abolition. For who, now, would embrace the cause of a madman?"

"Had I interfered on behalf of the rich and powerful, instead of God's lowliest of creatures, the court would have deemed it an act worthy of reward rather than punishment."

The jailer came to the cell then. "It is time," he said quietly.

Dan stood up.

"Tell me, Mr. Morris. When you intervened on behalf of the slave against Angus Malloy . . . was that an act of your heart? Or were you merely trying to find some way to curry my favor?''

"I do not approve of slavery, nor of cruelty to our fellow human beings," Dan replied. "I acted in good conscience."

"Yet it is true, is it not, that you are on the Missouri–Kansas border to prevent bloodshed?"

"If possible," Dan answered.

Brown shook his head. "It is not possible. I am now quite certain that the crimes of this guilty land will never be purged away but with blood."

"Come, Mr. Brown," the jailer said.

"So now I am to become a martyr to this glorious cause," Brown said. "It has become necessary that I mingle my blood with the blood of my children, and with the millions in this slave country whose rights are disregarded by wicked, cruel, and unjust enactment. I submit. Let it be done."

The jailer led John Brown out of his cell, but just as he stepped into the hallway, he looked back at Dan.

"Lieutenant Morris, will you do me the honor of watching my execution?"

Dan cleared his throat. "I do it, sir, not in any show of honor to you, but because I have been ordered to do so by the president of the United States."

Brown smiled. "The president of the United States? Then my efforts have not gone without note in the highest office in the land. I feel vindicated."

Two officers bound John Brown's arms at the elbows then and led him outside. Dan followed, watching as they helped Brown into a furniture wagon, then seated him on his coffin.

As the wagon proceeded to the gallows, John Brown stared straight ahead, not once looking over at the crowd of people who had gathered alongside the road to watch this, his last ride. His face, Dan noticed, was set almost in the expression of a smirk.

The gallows was a rough-hewn, unpainted wooden affair of thirteen steps and a crossbeam. He was helped down from the wagon, then went easily and resolutely up the steps. His hat was removed and a rope put around his neck, then a white muslin mask slipped down over his face.

"Would you move over the trap, please, Mr. Brown?" the sheriff asked.

"You will have to guide me there," Brown replied.

The sheriff put his hands on Brown's shoulders, then moved him into position.

"Mr. Brown, if you wish, I will give you a handkerchief to hold. You may drop the handkerchief as a signal for me to cut the rope."

"No, I don't care to do that," Brown replied. "But I don't want you to keep me waiting unnecessarily."

Dan stood in the first rank of the military, looking up toward the gallows. These were the last few moments of John Brown's life, and Dan couldn't help but wonder what the old man was thinking. Was he at peace with himself? Did he truly consider himself a martyr, justified to enter heaven? Was he thinking about his sons?

Out of the corner of his eye, Dan caught the movement of the sheriff's arm. He heard the *thunk* of the ax blade cutting through the rope, then the rattle of the trapdoor falling open. John Brown's body dropped sharply through the hole, jerked up short, then began twisting, slowly, to the left. The drop had been perfectly calculated for instant death, and John Brown made not one twitch after his fall.

Dan heard the expulsion of breath of a hundred or more onlookers and realized at that moment that he, too, had held his breath during the last, terrible moment.

As he left the scene of the execution, he saw a sketch artist finishing up his drawing. Above the gallows, in ghostly rendering, the artist had John Brown being escorted by two angels into heaven. The old man was right, Dan thought. The making of martyrdom was already under way.

✦ ✦ ✦

Seven

TRADING POST, KANSAS; NOVEMBER 1860

Despite Burke's assurance to Catherine that the Jackson County Regulators were "only setting things right" by intercepting contraband, the truth was that Russell Hinds was becoming more and more volatile. Three times his band had attacked innocent people in Kansas, for no more reason than that they were Kansans. Neither Burke, nor Lonnie, nor Vern had been with Hinds. And in each case Russell Hinds's raid had been reciprocated by Doc Jennison, Hinds's counterpart on the other side.

Burke had hoped that he would be able to, as President Buchanan instructed, ameliorate Hinds's behavior, but he had been unable to do so. Now there seemed no solution to the problem, short of arranging for federal troops to arrest Hinds. To that end, he had informed the U.S. marshal who was his contact that Hinds was planning to turn back a load of contraband today. When he told the marshal how uneasy he was feeling about this act of betrayal, even though it was for a good cause, he received the marshal's assurance that only Russell Hinds was to be arrested. No harm would come to any of Hinds's followers.

"Yes," Burke said. "I am very familiar with the concept. As I recall, Judas betrayed only Jesus."

Burke Phillips looked over at Russell Hinds and the others who made up the membership of the Jackson County Regulators. Although he knew all of them, he had become particularly friendly with two of them, Vern Woods and Lonnie Butrum, and he was glad he had arranged that no harm would come to them. He knew, however, that if they ever discovered that he was the one who had betrayed them, the friendship would be terminated.

Vern Woods stood in his stirrups, scratched his crotch, then settled back again. He looked over toward Burke.

"What's the matter with you?" Vern asked him. "I swear you ain't said more'n three or four words ever since we left Independence."

Lonnie laughed. "Hell, it ain't hard to figure out what's wrong with ol' Burke here, Vern. He ain't makin' no head-way with that pretty schoolteacher. Way I hear it, she don't hardly give him the time o' day."

"That right, Burke?" Vern asked. "She leavin' you out in the cold?"

"Out in the cold," Lonnie said, laughing again. "That's a good one, Vern. Ol' Burke is bein' left out in the cold."

Vern and Lonnie were correct in their appraisal of Burke's relationship with Catherine. Actually, nonrelation-ship was more like it. Although Catherine always managed a friendly reply to his greetings, those same friendly replies never seemed to open the door for anything more.

"I would rather not discuss Miss Darrow, if you don't mind," Burke said.

Vern laughed, then looked over at Jerry Logan, one of Hinds's regular riders. "He'd rather not discuss the school-marm, if we don't mind," he teased.

They were quiet for a few more minutes, then Vern spoke again.

"You're a smart man, Burke. Do you think they's goin' to be an all-out war?"

"I don't know if there's going to be or not," Burke replied.

"The reason I asked is, folks been sayin' that if that ape Lincoln got elected, the South would more'n likely secede. Well, he got elected."

Lonnie Butrum squirted a stream of tobacco juice toward a mud puddle, where it swirled brown for a moment, then was quickly washed away. "Hell, Vern, what does it matter to us whether they's a war between all them other states or not? We been fightin' one with Kansas now for two or three years. Nothin's goin' to change here, just 'cause a few states decides to pull out of the Union."

"Yeah, I guess you're right," Vern said. He raised up

to scratch his crotch again, then looked over at another of Hinds's party.

"Say, Emmitt, how many nigras you reckon'll be comin' through here this time?"

"It don't matter none," Emmitt answered.

Vern looked surprised by the answer. "What do you mean, it don't matter none?" he asked. "Of course it matters. We get five dollars apiece for ever' one we take back. The more nigras we catch, the more money we'll make."

"Hey, Russell, listen to this," Emmitt said. "Ol' Vern here thinks we're actually going to take them niggers back."

Russell, Emmitt, and Logan laughed.

Lonnie had been quiet until now, but he, too, was surprised by the answer. "You mean we aren't returning any of the coloreds?"

"Not a one."

"What are we goin' to do with them?"

"We're goin' to kill 'em," Logan said easily. "All of 'em. The niggers, and the nigger-lovin', white, Underground Railroad conductors that's been stealin' 'em from their rightful owners."

"But what about the bounty money?" Lonnie asked. "We would be givin' that up if we did that."

"Don't need no bounty money. We'll make just as much by sellin' the wagons and horses."

"Listen, me'n Lonnie an' Burke ain't never done nothin' like this, before," Vern protested. "I mean, just shootin' 'em down in cold blood. I don't know as I can do that, be it a white man or a nigra."

"Well, if you ain't got the stomach for it, why don't you three fellas jus' ride away?" Emmitt suggested.

"Yeah, when we sell the horses and wagon it'll just be more money for us," Logan said.

"You men hush your jawbonin'," Hinds cautioned. "I hear the wagons a-comin'."

The group grew quiet, and Burke could hear the whistling and shouting of the drivers as they urged their teams on.

"Logan, you got your tree notched?" Hinds asked.

"Yeah. All it'll take is about two whacks, and it'll drop right across that road, clean as a whistle."

"What about behind 'em, Russell?" Emmit asked. "What'll keep 'em from gettin' away that way?"

"We don't have to worry none about that," Hinds answered. "They ain't no way they can get them two wagons turned around on this road. The tree will keep 'em from goin' forward, and we'll keep 'em from goin' back."

"What are we goin' to do with 'em, after we shoot 'em?"

"Leave 'em for the buzzards," Hinds answered easily. "All right, ever'body get into position."

The men melted back into the woods and waited as the two wagons continued up the road. It had rained during the night, and from the shouts and whistles, Burke knew that the drivers were having to work their teams exceptionally hard to pull the wagons through the mud.

He also knew what no one else knew: that it was Federal troops under the canvas covers, not contraband.

When the wagons were on the road, in plain view, Hinds held up his hand, preparatory to giving the signal to attack. Unexpectedly, however, the lead wagon stopped and the driver sat there for a long moment, looking down the road.

"Look at the son of a bitch," Hinds said. "If I didn't know better, I'd say he was expectin' us."

"What do you want to do, Cap'n?" Emmitt asked.

"We won't do nothin', I reckon," Hinds replied. "Other'n just wait right here until they come on."

The driver climbed down from the wagon seat, then walked up the muddy road for several feet. Hinds and his men slipped a bit farther back into the woods. The driver stopped, and though he appeared to be staring right at them, Burke was convinced that he didn't see them.

If the driver had been more observant, however, he might have seen the freshly cut wood chips that were floating in the water on the road, put there from the notching of the tree. But the driver didn't notice them. Finally he turned and walked back to his wagon.

"Do you see anything, Pugh?" the driver of the second wagon called. His voice sounded thin and high-pitched.

"Naw," Pugh replied. He climbed back onto his wagon, then untied the reins from the brake lever and whistled. "Haw, there! Giddup!"

"He had a hunch," Hinds said under his breath. "I'll

give him that. The son of a bitch had a hunch.''

The wagons began rolling up the road once more, and as they drew closer, Hinds again held up his hand. At the appropriate time he brought his hand down. There were two sharp reports as the ax took the final two bites from the towering tree. Then, with groans, creaks, and loud snapping noises, the tree started down, falling across the muddy road with the crashing thunder of an artillery barrage. At the same time the tree hit the road in front of the wagons, Hinds's men moved out onto the road.

''Get the niggers out of them wagons!'' Hinds shouted.

Suddenly the two drivers jumped down from their seats onto the road on the opposite side of the wagons. At the same time, the canvas covers were raised, and a dozen or more men, in each wagon, stood up and aimed rifles at Hinds and his men.

Shocked by the sudden turn of events, Hinds realized at once that his entire band could be taken out with one volley from the wagons. Quickly he threw down his own weapon and put up his hands.

''Don't shoot!'' he shouted. ''Don't shoot!' We surrender!''

When the others saw Hinds drop his weapon and throw up his hands, they followed suit.

With a shout of victory, the men who had been hiding in the wagons jumped down and rushed forward, their weapons at the ready. As they got closer, Burke realized that they weren't the Federal soldiers he had been expecting. From the rough, ragtag look of them, they weren't even militiamen. They were Jayhawkers!

''Who is in command here?'' Burke asked when the Jayhawkers gathered around all of them, pointing their weapons at the six disarmed men.

''I am,'' someone answered. ''Folks call me Doc Jennison.'' Jennison was, perhaps, one of the shortest full-grown men Burke had ever seen. Less than five feet tall, he was wearing knee-high, yellow leather boots and a high-crowned fur hat that seemed to be half as tall as he was. The effect was ludicrous, as if Jennison were little more than boots and hat.

''Caught by a goddamned redleg,'' Hinds said, spitting.

"Well, I got to hand it to you, Jayhawker. You set us up. You set us up good."

Jennison chuckled. "It wasn't I who set you boys up. It was one of your own."

"What?" Hinds asked.

"Which one of you would be Lieutenant Burke Phillips?"

Hinds turned in his saddle and looked accusingly at Burke. "That you he's talking about, Burke?" Hinds asked.

Burke cleared his throat. He could feel his cheeks burning. "I am Lieutenant Phillips," he said.

"*Lieutenant* Phillips?" Lonnie said with a nervous laugh. "Burke, what the hell you talkin' about? You ain't no lieutenant."

"I'm afraid I am, Lonnie. I am a first lieutenant in the United States Army," Burke said.

"What the hell is a lieutenant in the army doin' way out here?" Vern asked.

"I'm on a special mission for the president of the United States," Burke said.

"Ain't you figured it out, yet?" Hinds asked. "Your friend Burke Phillips is a traitor. He sold us out!"

"I was just doing my duty," Burke said quickly. "Men like you, Hinds, are doing our side more harm than good."

"Just which side is 'our side'?" Lonnie asked accusingly.

"Our side, the side of law and justice," Burke replied. He looked at Lonnie and Vern. "You two ought to understand that. When you learned that he intended to murder the coloreds, you were as disgusted by the idea as I was."

"Maybe I was," Vern replied bitterly. "But I sure as hell wouldn't have turned my friends over to the goddamn Jayhawkers. Besides, you know them goddamn Jayhawkers, Burke. And you know there ain't a one of 'em what isn't as bad as Hinds."

"It wasn't supposed to be Jayhawkers," Burke said. He looked pointedly at Jennison. "What are you doing here, anyway? Where are the Federal soldiers?"

"We don't need any Federal soldiers," Jennison said. He twisted in his saddle and yelled back to the driver of the first wagon. "Pugh, bring that wagon up here!"

Pugh whistled and slapped the reins against the back of his team, and the wagon started forward.

"Hey, I know you, don't I?" Hinds said, looking closely at the driver of the wagon.

"I hope you know me," the driver replied. "The name is Pugh, Horace Pugh. When you killed every one of the colored men and women my wife and I were taking to freedom, you asked me to remember you. Well, Mr. Hinds, by God, I remembered."

"Hush up your palaverin', Pugh," Jennison said. "This son of a bitch don't need no explainin'." He pointed to a tree, which had a long, stout limb growing at right angles to the trunk about ten feet above the ground. "You see that tree there? Put your wagon right under the limb." Looking back up at Hinds and his men, Jennison said, "You men want to get down off your horses?"

Burke started to dismount with the others.

"You can keep your saddle, Lieutenant Phillips," Jennison said. "My business is with the others." He turned to some of his own men. "Tie their hands behind them," he ordered. A couple of men stepped forward to carry out the order.

The wagon was moved into position under the tree; then, from the bottom of the wagon, five ropes were produced. The ropes had already been woven into hangman's nooses, and the noose ends were thrown up and over the tree limb, then passed through a slipknot so that the rope end could be drawn tightly against the tree limb. A brief moment later, five hangman's ropes were dangling over the wagon.

"What the hell?" Hinds asked. "You plannin' on hangin' us?"

"What an astute observation," Jennison replied with a hollow, evil laugh.

"Hold it, Jennison, I forbid this!" Burke called.

Jennison chuckled. "You *forbid* it?"

"Yes, I'm in command here, and I demand that you turn these men over to me. That was my arrangement with the United States marshal."

"Well, you ain't dealin' with the United States marshal, Lieutenant Phillips, you are dealin' with me. And you are hardly in a position to demand anything. You should be glad I don't hang you with the others," Jennison said.

"Burke?" Vern asked, his voice now laced with fear. "Burke, you ain't goin' to let this redlegged son of a bitch hang us, are ye?"

"I warn you, hanging these men under these circumstances is an act of murder. If you do so, I will report you to the highest authority," Burke said.

"You ever heard of Lane? Senator Jim Lane?" Jennison asked.

"Yes, of course I have."

"Well, Lieutenant Burke, he *is* the highest authority. And he is the one who ordered this execution to take place."

Hinds, Lonnie, Vern, Logan, and Emmitt, their arms now tied behind their backs, were led over to the wagon, then lifted onto it. One by one they were positioned under the tree limb, then the nooses were placed around their necks.

"Do you five men have anything to say before we send you off to meet your Maker?" Jennison asked.

"Please!" Vern whimpered. "Me'n Lonnie . . . we ain't never done nothin'! This here was our first time to ever ride with Hinds. Tell 'em, Burke! You tell 'em!"

"It will avail you nothing to cry to him," Jennison said. "He cannot help you. What about you? Do you have anything to say?" he asked Logan.

Logan, whose eyes were wide in fear, shook his head no.

Jennison looked at Hinds. "And you, murderer of colored women and children. What have you to say?"

"I say I'll keep the fires in hell stoked up for you, Jennison," Hinds growled.

Jennison chuckled, then stepped back from the wagon and nodded toward the wagon driver.

Pugh slapped the reins and shouted at the team. The horses responded, and the wagon, rather than jerking out from under the men, lumbered forward, clumsily. Awkwardly the five men were dragged clear of the wagon bed to hang from the limb. For several long, stomach-turning moments, the ropes creaked while the men gasped in ragged, dying rattles as they bent their bodies at the waist trying to relieve the pressure and swung back and forth, jerking and twitching.

Eight

From *Harper's Weekly,* Domestic Intelligence; April 20, 1861:

FORT SUMPTER FALLEN

Major Anderson has surrendered, after hard fighting, commencing at 4 ½ o'clock yesterday morning and continuing until five minutes to 1 today. The American flag has given place to the Palmetto of South Carolina.

Major Anderson surrendered after heavy bombardment, when his quarters and barracks were destroyed and he had no hope of reinforcements. The fleet lay idly by during the thirty hours of the bombardment and either could not, or would not, help him. The gallant major's troops were prostrate from exertion. There were but five of them hurt, four badly and one, it is thought, mortally, but the rest were worn out.

President Lincoln issued the following proclamation: Whereas the laws of the United States have been for some time past, and now are, opposed, and the execution thereof obstructed in the states of South Carolina, Georgia, Alabama, Florida, Mississippi, Louisiana, and Texas, by combinations too powerful to be suppressed by the ordinary course of Judicial proceedings, or by the powers vested in the Marshals by law, now, therefore, I, Abraham Lincoln, President of the United States, in virtue of the power in me vested by the Constitution and the laws, have thought fit to call forth, and hereby do call forth, the militia of the several States of the Union to the aggregate number of seventy-five thousand, in order to suppress said combinations, and to cause the laws to be duly executed.

From *Harper's Weekly,* Domestic Intelligence; June 29, 1861:

A PROCLAMATION BY GOVERNOR JACKSON

Governor Jackson, of Missouri, last week issued a proclamation which fully exhibits his desire to precipitate that state into secession, if any doubts of that fact had previously existed. After reciting various acts of the Federal authorities nullifying the legislation of the state, such as taking state troops prisoners, and putting an embargo on southern commerce, and reciting the agreement between General Harney and ex–Governor Sterling Price with the subsequent removal of Harney and his own recent interview with General Lyon, etc.

Governor Jackson calls for 50,000 men, to be enrolled as state troops, to repel the invasion of their soil by the United States troops, and drive them out of the state. He admits that Missouri is still a member of the United States, and that it is not for him to disturb that relation; that a convention would, at the proper time, express the sovereign will of the people in relation to it; that in the meantime it was the duty of the people to obey the constitutional requirements of the United States Government: but he advises them that their first allegiance is due to the state.

After settling his account with the packet steward, Burke Phillips came back over to stand beside his friend Dan Morris, who was leaning against a rail fence, looking down the cobblestoned riverbank toward the boat. Smoke was billowing from the twin chimneys, and little wisps of steam escaped from the opening and closing relief valve.

Dan was in the uniform of a captain in the U.S. Army. Burke was in civilian clothes.

"I've got my luggage checked all the way through to

Charleston," Burke said. "Of course, with South Carolina being one of the states in rebellion . . . I'm not sure it will get there." He chuckled. "Hell, I'm not even sure I'll get there."

"I wish you would reconsider your resignation, Burke," Dan said, handing his friend one of the two mugs of beer he had just bought. "And stay out here with me."

"And I wish I had never come out here in the first place," Burke said. "Dan, you don't know how that made me feel, watching my friends be hanged like that."

Dan took a drink of his beer, then wiped the foam from his lips before he answered. "I think I do. I went through it as well, remember?"

Burke shook his head. "No, you didn't. John Brown was legally tried and hanged. And you could hardly call him your friend. As I understand it, you had just met him."

"Yes, but Hank Byrd was my friend. And I respected the aims of Brown and his men, even if I didn't approve of his methods."

"But you weren't the instrument of his capture, or the cause of his execution," Burke replied. "I was. I was a betrayer, Dan, and the stench of what I did is still in my nostrils."

"We both did things that we would rather not have done. But we were following orders."

"From a president who is no longer in office," Burke said.

"And thus, the orders are no longer in force. Don't you see, Burke? Your promotion came through on the same orders as did mine. We are through with the spy business. We would both be regular army officers, now."

"Officers in a state that is sure to secede."

Dan shook his head. "I don't think Missouri will pull out of the Union. St. Louis makes up over half the population of the entire state, and most in St. Louis are pro-Union."

"Only the foreigners," Burke said. "You read in the papers the reply Governor Jackson sent to Lincoln, when he requested that Missouri send its militia to the Union cause. I quote: 'Your requisition is illegal, unconstitutional, revolutionary, inhuman, diabolical, and cannot be complied with.' Besides which, he has submitted a bill of secession to the state legislature, and the word is it will be passed.''

"Don't forget about Jefferson Barracks. There is a very strong contingent of federal troops in Missouri, and they will not let the state secede, regardless of what the governor and the state legislature do.''

"Well, there is no doubt about my home state. North Carolina has joined her Southern sisters in secession.''

"We have no home state now, you and I, Burke. When we graduated from West Point, we stood out on the plain and took an oath of allegiance to the United States. The army is our home ... not North Carolina, and not Vermont.''

"Board!'' the steward called.

"And not Missouri,'' Burke replied, picking up the bag he would carry with him into his stateroom. "Dan, you ...'' He was quiet for a moment. "You know that if we meet again, we will meet as enemies.''

"No,'' Dan said, shaking his head. "The North and the South may be enemies. But you and I never will be.''

"Good luck, my friend,'' Burke said, extending his hand.

"God go with you,'' Dan replied.

The whistle blew, and the relief valve on the steamboat's engine boomed.

"Mr. Phillips! Mr. Phillips!'' a woman's voice called, and Burke turned to see Catherine hurrying toward him.

"Miss Darrow? What are you doing here?''

"I came to tell you good-bye,'' Catherine said.

"Haul in the gangplank!'' the steward shouted.

"I've got to go now,'' Burke said. "My boat is leaving.''

"I'm sorry I was late.''

"Cast off all lines, fore and aft!''

"Burke, you'd better get aboard,'' Dan warned.

"Dan, this is Catherine Darrow. Miss Darrow, this is my friend Dan Morris.''

The deep-throated whistle blew, and the paddle wheel slapped against the water. The boat started easing back.

"Burke, your boat?'' Dan said.

Burke looked at Catherine, then smiled and shrugged before he turned and ran down to the dock.

"He'll never make it,'' Catherine said.

"I've learned never to doubt him,'' Dan said.

Even as Dan was speaking, Burke made a mighty leap

from the dock to the boat, landing on a coil of rope. He turned and looked back, then, with a big smile, waved good-bye.

"He won't be coming back, will he?" Catherine asked.

"No," Dan said. "And I'm glad."

Catherine looked over at Dan in surprise. "What a strange thing for you to say. I thought he said you were his friend."

"I am," Dan replied. "And that's why I don't want him to come back here. You see, Miss Darrow, he is going home to join the Confederacy, while I shall remain loyal to the Union."

"Oh," Catherine said. "Yes, I see what you mean. If two friends are to be in opposing armies, it is best that they be as far apart as possible." She turned and started back toward her carriage. "It was a pleasure meeting you, Mr. Morris."

"Miss Darrow?" Dan called to her. Catherine stopped and looked back toward him. "I don't wish to be forward," he said. "But we have just told a mutual friend good-bye, and it is lunchtime. I wonder if you would do me the honor of dining with me. Unless, of course, you find my Union sympathies disagreeable."

"And why would you think I would find such sympathies disagreeable?"

Dan nodded toward the carriage where Willie sat, stoically, in the driver's seat.

"Your driver," Dan said. "Your slave?"

"Yes," Catherine admitted. "But I still hold to the belief that loyalty to the Union and slave ownership need not be mutually exclusive."

"Then you will have lunch with me?"

Catherine smiled sweetly. "I'm sorry, Mr. Morris, but I think it would be better if I declined. However, I do thank you for your kind invitation. Good day to you, sir."

Smiling back at her, Dan gave a half salute. "And to you, madam. Perhaps our paths will cross again."

Catherine nodded in reply, then climbed into the carriage. Dan watched her until the carriage turned the corner at the end of the block, then disappeared behind the warehouse.

Nine

From *Harper's Weekly*, Domestic Intelligence; August 3, 1861:

AFFAIRS IN MISSOURI

Our latest accounts from Missouri state that both Ben McCulloch and Governor Jackson have retreated, with all their available forces, across the Missouri line into Arkansas, for the purpose of drilling their troops. They were supposed to have a command numbering some 17,000, including the Texas Rangers and a Regiment from Mississippi. General Lyons, who was marching south to attack their force, at last accounts had 6,000 men and is expected soon to have 10,000 or 12,000. He had also, which is of the utmost importance, a large park of field artillery of various descriptions, an abundance of ammunition, and a full transportation train. Meantime, in north Missouri, secession appears to be entirely crushed out. General Pope has established the National Headquarters at St. Charles, having under his control about 7,000 troops, so posted that all important points are within easy reach. During the session of the State Convention at Jefferson City the national troops and the Home Guards will encamp outside the city limits.

THE LESSON OF DEFEAT

If we are true to ourselves, the disaster of 21st July will prove a benefit rather than an injury. The Bull Run tragedy is fraught with many valuable lessons.

It will teach us, in the first place, and not only us, but those also who have in charge the national interests at this crisis, that this war must be prosecuted on scientific principles, and that popular clamor must not be suffered to override the dictates of experience and the rules of strategy. We have the best evidence to prove that the march to Bull Run and the fight there were both undertaken against the judgment of Lieutenant General Winfield Scott, and solely in deference to the popular craving for action which owed its origin and main virulence to the *New York Tribune*. The wretched results must serve as a warning for the future. Hereafter our generals must not be hurried into premature demonstrations. If any portion of the press should attempt to goad them into setting in opposition to their judgment, public sentiment must rebuke the mischievous endeavor, and our officers and the Government must withstand it resolutely. No doubt, in the course of the next few weeks or months, it will often appear that our armies are sluggish, and their action dilatory. We must remember, when this occurs, that there may be reasons for delay which the public cannot discern. We must, in such cases, remind each other of the fatal twenty-first of July, and thank God that we can trust implicitly in Abraham Lincoln and Winfield Scott.

Burke, who was now a captain in the Confederate Infantry, sat on a tree stump, drinking a cup of coffee and writing a letter. It was a little after ten-thirty at night, and the mosquitoes were out in full force. He slapped at one on the back of his neck, then pulled it around to look at the little smear of blood in his hands.

"I hope you're bothering the Yankees as much as you are us," Burke growled.

He went back to the letter he was writing to Catherine Darrow:

Manassas Junction, Virginia, July 20, 1861
Dear Miss Darrow,
    You have been much on my mind since I departed Missouri, and I have but to close my eyes to see you standing on the riverbank, waving good-bye.

I do not know if you have ever thought of me, or, indeed, if you even remember me. But, on the eve of battle a soldier's mind often turns to more pleasant considerations than the reality at hand. My pleasant thoughts are of you, and my reality is that we are poised on the brink of what may be the first real test of the South's resolve to depart the Union, and the North's determination to hold the Southern States in bondage.

By the time you receive this letter this battle, if not the issue, will have been settled, and what I am telling you now will be of little consequence to you, or of value to the enemy. But, a description of the situation at hand may help you to better understand the events which are about to unfold.

Behind me the men of my company have already gone to bed for the night. Around the camp we have posted our pickets to keep an eye on the Federal troops who, under the command of General McDowell, are occupying ground to the northeast. We, under General Beauregard, are in fields to the southwest, and our two armies are divided by a small stream called Bull Run, which runs from the northwest to the southeast. The stream itself provides no defense, as it offers too many fords.

With two armies in bivouack, we cover the countryside like a cloud of locusts, as thick and as destructive. A plague of soliders can kill a crop in the quickest possible time. Our orders against plundering are very strict, and I think our boys are trying to minimize the damage, but the invaders from the North having no connection with the countryside, nor anyone in it, are destroying everything through which they pass.

Earlier tonight our camp was alive with lights, fires, songs, and shouts of laughter. Now, all is silence, fires are out, men talk, almost in whisper, and sleep on their arms.

What shall tomorrow bring? Will it be the shout of victory, the shame of defeat, the pain of wounds, or the closing scene of death?

> From your obedient servant,
> Burke Phillips
> Capt. CSA

Burke looked up when he heard one of his pickets call out.

"Halt! Who goes there?"

"Sergeant Dawes, returning with the scouting party," came the muffled reply.

"Coffee," the picket challenged, giving the call sign.

"Biscuit."

Having heard the proper countersign, the picket let Sergeant Dawes and his men back into the camp. Burke signed the letter and folded it for later posting, then tossed the bitter coffee grounds from his cup. He stood up and walked over to meet the scout.

"Hello, Sergeant Dawes, did you see anything?"

"Yes, sir, we seen a body of troops crossing Bull Run about two miles north of Stone Bridge. We could see the head of the column in the woods on this side, and the rear of the column in the woods on the other side. There was about half a mile in between, and the open area was solid with troops."

"Any artillery?"

"Yes, sir, we seen that, too."

"Well, I'd better send a report up to General Bee. Have you and your men had your supper?"

"No, sir. We been out since about three."

"Get yourselves something to eat, then try to get some rest if you can. The way the Yankees are bringing up support, I expect the ball is going to open tomorrow."

"Yes, sir," Sergeant Dawes said.

Burke returned to the coffeepot that sat on a flat rock near the flickering campfire and refilled his cup. Then he wrote out a report for General Bee and called for a courier.

"Take this to General Bee's headquarters," he ordered. He handed him the letter he had written to Catherine Darrow. "And see that this goes out with the mail, will you?"

"Yes, sir," the courier replied, taking the note and letter, then starting toward the horse that was already saddled just for this purpose.

Burke watched the courier ride off, then he walked down to the edge of Bull Run creek and looked across toward the Federal positions. Less than one mile separated the two armies, and from here he could quite easily see their campfires, as he knew they could see his. No doubt there were, on that side of the stream, couriers riding quickly among commands, bearing messages just like the one he had just sent. In fact, one of the messages on the other side might very well have come from a friend or classmate.

If battle did come tomorrow, it would be Burke's first. He had trained all his life to be a warrior, and now he was about to put that training into effect. But the irony was, he would be going into his first battle not in defense of the flag that had trained him, but against it. In fact, one of the units across from him was Tyler's division. Within Tyler's division was the very company, and the very men, Burke had once commanded.

The idea did not sit well with him. It did not sit well at all.

"How did it get this far?" he asked aloud, though speaking so quietly that no one could hear. "Dear God in heaven, how did it ever get this far?"

Burke was awakened the next morning by the roar of cannonfire. He ran down to the edge of the creek to see, if he could, what was going on. The firing was coming from his left, and when he looked in that direction he could see great billowing clouds of white smoke, accented by flashes of light as the Confederate artillery opened fire on the Union lines. The Union artillery returned fire almost at once, and some of the incoming shells struck the nearby trees, breaking off huge limbs that came crashing down into Burke's camp.

"Captain Phillips! Captain Phillips, sir!" a rider said, galloping into the camp.

"Yes?"

"General Bee's compliments, sir, and he asks that you bring your men at once to Stone Bridge!"

"Right away!" Burke replied.

"Let's go, men! Quickly, quickly!" Burke shouted, rallying his men from their early morning slumber.

General Bee had put his two brigades in position in a small depression overlooking the bridge, and when Burke arrived, Bee sent him forward to join with Major Wheat, whose battalion would be the first to engage the Federal troops when they attacked.

"Forward men, at a run!" Burke called, and, holding their rifles at high port, his men sprinted, their equipment jangling and clanking, to join the line with Major Wheat. As soon as they were in position, Burke reported directly to the major. The sound of cannonfire was intermixed with the rattle of musketry coming from the treeline just across the creek.

"Captain Phillips reporting, sir!" Burke said. He had to shout to be heard above the gunfire. "I've added my men to your line."

"Very good, Captain," Wheat shouted back. "Go back to them and take your position, for the enemy shall soon be upon us!"

Burke returned to his men; then, with his saber in one hand and his revolver in the other, he waited.

From out of the trees on the opposite side of the creek appeared a long line of soldiers. They were coming forward at a trot, firing as they came.

"Steady," Burke said. "Steady, men! Hold your fire until I give the word."

All up and down the line the Confederates waited as the men in blue advanced. The numbers of attacking soldiers grew as line after line of them came out of the trees.

The Federal attack was supported by a devastating bombardment of artillery as shot and shell dropped into the Southern ranks. Some shells exploded over the line of infantrymen, sending out deadly shards of shrapnel, while the solid shot unlimbered Confederate cannon, ripped limbs from trees, and crashed into the few houses and structures that occupied the ground.

"Now, men, fire!" Burke shouted, bringing his sword down sharply.

The sudden volley of musketry brought down several Union soldiers, and a barrage of grapeshot from the Southern artillery brought down more. The Federal advance was halted, but the soldiers didn't turn back. Instead they took positions just on the other side of the creek and began pouring a brutal fire into the thinly stretched Southern lines. For three hours the battle raged as the sound of musketry and the thunder of artillery filled the valley with a roar. Thick white gunsmoke boiled up out of the dust. From both armies, wounded and frightened men, dazed and bloodstained, began streaming to the rear, while all around them the battle raged in a panorama of fire, smoke, dust, and swirling men.

"Captain Phillips! Captain Phillips!"

Burke turned to see a young, frightened courier. "What is it!" he shouted above the din of battle.

"Captain Peters asked if you will support him in an organized withdrawal!"

"You mean retreat?"

"Captain Peters says that the Yankees are carrying the field!"

At that moment Burke saw a Yankee soldier kneel to fire his musket; taking careful aim with his revolver, Burke shot him down before the Yankee could fire. He looked back at the courier.

"You tell Peters I am too busy to think about retreating. He may withdraw if he wishes, but here I am, and here I shall remain until ordered out by General Bee."

"Yes, sir, I'll tell him!" the courier replied. Holding his hat on his head, he turned and ran back toward his own commander.

A few moments later another courier brought the message that General Bee wanted to see Burke. Leaving his first lieutenant in command, Burke moved quickly along the skirmish line until he reached General Bee. General Bee was striding up and down the line, urging his men to keep up the fire.

"Captain Phillips, are you prepared to move forward when you receive the word?"

"Yes, sir," Burke replied. He chuckled.

"What do you find so funny, sir?" Bee asked.

"I was afraid you had called me up here to coordinate a retreat."

"Retreat? You don't win battles by retreating." Bee pointed to General Jackson. "There is Jackson, standing like a stone wall! Let us determine to die here, and we will conquer."

"Give me the word, sir, and my company and I will lead the attack," Burke said.

"Go back to your men, strengthen their resolve," Bee ordered. "I'll send you word directly."

"Yes, sir," Burke said, and returned to his part of the line.

By now the battle was no longer a long, static line of gray facing a long, static line of blue. Instead it had evolved into a disconnected series of individual battles, even involving hand-to-hand fighting, as groups of men clustered around their shot-scarred flags.

Perhaps General Bee was right, Burke thought. Perhaps now would be the time for an attack, for surely the Federals had to be dispirited by the fact that their own attack had broken down.

Burke had no sooner returned to his own position than he received word that General Bee had been killed, shortly after he'd left him.

"Who has assumed command?" Burke asked.

"General Jackson."

Burke thought of the coolness Jackson was displaying under fire, and he nodded. "We'll be all right, then," he said. "General Jackson is a good man."

The fighting continued without resolution until about three-thirty in the afternoon, when the Federals pulled back, received reinforcements, then regrouped for another attack.

General Jackson, on horseback now, rode up and down the entire line, talking to the men under his command.

"Steady, men, all's well," he said over and over again.

"General, are them Yankees comin' agin?" asked one of the soldiers in the ranks.

"I expect they will, men, I expect they will," Jacson said. "But we've already taken the measure of the best they have, and I expect we'll handle them all right if they come again."

Then, as he continued his ride down the line, Burke could hear the same lines over and over again. "Steady, men, all's well. Steady, men, steady."

"Here they come!"

"Hold your fire, men, hold your fire!" Burke called, and all up and down the line other officers were telling their troops the same thing.

From out of the trees on the far side, a long, solid mass

of blue moved forward, marching to the measure of their drummers' beat.

The shooting stopped, and for a long moment nothing could be heard but the repeated drum cadence and the jangle of equipment. The Federal troops came across the open area, dressing up their line as if they were on parade. It was one of the most magnificent sights Burke had ever seen.

Burke looked at his men and was pleased to see, not fear, but determination. They had performed well thus far, and he had no doubt that they would be equal to the task before them.

"Hold your fire until they're on you!" General Jackson called. "Then fire and give them the bayonet. And, when their attack falters, you charge, and yell like the furies!"

Burke waited until the advancing troops were within pistol range, then he lowered his pistol and fired. His shot was the signal to the others, and all up and down the line, a devastating barrage of musketry and grapeshot slammed into the attacking Federal troops. The attacking troops were staggered, then stopped.

"Forward!" Burke shouted, seizing the advantage. "After them!"

Burke's company started forward first, then it was joined by the other companies in Wheat's line. Soon the entire gray line started forward, so that the Confederates, screaming at the top of their voices, ran pell-mell through the stream, then up the opposite side, across the open pasture, and into the face of the now dispirited Federal attack.

With bayonets gleaming in the sunlight, and a high, shrill yell coming from their throats, the Confederates moved forward like an unstoppable gray avalanche.

The orderly Yankee line broke. The soldiers in blue turned and fled, running past their own officers who were following on horseback, flailing at them with their sabers, screaming at them to stand and fight.

"Keep after them, men! Keep after them!" Burke shouted excitedly.

The Yankees continued to run, many of them throwing down their rifles and equipment in order to run faster. Burke and his men kept after them, moving around the bewildered Yankee officers on horseback like a swiftly flowing stream around isolated rocks.

The pursuing Confederate soldiers encountered the carriages and victorias of the civilians who had driven out from Washington with picnic baskets to watch the day's entertainment.

"Go back! Go back!" the Yankee soldiers shouted to the bewildered civilians as they ran by them. "We are whipped! We are whipped!"

The rout continued until nightfall, when, at last, the Confederate officers, seeking to reestablish control over their army, called a halt to the pursuit.

Burke's men, elated over their victory, began cheering and laughing and running back and forth on the battlefield, picking up the weapons the Yankees had abandoned. They also began helping their wounded back to the aid stations; Major Wheat, who had been in charge of the line where Burke's men had fought, was among them. Hearing that Wheat was in the field hospital, Burke hurried to see him.

When he reached the tent, he saw Wheat lying in the flickering yellow light of a lantern. An operating table had been made by placing a door from one of the destroyed houses across two sawhorses.

Wheat was quiet, and his breathing was coming in ragged gasps. A doctor was leaning over him.

"Are you a religious man, Major Wheat?" the doctor asked.

"As religious as the next man, I suppose," Wheat answered painfully. "Why?"

"Because, my friend, I think you would do well to make your peace with God. I have stopped the bleeding and bandaged your wounds, but the bullet passed through both of your lungs, and you are going to die."

Wheat was silent for a moment before he replied. "I don't feel like dying yet," he wheezed.

"Nevertheless you must prepare yourself, for there is no instance on record of anyone ever recovering from such a wound."

There was another beat of silence before Wheat answered. "Well then, I will put my case on record."

The doctor shook his head, then looked toward a couple

of the orderlies. "See if you can find a place to make him comfortable, then bring the next patient to me."

The two orderlies picked Wheat up and carried him into a nearby barn, then laid him in a stall on a bed of straw. Burke followed, staying out of the way until Wheat was put down. Wheat looked around at his surroundings.

"Well, our Lord started his life in a place like this," he said. "Seems to me it's a good enough place to end mine."

It began to rain, and almost unconsciously Burke glanced back toward the battlefield.

"Tell me, Captain Phillips, how many are still out there, lying in the rain?" Wheat asked.

Burke was surprised, not only that Wheat realized that it was raining, but that he knew and recognized him.

"I don't know for sure. Two or three thousand, I guess, counting the wounded from both armies."

"Poor devils," Wheat said.

"How are you doing, sir?"

"You heard the doctor. I'm dying," Wheat said. He gasped a few times. "Only, I don't plan to do so." Wheat tried to laugh. "We had them on the run, didn't we, Captain? Think about it. They're probably roaming through the streets of Washington City right now, exhausted, sleeping on porch steps, and crowding under the eaves for shelter."

"Yes, sir."

"We should've continued the chase, you know."

"Beg pardon, sir?"

"We should've run them all the way through Washington City. We could've captured Congress, the president, and his cabinet, the whole bunch of them. And we could've ended the war tonight."

Burke shook his head. "I agree, it would've been good had we been able to do it. But in truth, Major Wheat, our army was as disorganized in victory as was the Union Army in defeat. Not even Alexander the Great or Napoleon could've held them together long enough for a march to Washington."

"That's too bad," Wheat said. "For I fear that never again will we have an opportunity so golden."

★ ★ ★

Ten

From *Harper's Weekly,* Domestic Intelligence; August 31, 1861:

THE BATTLE AT SPRINGFIELD, MISSOURI

The following account of the battle is furnished by an eyewitness who left Springfield on Sunday morning and came through to Rolla on horseback:

Our army marched out of Springfield on Friday evening only 5,500 strong, the Home Guard remaining at that place. Our forces slept on the prairie a portion of the night and about sunrise on Saturday morning drove in the outposts of the enemy, and soon after the attck became general.

The attack was made in two columns by Generals Lyons and Sturgis, General Siegel leading a flanking force of about 1,000 men and four guns on the south of the enemy's camp.

The fight raged from sunrise until one or two o'clock in the afternoon. The Rebels, in overwhelming force, charged Captain Totten's battery three distinct times, but were repulsed with great slaughter.

General Lyons fell early in the day. He had been previously wounded in the leg and had a horse shot from under him.

The Colonel of one of the Kansas regiments having become disabled, the boys cried out, "General, you come and lead us on!" He did so, and at once putting himself in front, and while cheering the men on to the charge, received a bullet in the left breast and fell from his horse. He was asked if he was hurt and replied, "No, not much," but in a few minutes he expired without a struggle.

General Siegel had a very severe struggle and lost three of his four guns. His artillery horses were shot in their harness and the pieces disabled. He endeavored to haul them off with a number of prisoners he had taken, but was finally compelled to abandon them, first, however, spiking the guns and disabling the carriages.

About one o'clock the enemy seemed to be in great disorder, retreating and setting fire to their train of baggage wagons. Our forces were too much fatigued and cut up to pursue, so the battle may be considered a drawn one.

A letter from Dan Morris to Catherine Darrow:

Springfield, Missouri, August 9, 1861

Dear Miss Darrow,

I know you must be wondering who has the effrontery to send you an unsolicited letter. Please allow me to resolve that mystery for you. I am Dan Morris. We met when our mutual friend, Burke Phillips, left Missouri to take up the cause of the Confederacy. At that time, you may recall, I invited you to have lunch with me, but you declined.

While such a brief meeting does not give me the right to impose myself upon you, I must confess as to being so struck by your charm and beauty that I could not resist this temptation to open a correspondence with you.

Tomorrow, I will join many others in debating upon the field of battle, the issue which divides North from South. As I stated, our mutual friend, Burke Phillips, has taken up the Southern Banner, whereas I shall continue to serve the same flag to which I swore loyalty upon the plain at West Point some years past.

I do not know how you stand in the great question which has sundered our nation. But if that weighty issue may be set aside so that you and I could be-

come, not political pawns, but merely two people
seeking an innocent discourse, then I would greatly
enjoy the opportunity to correspond with you. If,
however, you would consider such a correspondence
inappropriate, please destroy this letter and accept the
apologies of one who will bother you no more.

> From one who wishes to be your friend,
> Dan Morris
> Captain, U.S. Army

Sealing his letter, Captain Dan Morris looked up as an
arriving scout poured rain out of his hat, then took off the
rubber poncho and hung it on a hook on the tent pole.
Outside, the rain continued to drum against the canvas of
the headquarters tent, and little streams ran across the dirt
floor, despite the trench that had been dug around the tent
to divert the pooling water. The scout saluted General Lyons, who was sitting at his field desk on the other side of
the tent.

General Lyons, his red hair glowing in the lantern light,
began examining the map as the scout rendered his report.

"And you say they are north of the Cowskins Springfield
Road?" Lyons asked.

"Yes, sir."

"What is their strength?"

"It could be as high as twenty thousand," Dan replied.

"Damn that Sterling Price," General Lyons said. "How
could he raise such an army so quickly?"

"Well, he is the governor of Missouri, General," Dan
explained.

"Former governor," General Lyons replied. Then, to the
scout, he added: "Have you eaten?"

"No, sir," the scout answered.

"Captain, have we anything for this man to eat?"

"I think so, sir," Dan said. Then he continued: "I admit
that Price is a former governor, but he is as popular with
the people now as he was when he held office. And outside
of St. Louis there is strong support for the South."

"That is true," General Lyons admitted.

"Here you go, Sergeant," Dan said, handing a cloth-
wrapped parcel to the scout. "It's a cold biscuit with a

piece of salt meat. Not much, I'm afraid, but it's all we have here.''

"Thank you, Captain, that'll be just fine,'' the sergeant said, unwrapping the biscuit to take a bite.

"Captain Morris, you have some experience fighting against these Missourians, I think?'' General Lyons asked.

"Yes, sir, I was involved in some of the border skirmishes before the war.''

"I would be interested in your opinion of General Price's army. Are they to be reckoned with?''

"Yes, sir, I would say so,'' Dan answered.

"Surely, sir, you joke. Why, there is scarcely a modern weapon in the whole lot of them,'' General Lyons said.

"I do not joke, General. Admittedly, General Price's army isn't very well armed. I mean, they are out there with nothing but flintlocks, shotguns, squirrel guns . . . hell, some of them have nothing more than Arkansas tooth-picks.''

"Arkansas toothpicks?''

"Knives.''

Lyons snorted. "Knives, on a battlefield.''

"Don't dismiss those knives out of hand, General. If the fighting gets to be hand to hand, a good man with an Ar-kansas toothpick is far superior to a soldier trying to use a bayonet.''

"Yeah,'' Lyons agreed. "Yeah, I guess you are right.'' He walked over to the opening of the tent and stood there, looking out at the rain. "Will this damn rain never stop?''

"It does seem to continue without letup,'' Dan said.

"You know, I have a theory about that. I believe that God puts his most cantankerous angel in charge of battles,'' Lyons said. "And that cantankerous gentleman's only job is to look down upon us lowly humans when we are at war, and create the worst conditions imaginable, in order to make the battle more miserable.'' The general turned away from the opening and smiled at Dan. "God has to do that, you see, otherwise war would become much too attrac-tive.''

"Attractive?''

"Oh, yes, Captain, war is very attractive,'' Lyons in-sisted, returning to his table to look at the map again. "Where else would we get our heroes, our stirring songs, our patriotic zeal, if it weren't for war? Why, just consider your own situation. You attended West Point, did you not? What attracted you to that institution, if not patriotism?''

"Perhaps there is something to what you say, sir."

"Of course there is. Now . . ." Lyons stroked his red beard as he studied the map. "Let me share my plan of battle with you. I'm going to send one column, under Colonel Siegel, in a wide sweep around the enemy to hit them in the rear. Then, when Colonel Siegel gets their attention, I'll hit them from the front with the main body."

"General, are you sure you want to split your forces like that? We are already outnumbered," Dan suggested.

"I know, I know, and I am disregarding one of the first things you learn in military tactics," Lyons said, dismissing Dan's objection with a wave of his hand. "In the classic military sense, you would be right. But this will not be a classic military engagement, Captain. Though we have twenty thousand men against us, they are not trained soldiers. They are nothing but small farmers and clerks, field hands and mechanics, led by an ex-governor with grandiose ideas. And, as you said yourself, they are not very well armed. It is my belief that they will be so dispirited by being hit from both sides that they will bolt and run. Thus, the tactical advantage of splitting our forces will far outweigh any negative."

"I hope you are right, sir," Dan said without enthusiasm.

"Besides, the angel God sent to send the rain down on us? Why, he is on our side, Captain. The rain will cover Colonel Siegel's movement. I've no doubt but that Siegel will be in position long before the Rebels even suspect anything is up."

Sometime after midnight the rain eased up a little, and when Dan and the others broke camp just before dawn the next morning, the rain had completely stopped.

Advance scouts brought back word that nothing was stirring in the Rebel camp. In fact, the Rebels had not even put out pickets.

"No sentries on duty?" Lyons asked in disbelief.

"Not a one, General."

"What did I tell you, Captain Morris?" Lyons snorted.

"We aren't attacking an army. We're attacking an unorganized mob."

"I beg of you, General, don't underestimate them," Dan said.

"Thank you for your word of caution, Captain," Lyons said by way of dismissal. "Major Sinclair," he called.

"Yes, sir?" his adjutant replied.

"Send word down to all commanders. We will attack when we hear that Siegel is engaged."

"Yes, sir," Major Sinclair replied.

Couriers, dispatched by Major Sinclair, hurried through the camp, carrying General Lyons's message. Within half an hour every Union soldier was armed and waiting, patiently, for the battle to begin. Dan rode through the camp on horseback, inspecting the readiness. As he did so, he caught parts of many conversations.

"I hear they don't even have any guns. Nothin' but knives and clubs. . . ."

"They don't have any guards posted a'tall. Why, like as not, when General Lyons gives us the word, we'll just wade right on through 'em. . . ."

"When we're through with 'em today, they'll run down into Arkansas, you can bet on that. Why, after this, I'll bet you won't be able to find a Reb in the entire state of Missouri."

"Nary one alive, anyhow. . . ."

Eventually the banter stopped, and the soldiers began to wait for the battle to come.

As the first pink fingers of dawn colored the eastern horizon, there were several flashes of what looked like summer lightning, followed by a deep-throated roar.

"Damn, it's going to rain again," someone said.

Dan shook his head. "No, that's artillery," he explained. "Colonel Siegel is engaged."

"Forward, men!" General Lyons called. "To the attack!"

Lyons's regular army troops swept forward, confident of an easy time of it with the ragtag army they were facing. After all, the Rebels were all snug in their blankets, what could they do?

To the surprise of the Federal soldiers, however, the Rebels came out of their sleeping rolls, half-naked, half-asleep, and fighting mad. Quickly, much more quickly than even Dan would have believed possible, General Price rallied his men to establish a line of resistance, his white hair streaming in the wind as he rode up and down just behind the line of the embattled Missourians, shouting encouragement to them. The defenders were easily able to meet the attacks from both directions.

The fighting moved to close quarters, made necessary by the fact that the Confederate weapons weren't capable of stand-off fighting. Squads, platoons, companies, and entire battalions of Confederates would move right up to the Federal lines, deliver a volley, then reload and deliver another. Unlike their brother Confederate soldiers at Bull Run, two weeks earlier and a thousand miles away, there was no cheering. Instead the men went about their grim task of firing and reloading and firing again in deadly determination, accompanied only by the sustained rattle of rifle fire, the deep roar of cannons, and the agonizing screams of pain from the wounded.

The soldiers in blue, stunned that the Rebels had not run at the first onslaught, and now shocked by the boldness the Rebels were displaying by coming right into their faces, quickly lost the advantage.

The Federal attack from the South faltered almost from the very moment it encountered resistance. Siegel's men broke, then began running, leaving behind their flags, hundreds of rifles, and all but one of their cannon.

With the threat from their rear alleviated, General Price was able to turn all of his men toward the main attack, instantly doubling the number of effectives against Lyons. Dan saw that his men were beginning to waver as, across their front, the Confederates grew thicker and thicker as new regiments, fresh from their victory over Siegel, arrived moment by moment.

"Stand steady, men, stand steady!" Dan shouted.

Behind the Federal line, which was still holding, General Lyons was riding back and forth, shouting his own encouragement. Suddenly a bullet took off his hat, creasing his scalp and sending a trickle of blood down from his red hair. Almost immediately after that another bullet hit him in the thigh, and a third hit him in the ankle. At the same time, his horse was shot and fell dead under him.

"General Lyons!" Dan shouted, running to him.

"Help me up, lad," Lyons said in a strained voice. "Help me up and get me mounted, or I fear the day is lost."

Dan commandeered a horse from one of the couriers and helped the general remount.

"Let's go, men!" General Lyons shouted, taking off his hat and waving it over his head. "Follow me!"

General Lyons galloped to the front, then started riding toward the Confederates. For a brief moment, his men, inspired by the bravery of their general, started after him, and Dan had a glimmer of hope that the tide of battle would change. Then another bullet struck General Lyons, this time in the chest, and he went down again, this time for good.

Seeing their leader go down, the Federal troops were so badly shaken that they turned and ran. Dan and a few of the other officers tried desperately to stop the wholesale retreat, but it was too late. The retreat turned into a full-scale rout as the fleeing men left their general and their fallen comrades, both dead and wounded, on the field behind them. Suddenly Dan was caught between the lines as the Federals retreated and the Confederates advanced. In order to avoid being taken prisoner, he had to spur his horse and ride at a gallop to catch up with the retreating blue line.

By the time the general retreat halted, and the troops regrouped, they were several miles away from the battle, in the small town of Rolla, Missouri. Here, Colonel Siegel assumed command. That night Siegel held an officers' call, bringing all of his officers together to formally take command and to issue new orders.

When the business was over, Siegel lit his pipe from a burning stick he took from the flickering flames of a campfire. He saw Dan getting ready to return to his own company.

"Captain Morris, stay a moment, won't you?" Siegel asked around puffs.

"Certainly, sir," Dan answered, and remained behind as the other officers returned to their commands.

Siegel drew several puffs before he had the pipe going to his satisfaction. "What did you think about today?"

"It was a disaster," Dan replied.

"I am told that you are a West Point graduate. A regular."

"Yes, sir, that is true," Dan said.

"You should have cautioned General Lyons not to split his command."

"I did caution him, sir," Dan replied. "But he did it anyway."

"You should have insisted."

"Colonel, you were second in command. If you felt that way, why didn't you say something?"

"Because it is my belief that the second in command should show absolute loyalty and obedience. My hands were tied. But you are a West Pointer. I think he would have listened to you."

"I'm not sure he would have listened to General Fremont himself," Dan said, and shook his head. "But it would not have mattered anyway. Even if we had kept the force together, I don't think we would have carried the day. The Rebels are well-led, determined, and courageous, and contrary to what some people believe, I think we have more than a minor insurrection on our hands. I think the United States is engaged in a full-scale war."

"But surely the war will amount to nothing," Seigel suggested. "This, this . . . debacle today is not representative of how things will be. And by the way, I take full responsibility for my own failure to prevent my men from running from the field—"

"No, sir, that is a responsibility that should be shared by every officer in the command, for all of us failed in that department," Dan interrupted. "But as for the battle we fought today, we must add to it the battle fought at Manassas Junction a couple of weeks ago. There, too, our army fled from the field."

"Yes, that is true, isn't it?" Siegel said, shaking his head. "God help us, Captain."

"And God help the United States," Dan added.

★ ★ ★

Eleven

Independence, Missouri, August 21, 1861
Dear Captain Phillips,

I must confess that I was surprised, though pleasantly so, to receive your letter of the 20th ultimate,
in which you described your feelings and the conditions on the eve of battle.

Much has been written of the battle of Bull Run,
and your brilliant description of the creek bearing
that name, and the disposition of forces has helped
me to understand more easily the stories that I have
read.

Even though the battle had long been decided
when I received the letter from you, the clarity of
your words took me back so that it was as if I, too,
were awaiting the morrow. But your letter had a
frightening effect, too, for I can but wonder if you
survived the battle without harm. That you did, is my
earnest prayer.

Your friend,
Catherine Darrow

"Richmond! We're comin' into Richmond, the capital of
the Confederacy!" the conductor called proudly as he
walked through the lurching train car.

Upon hearing the station announced, Burke refolded the
oft read letter and prepared to detrain. After the battle at
Bull Run, Burke had gone home to see his parents. Now
he was returning to Richmond from Charleston, South Carolina. The trip from Charleston had taken over thirty-six
hours, whereas one year ago the same trip would have eas-

ily been accomplished in much less time. Then the trains
often traveled at nearly forty miles per hour. That was no
longer the case, however, as a new law designed to protect
the railroads from undue wear limited all trains to ten miles
per hour.

Burke looked through the window of the car as the train
crossed the James River on its approach to Richmond. The
city was spread out on the opposite bank of the river.

The capital of the Confederacy was normally a city of
thirty thousand, though its numbers were greatly swelled
by its position as capital of the South and by the advent of
the war. It was, the politicians liked to point out, just like
Rome, in that it was built upon seven hills.

The principal part of the city, however, was built upon
one hill, and on that hill was located Capitol Square, with
the Capitol Building, which was designed by Thomas Jefferson and guarded by a mounted statue of George Washington.

As Burke's mother was originally from Richmond, he
actually knew the city quite well. He knew that there was
really only one business thoroughfare, a north-and-south
street known as Main Street. And he knew that all the hotels, banks, newspaper offices, and principal stores were
located along this avenue.

Burke had come to Richmond in response to a telegram
sent to him by President Jefferson Davis. Like Burke, Davis
was a graduate of West Point. Davis had also been secretary
of war and had gone to West Point at least half a dozen
times while occupying that position. Burke had met him
first during one of those trips, then met him again shortly
after the successful conclusion of the fighting at Bull Run,
when President Davis visited the battlefield.

"This young man will go far," Major Wheat had told
President Davis from his bed in the field hospital. Wheat
had astounded the doctors, not only by not dying, but by
actually getting stronger. "He was the ablest and bravest
officer in our line."

"Good for you, young man," Davis said, shaking
Burke's hand. "I'm sure the South will have much use for
a young man of your courage and ability."

The South's "need" for Burke came very shortly after-
ward when, while home on furlough, he received a telegram

from President Davis. Now, on the train en route to Richmond, Burke pulled out the telegram to read it one more time.

Have proposal I think will interest you. Requires bravery and dedication of the kind you displayed at Bull Run. Please visit me in Richmond soonest. J. Davis, Pres. CSA.

Burke put away the telegram and wondered, for perhaps the twentieth time, what the president's proposal was.

As soon as the train stopped, Burke hurried to find a hack and, providing a generous tip, ordered the driver to take him swiftly to Capitol Square. Once there, however, any further attempt at swiftness was impossible because of the red tape of the bureaucracy already in place in the new government.

"I don't care whether the president sent for you or not, you don't get in to see him without an appointment."

"And how do I make an appointment?" Burke asked.

"I make the appointments," the clerk said with an air of self-importance.

"Then I should like an appointment at the soonest possible time."

"I can fit you in on Friday next," the clerk said, looking at his ledger book.

Burke sighed. "Very well, do what you can."

"Where will you be staying?" the clerk asked. "If something opens sooner, I will get in touch with you." He was being more generous now that Burke had given in to him.

"I don't know," Burke admitted. "I haven't thought about it."

"May I recommend the Hotel Crillion? They have the cleanest rooms at the lowest rates."

"Thank you," Burke said.

The hotels and restaurants of Richmond were crowded with men in colorful braided uniforms, representing units with such bombastic names as Bailey's Battlers, Morgan's Marauders, Wilson's Warriors, and perhaps a dozen or so others, none of which had ever seen combat. In fact, Burke quickly learned, many of these units didn't even exist on the South's tactical table of organizations but were simply elite social clubs organized to provide elegant uniforms for their gentlemanly members.

The Hotel Crillion, like all the other hotels in Richmond, was exceptionally crowded. Uniformed men and well-dressed women were so numerous in the lobby that a normal conversation was out of the question. The only way one could be heard was to yell just a little louder than his neighbor, and that, of course, only intensified the bedlam.

Captains, majors, and colonels who had never commanded a man, or heard a shot fired in anger, waved drinks and cigars as they discussed tactics and strategy. The women, who were also caught up in the excitement, were just as noisy as the men. Occasionally the high-pitched shrill of a woman's laugh could be heard above all else.

"You are in luck, sir," the hotel clerk said. "A room was just vacated."

Burke took the key and his grip up to his room. He had not worn his uniform on the train, though he had brought it with him. He intended to wear it when he met with President Davis. When he reached his room, he took his uniform out of the grip and hung it up to smooth out the wrinkles. He looked at it, still not quite used to its color, cut, and design. It was gray, not blue. His rank of captain was denoted not by two joined silver bars on a shoulder tab, as he was accustomed to, but by three golden bars on a choker collar. It was attractive, but it looked more like the uniform of a military school than that of an active-duty officer.

Someone knocked on his door. When he opened it he saw the same clerk who had, earlier in the day, refused to allow him in to see the president. Now the clerk was wearing a look of concern.

"I beg your pardon, sir," he said. "But when the president learned of your arrival, he asked that I bring you to him immediately. Would it be convenient for you to come now?"

"Yes, of course," Burke said, reaching for his jacket.

"There are so many colonels and even brigadier generals trying to get in to see the president for their own reasons that, I'm sure you understand, a mere captain made not the slightest impression upon me."

"Ah, but the difference is, I am a *real* captain," Burke

said. "Whereas all these others running around here are little more than characters in a theatrical of their own production."

The clerk laughed. "Yes," he said. "Yes indeed, you are right, sir."

When he walked out of the front door of the hotel, Burke saw that a carriage was waiting in the street to take him directly to Capitol Square. Fifteen minutes later he was shown into President Davis's office.

President Davis and a silver-haired man in a general's uniform were bending over a table, studying a map. Davis straightened and smiled as Burke was led in.

"Captain Phillips, welcome, sir. It was good of you to come," President Davis said warmly.

"I thank you for providing the transportation," Burke replied. He looked at the large, handsome, white-haired man. "I believe I know you, sir," he said.

The white-haired man smiled. "President Davis tells me you spent some time in Missouri."

Burke snapped his fingers. "That's it! You are Governor Sterling Price!"

"I *was* Governor Price. Now I am General Price, of the Confederate Army of Missouri."

"It is good that you two should meet now," Davis said. "Not only because both of you are from Missouri, but because you are both genuine heroes of the Confederacy. General Price, it was reported to me by Captain Phillips's commanding officer that his valor had no superior during the battle of Bull Run. And, Captain, surely I need not tell you of General Price's exploits at Wilson Creek."

"They have been well reported in all the newspapers," Burke said, extending his hand. "I congratulate you, and may I say that it is a pleasure to meet you, sir?"

"The pleasure is all mine."

"General, suppose you fill Captain Phillips in on the situation in Missouri now," President Davis suggested.

"Yes, sir," Price answered. "Captain, you want to come over here and take a look at Missouri on this map? As you can see, the Mississippi River runs the full length of its eastern border." Price pointed to the map. "And as long as we can control the state, we can control the river."

"I know that the Yankees' strategy is going to be to

occupy the river as quickly as they can," President Davis put in. "For if they can take the river, they will not only cut our nation in two, they will also have a wide roadway, straight into the heart of the Confederacy."

"Yes, sir, that is true," Burke said. "Correct me if I'm wrong, General, but don't the Yankees already control St. Louis?"

"Sadly, that is true," General Price conceded. "And they also control their capital at Jefferson City."

Burke looked up in surprise. "*Their* capital?"

"As you know, the Missouri State Legislature voted to secede, only to have Federal troops move in and declare immediate martial law. So, we moved the legislature lock, stock, and barrel to Neosho, and that is the new capital of Missouri."

"*Confederate* Missouri," Davis pointed out. "We have added a star to our flag, representing the state of Missouri, and her delegates sit in our Confederate Congress."

"But that still leaves St. Louis under Yankee control," Burke said. "And there are more people in St. Louis than there are in all the rest of the state."

"Foreigners, mostly," Price said derisively. "But it isn't just St. Louis. The Yankees more or less control Sainte Genevieve, Perryville, and Cape Girardeau as well. But the area south of Cape Girardeau belongs to us. Commerce, Sikeston, Charleston, New Madrid, and the ten Bootheel counties are well in hand, and under the command of General Jeff Thompson."

"In addition to which, we have fortified Island Number Ten, which is located in the great bend at New Madrid," President Davis added. "Thus far we have the river well under control."

"And we will continue to control it, as long as we can keep the Yankee army tied up, fighting engagements throughout the rest of the state," Price said.

"That's where you come in," President Davis suggested.

"How, sir?"

"I understand that before the war you spent some time on the Missouri–Kansas border," Price said. "Is that correct?"

"It is, sir."

"Then you know that there are already several bands of

armed men who are fighting for the Southern cause,'' Price said. ''They are bold and courageous men, but they are of little help to our cause now, for their activities are so isolated that we are unable to take advantage of them.''

''What we need,'' President Davis said, ''is someone who knows and understands that type of irregular warfare. Someone who can coordinate their operations so that they are for the good of the whole.''

''Mr. President, the men you are talking about have already been fighting this war for four years. They are all individuals who can scarcely be made to cooperate with each other, let alone with some distant commander for some strategic purpose.''

Price laughed. ''He knows the men, Mr. President, I'll tell you that for sure.''

''Don't misunderstand your mission, Captain,'' President Davis said. ''I don't expect you to bring them under some military umbrella. I know that is impossible, and I'm not even certain I would want you to do it if you could. I am told that they are ferocious fighters.''

''Man for man, Mr. President, they are the most ferocious fighters in the entire army.''

''I will vouch for that,'' General Price said.

''Then I fear any attempt to control them would not only fail, it might also quench their fighting spirit,'' President Davis said. ''And that I do not want to do. All I want you to do is to join them, fight with them—but, any time you can exert some influence over them to see to it that their efforts contribute to the overall fight for independence, then do so.''

''I must tell you, Mr. President, that I have received similar orders before.''

''You are talking about the mission President Buchanan sent you and your friend on, before the war,'' President Davis said.

''You *know* about that?'' Burke asked in surprise. ''But how? I thought our mission was secret.''

''It was, but I had my sources,'' President Davis said.

''Yes, well, carrying out that mission put me in a situation that I hope never to repeat.''

''You are talking about your part in capturing Russell Hinds?'' Sterling Price asked.

"Not just Hinds. That murdering bastard deserved to hang," Burke said. "But Lonnie Butrum and Vern Woods were innocent."

"The man who hanged them, Doc Jennison, was riding under orders from then senator, and now general, Jim Lane," General Price said. "Would it make your mission any easier if you knew that Jim Lane would be your principal adversary?"

"I don't mind telling you that's one redlegged son of a bitch I would like to have in my sights," Burke admitted.

"Then you'll take the assignment?" President Davis asked.

"Mr. President, I am an officer in your army, sir. I will take any assignment you give me."

"Good, because that is the assignment I want you to take."

"Very well, sir," Burke said without too much enthusiasm.

"Captain, I know you would like to remain a part of the regular army, to participate in future battles like the one we had at Bull Run. But I honestly consider the fate of Missouri to be vital to the future of the Confederacy, and I can think of no assignment in the army that would be more important to our cause than the one I am giving you now."

Burke smiled, then stuck out his hand. "I accept the assignment with pride, Mr. President. How soon do I leave?"

"How soon can you be ready?" General Price responded.

"I'm ready now, sir."

"Good. We'll take the cars at six."

Sitting in his saddle, Dan ran the letter that had just, by a most circuitous route, been delivered to him.

Independence, Missouri, September 4, 1861
Dear Captain Morris,

Of course you may write to me whenever you wish. I will be most happy to correspond with you, though I must confess an ignorance of things military and a complete intolerance for things political.

It may be of interest to you to know that, in ad-

dition to your letter, I also received one from our
mutual friend, Burke Phillips. Captain Phillips' letter
was posted from Virginia, where he took part in the
battle of Bull Run.

It is terribly distressing to me that the two of you,
who are great friends, should be divided by this war.
I do take comfort, however, in knowing that he
fought a battle in Virginia, while your battle took
place in Missouri; thus there seems to be no chance
of the two of you ever actually meeting in battle.

I close my letter to you as I did my letter to Mr.
Phillips. I know not if you survived the fight in
Springfield. That you did, is my earnest prayer.

Your friend,
Catherine Darrow

After folding the letter and putting it in his jacket pocket,
Dan turned his attention to the task at hand, that of escorting a Federal supply train.

The ox-drawn wagon train stretched a quarter of a mile
from the first wagon until the last. The wagons were well
loaded with uniforms, food, blankets, rifles, powder, and
ball ammunition. Captain Dan Morris, who had been detached from duty with General Halleck's army, was now
assigned to the Seventh Kansas Volunteer Cavalry Regiment. The Seventh was made up of former Jayhawkers who
had been taken into the army, and Dan's job was to provide
some liaison between them and the regulars.

"Cap'n Morris," one of the wagon train drivers called
to Dan as he rode by on an inspection. "You fellas are
goin' to stick real close, aren't you? I mean, the Secesh
would like nothin' better'n to get their hands on what we're
a-carryin'."

"We'll be right here if the Rebs jump you."

"*If* they jump us? Hell, man, they ain't no 'if' about it.
You ask me, us drivers ain't no more'n bait in a trap."

Dan smiled. "Well, if you are, it's a trap for the Rebs,
not for you."

"You ever run a trap line, Cap'n?"

Dan shook his head. "No, I can't say that I have."

"I used to trap muskrat along the Blue. An' the one thing

I always noticed is that even when you trapped the critter, the bait was pert' near always et. I don't want to get et.''

Dan laughed. ''Don't worry. We won't let it go that far.''

The driver leaned over to spit out a quid of tobacco. ''I sure's hell hope not.''

Dan rode on down the line of wagons, watching as the last minute preparations were being made. Here a wheel was being greased; there a load was being tied down; at another wagon a team of oxen was being put into the yoke.

Most of the citizens of Kansas City had turned out to see the departure of the wagon train, which was carrying the goods to the Federal troops in Georgetown. The train departure was the most excitement the little town had ever seen, and an almost partylike atmosphere developed as the townspeople moved up and down the wagons, providing coffee and sandwiches and cake to the teamsters and their escort.

About three-quarters of the way toward the end of the long train, Dan saw Doc Jennison, now Lieutenant Colonel Jennison, talking to several of the men in his newly constituted command. Dan dismounted and walked over to report to Jennison. He saluted, and Jennison, who was holding the reins of his horse with his right hand, returned the salute with his left. Dan cringed at Jennison's lack of military bearing.

''I have inspected the train, sir, and can report that we are ready, in all respects, to get under way.''

''Good, good,'' Jennison said. ''Then they won't need us.''

Dan looked surprised. ''I beg your pardon, sir?''

''The wagons,'' Jennison said, taking in the train with an impatient wave of his hand. ''They'll get along fine without us.''

''Colonel, are you saying you don't intend to escort them to Georgetown?''

''Now, why would I want to do something like that?'' Jennison asked. ''Look at these men, Morris.'' He pointed to his Jayhawkers. ''They are fighting men, by God. They aren't teamsters and draymen! We've got better things to do.''

''Don't you understand that this train could be attacked?''

Jennison looked at his second in command. "Anthony, ride up and down the street. Let the people know that we expect this wagon train to get through to Georgetown unmolested."

Nodding, Anthony mounted his horse, then rode down the street alongside the waiting wagons.

"People of Missouri! Hear my words!" he called at the top of his voice. The teamsters and the citizens who had been milling around alongside the wagons looked over at him.

"These here wagons are travelin' under the protection of the Seventh Kansas Cavalry. We won't actually be ridin' with 'em, but if any harm comes to them while they are going to Georgetown, our retribution will be swift and terrible!"

"Hold on there!" the lead driver called. "We was told we would have your protection!"

"You have got our protection," Jennison said, hearing the man's protest. "You think any Rebels would dare to attack you knowing that they'd have to deal with us?"

"Is that supposed to make us feel safe?" the lead driver asked.

"It should," Jennison insisted. "I assure you, the Rebels will be severely punished if this train is attacked."

"Well now, Colonel, we're already at war with the Rebs. What you goin' to do to 'em that you ain't already doin'? Besides which, it won't matter much to us, since they will have already done what they're goin' to do in the first place."

"Colonel, maybe you would let me have a platoon to go with them," Dan offered.

"No," Jennison replied. "You're my liaison with the regular army. I want you with me. Besides, what could a platoon do for 'em?"

Dan looked at the lead driver, then shrugged as if to say he was sorry. The lead driver made no sign of recognition of Dan's expression of regret. Instead he stood up on his seat and shouted back to the wagons behind him, his call picked up and carried for the entire length of the train.

"Wagons ho!"

"*Wagons ho!*" came the repeated call.

"Wagons ho!" softer now, as it carried up the line until the final call could barely be heard.

Feeling almost as if he, personally, had failed them, Dan watched the train roll slowly out of Kansas City.

"Come on, boys!" Jennison yelled a short time later. "We've got some raiding to do!"

INDEPENDENCE, MISSOURI

Tom Peters was in front of the livery stable, brushing down a horse, when he saw the riders coming into town. There were nearly one hundred of them, all heavily armed, in uniform, and riding by twos. He paused to watch them pass by the livery, wondering what they were doing in town.

Wentworth Caldwell, proprietor of the general store, was sweeping his porch when the riders passed by. He continued with his sweeping, but he kept an eye on them as they stopped in front of the bank.

"Soldiers . . . get down!" Jennison shouted what he assumed to be a military order.

"What's that, Doc?" one of the men called.

Jennison looked at Dan. "You're the soldier around here. What's the right words?"

"Troop, dismount," Dan told him.

"Yeah, that's it. *Troop, dismount,"* Jennison called, and the riders all dismounted. Several of them led their animals over to the watering troughs placed strategically up and down the street. By now most of the town had turned out, curious as to why such a large troop of men had ridden into their town.

Jennison climbed up onto the front porch of the bank. "Where at's the mayor of this here town?" he shouted.

A man hurried out of the barbershop from the other side of the street, still wearing the barber's apron. He picked his way through the newly deposited and still steaming horse droppings, toward the bank.

"I am the mayor," he said. "What can I do for you gentlemen?"

"Mayor, I want you to call a town meeting," Jennison said. "I want ever'one in this town, and that means ever' man, woman, and child, black and white, to gather round right here, in front of this bank.''

"Why on earth would I want to do a thing like that?" the mayor asked.

Jennison pulled his revolver and leveled it toward the mayor. "Because I aim to blow a hole through your traitorous Rebel head if you don't. Is that a good enough reason?"

"Yes, yes, whatever you say," the mayor answered in a frightened tone of voice. "Tom, Wentworth, go and gather the people," he ordered. "Quickly! Call everyone together."

"You fellas," Jennison said to his soldiers. "Spread out up and down the street. Make sure there ain't no one left who don't join us."

Over the next half hour men, women, and children were called out of their places of employment, homes, and school and herded down the street, where they began to form a large and uneasy crowd.

"Here, missy!" one soldier called, leaning down from his saddle to scoop up a woman who was leading the schoolchildren. "I'll give you a ride down to the bank."

"Help!" the woman shouted, struggling against the man who had grabbed her. "Put me down!"

The man laughed. "Why, you're a little wildcat, you are!" he said.

"You! Put that woman down!" Dan shouted in a voice that sounded like the crack of doom.

"Who says so?"

"I'm not just saying, I'm ordering," Dan said.

"This here ain't the reg'lar army," the soldier said. "We don't pay that much attention to orders."

Dan cocked his pistol, and the deadly click of the rotating cylinder could be heard clearly. "Put her down, Collins. Now!"

Collins grinned. "You don't want her dropped in the horseshit, do you? If you shoot me, I'll drop her."

"She can clean up. You'll still be dead," Dan said coldly.

Collins held her for just a second as he contemplated Dan's words; then, sullenly, he put the woman down.

"Rejoin the troop," Dan ordered.

"Doc Jennison, he don't like no one messin' with us," the man said, pointing a finger at Dan.

"I said, rejoin the troop," Dan ordered coldly.

Collins stared at Dan for a long moment, then slapped his heels against the side of his horse. The horse bolted forward, leaving the woman and the schoolchildren behind.

"Thank you," the woman said in a shaken voice.

"Miss Darrow, I apologize for the beastly behavior of that man," Dan said.

At first Catherine was surprised to hear her name called; then, looking at Dan more closely, she gasped. "Captain Morris, is that you riding with such men?"

"I cannot tell you how ashamed I am by what is happening here," Dan said. "Unfortunately, I have no control over all of this. I am not in command."

At that moment there was a crash of glass, followed by raucous laughter. When Dan and Catherine looked in the direction of the noise, they saw several of Jennison's men pulling merchandise through a broken window in front of Caldwell's General Store. One man had an armful of ax handles, another was sporting a new hat, a third clutched a side of cured bacon, while a fourth, with a wide, foolish grin on his face, was running down the street carrying a dressmaking dummy under his arm.

"It looks to me as if no one is in command," Catherine said.

Dan sighed. "For all intents and purposes, that is the truth," he admitted. "Miss Darrow, I think you and the children should return to the school. I'll see to it that no one bothers you again."

"And the other innocent citizens of this town?" Catherine asked. "Will you protect them as well?"

"I will do all that I can." Dan sighed. "But I am only one man. . . ." He shrugged.

"I understand," Catherine said.

"I hope you *do* understand. I would not like to be the villain in your eyes."

"For the moment, Captain, I shall reserve judgment on that," Catherine said. "Come along, children."

Dan watched until they were all safely back in the school building, then he rode back to the bank, where, by now, the rest of the town had gathered.

"Was that the schoolmarm and schoolkids goin' back?" Jennison asked.

"Yes," Dan answered. "I sent them back."

"Now, why did you do a fool thing like that?" Jennison asked. "I specifically ordered that everyone be brought out."

"And I gave the teacher my word that they would be left alone," Dan said.

The two men stared, hard, at each other, then Jennison broke off the contact and snorted.

"All right, all right, we don't need them, anyway," he said. He turned to the townspeople.

"Now, folks, I know that most of you in this town are Rebels. And even if you ain't, you're Missourians, and to my way of lookin' at it, there ain't a Missourian worth a nickel, be he Rebel or not. So I tell you what we're goin' to do. We're goin' to take a little tax from the town. But first, we're goin' to make you all loyal Union people. So, the first thing I want is for you to hold up your hands."

A couple of people in the front row raised both hands over their head, as if they were getting robbed.

"No, no, not like that!" Jennison insisted. "What I mean is, hold up your right hand. You're all goin' to take an oath!"

The townspeople looked at each other in confusion for a moment.

Jennison fired a shot into the air, and a few women screamed and one or two men cursed out loud as the sound of the pistol shot echoed back through the street.

"I'm not goin' to ask you again," he said. "Hold up your right hands."

Tentatively one or two put up their hands, then a few more, and a few more, until, under the urging of Jennison's men, everyone in town was standing out in the street in front of the bank, right hands raised.

"Now, that's more like it," Jennison said. "All right, repeat after me. 'I swear to be loyal to the Union.'"

"I swear to be loyal to the Union," the people repeated.

"And I swear to be against the Rebels."

"And I swear to be against the Rebels."

Smiling broadly, Jennison lowered his pistol. "Well,

now that we got that part took care of, all we have to do is collect a little tax. Mr. Banker.''

"Yes?'' one man in the crowd said.

"I'm goin' to send a couple of my men into the bank with you,'' he said. "And I would appreciate it if you would be so kind as to put all the money you got in that bank into a couple of sacks and hand it to 'em.''

"Hold on here!'' Wentworth Caldwell shouted, stepping out of the crowd. "You can't do that! You've already cleaned out my store. How'm I goin' to restock if you take all the money besides? Everything I have is in that bank.''

Jennison turned his pistol toward Caldwell and without so much as a second thought pulled the trigger. The heavy slug caught Caldwell right in the middle of his chest, and he died with an expression of surprise on his face.

"Well, now he don't have to worry about restocking his store, does he? Anyone else wish to say that we don't have a legal right to this money?''

No one said a word.

"That's what I thought. Okay, a couple of you boys, go inside with the banker. I'm sure he's ready to be just real accommodatin'.''

Two men grabbed the banker and pushed him into the store. Jennison looked over at the building next door to the bank and saw a loaded freight wagon sitting parked in front.

"What's in that there wagon?'' he asked.

No one answered.

"Collins, climb up onto that wagon and break open one of the crates. Tell me what's inside.''

Collins rode his horse over to the side of the wagon, then slipped from the saddle into the wagon. Using his knife, he pried up a couple of nails, then took off the top.

"I'll be damned!'' he said, laughing.

"What is it?''

"Bibles.''

"Bibles?''

"This whole wagon is loaded with nothin' but Bibles.''

"Which one of you is the freight operator?'' Jennison asked.

"I am,'' a gray-haired, gray-bearded man answered from the street.

"What are you doin' with all these Bibles? Is this town that full of sinners?"

Jennison's men laughed uproariously at his joke.

"It's a consignment for all the Episcopal churches in the diocese," the freight operator answered.

"Take 'em," Jennison said to Collins.

"Damn, chief, what do we want with a wagonload of Bibles?" Collins asked.

"Maybe we can sell 'em somewhere. If not, some of you fellas could profit from readin' 'em," Jennison answered.

The two men Jennison had sent into the bank came back outside now, carrying a small cloth bag.

"All right, men, we've finished our business here," Jennison said. Assuming a commanding voice, he gave another one of his convoluted military commands: *"Get back . . . on your horses!"*

With a few shouts and a lot of laughter, Jennison's men remounted.

"Let's . . . go!" he commanded.

At Jennison's order, his raiders rode out of town at a gallop, with the wagonload of Bibles lumbering along behind, leaving the stunned population of Independence standing forlorn in the street.

In a heavy snowstorm, Burke Phillips waited under a cluster of trees with a group of horsemen. All wore sheepskin coats and scarves wrapped around their necks and hats that were filled to the brim with snow.

"What the hell we doin' out here, anyway?" one of the men asked. "Don't make no sense to be out in weather like this."

"You know why we're here," Burke replied. "We can cut enough supplies out of that wagon train to keep us going for another year."

"What wagon train?" the man scoffed. "You ask me, they're prob'ly holed up somewhere, waitin' out the storm." He squirted a stream of tobacco juice toward the snowbank, where it was quickly buried by new snow. "It's damn near nightfall anyhow. They prob'ly done put in for the night," the man continued. "Which is where we ought to be, rather than runnin' around like we're on some snipe hunt."

"The chief said they'll be here, they'll be here," another answered.

"You think the chief cain't do nothin' wrong?" the complaining man asked. "What's he got for you, boy? A pocket full o' sugar titties?"

The fifteen-year-old boy who had defended his chief unbuttoned his coat and faced his taunter. His gun was now clearly visible, and he moved his hand to hover menacingly over it.

"Pull your gun, you son of a bitch," the boy said.

"You crazy?" the man asked. "I ain't pullin' my gun."

"Pull it, or ride out of here," the boy said coldly.

"Jesse, come on, he didn't mean nothin' by it," Burke said.

"Maybe not, but I aim to kill him for it," the boy said again, looking at the man with cold, calm blue eyes.

"Dingus, we have enough Yankees to fight without killing any of our own," Burke said. He was using Jesse's nickname as a placating gesture, but Jesse wasn't put off by it.

"Burke, get out of the way," the boy said. "I don't want to shoot you."

"Then call this thing off," Burke said. "Leastwise till we get somewhere where you two can settle it between yourselves without putting the rest of us in danger. Frank, talk to your brother."

Frank James rode over to his younger brother and put his hand on Jesse's arm. "Close up your coat, Dingus," he said quietly. "You're goin' to catch your death with a chill."

There was a tense moment, then Jesse relented. "Sure, Frank," he said. "Whatever you say." He buttoned his coat back up, then stuck his hands in his pockets to warm them.

"I don't know why he got so mad," the other man began. "All I said was—"

Burke twisted in his saddle and cuffed the man on the jaw, stopping him in midsentence.

"Hey, what'd you do that for?" the man asked.

"Figured I'd save your life, you damned fool," Burke answered. "We don't want to hear what you said. Just shut up and wait for the wagons."

Burke settled back in his saddle and tried to fight off the

cold. Since returning to Missouri with General Price, he had, at the general's insistence, joined with one of the many irregular outfits. The group he had joined was that of William Clarke Quantrill. Quantrill, who often used the alias Charles Hart, had collected the deadliest gang of cutthroats and brigands ever assembled into one company. Quantrill, and men like Bloody Bill Anderson, Frank and Jesse James, and Jim and Cole Younger, were little more than cold-blooded killers and thieves, and Burke would have left the group long ago if he had not been there on direct orders from General Price.

"Here comes the chief now," Cole Younger said.

Burke looked over to see a young man with a Vandyke beard riding toward them. Granted a captain's commission by the Confederate Congress, Quantrill had promoted himself to major. He had promoted Anderson to lieutenant colonel, until Burke informed him that a lieutenant colonel outranked a major.

"But it has the word 'lieutenant' in it," Quantrill had said. "I know for sure that a major outranks a lieutenant."

"Yes, but not a lieutenant colonel."

"All right, I'll leave the colonel part off, and make him a lieutenant. . . ."

"All right, boys, get ready," Quantrill said when he reached them. "Remember, we'll let the first part of the train go by, then we'll hit the rear end. That way the ones up front won't be able to help the ones in the rear."

"What about the escort?" Burke asked. "Any soldiers escorting them?"

Quantrill grinned. "No," he said. "That fool Jennison sent 'em off with a warning of what he would do to anyone who attacked the train."

"Oh, I'm real scared," Cole Younger said, and the others laughed.

"All right, now, ever'one quiet," Quantrill ordered. "I think I hear 'em comin'."

Burke strained to hear. In the softness of the snowfall, he could hear the drivers whistling and calling to their teams, urging them on.

"Chief, look," Frank James said, pointing to the train as it passed by. "There's a big gap between those two wagons."

"You're right," Quantrill said. "That's where we'll hit 'em. Tell you what, Burke. You ride on down there and hold up your hands to stop the wagon. Don't do anything to spook the driver. Tell 'im you've got a message for 'im. Once we get the ones to the rear stopped, the rest of us will ride out of the woods and get the drop on 'em. We might even be able to pull this off without any gunplay."

"Hell, why don't we just shoot 'em and be done with it?" Anderson asked.

"We'll try it my way," Quantrill insisted. "Now, all of you but Burke, here, get out of sight."

The rest of the gang melted back into the woods to wait for Burke to do his job. Burke rode out onto the road and stood with his hand raised. Because the sheepskin coat covered his uniform, there was nothing threatening about his appearance.

"Whoa, there," the driver called, stopping his team. "What can I do for you, mister?"

"I've got a message for you," Burke began, but he was interrupted because the rider who had been braced by Jesse a little earlier suddenly dashed out of the woods, brandishing his pistol. The driver saw something out of the corner of his eye and, realizing that something was up, raised his rifle and shot Burke.

Burke felt a searing pain tear into his shoulder, and his breath left him as the bullet knocked him off his horse. Almost as soon as he fell into the snow, he heard the guns of the others open up. He saw the driver pitch off his seat, then land spread-eagle in the snow, his blood making a red stain on the pristine white.

From Burke's vantage point on the ground he saw, despite his pain, a peculiar thing. The rider who had compromised their position suddenly tumbled out of the saddle, though not one more shot had come from the wagon train itself.

The riders reined up alongside the wagon train, their horses prancing about in excitement, kicking up clumps of snow and breathing clouds of steam into the cold air.

"You drivers, leave your guns behind and climb down off them seats!" Quantrill shouted.

Without protest, the drivers began to comply.

Cole Younger rode over to where Burke lay in the snow and looked down at him. "You hurt bad?"

"Just a nick. Help me onto my horse, Cole," Burke said, keeping his voice calm. He wasn't sure but that they might shoot him if they thought he was hurt badly enough to slow them down, so he was underplaying his wound as much as possible.

"You sure it ain't no worse?" Cole asked.

"No," Burke replied. "It's just a graze." The bullet was in fact buried deep in his shoulder, and he could feel the weight of it and the heat of it, like a hot poker being held to his flesh.

Burke followed the action around the wagon train as best he could, while Cole helped him mount.

"Gentlemen, my name is William Clarke Quantrill, at your service," Quantrill shouted to the wagon drivers. "Your job here is finished. My men will take over the wagons now. Please take off your coats and leave your weapons here. I will let you go ahead on foot to catch up with the wagons in front of you."

"We can't take off our coats! We'll freeze to death!" one of the drivers complained.

"I'm sure there are blankets in the wagons ahead. And if you aren't wearing your coats, you won't be getting any ideas about staying around here and making trouble for us. Be gone with you now."

For a moment or two the four remaining drivers looked at Quantrill as if they didn't quite understand what he was saying.

"You do have a choice, gentlemen," Quantrill said. "You can strip out of your coats and start running, or you can wind up lyin' dead in the snow, just like your friend here." He pointed with his pistol to the driver who had already been shot. "Which will it be?"

"You ain't goin' to get any trouble out of me," one of the drivers said, and he stripped out of his coat and left it and his pistol lying in the snow. When he started moving, the others quickly followed suit.

"Well now, that's more like it," Quantrill said. He watched until the drivers were all standing around, half-naked in the snow, then he waved his gun toward them as if he were about to shoot. The drivers started running then, slipping and sliding through the snow as they hurried to catch up with the wagons, which were now a quarter of a mile or farther in front of them. Even though they must have heard the shooting, they had continued ahead without stopping, exactly as Quantrill knew they would.

"Whoowee, lookit them boys run!" Jesse said, and the others laughed.

"Get the pack mules up here," Quantrill ordered. "We'll take off as much as we can haul away, then we'll burn the wagons and what's left."

"What about the driver?" Frank asked, pointing to the one who was lying facedown in the snow.

"Pull him away so he doesn't get burned up with the wagons," Quantrill said. "That way, when they find him, folks will know who he is." Quantrill looked over at Burke, who was now mounted. "How are you doin', Burke?"

"I'm doin' fine," Burke said, keeping his voice as light and as strong as possible, fighting against the pain so as not to show it.

"I'll watch over him, chief," Jesse offered.

"If he starts slowin' us down, you know what to do," Quantrill said.

"I know," Jesse answered.

"Chief, we got the pack mules loaded," Jim Younger said.

"All right, let's ride on out of here," Quantrill said, and the group of raiders, with their pack mules loaded with booty, rode away. Behind them the wagons burned fiercely, and five columns of thick, black smoke roiled upward into the snow-filled sky.

The terrible pain had stopped and a warning numbness set in. It was the numbness that allowed Burke to keep up with the others on their mad ride away from the scene of the wagon raid. But with the numbness came also a weakness from loss of blood, and by the time they were riding into Boonville, Missouri, just before dawn the next morning, Burke was managing to stay in his saddle only by supreme effort of will.

"Hey, chief, Burke's about to keel over here," Jesse called.

Although it had been Cole who had helped Burke mount,

Jesse was the one who had taken it on himself to ride along-side Burke, and for the last three hours it had been Jesse who'd held the reins to Burke's horse, while Burke had used both hands and all his strength to hold on the pommel just to stay in the saddle.

Despite the befuddling haze, Burke thought of the con-tradictions in Jesse James's makeup. Dingus, as some called him, was so young that he didn't even shave yet, and on more than one occasion he had disguised himself as a young girl in order to act as an advance scout for one of Quantrill's raids. His soft looks were deceiving, for Jesse James could kill a man without blinking an eye.

Jesse James could also be moved to acts of extreme kind-ness and gentleness, as he was proving now. His loyalty to his chief, his brother, and his friends was unqualified, even as his ruthlessness to his enemies was without peer. He was the youngest of Quantrill's band by at least four years and, Burke thought, clearly the most complex and fascinating of them all.

"I know a doctor in this town who'll patch him up," Quantrill said.

"Do we have the time?" one of the other riders asked.

"We won't wait for him. We'll just drop him off and ride on our way."

"What if the sawbones turns him over to the Yankees?" Jesse asked.

"We'll pay him enough to buy his silence," Quantrill answered. "Dingus, bring Burke and come along with me. Anderson, you and the rest of the boys ride on down to that farmhouse there. It belongs to a fella by the name of Matthew Poe. Tell him you're with Charles Hart and that we've come to Boonville to buy cattle. He'll have his woman fix you some hot grub."

"What about you, chief? Where you goin' to eat?" An-derson asked.

"Me'n Dingus'll take breakfast at the doc's house."

"All right, let's go, boys," Anderson said.

As they left, Quantrill, Jesse, and Burke headed for the doctor's house. Though it was still predawn dark, the snow on the ground made it appear light. As the three rode through the street, the beat of the hooves of their horses was deadened by the cushion of snow so that they glided in as silently as specters.

They could see squares of golden light on the snow, cast through the windows of the houses where early risers were already beginning to sit down to breakfast. Quantrill halted them when they reached the end of the street.

"What is it, chief?" Jesse asked.

"That's the doc's house down there," Quantrill said, pointing to a low, single-story building that sat nearly half a block away from the others. A wisp of wood smoke rose from the chimney, carrying with it the aroma of frying bacon. "I just want to make sure there's no one around."

The saddle squeaked as Jesse twisted in it to look around. Burke held on, telling himself that only a short time remained until he could lie down and rest in a warm house.

"It looks clear," Jesse said calmly.

Quantrill clicked to his horse, and the three of them slowly crossed the distance. They stopped just in front of the doctor's house.

"Tharon Swayne, M.D.," the sign read by the door. Quantrill didn't bother to knock, he just pushed it open. Then he and Jesse half carried, half supported Burke inside.

"What the . . . ? What is this?" the surprised doctor asked, looking up from his breakfast table. His wife was standing at the stove, frying bacon, and she looked around in alarm as well.

"Don't get yourself fretted none, Doc," Quantrill said quietly. "It's just me. One of my men got hisself shot up last night. He needs some doctorin'."

The doctor moved quickly to the door and looked around nervously before he shut it. "Did anyone see you bring him here?" he asked anxiously.

"No," Quantrill said. "We know it ain't healthy to be Secesh in this town."

Jesse laid Burke on the bed. Dr. Swayne sat beside him and opened his coat, then his shirt. "He's lucky," he said. "The cold stopped the bleeding, and it doesn't look like there's been any festering. But the bullet is going to have to come out."

Quantrill sat at the breakfast table without asking and began to help himself. Jesse stood by the bed for a moment longer; then, when the doctor's wife invited him to breakfast, he nodded.

"Thank you kindly, ma'am. That's real gracious of you."

"Here's a little laudanum," Dr. Swayne said to Burke, handing him a small bottle. "Take it. You'll need it when I start probing for the bullet. Martha, get over here. I'm going to need your help," he said to his wife.

With his wife helping him, the doctor removed Burke's shirt and then began digging into the wound for the bullet. Quantrill and Jesse ate their breakfast as if totally unconcerned with what was going on by the bed.

"Here it is," Swayne said after a few minutes. He held up the black slug between the end of a long pair of tweezers to show it, then dropped the bullet, with a splash and dull clink, into a pan of warm water. All the while, Quantrill and Jesse continued to eat their breakfast without comment and seemingly without concern.

"I think he'll be all right," Swayne said, washing his own hands.

"Can he ride out with us now?" Quantrill asked, getting up from the table and bringing over a biscuit and bacon sandwich to look down at the patient.

"Are you serious? I should say not. It'll be a few hours before he even wakes up."

Quantrill tugged at his beard for a moment, then reached into his coat pocket and pulled out a stack of gold coins. "Here, Doc. This is for fixin' up the boy and feedin' us breakfast. Tell Burke, here, that he's on his own when he wakes up. We can't wait around for him."

"Wait a minute! I can't keep him here," Dr. Swayne protested.

"You don't have to keep him here. Send him on his way."

"He needs at least a day's rest," Swayne said.

"Then give it to him," Quantrill said. "You've been paid handsomely enough."

"I can't! Don't you understand?"

Quantrill pulled out his pistol. "All right," he said. "I'll just kill him now, and you can bury him. But I want my money back." He picked up a pillow and wrapped it around his gun to deaden the sound.

"No!" Martha gasped. "What are you doing?"

"Trying to save you some trouble," Quantrill said flatly.

"He's no trouble. Tharon, tell him. The boy is no trouble," Mrs. Swayne insisted.

"Martha's right," Swayne said. "He's not that much trouble. You two go on. We'll take care of him."

Quantrill chuckled. "Which was it, ma'am?" he asked.

"I beg your pardon?" Martha asked.

"You savin' the boy because of Christian kindness? Or because you don't want to give that stack of gold coins back?"

"Please," Martha said. "Just go now, and leave us alone."

Quantrill laughed again. "Come on, Dingus," he said. "I don't want to get caught in this town come sunup."

Quantrill and Jesse left the small house, and Swayne and his wife stood there, looking at the door as if unable to believe what had happened to them this morning. They waited for a long moment, and when they were sure the horses had left, Swayne began to put on his hat and coat.

"Martha," he said, "if anyone comes by today, you tell them I was called to Jefferson City. Do you have that? I'm going to Jefferson City."

"What for?"

"Unless I miss my guess, there'll be a reward out for this man. I aim to bring a couple of soldiers back with me."

"Tharon, you aren't going to leave me with him, alone?" Martha asked, surprised by his statement and frightened at the prospect.

"Don't worry none. He'll mostly be out for the next twelve hours, and I figure to be back by nightfall. If anyone asks who he is, why, you just tell him he's your nephew, wounded in the war."

"What will they do to him?" Martha asked, looking at Burke.

"Hang him, most likely."

"Hang him? But he's hurt."

"He also rides with Quantrill. There's no tellin' how many men he's killed," the doctor said, wrapping a scarf around his neck. "You just do like I told you, and I'll see you tonight." He smiled. "Countin' the gold Quantrill gave me, and the reward this fella is sure to bring, why, this'll be a pretty profitable day, don't you think?''

"Can you believe that damned bank only had three thousand and eleven dollars?" Jennison asked in disgust. "What kind of bank would only have three thousand and eleven dollars?"

"A bank where only poor, hardworking people and honest people keep their money," Dan answered. "I don't think we left many friends in that place."

"Who the hell needs to be friends with a Missourian, anyway?" Jennison growled.

"We do," Dan replied.

"How do you figure that?"

"We are irregular soldiers," Dan explained. "We move through the countryside like fish through water. The water is more hospitable if it isn't full of sharks. The more friends we make among the Missourians, the fewer sharks we will encounter."

Jennison laughed. "You've got that backwards," he said. He made a fist and pointed to his chest with his thumb. "*We* are the sharks, and the people are the fish. I want mothers to be able to frighten their children by using my name."

"Doc! Doc!" someone shouted, riding hard into camp. He swung down from his horse and ran to the tent where Jennison was making his headquarters.

"I told you, men," Jennison said. "I ain't to be called Doc no more. I'm a colonel, by God, and that's what you men will call me."

"Sorry, Doc, uh, Colonel, I forgot."

"Now, what's got you so all-fired excited that you come riding into camp like this?"

"It's the Rebels, Colonel. They jumped the last five wagons of the train just before it got to Georgetown, and robbed them, then burned them. Must've got near a hundred rifles and all the ammunition."

"Those bastards! Who do they think they are!" Jennison swore angrily.

"They think they are soldiers who found a ready source of resupply," Dan explained. "I told you, we should've provided an escort."

"And I told you we had better things to do than play nursemaid to a bunch of wagons. Well, never mind. I guess now we'll just have to teach them boys a lesson," Jennison growled.

"How are we going to do that, Colonel? We have no idea where they are."

"Hell, it don't matter none where they are. 'Far as I'm concerned, one Rebel is pretty much like another," Jennison said. "All right, boys, get on your horses! It's time for revenge!"

After Swayne left, Martha put the "Doctor Out of Town" sign on the front door, then cleaned up the breakfast dishes and then the house. But throughout the morning her eyes kept wandering over to the man on the bed. His hair was sandy, there was a thin blond mustache over lips that were almost too full for a man, and there was a dimple in his chin. His chest, though adorned with only the sparsest blond hair, was full and muscular, and the skin was clear and smooth.

Whenever Martha caught herself looking at him, she would scold herself mentally and look away. She was certain that the young man couldn't be much over twenty-five or twenty-six, and she was forty-two. Not only that, she was a married woman who had no right to think about how handsome a man might be.

But she couldn't keep the disturbing thoughts of him from creeping into her mind, and before she knew it, she would be looking at him again.

Martha stoked up the fire in the fireplace, not because it was cold in the house—in fact, it was quite warm—but just to keep herself occupied so that she wouldn't look at him.

But it didn't work. Once more she turned to see him, and this time as she stared, she could feel a warmth in her body that wasn't brought on entirely by the fire she had built.

She took off her sweater.

She felt some respite from the increased temperature but no relief from the heat that was building within. That heat drove her to unbutton the top six buttons of her dress, and she folded the collar back, almost all the way down to the swell of her breasts. She knew it was a scandalous move, but as she was alone, she didn't care.

No, she thought. She wasn't alone. The young man on the bed was with her. But he's sleeping, she decided, to justify her scandalous action.

Martha walked over to the stove and poured a kettle of hot water into a basin, then carried the basin to the bed. She sat on the edge of the bed and began giving the young man a bath.

She was doing no more than ministering to a patient, she told herself. But her breathing began to be more labored, and she felt such a churning within that it could scarcely be contained.

The man's eyes opened.

Burke started to sit up, but so abrupt was his movement that it sent a searing stab of pain into his shoulder, and he fell back on the bed.

"Lie still, sir, and you will be more comfortable," Martha instructed him.

"Who are you?" Burke asked. He looked around. "Where am I? What is this place?"

"Don't you remember coming here earlier this morning?"

Burke looked into the face of the woman who was bathing him. It was a pleasantly attractive face, he decided, and it eased some of the fear that shot through him.

"No," he finally said. "I remember only the cold. The cold and the pain. And the riding. I seem to recall riding almost all night. Where am I?"

"You are in Boonville, and this is the house of Dr. Tharon Swayne."

"Where are the others?"

"Your friends have gone," Martha said. "They left you here to mend."

Burke looked around. "Where is the doctor?" he asked.

"He's . . . gone . . . on business," Martha said. "There are just the two of us here." As she talked, she continued to bathe Burke, and now the washcloth was on Burke's stomach. The action caused Martha to bend over, and as she did, her unbuttoned dress fell forward slightly, exposing the curve of her breast all the way out to the nipple, which had stiffened and was pushing into the material of the dress.

She felt a heat there, then looked up to see that Burke was staring at her.

"I . . . I'm sorry," she mumbled, and reached up to adjust her dress, to cover the breast. "It is so hot in here, and I . . . I wasn't thinking."

"No," Burke said, putting his hand on hers gently. "Please, don't apologize."

"I'm a silly old woman," Martha said. She turned her head away from him, closing her eyes tightly and biting her lower lip.

"You are a beautiful woman, without age," Burke said easily. He reached up, put his hand behind her neck, then gently pulled her head down to his, pressing his lips to hers.

Martha let out a small whimper and returned his kiss with surprising ardor. Her skin was incredibly warm, and he could feel the pulse in her neck, beating rapidly. Finally, with a gasp of breath, she sat up.

"I beg of you," she said. "Don't you know what you are doing to me?"

"No more than you are doing to me," Burke replied with a smile. Again he reached for her, pulling her back to him for another kiss. This time he began unbuttoning the remaining buttons. Without mind or will of her own, Martha helped him, so that within a moment she lay beside him on the bed . . . the bed she shared with her impotent husband.

Martha tried to fight against the terrible need that was consuming her body, but she was too weak, too invested with desire, to be effective. The warmth spread through her with dizzying speed, and she surrendered herself to it, no longer putting up the pretense of fighting.

Burke tried to change positions, to move over her, but the pain in his shoulder stabbed at him again. When Martha saw that, she smiled gently, put her cool fingers on his shoulders to indicate that he should stay where he was, and moved over him, taking him into her, orchestrating the unfolding events on her own.

Burke felt Martha over her, and he thrust up against her, helping her as she began to make love to him. Then he felt her body begin to jerk in convulsive jolts, and she fell across him with a groan of ecstasy even as he was spending himself in her in final, orgasmic shudders.

They lay that way for several moments, with Martha on

top. They allowed the pleasure to drain from their bodies slowly, like heat leaving an iron. Finally Martha got up and looked down at him.

Burke smiled. "Your husband is a lucky man, madam," he said.

Martha gasped and put her hand to her mouth. "Oh," she said. "I almost forgot! You can't stay here! You must leave."

Burke chuckled. "Why? Are you afraid he can see it in our faces?"

"No, it isn't that at all," she said. "But my husband has gone after Union soldiers. He intends to turn you in for the reward money!"

The smile left Burke's face. "How much time do I have?" he asked.

"He said he wouldn't be back until tonight."

"Then we've got plenty of time."

"No. If he finds soldiers between here and Jefferson City, he'll be back much sooner than that."

Burke reached for his pants. "Help me get dressed," he said, and Martha, still naked herself, bent down beside him to help him into his clothes.

After Burke was dressed, Martha dressed quickly, then made him several sandwiches and wrapped them in a cloth to give to him.

"Here's something for you to take with you," she said.

"Thanks," Burke replied, taking the proffered package. "Is my horse still here?"

"Yes, Tharon took him to the barn."

"Still saddled?"

"I'm sure it is. Tharon didn't stay out there long enough to unsaddle it."

"That's bad for my horse, but good for me. I don't know if I could get him saddled myself."

With Martha's help Burke put on his coat, then started out the back door. Just before he opened it, he looked at her and smiled. "Thanks," he said.

Martha kissed him good-bye, then watched him crunch through the new-fallen snow to the small lean-to that served as a barn. When Burke swung onto his horse and rode away, his last sight was of Martha standing in the doorway, watching him.

★★★

Twelve

From *Harper's Weekly;* March 1, 1862:

THE UNION EXPEDITION UP THE TENNESSEE RIVER

After the capture of Fort Henry, the *Lexington, Conestoga,* and *Tyler* gave chase to the Rebel steamer *Dunbar,* and on reaching the Memphis & Louisville Railroad bridge set fire to a portion of it and captured some stores, etc. They then passed on in chase of the *Dunbar,* but did not overtake her. It is supposed that she escaped by running up some creek.

During the night the gunboats went to Florence, Alabama, the head of navigation, and two hundred and fifty miles from Paducah. Everywhere along the river they were received with astonishing welcome by numerous Union families in southern Tennessee and northern Alabama and at towns along the river the old flag was looked upon as a redeemer, and hailed with shouts of joy.

At Savannah, Eastport, and Florence the officers and men of our gunboats went ashore without arms and mingled freely with the people.

The Union men along the river constitute the wealthy and best portion of the inhabitants, large numbers of whom have American flags.

Not a gun was fired either going or coming.

Dan Morris was at the window of the Federal Building in St. Louis, waiting to talk to General Halleck. From where he was standing, he could see the Mississippi River as it flowed by. It was very cold, and chunks of ice joined with the other debris that floated downstream.

The cobblestone levee, where several boats were tied up, was slick with winter ice, and the several men working there, loading and unloading the boats, were having to move around cautiously to avoid slipping down. Dan could see their breaths, and the breaths of the mules and horses, forming little clouds to flare and drift away.

"Captain Morris, General Halleck will see you now," a staff officer said, coming into the room behind him. Dan thanked him, then followed him down a hall and into another room that also overlooked the river. This was the general's office, and Dan took three steps into the room, then stopped and saluted. General Halleck returned his salute, then walked over to offer his hand.

"Captain Morris, it is good to see you again. As I recall, you are the young cadet who wrote the brilliant dissertation on Napoleon at Waterloo. I believe it was your contention that had Napoleon attacked Wellington in the morning instead of waiting until noon, he would have carried the day."

"Yes, sir, he would have defeated Wellington long before von Blucher arrived with reinforcements," Dan said. He smiled. "I must say that I'm surprised, and flattered, you would remember that, General."

"Why shouldn't I remember it? You were exactly right. But then you were one of my best students. You and your friend Burke Phillips."

"Could it be that the general's recollection has mellowed with time? You were not always that generous with praise then," Dan suggested with a smile.

"Perhaps so, Captain, perhaps so," General Halleck admitted, laughing. "I do recall, with fondness, however, my days as professor of military theory at the United States Military Academy. And now, here we are, you and I and so many more of our friends and classmates, putting those theories to the test."

"Yes, sir," Dan replied, his expression growing somber. "We are putting them to the test."

General Halleck read the expression on Dan's face. "I know about your experiences at Wilson Creek. According to General Siegel, your performance of duty was one of the few bright spots of that battle. There is a great difference between war in the field and war on paper, isn't there, son?''

"Yes, sir," Dan replied. He thought of General Lyons and of the men they'd left behind on the battlefield, screaming in pain and dying in agony.

"But, for the moment, let's put that behind us, shall we?" General Halleck suggested.

"Yes, sir, I would like to. General, I appreciate your agreeing to meet with me."

"Well, you have brought some serious matters to my attention," General Halleck responded. "And while normally I don't like to receive a junior officer's criticism of his commanding officer unless it has gone through all the proper channels, in this case I believe your action is entirely warranted. Especially as you are a regular army officer with a spotless reputation and this man Jennison is nothing but a border ruffian who holds his commission through the Kansas militia. Tell me, Captain, is it true that he shot down a civilian in Independence, then robbed the bank there?"

"Yes, sir. The civilian he killed was Wentworth Caldwell, a local merchant."

"And then he attacked another town in retribution for a Rebel attack on a wagon train?"

"General, 'attack' is a military term. To say that Jennison attacked the town of Pleasant Hill is to bring shame and dishonor upon a proud profession," Dan protested. "He *sacked* the town, burning and pillaging with as much ruthlessness as was ever shown by the hordes of Genghis Khan."

"Was there some reason that he chose Pleasant Hill? Was it the headquarters of the Rebel raiders?"

"No, sir. Pleasant Hill is seventy or eighty miles away from where the Rebels attacked the wagon train. I doubt if there was one person in that town who even knew any of the Rebels."

"Other than you," General Halleck stated.

Dan looked surprised. "Other than I? I beg your pardon?"

"My informants tell me that Burke Phillips was one of the men who took part in the attack on the wagon train. That he was, in fact, wounded, though not seriously."

Dan was silent for a moment, then he walked over to the window to look down upon the river.

"I take it you did not know Burke Phillips was back in Missouri?"

Dan shook his head. "No, sir," he answered. "I thought he was back east somewhere."

"Well, he was, for a while. As I understand it, he was back there during the fight at Manassas," General Halleck said. "But he returned to Missouri with Sterling Price."

"I had hoped that we . . ." Dan let the sentence hang.

"Wouldn't meet on the battlefield?"

"Yes, sir."

"I'm sorry, Captain, but that seems to be the way of this war. I am told that even in some families there is a division of loyalties. It might also interest you to know that I am not exempt from this. I am the commanding general of the Army of the West. My opponent on the other side is General Albert Sidney Johnston, who also happens to be my oldest and dearest friend. Six months ago Al and I had dinner together in San Francisco, then each of us left to accept our commands, he with the South, I with the North."

Dan turned away from the window. "Fighting among ourselves. General, how did our country ever get to this point?"

"I would think you would understand better than most, Captain. After all, you have been on the Kansas–Missouri border for two years. You are a personal witness to the hatreds that differences in politics can bring about."

"But there are many—Burke and I are just one example—who hold opposing beliefs but still manage to maintain a friendship."

General Halleck held up his finger. "And yet despite that, the two of you are now fighting on opposite sides of the question. Tell me, Captain, if you and your friend Burke Phillips met in battle, what would you do?"

"I would do exactly as I would expect Burke to do," Dan replied. "I would attempt, by all means necessary, to gain victory for my side."

"In other words, you would be enemies in the field."

"Yes, sir, I suppose we would," Dan admitted.

"Of course you would. And no less would be expected from a soldier. That is the tragedy of this war."

"Yes, sir," Dan said.

General Halleck stroked his beard in silence for a long moment. "Captain Morris, what would your reaction be if I told you I would like to pull you away from your duties in the western part of the state for a while?"

"I serve at the general's discretion," Dan replied. "My reaction would be to go, without question, anywhere you send me."

"Good. The assignment I have in mind for you is very important if we are to wrest control of the Mississippi River away from the Rebels. And it will also give me an opportunity to investigate the activities of Mr. Jennison. I have a feeling his military career is about to come to a close, and it might prove to be uncomfortable for you to be there. More than that, given his volatile nature, it might even be dangerous."

"General, I have no fear of the man. If my being there would help you with your investigation . . ."

"No, no, for the time being I have a greater need for you elsewhere."

"Very good, sir."

General Halleck walked back over to a table to study a map. "Have you ever heard of a place called Island Number Ten?"

"Island Number Ten? No, sir, I don't think I have."

"It is an island in the Mississippi River, so called because all islands are numbered in order from north to south," General Halleck explained. "The tenth island is here, at New Madrid, right in the middle of this great bend of the river. Because of its strategic location, it acts very much like a cork in a wine bottle, closing up the river below it. And, as long as the Rebels control that island, absolutely nothing can proceed downriver without coming under their guns."

"Cork in a wine bottle," Dan said as he studied the map. "I can see that that is quite a good analogy, General."

"I want you to help pull that cork," General Halleck said. "And to that end I will be sending you downriver to Sikeston, where you will be assigned to Major Lathrop."

"Sikeston?"

"It's a small town, located right here at the end of the railroad that connects the town to the river. From Sikeston a corduroy road passes through the swamp to New Madrid. You will be going as second in command to Major Lathrop. Major Lathrop is an artillery officer. His job will be to transport and assemble artillery pieces in Sikeston. Your job will be to make certain that the road that runs from Sikeston to New Madrid stays in our hands.''

"Yes, sir,'' Dan said, quickly taking in the tactical situation.

"As soon as the guns are assembled, we will attack, and capture, New Madrid,'' General Halleck continued. "Once we have New Madrid in hand, we will be able to bombard the island and drive the Rebels out.'' General Halleck straightened. "Do you have any questions?''

"Are the Rebels occupying the road now? Or are they remaining holed up in New Madrid and over on the island?''

"Good question,'' General Halleck replied. "And I brought along a man who should be able to answer that for us. His name is John Sikes.''

"Sikes? As in Sikes town?''

Halleck smiled. "Sikeston,'' he corrected. "But, yes, Mr. Sikes is the town founder. Would you like to meet him?''

"Yes, sir, I would.''

A moment later a tall, thin man stepped into the room. He had piercing brown eyes and rather prominent cheekbones, and he extended his hand in a perfunctory, businesslike way when Dan offered his.

"The road between Sikeston and New Madrid,'' Dan began. "Who occupies it?''

"It belongs to whoever is on it,'' Sikes answered. "Although the Rebels stay pretty much in New Madrid, they have sent their cavalry as far north as Sikeston on several occasions.''

"What can you tell me about the road itself?''

"It's part of the old El Camino Real,'' Sikes said. "King's highway, we call it now. It's a road that stretches from St. Louis to New Madrid, and though much of it has fallen into disrepair, the stretch from Sikeston to New Madrid is quite good.''

"Is it surfaced?''

"Yes, it's a plank road, made of crisscrossed logs.''

"The trouble is, we don't know whether or not the Rebels have torn it up," Dan mused.

"I don't think they've damaged it. At least, the road was in good repair as of last week," Sikes commented. "I rode it myself then."

"The riverboat *Cairo* leaves LaClede's Landing early tomorrow morning," General Halleck said.

"How early?"

"Three A.M."

Dan smiled. "That *is* early," he said.

"Not too early, I hope," General Halleck said. "I intend for you to be on it."

"I'll be there, General," Dan promised.

"And so will I," Sikes added.

"Good," Dan replied. "Perhaps we can visit during the trip down. I may have some more questions for you."

"I will endeavor to be as helpful as possible," Sikes promised.

"In the meantime, Captain, I am giving a small dinner party tonight. I would like you to attend."

"I would be honored," Dan answered.

Once back in the Boatman Hotel, where he was staying, Dan threw a towel over his shoulder and picked up a little kit containing soap, shaving brush, and razor. Then he walked down to the end of the carpeted hallway, where he had been told he would find a room with a bathtub and a stove for heating water.

In the bathroom at that precise moment, Catherine Darrow was just finishing her own bath, and she stood up in the tub and reached for a towel, humming a little song as she did so. She interrupted the song when she found the towel just out of reach, and she had to step out of the tub to get it. Because of that, her nudity was fully exposed when the door was suddenly, and unexpectedly, thrown open.

Catherine looked around in surprise, then gasped when she saw Dan standing there, carrying a towel draped across one arm, and looking as surprised to see Catherine as she was to see him.

"Miss Darrow! I beg your pardon!"

"What . . . what are you doing here?" Catherine asked

in a choked voice. She was so shocked by Dan's sudden appearance that for a long moment she made no attempt to cover herself. Only when she saw him continue to stare at her in obvious appreciation did she fully realize her situation. Quickly she grabbed the towel and managed to restore some modesty, if not dignity, to the scene.

"I came to take a bath," Dan said, holding out his bath items as if in justification.

"As you can plainly see, Captain, this bathroom is occupied."

"Yes, so it is."

"I cannot believe the letters we exchanged would embolden you to such liberties! To barge into a lady's bath! One would never expect a gentleman to do such a thing!"

"I'm . . . I'm sorry," Dan sputtered. "But in my defense, Miss Darrow, I could say that one does not expect a lady to take a bath in a public place without first locking the door."

"You mean the door wasn't locked?" Catherine asked.

Dan shook his head without speaking aloud.

"I . . . I thought I did lock it," Catherine said meekly.

Dan shook his head no. "Nevertheless, finish your bath in peace, Miss Darrow. I shall stand sentry duty outside your door."

"Thank you, Captain," Catherine said.

Fifteen minutes later, when Catherine opened the door, Dan was still standing guard, faithfully discharging his self-appointed duty of protecting her from any further unwanted entries.

"I see you are still here," Catherine said, trying to make her voice sound flat and unemotional.

"Yes, and lucky for you I am," Burke replied. "There was yet another who would have intruded upon your bath, had I not turned him away."

"I thank you, Captain," Catherine said, still keeping the tone of her voice flat.

"Miss Darrow," Dan said seriously, "I beg of you, do not think my ill-timed intrusion was planned. It was a mistake for which I most heartily apologize."

Catherine looked at him for a moment; then, unexpectedly, she chuckled.

"In truth, sir, the fault was mine, for I had indeed failed to lock the door. I am the one who should apologize, for my stupidity and for my rudeness. Only, next time, do be a good man and knock before you enter, won't you?"

"Absolutely," Dan replied with a sly smile. "I promise. *Next time,* I will knock before I come into your bath."

Back in his room after his bath, Dan had just finished buttoning his tunic and was checking his image in the mirror when there was a knock on his hotel room door. Thinking it was one of the hotel staff informing him that the carriage had arrived to take him to the general's dinner, he called out.

"The door is unlocked. Come in."

He heard the door open and close behind him.

"My, Captain Morris, you seem to be as careless about locking your doors as I am," a woman's voice said.

Startled, Dan turned to see Catherine Darrow standing there.

"Good evening, Miss Darrow," he said, and cleared his throat. "I must say that I was surprised, earlier, not only by my untimely intrusion upon your privacy, but also at finding you in St. Louis. What are you doing here?"

"I came for the same reason you did," Catherine said. "To see General Halleck."

"I don't understand."

"After what happened at Independence, I wrote a letter to General Halleck, complaining of Colonel Jennison's beastly behavior and praising you as the only gentleman of the lot," Catherine said. "To my surprise, I received an answer from General Halleck, asking me if I would come to military headquarters in St. Louis to testify before a military tribunal."

"Good for you," Dan said. "If more citizens would complain about behavior like that, I've no doubt but that the army would quickly get rid of such men."

"I was glad to learn, when I met with General Halleck this afternoon, that you had also filed a complaint. The general assured me that such a complaint, from both civilian and military sources, was certain to bear fruit, and Colonel Jennison would no doubt be relieved of his command."

"Command," Dan scoffed. "Jennison doesn't deserve to even have that word spoken in conjunction with his name."

Catherine smiled. "I am glad to see that we agree on that, Captain," she said. "Oh, and General Halleck was kind enough to invite me to his dinner party tonight, provided I could find someone to escort me. That explains my presence in your room. It is my hope that you would escort me."

Dan smiled. "You mean, after . . . what happened . . . you are still willing to let me be your escort?"

"Yes, of course. And Captain, please, you make me blush," Catherine said as she did blush. "Let's not bring up the incident again, shall we?"

"You have my word on it. And as for escorting you? It would be my honor and privilege, Miss Darrow. There isn't a duty in the world I can think of that would be more pleasurable," he said.

Dan was keenly aware of being the envy of nearly everyone present when he arrived at General Halleck's dinner party with a beautiful young woman on his arm. It was a small party, with few enough guests that they could all be accommodated around one long table. And as they ate, they listened to General Halleck explain how he thought the war should be fought.

Although Dan was the only one present who had been a student of Halleck's at West Point, all knew of the general's reputation as a military theorist. His expertise was such that General Halleck had written a highly regarded textbook on military strategy that was being used not only by the United States Army, but by European armies as well.

"My biggest fear," Halleck was saying as he spread butter on a roll, "is that the eastern press will get too impatient with the progress of the war and force us into a large, set-piece battle with the Rebels. That would be a great mistake."

"Why is that, General?" asked a reporter from one of the St. Louis newspapers. "Surely you don't believe the Rebels can stand up to us in a classic battle?"

"It doesn't matter whether they can or cannot, sir," Halleck replied. "Their only chance for victory would be to engage us in a few large battles, much larger than either Manassas or Wilson Creek. In such a battle the casualties would be very high on both sides. And it is my belief that the South, because of its motivation to quit the Union, would persevere through such setbacks, whereas in the North the public mood would quickly turn to one of peace at any cost . . . even if that cost meant the disunion of our nation.''

''Then how do you propose this war be fought, if not in the classic manner?''

''We must obtain several strategic positions and hold them,'' Halleck answered. ''Island Number Ten is a case in point. Once we have that island we will control the Mississippi River all the way to Memphis. After we take Memphis and Vicksburg, the entire river will be ours. And thanks to General Grant, we already have the Cumberland and the Tennessee. With all the South's waterways under our control, we can then start to dismember the Southern states' railroad system. That will shut off all internal means of transportation. At the same time, we will blockade the seaports so that no supplies can come in and the so-called Confederacy is trapped, like a raccoon in a bag.''

As Halleck spoke he demonstrated with a napkin, forming it into a sack, then drawing the neck tight and squeezing it.

''All we have to do is close the neck of the bag, and hold it until the South quits struggling.''

''General, the plan you propose is a brilliant one, to be sure,'' one of the dinner guests said. ''But what about people like Johnston, Beauregard, and Lee? Don't you think they have considered the very thing you are speaking of?''

Halleck laughed easily. ''I'm certain they have thought of it,'' he said. ''Indeed, I would be upset if they hadn't, because this is just the type of concept I have preached in my lectures and advanced in my textbooks. I would hope I have had some influence on them. But our task will be to accomplish this, while the South knows about it, but is unable to do anything to prevent it. And to do that, we must avoid a set-piece battle at all costs.''

''At all costs, General? Even if it means fleeing to avoid a battle?'' the reporter asked.

''Yes,'' Halleck answered. ''Though in this case, I

wouldn't say we are fleeing to avoid the battle. I would prefer to say we are merely strategically repositioning our forces."

"What is your next objective after Island Number Ten?" the reporter asked.

"In northern Mississippi, right on the Tennessee border, there is a flyspeck on the map that is the site of a very strategic railroad junction," Halleck said. "If we control it, we will cut off all transportation between Memphis and Charleston, and from Mobile to the Ohio. In fact, within a triangle of about twenty miles, we can totally disrupt nearly one-third of the South's railway system."

"Where is this place?" the reporter asked.

Halleck laughed. "Surely, sir, you don't expect me to tell you that. I believe, at the present time, that the South is unaware of just how strategic that railroad junction is, and if you wrote about it in your paper, then Generals Johnston and Beauregard would be able to move forces in to defend it. I would much prefer to occupy that place without a major battle."

"Do you not fear that you have already said too much?" one of the other guests asked. "After all, your dinner guests tonight represent quite a diverse group."

"No," Halleck answered. "I am certain that what you have all heard here tonight will not be printed in the newspaper, or spoken of in public places."

"What about the woman?" the reporter asked. There were actually three women at the dinner, but everyone knew that the reporter was talking about Catherine, and they all looked at her.

"What about her?" General Halleck replied.

"I happen to know that she is a slave holder. Also, she is from the western part of the state, and there seem to be as many Rebels over there as there are anywhere in the southern part of the state."

"Gentlemen, I have not spoken lightly here, tonight," Halleck said. "Perhaps my intelligence is superior to yours. I am not worried that information will reach unfriendly ears. Believe me when I say that Miss Darrow is entirely trustworthy."

"That's good," the reporter teased. "I would not want to think of putting such a beautiful lady into jail as a spy."

Dan looked over at Catherine and saw her cheeks pinken slightly in embarrassment.

When the carriage let Dan and Catherine off back at the hotel after the dinner party, Dan held Catherine's arm as they started up the front steps.

"Miss Darrow, one of the things I learned about Missouri since arriving here is that not only is it the leading beer-producing state, it is also our nation's third leading wine-producing state. I have a bottle of Missouri's finest red wine in my room. Would you consider it too presumptuous of me to invite you to test this commodity?"

"I beg your pardon?"

Dan laughed. "In my awkward way, Miss Darrow, I was inviting you for a drink."

"Do you mean in your room?" Catherine replied.

"Yes. Perhaps it was too presumptuous of me. I'm sorry if the invitation offends you," Dan said. "I mean, I wouldn't want to embarrass you any more than I already have today."

Catherine smiled and held up her hand to interrupt Dan's apology. "You do seem to be a man of presumption, don't you?"

"It was presumptuous. I apologize if I have given offense," Dan said.

Catherine chuckled. "I consider the suggestion presumptuous," she said. "But I don't consider it offensive. And I do not believe coming to your room would embarrass me. Actually, I think we have moved beyond embarrassment now."

The Otis elevator let them off on the fourth floor. Then, as the elevator doors closed behind them, they walked arm in arm down the hall toward Dan's room. For the first time that evening Dan became aware of Catherine's perfume. It was subtle, though effective enough to titillate his senses.

Dan opened the door with his key, then they stepped inside. When he closed the door behind them and turned up the gaslight, Catherine looked up at him and smiled. Their gaze held for just a moment, then a sudden, almost overpowering feeling made Dan want to take her in his arms and kiss her. Only his own sense of propriety kept him from doing so. Catherine's face flushed, and Dan realized that she knew exactly what he was thinking.

"Aren't the gaslights marvelous?" Catherine asked.

"What?" Dan replied. He was drowning in her eyes and scarcely heard what she said.

"Nothing," Catherine admitted. "I was just making nervous conversation, that's all."

"There's no reason to be nervous, Catherine," Dan said. It was the first time he had ever called her by her first name. "You don't have to be afraid of me. Nothing is going to happen unless you want it to happen."

"Maybe you aren't the one I am afraid of," Catherine suggested.

The urge to kiss her came over Dan again, and this time it was so overpowering that he didn't know whether or not he would be able to resist it.

"Dan?" Catherine said softly, looking deep into his eyes and reading his very thoughts.

Almost as if the action were beyond him, Dan put his arms around her and pulled her to him. It was not a hesitant kiss, soft and apologetic, as first kisses often were. It was a deep kiss, joined in with a fervor that surprised them both. The kiss deepened until their senses were reeling, then, suddenly and unexpectedly, Catherine twisted away from him.

"No!" she gasped. "Dan, not like this. I don't want to be some casual wartime dalliance, to be used as you would use a trollop."

"Catherine, I don't think that at all. Please believe me. Look, if you are afraid, I'll take you back to your room. I want neither to frighten nor to hurt you."

"No, it's all right," Catherine said. "I don't have to go. You invited me for a drink of wine, and I'll stay for that. But for that only," she added.

"Yes, wine," Dan said, as if jerking himself back to reality. He pointed to one of the two wing-backed chairs around a small table. "Sit there," he invited. "I'll pour."

The next morning Dan was leaning over the railing of the riverboat *Carondolet,* looking down at one of the huge paddle wheels, now lifeless in the water. He studied a twig as it floated along the waterline of the boat, then got caught in the wheel.

It was funny, he thought. He had met Catherine Darrow twice previously, and though he had found her to be an exceptionally pretty woman, and a woman of courage and spirit, he had never thought of her in connection with himself, until last night.

Nothing had happened last night. They'd drunk wine together and talked about many things, exchanging histories. They'd also talked about Burke, who was the one person they both knew, and Catherine had remarked on the tragedy of a war that would force such close friends to choose opposite sides of the question.

Nothing else had happened, though Dan had known, before she'd left his room, that someday it would. And when he'd kissed her good night—a very subdued, chaste kiss— he'd told her what he had come to realize before the evening was over. Catherine Darrow was the woman he wanted to spend the rest of his life with.

"Dan, such things are not to be joked about," Catherine had replied.

"I'm not joking."

"But we have known each other for so short a time."

"The length of time is less important than the fullness of it. At the heart of it, there is no difference between a flower that lives and dies in one day, and a tree that stands for a thousand years," Dan had said.

"Please, Dan, don't make me answer such a question now."

"No answer is needed, for I have not yet asked the question. But one day I will," Dan had promised. . . .

John Sikes walked over to stand beside him. "You seem deeply immersed in thought, Captain Morris," he said.

Dan looked around at him, not sure whether he welcomed the interruption in his thoughts or resented it. "I suppose I am," he admitted.

"Well, it's understandable. Sikeston isn't like St. Louis. When you get down there, you are going to be right in the heart of Rebel country."

"Has there been much military activity around Sikeston?" Dan asked.

"There was heavy fighting over around Belmont, just a few miles away. But nothing in Sikeston that you could call a real battle. Although my little town has suffered terribly from the ruffians. Raiders come riding through the town, first under one flag, then under the other, it doesn't seem

to matter to them, terrorizing our citizens, shooting, rob-
bing, and burning. In truth, Captain, by now more than two-
thirds of the townspeople have abandoned Sikeston.''

"And yet, you are staying on.''

"Yes, I will stay for as long as I can,'' Sikes said. "Although if this war continues much longer, I fear there will
be little left to stay for.''

The *Carondolet* sounded its whistle then and started reversing the paddle wheel on the left while going forward
with the one on the right. That action turned the boat away
from the dock. Then, when both paddles started slapping
at the water together, a frothy white wake bubbled up
alongside as the boat moved majestically into the center of
the river, then turned its bow downstream.

Although the *Carondolet* would ultimately be going into
battle as a gunboat, and indeed cannon were protruding
from both sloping sides of the ironclad, it was now being
used as a troop boat, for in addition to Dan there were
nearly one hundred other soldiers on board the vessel.

As the boat steamed downriver the soldiers sat or lay
around anywhere they could find a place, playing cards,
writing letters, talking, or just staring off into space, lost in
their own private thoughts. Dan found a small corner where
he could stretch out, and he lay down to take a nap, thinking
of Catherine as he fell asleep.

Sometime later he was awakened by the heavy blast of
the boat's whistle, and when he opened his eyes he saw the
red smear of an early morning sky through one of the gun
ports. He stood up, stretched, then walked out onto the
small afterdeck, which was unprotected by the iron plate.

Dan had no sooner reached the deck than he heard a
*ping*ing sound against the plate behind him. He turned in
curiosity to see what had made the noise.

"Better get down, Cap'n!'' a voice called. "They's Rebs
on the bank.''

Almost immediately after the soldier's warning, a large
splinter of wood was torn from the rail near where he was
standing, and this time Dan heard the unmistakable sound
of a rifle shot, a flat sound that echoed across the water.
He dropped to the deck.

"Wh'on't stand up ag'in, Yank, 'n give me another
potshot at ye?'' a voice called from the shore. The voice

rolled with amazing clarity across the river, aided by the
sound-carrying property of the water.

From his position down on the deck of the boat, Dan
looked over to see the private who had cautioned him to
get down. "What's your name, soldier?"

"It's Tinker, sir."

"Thanks for the warning, Tinker," he said.

"Yes, sir. Well, the bastards done got one of us," Tinker
said, nodding his head toward the other side of the boat.
When Dan looked over, he saw a canvas-covered body lying very still on the deck. "Don't want to give 'em the
chance to get another, even if you are an officer."

Dan laughed. "Well, I thank you again," he said.

It was midmorning of the second day when the paddle
wheels stopped to allow the boat to glide up to a mooring
at Bird's Point Landing, on the Missouri side of the conflux
of the Mississippi and Ohio Rivers. There was a small
scrape as the *Carondolet* rubbed against the bottom, then a
rush of steam and a frantic beating of paddle wheels as the
captain pegged the boat to the bank. Just up the bank from
the river's edge, a train sat on the track, waiting, the engine's relief valve opening and closing in loud puffs.

Prodded by the orders of their officers and the curses and
threats of their sergeants, the soldiers loaded the artillery
and wagons onto the flatcars. When the work was done they
climbed into the cattle cars, handing up their long rifles, all
the while jostling and joking with each other to take the
edge off their nervousness. Dan also started toward one of
the cattle cars.

"We don't have to ride back there, Captain. There's
room in the engine cab for us," Sikes said.

"The engineer won't mind?"

Sikes chuckled. "Seein' as I own one-third of the railroad, and he works for me, I don't think he has much
choice in the matter."

A moment later the train got under way, puffing loudly
and throwing great pillars of smoke into the sky.

Riding in the cab, Dan looked back along the string of
cars, where he could see the soldiers shouting at each other,
trying to be heard over the sound of the train. They approached a long trestle, which stretched out over swamp-

land, and the train roared and clacked out onto it.

Suddenly the other end of the trestle erupted in a concussive sheet of flame!

"Engineer! Back down!" Dan shouted. "The Rebels have the other end. It's on fire!"

The engineer threw the lever into reverse and opened the steam valve full. The wheels began reversing, throwing up a shower of sparks that bathed the inside of the cab in a glow of orange.

The sudden stopping of the train threw many of the soldiers against each other, cursing and shouting. Some of those riding in the open door fell out, and Dan saw one unfortunate soldier get crushed by the car wheels.

From across an open field, a mounted band broke out of the woods and raced toward the train, firing and yelling as they approached. Bullets began crashing against the engine cab, and Dan and the others ducked down. One bullet hit the steam gauge, and a hissing rush of white steam spurted out. Dan pulled his pistol and began returning fire.

The Rebels made only one pass, then they broke away and rode back into the woods, still shooting and yelling. Dan raised up and looked in the direction they had gone for a moment, then realized that the troops were still firing into the woods, now just wasting ammunition.

"Cease firing!" he yelled, finally leaving the engine cab and waving his arms at them until they heard his order. Their guns fell silent.

Dan and John Sikes walked down the track to inspect the damage. They were surprised to see that there was practically no damage at all.

"Whoever laid the charge didn't know what the hell he was doing," Sikes commented, kicking at a singed but still intact railroad tie. He turned and waved at the engineer. Then, moving slowly, he and Dan walked in front of the train until it was safely across the trestle. Thirty minutes later they were in Sikeston.

Thirteen

Back again.

My visit to St. Louis was an exciting one, made more so because of an unexpected encounter with Captain Dan Morris. That he was there to complain to General Halleck about the beastly behavior of Colonel Jennison during his "raid on Independence" renews my faith in him as a gentleman. It does a disservice to their cause that Jennison wears the uniform of the United States. I am pleased that the Union Army does not consist, in the main, of such people as Colonel Jennison, but has gentlemen like General Halleck and Captain Morris.

Something happened in St. Louis that is too embarrassing even for me to inscribe in the pages of this diary. I know that I keep this journal for myself, but who knows what eyes may read these words in some distant future? I will say only that the incident involved Captain Morris, and though it was embarrassing I must also confess to a certain degree of titillation from the incident. Captain Morris was the perfect gentleman throughout. If I be honest with these entries, however, then I must confess that there were a few seconds when I almost wished he had put gentlemanly behavior aside. But, I will say no more on that subject, for I fear I have already divulged too much.

Before we left St. Louis Captain Morris all but asked me to marry him. Not in so many words, perhaps, but he did tell me that I was the one he wanted to spend the rest of his life with.

I hope the few letters we have exchanged have not led him on. Dan is a handsome and exciting man, and he has proven on more than one occasion that he is also a perfect gentleman. But as long as I am involved in my work with the "Railroad," I cannot even think of marriage.

There is also the problem with Captain Burke Phillips. Like Dan, Burke has been sending me letters, and I have been answering them. And, like Dan, Burke is handsome, exciting, and a gentleman. But Burke has committed himself to the cause of defending slavery, a position I abhor. Of course, Burke denies that he is fighting in defense of the institution of slavery, pointing out that neither he nor his family has any slaves. He says that he is fighting to defend the rights of the individual states to self-expression, and I must admit that were it not for the slave question, I would, in all likelihood, be a staunch ally of that position.

Upon my return, Willie and Thelma reported that during my absence they helped six passengers through to freedom. How courageous Willie and Thelma are! Both could leave and live their own lives, free of danger, yet they stay on to help others. The penalty if I get caught is, at worst, imprisonment. But for Willie and Thelma, it would surely be death by hanging. That I have two such wonderful friends is one of God's greatest blessings to me.

Entered in my diary this 3rd day of March, in the Year of Our Lord 1862, by Catherine Darrow.

In Sikeston, Missouri, some three hundred and fifty miles away from where Catherine was writing her diary, Dan formed up his company to inspect the road that led to New Madrid. They began riding down the road and were approximately one mile south when one of Dan's advance scouts came galloping back, his horse's hooves drumming on the plank road like the beating of a drum.

"Captain! Rebels!" the soldier warned. "They're comin' up fast!"

"Horse holders to the rear!" Dan shouted. "The rest of you, form a skirmish line!"

With every fourth man moving the horses back out of the way, the remaining men spread out onto either side of the road to wait for the Rebels. Dan took a position behind the line, watching down the road.

They could feel, in the road planks, the vibrations of the approaching cavalry before they could hear them, and they could hear them before they could see them. Then, finally, they saw them, moving up the road en masse, a tiny dot of blue waving above the column. Dan recognized the flag as the same one he had seen at Wilson Creek. It was solid blue, with a red border across the top, bottom, and down the right side. A large white cross filled the left one-third of the flag. This was the flag not of the Confederacy, but of the Missouri Brigade.

"Lord, look at 'em comin'!" one of the men said nervously. It wasn't until that moment that Dan thought about the fact that he was the only one of them who had already seen battle. He wondered how his men would do.

"Easy, men, just wait until I give you the word," he said, keeping his voice as calm as possible to give them confidence.

Across the open area between them, Dan heard the faint, tinny sound of a bugle. At the bugle call, the Rebels urged their horses into a gallop.

At first, Dan could hear only the beat of the hooves, then the jangle of their gear and the rattle of sabers. Then he heard the Rebels themselves, shouting and screaming at the top of their lungs as they approached his line of soldiers.

Dan knew that his men had the more favored position. They had cover behind trees, logs, and mounds of earth. But he knew also that the Rebels advancing toward them were hardened veterans who had been fighting in one form or another for several months.

"Hold your fire, men. Hold your fire until I give the word," Dan said again. He raised his pistol and leveled it at the approaching army. Closer and closer they came, until the great, gray mass became distinguishable as horses and riders, then closer yet, until even the Rebels' faces were visible.

"Now, men, fire!" Dan yelled, shooting even as he spoke.

There was a deafening rattle of musketry as Union and Confederate soldiers opened fire. A soldier standing less than two feet from Dan suddenly spun around with blood spurting from his forehead. Dan took careful aim, then fired and saw one of the Rebels pitch forward from his saddle.

The Rebels advanced far enough to take several saber slashes at Dan's men; then, just as Dan was afraid some of his men might turn and run, the Confederates suddenly and inexplicably wheeled and started back down the road.

Dan's men began cheering.

"Mount up, men!" Dan shouted. "We'll chase them down!"

With a shout, Dan's men leaped into their saddles. Seconds later they were pounding down the plank road in hot pursuit.

Dan kept up the pursuit for several minutes until he suddenly realized what he was doing. He wasn't chasing the enemy! He was being led by them! They were taking him right into New Madrid, where all the Confederate forces were concentrated.

Dan held up his hand, signaling for his men to stop.

"Why stop now, Captain? We've nearly caught them!" his sergeant yelled.

"Sergeant, we have to stop now," Dan said. "Do you know how many of us there are?"

"About eighty," the sergeant answered. "And I didn't count more'n fifty of them."

"But in New Madrid, and around Island Number Ten, there are nearly ten thousand of them," Dan reminded his sergeant.

"Damn!" the sergeant said, his eyes growing wide with fear. "We're riding into a trap!"

"Not if we get out of here," Dan said.

He turned his men around and led them back up the road toward Sikeston, feeling very exposed and very foolish.

But he had accomplished one thing. He had reconnoitered the road almost all the way to New Madrid, and he could report to Major Lathom that the cannons could be brought down and put into position immediately.

*   *   *

Burke Phillips was less than ten miles away from where Dan halted his reconnaissance ride. Totally unaware of the close proximity of his friend, Burke went across the water to Island Number Ten in a small skiff. Large cannon protruded from earthen works on the island, pointing upstream to turn back the gunboat flotilla of the Union. But the guns were heavy and mounted in fixed positions that commanded the river approach only. That made Burke feel uneasy, and he commented on it.

"Don't worry about it, Captain. We control the Tennessee side of the river," General McCown said. "We're safe on the Missouri side, because there is no way heavy artillery can be brought through the swamps to threaten us at New Madrid. And as for the river, well, we can hardly expect an attack from the southern approach, now, can we? Therefore, the guns are pointed in the only direction that could possibly offer a threat."

Island Number Ten was the western end of a line of defense established by General Beauregard. The eastern end of the line was at the town of Corinth, Mississippi.

Burke was in New Madrid, Missouri, because when he'd recovered from his wound, he was detached from Quantrill and assigned as liaison officer to General Sterling Price. General Price took the Missouri Division south to effect a linkup with General Van Dorn, in Arkansas. He left Burke in New Madrid with the Thompson Brigade, commanded by General Jeff Thompson, and General Thompson was second in command of the overall defense of New Madrid and Island Number Ten.

Shortly after he arrived, Burke learned from General Thompson's scouts that the Yankees were busily assembling cannon in Sikeston. Once all the guns were assembled, it would be an easy job to bring them down the road to lay siege to New Madrid. The only way to prevent that would be to destroy the road, and though General Thompson agreed that it should be done, he told Burke that they would have to have General McCown's permission to do so. It was to obtain that permission that Burke had one of his men row him out to the island.

It proved to be a wasted trip.

"Permission denied," General McCown said when Burke laid out his plan.

"General, if you don't let us destroy that road, we will be dodging cannonballs in less than twenty-four hours," Burke insisted.

"I'm afraid you don't understand the big picture, Captain Phillips," McCown said. "Governor Jackson has announced his intention to convene the Missouri State Legislature here, in New Madrid. If the road from Sikeston is cut, New Madrid will be isolated from the rest of the state and none of the legislators will be able to get here."

Burke ran his hand through his hair in exasperation. "The legislature meet in New Madrid? Governor Jackson is a damned idiot! He's been run out of Jefferson City and the state government has been taken over by the military. Who the hell does he think he's kidding?"

"Nevertheless," McCown said, "it is Governor Jackson's civilian government, the legitimate government of the people of Missouri, which is recognized by the Confederacy. It is of great political importance that Governor Jackson holds a meeting of the general assembly. We must show the rest of the South that the democratically elected government of Missouri is a bona fide member of the Confederacy."

"General, if you don't let me destroy that road, the only people who will come to Governor Jackson's meeting will be Yankee cannoneers."

"You have my answer, Captain. The road is to be left intact."

"Yes, sir," Burke said. He saluted. "By your leave, sir, I'll return to my post."

"Have faith, Captain," General McCown said. "Have faith."

The sun had set, but it wasn't quite dark as Burke walked through the island fortifications toward the little skiff that was tied up on the western side of the island. Half a dozen fires were burning as the Confederate defenders cooked a supper of catfish snagged from the river. Up on the parapets, huge guns loomed darkly against the sky while the lookouts stood in their observation posts, their eyes scanning the broad expanse of the Mississippi, now a luminescent pearl gray in the fading light.

Just beyond the bend, some two miles upriver, a flotilla of Union gunboats was anchored against the shore. The gunboats mounted thirteen-inch mortars, which kept up a steady lob of two-hundred-pound shells. Because of the range, and the fact that the boats were not in line of sight with the island, most of the missiles exploded harmlessly in the swampy woods on the Tennessee side of the river, providing the Confederate defenders with more entertainment than fear.

"The general didn't listen to you none, did he, Cap'n?" the boatman asked.

"No, Private Coates, he didn't."

"Didn't much figure he did, from the way you was lookin'," Coates said.

"Let's go back," Burke said.

As Burke got into the boat, he heard the heavy thump of a couple of mortars firing, and he looked toward the north.

"There they go, Cap'n. Two of 'em," Coates said, his finger pointing toward the northern sky.

The mortar shells were easy to pick out as they hurtled up, black balls against the gray sky, trailing a little line of sparks and smoke from their sputtering fuses. They climbed to a height of a thousand feet or so, then arced sharply back down. Burke watched them through their entire flight. One ball hit on the edge of the river just at the line between water and the Tennessee shore, and when it exploded it sent up a shower of water and mud. The other crashed into the treeline, taking out half a cypress tree with its fiery detonation.

"Them damn Yankees can't hit a bull in the ass with them things," Coates said derisively.

"That's because they can't see the target," Burke replied. "If they manage to improve their position, they can unleash an accurate fire on the island that would reduce it in no time at all."

There were two more thumps, and two more mortar shells made the long arcing flight from the bend to the island. One of these actually hit on the island, but it hit on the southeastern end so that no damage was done. The other struck in the water, very close to the island. These were so close that Burke and Coates could actually feel the shock waves of their explosion.

"I see what you mean, sir. You think they're goin' to be able to improve their position?"

"I don't know," Burke replied. He wasn't being truthful. As long as Sikeston Road was intact, there was no way the Federals wouldn't improve their position. But he saw no need to frighten the private.

Both men grew quiet then as the boat was rowed back to New Madrid. They had just touched shore and Burke was getting out of the boat when there was a sudden rushing noise, followed immediately by several loud explosions. These weren't random mortar shells fired by distant gunboats; this was a well-aimed artillery barrage.

"Cap'n Phillips! Cap'n Phillips!" one of his men shouted, running toward him. "There's about a million Yankees out there, and they've got the biggest goddamn cannons I've ever seen!"

Although it had grown dark, the night was intermittently pushed away by the lightning flash of firing cannons whose explosions shook the ground. Burke ran for shelter in the bombproof of the fort.

A short time later it began to rain, and the boom and flash of artillery was augmented by the thunder and lightning of a violent storm.

At around two o'clock in the morning General Jeff Thompson sent for Burke. When Burke reported to him, General Thompson was sitting on a log, eating a piece of cornbread.

"This is exactly what you were warning General McCown about, isn't it?" Thompson asked, shielding his cornbread from the rain by holding it under the apron of his poncho.

"Yes, sir, it is," Burke replied.

"Well, McCown is a hard man to figure out sometimes," Thompson said. "Like, well, you take now, for instance. He's determined to make a fight for Island Number Ten, when any fool can plainly see the writing on the wall."

"He is either a very brave man or a very foolish one," Burke said.

Thompson finished his cornbread, then wiped his hands on his pants. "Yes, well, the island is going to fall, there's no doubt about that," he said. "The truth is, I get the impression that he's ready to abandon not only New Madrid, but the whole state of Missouri. And if that is so, then I say to hell with him. I'm pulling my division out tonight."

"You're leaving New Madrid?"

"I don't intend to stay here and fall into the Yankees' lap, like a ripe plum from a tree," General Thompson said.

"I suppose you have a point," Burke replied.

"Do you want to come with me? I'm going down into Arkansas to join up with Generals Price and Van Dorn."

"No, sir. General Price put me here, so here is where I'll stay."

"Speaking of General Price, I'm glad McCown doesn't know about the one hundred thousand dollars in gold General Price gave me."

"You didn't tell McCown about the money?"

"Why should I? It was Missouri money for Missouri troops," Thompson said.

Burke nodded. "Yes, sir, you're right about that."

"That's why I sent for you, Burke. I want you to get the money out of here."

"And do what with it?"

"Hide it, or take it to someone in Missouri, who can use it."

"All right, General, if that's what you want, I'll do what I can," Burke promised. "When do you want me to do it?"

"What's wrong with right now?" Thompson answered. "Pick out the best horse you can find, then sneak out of here. But be careful. General Pope has an entire army moving this way. No doubt he'll have scouting parties out on both sides of the river, and you're more'n likely going to be running into them."

"I'll get through, General."

"I don't have any doubts."

"General Thompson, sir," called an approaching officer. "General McCown's respects, sir, and he would like a word with you." The new officer was dressed in the gray-and-gold–trimmed uniform of McCown's regular troops, and he looked with ill-concealed contempt at Thompson's butternut clothes.

Thompson stood and pointed to a pair of saddlebags. "Take care of that for me, will you, Captain?" he asked Burke, pitching his voice in a careless inflection that told the visiting officer nothing of the contents of the bags.

"Yes, sir, right away," Burke replied.

After General Thompson and the staff officer left, Burke hefted the saddlebags, surprised at their weight, then went to the remuda, where he saw Sergeant Conley. Like Burke, Sergeant Conley was on General Price's personal staff, and like Burke, he had been left to help in the defense of New Madrid.

"Sergeant Conley, help me pick out two horses," Burke said.

"All right, sir," Conley said. He didn't ask what the horses were for.

"Didn't you tell me you were raised in this part of the state?"

"Yes, sir, I was borned up in Charleston," Conley replied.

"Then you're just the man I want with me." Burke looked around to make certain no one could overhear him. "You and I have to find a place to hide this gold. Otherwise, it's going to fall into Yankee hands. Think you can help me with that?"

"Yes, sir, I can find a place all right," Conley said easily.

A few moments later Burke and Conley mounted their horses and rode through the abatis construction into the dark, rainy night. They moved north, along the Missouri side of the river. Mingled with the crump of artillery and the heavier boom of the mortars on the gunboats were the sounds of the Federal troops in the area. In the night they could make out several campfires, but they had no way of knowing whether they were Northern or Southern fires. Occasionally they would hear a shout or a guttural laugh. Once a skiff moved down the river quickly, a dark shadow slipping through the night rain.

"You're crazy! Grant ain't half the gen'rul Pope is," a strange voice said loudly.

Burke held up his hand, and the two riders stopped. "Yankees," he hissed at Conley.

The two men rode into the shadows of the trees and waited while the patrol moved through. Burke and Conley were veterans of many raiding campaigns. They knew how to use the night to mask their moves, how to strike and then melt back into the trees before the advancing Federal troops. The Yankees they had just encountered had evi-

dently spent their entire period of service in garrison, for
they were moving through the woods and across open fields
as if on parade, talking in loud voices.

Union troops were now occupying all of the ground
around New Madrid, so Burke and Conley slowed their
horses to a walk as they moved through the thick, tangled
undergrowth, picking their way around swollen sloughs and
patches of quicksand.

And always, as they moved, they could hear the constant
sound of artillery fire as the duel between the Union and
Confederate cannoneers continued. Then they heard an explosion so close that they were sure a cannonball had
landed right between them. To their surprise, they discovered that they had blundered into a Union battery. The gun
had just been fired, and one of the soldiers was swabbing
the barrel with water to prevent the premature detonation
of the next charge. The soldier looked up just as Burke and
Conley burst upon them. As it was dark, and both Burke
and Conley were wearing irregular uniforms, the soldier
didn't immediately recognize them as Confederates.

"Hey, you two civilians, get the hell out of here! There's
a battle going on!" the Yankee soldier said.

"Sorry, Colonel," Conley answered, exaggerating the
flat southeast Missouri twang. "We'uns is'a lookin' for
some stray hawgs."

"Colonel?" the Yankee soldier chortled. "Law' now,
don't I wish I was a colonel!"

The battery commander came toward them then. "We
haven't seen any pigs around here," he said. "You'd best
get on out of harm's way."

"Thank'ee. We'll be a-goin', then," Conley said.

"Who the hell ever heard of goin' out at night in a rain-
storm, in the middle of a battle, just to look for some damn
pigs?" one of the soldiers commented suspiciously.

"Hey!" the battery commander said. "Wait a minute!
That's right! Maybe you two fellas better climb down off
those horses."

"Go, Conley!" Burke shouted, and he and Conley
slapped the reins and spurred their horses into a gallop. The
Union soldiers yelled at them to stop, but as they had been
working the cannon, none possessed sidearms, and they had
no way of stopping them.

Burke and Conley managed to get away from the Federal battery, then they rode north along the riverbank. The riverbank was badly overgrown, and the established roads were full of Union soldiers, so progress was very slow. Finally Conley held up his hand.

"You got any place in particular you wantin' to hide that gold?"

"Just so long as it is some place where it won't be found," Burke replied. "Why, do you have a place in mind?"

"Yes, sir. Right over there is a place that is protected from the river, but will never be farmed. It could stay there a hunnert years or more, without anyone finding it."

"All right," Burke agreed. "Let's bury it."

Burke followed Conley to the place he was talking about, then stood guard while Conley buried the saddlebags. Once or twice Burke looked back and saw Conley by the light of a lightning flash, busily shoveling wet sand. After a while Conley came back, brushing his hands together.

"It's all took care of," he said.

"Good. Let's go."

Just before dawn their luck ran out. They blundered into another Union column and were challenged by the pickets. The two men spurred their horses in an attempt to run away, but the terrain was so badly undergrown that the horses couldn't run much faster than a man on foot. The pickets fired, and with a grunt, Conley fell from his horse, mortally wounded. Burke's horse was shot out from under him, and he pitched over the animal's head onto the ground. When he came to a moment later, there were four bayoneted rifles pointed at him.

"Easy, boys, easy," Burke said. "I know when it is foolish to keep on running. You've got me."

"He's alive, Sarge," one of the Union soldiers yelled. "What do we do now?"

"Take him to New Madrid," the sergeant answered. "General Pope will know what to do with him."

Burke was jerked to his feet and prodded in the rear with one of the bayonets, just hard enough to make him wince and elicit a bit of laughter from the soldiers who were guarding him.

"You just keep it movin' right along there, Reb, and I'll try'n keep my bayonet outta your ass."

The others laughed, and the prodding soldier, enjoying being the center of attention, added a bit to hold the limelight as long as possible.

"Mind you, now, I'll just try. But my arms is awful itchy, and ever' now'n then I'm liable to lose control, 'n the next thing you know, somethin' like this will happen."

The soldier jabbed Burke again, this time more painfully than before. But Burke refused to give them the pleasure of watching him wince a second time.

On the Union side, Dan Morris had his men in position to repel any counterattack by the Rebel troops. He and his men were being heavily bombarded by the Confederate gunboats, and he mistakenly assumed that the firing was coming from the Rebels ashore, not realizing that by now General Thompson had withdrawn his entire brigade.

In addition to the bombardment, Dan and his men also had to endure a cold, drenching rain that filled the shelters with water and turned the ground into quicksand. He shivered in the cold and pressed himself into the mud to avoid the shrapnel of incoming fire.

The rain stopped just before dawn, but daybreak itself was masked with a thick fog, which rolled in off the river and laid its oppressive blanket about everything. The fog was so thick that Dan could see no more than fifty feet in front of him. This would be the perfect time, he thought, for the Rebels to counterattack.

"Sergeant Martin," he called quietly.

"Yes, sir?"

"Pass the word to all the men to be especially watchful of a counterattack. I couldn't think of any better time to do it than right now."

"Yes, sir," the sergeant replied, and Dan heard the word being passed down the line until the entire company was alerted.

Strange, muffled sounds floated up to Dan's ears, distorted by the fog until even his own breathing sounded like the approaching footsteps of an army. Finally the fog began to roll away, and he could see trees and bushes and, after nearly two hours, the river itself.

And the fort.

All was quiet in the fort. No flags were flying, and from his vantage point Dan could make out no sign of life.

"Sergeant," he yelled.

"Yes, sir?"

"Pass the word back to General Pope that I believe the Rebels have abandoned the town."

Upon discovering the Rebel fort was abandoned, the Union forces moved into the town. Quickly they set up their field guns and began firing at the Rebels out on the island.

Although the fixed guns on the island were in no position to return fire, the Rebel gunboats were, and they began steaming in big circles, bringing their guns to bear to deliver a broadside that rent the air with its thunder. The battle continued for an hour and a half, with one shell exploding not ten feet from Dan, killing six of his men, including Sergeant Martin.

"You two, keep the prisoner right here while I go see what we're to do with 'im," the Yankee sergeant ordered the soldiers who had captured Burke.

The private who had been jabbing Burke with his bayonet looked at his prisoner. There were spots of blood on Burke's pants where he had bled from the wounds the private had inflicted upon him.

"Hey, Reb," the private said. "You got blood all over your ass, you know that?"

Burke said nothing.

"Looks like you shit in your britches," the Yankee said, and he laughed.

"Cole, wh'on't you leave him alone?" the other soldier asked. "He's a prisoner. You ain't supposed to treat him that way."

"Why don't you mind your own business?" Cole replied. "The sergeant left me in charge, not you." Cole motioned toward a tree with his rifle. "Sit down over there, Reb. And don't you be tryin' nothin', neither, 'cause if'n you do, I'll blow a hole right through you."

Burke sat on an exposed cypress root.

Almost immediately after he sat down, an incoming cannonball from one of the Confederate gunboats landed between Cole and the other guard. The explosion killed Cole instantly and wounded the other soldier. Because of Burke's position under the tree, he wasn't even scratched.

This was it! This was Burke's opportunity to escape! He stood up, then looked back at the two men. The soldier with Cole was bleeding profusely from a wound in his leg. He was also in shock, and he looked at Burke as if not fully comprehending what had happened to him.

Burke turned to run, then he stopped and went back to the wounded man. Quickly he took the shirt off Cole and wadded it up to put on the wound. Then he took Cole's belt and strapped it around the wad to make a pressure bandage to stop the bleeding.

"Don't take that off until you get your wound tended to," Burke ordered the wounded soldier. "Otherwise, you'll bleed to death."

The soldier nodded.

"Good-bye," Burke said. He stood and started to leave.

"Reb, wait!" the wounded Yankee called.

Burke stopped, then looked around. When he did, he saw that the wounded soldier was pointing his rifle at him. "I can't let you go," he said. "You're my prisoner. It's my duty to keep you here."

"I respect that," Burke replied. "But it's my duty to get away, and that's what I'm going to do."

The Yankee cocked his rifle. Burke stared at him a moment longer. "Do whatever you think you have to do," he said. He turned and started to walk away.

"Reb!" the soldier called a second time.

Again Burke stopped, and again he turned. When he did, he saw the Yankee soldier putting down his rifle.

"Good luck, Reb," the soldier said. His voice strained through teeth that were clenched in pain.

Burke smiled. "Good luck to you," he replied. He ran down to the river, then dove in. It was a long, hard swim, but the current became his ally, pushing him downstream toward the island. Twenty minutes later one of the sentries on the island was startled to see Burke come crawling ashore, cold, wet, and exhausted.

"Halt, who goes there?" the sentry challenged.

"Relax, I'm one of you," Burke replied.

"Yeah? How the hell do I know that?"

Breathing hard, Burke walked right by the nervous sentry. "Do I look so damn dumb that I would swim out here without a gun to attack the island? Where's General McCown? He'll vouch for me."

"He's down there, in the bombproof," the sentry said, convinced now that Burke represented no immediate threat.

★★★

Fourteen

From *Harper's Weekly;* March 15, 1861:

HUMORS OF THE DAY

"What kind of ball do the Rebels play on Island Number Ten?"

"I don't know."

"Do you give it up?"

"Yes."

"They play (Commodore) Foote ball."

Island Number Ten fell under constant bombardment for the next week, but despite the terrible rain of shells upon the defenders, the island fort held fast, accomplishing its avowed purpose of keeping the Union fleet bottled upriver above the New Madrid bend.

Commodore Foote made several sorties against the island with his gunboats, but each attack was driven back by deadly accurate cannonfire. Finally, in frustration, Foote withdrew his gunboats and asked for a conference with General Pope.

"You don't seem to understand the problem," Foote said when he responded to Pope's question as to why the boats couldn't be as effective against Island Number Ten as they had been against Fort Donnelson. "That was the Tennessee River. This is the Mississippi."

"What's the difference? A river is a river. They are both water, and a boat goes on water."

"General, there is one hell of a difference," Foote explained. "The Mississippi has a much stronger current, and we would be fighting downstream, which means that the slightest mishap, a damaged rudder, or a hole in our boiler would cause us to lose control of the boat. That would most certainly result in our destruction, or capture.

"Also, we carry armor only at the head, there is little armor plate on the side, and none at all at the stern. And weighted down with armor, guns, and shot, we cannot maintain a stationary position under reverse power, even with anchors, because there is nothing on the slimy river bottom that will afford purchase for the flukes."

"Nevertheless, we have to capture that island," Pope insisted. "Halleck wants it. Grant wants it. Hell, even the secretary of war has sent a telegram asking when we might expect it to fall."

"General, if I could sink that damn island for you, I would readily do so," Foote said. "But it won't sink, and unfortunately, my boats will. I've already lost eleven boats and a goodly number of men. I'm telling you, I cannot take that island with a frontal attack."

"We've captured the Rebel position at New Madrid," Pope said. "We've at least relieved the pressure against you from the Missouri side of the river."

"The guns at New Madrid don't bring enough pressure on the island," Foote said. "What I need is a few batteries on the Missouri shore, just opposite the island. Perhaps then the combined effort of your shore batteries and my gunboats would reduce it."

General Pope unrolled a map on the table in his tent and held down the corners with a pistol, his coffee cup, his field glasses, and a book. "Then you are asking the army for help. Is that it?"

"If it is within your power to do so, then please help," Foote said.

"What about this?" Pope asked, pointing to the map. "I propose to build a road from the Sikeston Road, stretching over to the riverbank at this point, which is quite close to the island. If we erected batteries here, we could aid in the bombardment."

Foote put down the cup and looked at the map where Pope had indicated. "I agree. It would be a great help," he said. He rubbed his chin. "The question is, how are you going to build a road across the swamp?"

"Simple, my dear fellow," Pope replied, smiling. "I am

going to order it done. That is the way we do things in the army.''

"Ordering it and doing it are two different things," Dan said a bit later, after he heard of General Pope's comment. Dan was talking to Colonel Bissel, who was chief of Pope's engineers, and to Bissel had fallen the task of examining the area where Pope wanted his road built. Because of Dan's engineering background at West Point, Bissel had asked for his help.

"Perhaps we could fell enough trees to lay a foundation," Bissel suggested. "We could build a corduroy road, like the one from Sikeston."

Dan shook his head. "That road follows a ridge line of high ground," he said. "Look at this swamp, Colonel. It is absolutely impassable. A man on foot would do well to make it to the river. There is just no way we can build a road good enough to haul in cannons and ammunition. The only thing we can do is disassemble the artillery and pack it in by hand."

"I suppose you're right," Bissel said. "But that limits us to the smaller guns, and I don't know how effective they will be against the island."

Dan stood alongside a winding slough of water, looking at it, lost in thought.

"Colonel, could I take a look at that map for a moment?" he asked at last.

"By all means," Bissel answered easily. "Do you think you've found a route for the road?"

"Not a road, Colonel. A canal," Dan replied.

"A canal?" Bissel mused. He tugged at his beard as he looked at the map. "You may have something, Dan. Of course, why didn't I think of it? We could follow these low-lying areas right here, from the river bend to Wilson's Bayou." Bissel laughed. "Come on, let's take our idea to General Pope!"

When Dan and Bissel reached Pope's headquarters, they found the general posing for Mr. Simplot, a staff artist from *Harper's Weekly.* General Pope was sitting stiffly in a chair, gazing off into space, one hand thrust inside his tunic jacket in a pose that was considered very appropriate for military pictures.

"Well," Pope said. "Colonel Bissel, my road builder. What have you come up with?"

"General, there's no way a road can be built through that swamp."

"What?" Pope asked, jerking his head around toward them. "That's not the answer I wanted to hear."

"General, please, just a moment longer," Mr. Simplot pleaded.

General Pope returned to the original pose. "What do you mean, a road can't be built?"

"General, what we are dealing with is swampland, pure and simple. We'd have to lay a roadbed fifteen feet thick, just to keep from sinking," Bissel explained.

"Then, by God, build the road fifteen feet thick," Pope demanded, taking a sidelong glance at the artist's sketch to see how Simplot was depicting him.

"General, Captain Morris has an idea that I think has merit," Bissel suggested.

"All right, let's hear it," Pope said. "What is your idea?"

"Instead of a road, General, a canal," Dan said.

"A canal? Where? What would that do?"

"General, a canal would allow boats to pass through the swamp, cut across the bend the river makes here, and land soldiers and matériel on shore, below the island."

"Do you think you can do it?" Pope asked, looking directly at Bissel.

"General, please, your pose?" Simplot said.

"Yes, sir, I am positive we can build it," Bissel replied.

Pope resumed his pose. "Then do it," he said without looking around again.

It was a formidable task to build the canal. Colonel Bissel had to cut a channel through the forest that was fifty feet wide, four and a half feet deep, and twelve miles long. In order to accomplish this, he and his men waded through mud and stood waist deep in icy water to saw through the trunks of trees. The trees, once felled, had to be cut up and disposed of. The overhanging boughs of other trees that were standing outside the channel had to be lopped off and their limbs cleared away. Shallow places were excavated, and men worked around the clock in three shifts. Bissel drove himself and his men relentlessly, often working two full shifts himself, then showing up to oversee a portion of the third.

Halfway through the construction of the canal, General Grant came by to inspect the forces at New Madrid. Bissel was too busy with the canal to get away to meet with General Grant, so he sent Dan.

"General Pope told me about the engineering project you and Bissel are undertaking, Captain," Grant said.

"Actually, it's Colonel Bissel's undertaking, General. I am just providing assistance."

"How is it coming?" Grant asked.

"It's coming along very well, sir," Dan answered. "I think we'll have it completed pretty soon now."

"The sooner the better," Grant replied. "If we can control this river, we'll have a waterway that heads right into the heart of the South. But we'll have something else which right now is even more important."

"What's that, General?"

Grant put both hands behind his back and looked southeast. "There's a big battle brewing down there, Captain. By far the biggest of this war. Johnston and Beauregard have been fortifying the railroad junction around Corinth. They're pulling in troops from all over the South. But if we can control this river, we'll have General Price, General Van Dorn, and some thirty-five thousand Confederate soldiers trapped west of the Mississippi. That would be thirty-five thousand people that Johnston won't be able to use. You can see, then, the importance of capturing Island Number Ten and establishing control of the river."

"Yes, sir," Dan agreed.

"Fire in the hole!" someone yelled. The yell was repeated down the line until one of the men nearest them picked it up and passed it on.

"What is that?" Grant asked. "What is going on?"

"They are about to blast some more trees," Dan replied.

Seconds later there was a deep, stomach-jarring explosion as water, mud, smoke, and small pieces of tree flew into the air where the blast occurred.

Grant, who had stepped over to watch the results of the explosion, chuckled. "It's too bad we can't get the Confederates to fire a few explosive shells just where we can best use them."

Dan laughed. "Maybe we can come to some arrangement with them, General."

"Captain, General Halleck speaks very highly of you," General Grant said.

"I am grateful to General Halleck for his kind words."

Grant shook his head. "They aren't just kind words, Captain, they are recommendations. I want you to come with me to Pittsburg Landing."

"I serve at the general's pleasure, sir," Dan replied.

"Yes, well, don't come yet. Wait until all this is over," Grant said. "Once the canal is completed and you have the island invested, come right away, whether the island yet stands or not."

"I'll be there, sir," Dan said.

Grant waved good-bye, then began walking slowly, picking his way back through the swamp. Within a few moments he was swallowed up by the twisted tangle of trees and vines. Dan thought how easy it would be for a lone Rebel soldier to sneak into the swamp, hide, and kill General Grant, then escape without ever being caught. It would be a small act, but one with a tremendous consequence. He shuddered at the thought.

"Hey, Cap'n, was that feller really Gen'rul Grant?" one of Dan's men asked.

"He sure was," Dan replied.

"I'm goin' to write my pa 'n say that I seen him," the soldier said. Then he looked at his rope-burned hands. "That is, if I got 'nything left to write with after diggin' this here damn canal."

Over the next two weeks, and across twelve tortuous miles, Colonel Bissel worked his men twenty-four hours a day, in every condition of weather, without letup. Finally, thirteen days after the first spade of dirt was turned, Colonel Bissel reported to Commodore Foote that the canal was open.

"We have your guarantee that safe passage can be effected through your canal, is that it, Captain?" Commodore Foote asked, pulling on his chin whiskers.

"No, sir," Dan replied.

"What? You don't feel your canal is safe?"

"Commodore, I can't guarantee that some enterprising Confederate officer hasn't found a way to mine the canal with floating torpedoes."

General Pope lauged. "Let's hope, Colonel Bissel, that the Confederates don't have an officer as enterprising as you are."

"I would not wish to underestimate them," Bissel replied.

"Nor I," Pope agreed. "But decisions have to be made and risks must be taken. Commodore Foote, I declare the canal open, and I suggest you effect a passage as soon as possible."

"Of course, General," Foote replied. "Though I can't help but notice it is your declaration, whereas it is my risk. Or, rather, the risk of Commander Walke, who has already volunteered to take the first boat through."

"Balls of fire, Commodore!" Pope exploded. "What do you want? Colonel Bissel's men have been working waist deep in cold water and mud for two weeks for you. Theirs was the drudgery, but you stand to reap the glory. Were it my risk to take I would gladly take it!"

"I'm merely thinking of the *Carondolet* and its men," Foote replied. "They must face this alone."

"Commodore," Dan said, speaking for the first time, "I was a passenger on the *Carondolet* on the way down from St. Louis. I know Commander Walke, and I have already spoken with him. I intend to be in the boat when he effects the passage."

"We don't need an army officer to give us courage," Foote said rather stiffly.

"Courage has nothing to do with it, sir," Dan replied. "But I have worked on the canal and I know all the obstacles."

"The captain has a point, Commodore," Pope said.

Foote stroked his chin whiskers again, striking a thoughtful pose for a moment. He was clean-shaven around his mouth, and he pursed his lips. Finally he spoke.

"Very well, I have no objections. But I want it clearly understood that Commander Walke is in command. From here on, it is a naval operation."

"I appreciate that fact, Commodore," Dan said. "And

now, if I may be excused, I promised to help Commander Walke prepare the *Carondolet*."

The *Carondolet* was a beehive of activity by the time Dan returned to the boat. Its crew, along with Dan's men, were covering the decks with heavy planks. Chains were coiled over the most vulnerable parts of the boat, and an eleven-inch hawser was wound around the pilothouse as high as the windows. Barriers of cordwood were built around the boilers. Finally, protected in every way possible, the boat was ready to make the passage.

"Dan," Walke said, "are you absolutely positive you want to go with us? It could be quite dangerous, and you did your part when you cut the canal."

"I'm ready to go," Dan said.

"All right, it's your funeral."

"Thanks," Dan said, grinning dryly. "But couldn't you have chosen another metaphor?"

Walke returned the grin, then added with another touch of grim humor, "I'll make you an honorary member of the United States Navy," he said. "If you get killed, we'll bury you at sea, in the swamp."

"That'll make me the first sailor in history to have dug my own grave at sea," Dan replied, laughing.

"Commander Walke, Commodore Foote says you may proceed at your discretion," a sailor reported, coming aboard the *Carondolet* with the message.

"Very well, tell the commodore we will get under way just after sunset," Walke replied.

Clouds had been building all day. By the time the sun set, the sky was hazy and overcast. Walke called for the guns to be run back, and he closed the ports. The sailors were all armed with handguns and put in strategic positions to be used in resisting any attempted boarding. Men were also put in position to open the petcocks and sink the boat if she appeared likely to fall into enemy hands. Walke signaled the pilot, and the boat was cast loose to steam slowly downstream, heading toward the mouth of the canal.

By now a storm was gathering, and the boat was little more than a dark shadow against the night, practically invisible as it moved downriver.

"Leadsman, inform me of the depth at all times," Walke said. "Remember, we need at least six feet."

"Six feet?" Dan gasped. "Commander, no!"

"What is it, Captain?" Walke asked. "Does the canal not afford us six feet?"

"We were told four and one-half feet," Dan said. "The tree trunks are cut no lower than that."

"Four and a half feet for the barges," Walke said. "But the *Carondolet* draws a minimum of six feet. Are there stumps underwater?"

Dan nodded. "Hundreds of them. All at four and a half feet."

"All stop!" Walke ordered, and the pilot telegraphed the signal to the engine room. The paddle wheels stopped, then began turning in reverse, churning up the water as it did so. "That's no good," Walke told Dan. "Any one of those stumps will rip the bottom out."

"I'm sorry for the misunderstanding," Dan said. "I'm just glad we discovered it before you put the boat into the canal. I guess we had better go back."

"No," Walke said.

"Commander, you ain't plannin' on trying to go through the canal with all them stumps, are you?" the pilot asked. The pilot had plied the river for many years as a civilian, and he knew the river very well.

"No," Walke replied. "We're going to run by the island all right. But we're going to stay in the river."

"Damn. That's even riskier than the tree stumps," the pilot said.

"Pull the flue caps shut, Lucas," Walke ordered the pilot. "That'll keep the steam from puffing up through the chimneys. We won't make as much noise."

"Won't that make the boiler explode?" Dan asked anxiously.

"No," Walke replied. "The steam'll just vent through the cylinder ports, that's all. It's not terribly dangerous, though the steam is the only way we have of keeping the soot wet. If the soot dries out, there could be a chimney fire."

"Ain't no 'could be' to it. There *will* be a chimney fire, Commander," Lucas said. "I done seen it happen too many times."

"Nevertheless, we have to take the chance. Pull the caps shut."

The valves were pulled shut and the puffing noise ceased almost immediately, so that the boat, in addition to being practically invisible, was now nearly noiseless as well.

"Ahead slow," Walke ordered, speaking quietly as if even his voice might give them away. He pointed into the darkness through the pilothouse window. "The first Rebel position is right over that point. The gun they have there can throw a ball four miles."

Suddenly a sheet of flame, five feet high, shot up from the stack.

"Stack fire!" Lucas said. "I told you!"

"Open the flue caps!" Walke shouted.

A rocket darted skyward from the riverbank.

"It's too late! They've seen us!" Walke shouted. His shout was followed by the explosions of heavy cannonading.

As if on cue, the storm that had been threatening broke. Streaks of lightning flashed through the sky, commingling the flashes and thunder of the heavens with the flashes and thunder of men.

Shrapnel from exploding shells crashed through the window of the pilothouse. One of the armed sailors let out a scream, then crumpled to the floor.

"What is that?" Lucas shouted during one of the lightning flashes. "Commander Walke! There's an obstruction ahead!"

Dan strained to look through the broken window. Then he could see it, too, a long, low-lying mass stretched across the river in front of them.

"It's a chain!" Dan shouted. "They've stretched a chain across the water!"

"Lucas, back down!" Walke shouted.

A cannonball passed through the wheelhouse at that moment, not exploding, but crashing through with a ripping, smashing sound. The ball cut right through Lucas. When Dan looked, he saw the macabre sight of the top half of a man hanging from the wheel, still holding on tightly, while the bottom half was torn away and flattened against the bulkhead on the other side of the wheelhouse.

Walke moved quickly to take the wheel. "There's no time to reverse the engine," he shouted. "We're going to hit the chain!"

"Commander! Try and hit one of the supporting floats!" Dan yelled. "Maybe it'll give way there!"

Walke spun the wheel, heading them toward the nearest float. Seconds later the boat hit it with a jar that was great enough to pitch Dan against the front of the wheelhouse. He put out his hand to brace himself and was painfully cut by the jagged pieces of the remaining glass. The boat shuddered, then continued forward.

"We made it through!" Walke shouted happily.

The storm continued to vent its fury upon the river and combatants, but the fire from the shore batteries was no longer effective once the *Carondolet* passed beyond the point at which the Confederate guns could traverse.

Once the *Carondolet* was through, Walke fired a signal rocket and another boat started down. From the deck of the *Carondolet,* Dan and the others watched anxiously as the flashes of the batteries competed with the lightning to illuminate the night sky. Finally the second boat appeared, then another, and then another.

In the meantime, the mortar barges began working their way through the canal, so that by the break of dawn, in a still pouring rain, the defenders of Island Number Ten saw a ghost fleet materializing out of the swamp, steaming toward their island with all guns firing.

At the height of the cannonading, one of the guns burst on the island, killing three men and wounding four others. That left the commander of the artillery, Captain Jeremy Humes, with only seven working guns. When General McCown came over to check on them, Captain Humes made a desperate plea to have some of the guns moved from the Tennessee side of the river onto the island.

"No," McCown said. "I don't think that would be practical."

"But, General, with just a few more guns I believe we could hold the Yankees off indefinitely," Humes argued. "Look what we're doing now, with only seven."

McCown put his hand affectionately on Captain Humes's shoulder, then looked into the powder-blackened faces of Captain Humes's men. "Men, you have all done an admirable job here. You've stemmed the tide against impossible odds. But the truth is, this island is going to fall despite all we can do to hold it. And when it does, we'll lose everything on it. It would be folly of me to bring more guns into position where they are likely to fall into enemy hands.''

"But, General, with a spirited defense, the island need not fall at all," Humes protested.

"It *is* going to fall," McCown said flatly. "But we have accomplished our mission thus far. We have kept the Yankees bottled up here while Johnston and Beauregard have gathered our forces at Corinth. Now, I'm off to join them with what remains here.''

"You mean we are abandoning the island?" Humes asked.

"I'm leaving you in command, Captain Humes. You and your artillerymen. I'll take every remaining unit, slip across to the Tennessee shore under cover of darkness, and try to make it to Johnston's position.''

"I wish you luck, sir," Humes said.

"Jerry," General McCown said, looking at the junior officer with deep, sad eyes, "I wish there was a way we could all get out of here. But I must ask you to stay and hold the enemy off for as long as possible, in order to give us the chance to get away. I'm asking a great deal of you, I know.''

"We'll do the best we can, sir."

"I'm not asking for a stand until you die," McCown said. "After we've slipped away, your conduct will be up to your own discretion. You may slip away if you feel you can, or surrender, if need be.''

"General, you're askin' us to stay here and fight. But what are we goin' to fight with?" one of the enlisted men asked. "We ain't got but seven guns left.''

"We'll double the rate of fire," Humes said. "That will make seven guns do the work of fourteen.''

"We'll burst another breech," one of the others protested.

"Which gun is most likely to go?" Humes asked.

"Number three."

"Then I'll thumb the touchhole on number three myself," Humes offered. "If the breech bursts, I'll be the only one hurt. Let's go, men. We've got some fighting to do!''

Captain Humes' talk managed to instill a little spirit into

his men, and they let out a cheer of defiance and returned
to their guns. Though the rate of fire wasn't doubled, it was
increased, and moments later they let out a lusty cheer as
one of Foote's gunboats limped away, burning badly.

The increased rate of fire was enough to provide the
cover General McCown needed. He, Burke, and the others
slipped across the water into Tennessee, then started south
and east to link up with General Johnston.

Dan was still on board the *Carondolet*, standing behind the
iron-plated shields as the guns boomed away, throwing shot
and shell, not at Island Number Ten, but at some Confederate batteries on the Tennessee shore. The shore batteries
consisted of 3 sixty-four-pound guns, standing half a mile
apart, and they maintained a spirited contest for a couple
of hours until, finally, they were silenced by the gunners
on board the *Carondolet*.

"You want to go ashore and have a look around?"
Walke asked after the Confederate guns quit answering the
fire.

"I'd love to," Dan replied.

Walke headed the boat into a sandbar and grounded the
bow so that a reconnaissance party could disembark. Dan,
going ashore with them, found the Rebel guns, two of
which had been dismounted by fire from the *Carondolet*
and one of which had been spiked by the retreating Confederates.

The works were abandoned, though a few bodies had
been left behind. One of the bodies was that of a boy who
couldn't have been over seventeen. He was sitting in an
upright position against the destroyed gun carriage, his
arms by his side, his hands lying on the ground palms up,
his mouth hanging slightly open, and his eyes wide, as if
staring accusingly at the men who killed him. The sailors
spoke in hushed tones around the body, as if the boy could
hear them and would be disturbed by their conversation.

One cannonball had chopped through a tree, and the tree
was akimbo, leading to a great height and at an angle that
made it easy to climb. Dan, on impulse, climbed it. From
his position near the top, he could look far up and down
the broad, amber-colored river. He saw gunboats sailing in
circles, now owning positions both above and below the

island, firing as they came into position. And he could see the island returning the fire. The sounds of the cannons rolled across the flat space like thunder, and though he knew they were spewing out missiles of death, he was nevertheless thrilled by the sight.

Dan turned to start back down the tree when, from his vantage point, he saw something that made him gasp. A large body of Confederate troops, one of the largest he had ever seen assembled in one place, were moving south and east. Dan scrambled down the tree quickly. "Come on!" he shouted to the others. "We've got to get word to General Pope! The Rebels are getting away!"

The men ran back to the *Carondolet,* and Walke made a quick run across the river to New Madrid to communicate the news to General Pope.

"We've got 'em!" Pope said, hitting his fist into his hand. "Walke, General Paine's division is on board boats, ready to assault the island. Tell them to forget the island and land on the other side of the river. Move as quickly as they can to join up with General Grant."

"I'd like to go with General Paine, sir," Dan requested.

"Go ahead. It's just a matter of time now, before the island falls," Pope said. "You found them, you've earned the right. Besides, General Grant left word with me to send you to him as soon as you could be spared."

Dan hurried to board one of the boats carrying Paine's division, leaping onto it just as it pulled away from the bank. Half an hour later he stepped off on the Tennessee side, where the troops formed up, then, quickly, he took up the march south and east. The Yankees passed by abandoned camps and artillery. Straggling prisoners were gathered up. The Confederate army was now flanked and pinned against the swamp. They had no way out.

Confederate pickets brought news of the approaching Yankees to General McCown just before midnight. McCown, who suffered with malaria, was sitting on a log, wrapped in a blanket, fighting the effects of chills and fever. His troops had lit no fires for fear of exposing their position and had eaten no food since before leaving the island.

"What are we goin' to do, General? Fight 'em?" his adjutant asked.

"What is their strength?" McCown asked, shivering in the cold night air.

"I'd estimate two full divisions, maybe more," the adjutant replied. "They're fresh troops, too, prob'ly just brought down from St. Louis in the last week or so. They look awful healthy."

"Look at our men." McCown sighed. "We've but one recourse."

"I know, sir," the adjutant answered.

"Tell the officers I have decided to sue for surrender."

"General," Burke said anxiously. "General, have I your permission to lead as many men out of here as are willing to come with me?"

"Lead them out? Lead them out how?" McCown asked. "Where will you go?"

"We'll go through the swamp," Burke said. "And we'll join with General Johnston, just as you intended."

"You'll lose half your men. I can't order anyone to go with you."

"We'll lose all of them if we surrender. And I'll take only volunteers."

"I'll go with you, Cap'n," a private said.

"Coates, what are you doing here? I thought you were with General Thompson."

"Me'n Tim was out on the island when General Thompson pulled out," Coates said. "So we just stayed there."

"Tim?"

"That's me, Cap'n. Private Kelly. I'll go with you, too."

"Anyone else?" Burke asked.

At least one hundred more raised their hands.

"General, with your permission?" Burke said.

General McCown nodded, then hung his head to hide the tears now streaming down his face.

"God go with you, Captain," he said.

"Let's go, men," Burke ordered, and those who had .volunteered to go with him shouldered their arms, then began, laboriously, picking their way through the swamp. Behind them, the island, with its few, brave defenders, was still in Confederate hands, but Burke knew that it was only a matter of time before it fell.

Fifteen

From *Harper's Weekly,* Domestic Intelligence; April 12, 1862:

EXPECTED BATTLE NEAR CORINTH

According to intelligence received from Memphis, a large force of the rebels are concentrated at Corinth, Mississippi, where Generals Beauregard, Clark, Polk, and Cheatham are all located. They are said to have 70,000 men there.

General Buell, who has command of his army in person, had arrived at latest accounts within fifteen miles of Corinth, Mississippi.

The Union troops have possession of Florence and Tuscumbia, Alabama, and Iuka, Mississippi. The two latter places are on the Memphis & Charleston Railroad, Tuscumbia being about midway between Chattanooga and Memphis.

General Grant, with a force not far from 40,000 men, is understood to be at Savannah, Tennessee, so that we must have near 100,000 men threatening Corinth.

The commanding general of all the Confederate forces in the field at Corinth was General Albert Sidney Johnston, and though he wasn't even mentioned in the news article that alerted the rest of the country of an impending battle, he was not the kind who would consider the oversight an affront. In fact, had he read the *Harper's* piece, he would have been pleased, for it would have reassured him that the

Yankee intelligence had not completely compromised his position.

Arriving at Corinth with nearly all of the one hundred men he had led from Island Number Ten, Burke learned that General Braxton Bragg, with ten thousand battle-proven veterans, had also recently reported to General Johnston. In addition, the governors of several Confederate states had answered Johnston's call to provide more men, so that the army had grown to an even greater size.

"You say you are attached to General Price? Is the general coming?" Johnston asked hopefully.

"I am sure it is his intention to join you as quickly as he can," Burke said. "But his army is on the other side of the river, and the Yankees have now made it around Island Number Ten, so that nearly all of the river, all the way to Memphis, is in their hands."

"What about Island Number Ten? Has it fallen?"

"Not yet, General, but it can't hold out much longer."

"God bless the brave men who are besieged there," Johnston said. He sighed. "Very well, as you are here without your general, I shall appoint you to my own personal staff, if you have no objections."

"I would consider such an appointment a great honor, General."

"Good. Then the first thing I want you to do is to go on a recruiting mission to the surrounding farms. Ask them to send their Negroes and their mules to be used in defending our beloved South."

"Yes, General," Burke replied, and he left at once.

Burke's recruiting effort was an exercise in futility. He returned with the report that, while the area farmers would freely give their last son, they wouldn't part with one Negro or a single mule. Johnston shook his head in frustrated disbelief after hearing Burke's report.

"I so appreciate your effort, Captain," Johnston said. He nodded toward the kitchen of the elegant two-story house that was serving as his headquarters. "I think there is some cold chicken left, and some coffee. You are welcome to it."

"Thank you, General," Burke replied. He walked into the kitchen, where the general's orderly poured a cup of coffee, then nodded toward a plate that was covered by a cloth.

"There's the chicken, Cap'n," Coates said.

"Coates, you're the general's orderly?"

"Yes, sir. He give me the job after you left to look for the coloreds and mules."

Burke turned back the cloth to select a drumstick. He had just taken a bite when he heard a commotion in the living room. "What's going on out there?" he asked.

"The gen'rul has called all the other gen'ruls to a meetin'. Don't know what it's about, though, I didn't get invited," Coates said, laughing at his own joke.

"Nor did I," Burke said, smiling. "But I'm going to have a peek at what's all about."

Holding his coffee cup in one hand and his piece of chicken in the other, Burke stepped into the open door frame, then stood there, just out of the way, watching as Generals Beauregard, Bragg, Polk, Hardee, and Breckinridge conducted their conference.

There were not enough places for all the generals and their executive officers and aides to sit, so Beauregard, who was second in command only to Johnston, disdained a chair or a place on the sofa, to sit on the floor near the fireplace. When several officers of lesser rank offered their own seats, Beauregard waved them off, insisting that he was quite comfortable where he was.

"Gentlemen," Johnston said when all were assembled, "while I have guarded against an uncertain offensive, I am now of the opinion that we should entice the enemy into an engagement as soon as possible, before he can further increase his numbers."

"General, I think we should strike at Pittsburg Landing right now, while the Yankees are engaged in offloading their boats," Bragg suggested. "They haven't built any fortifications, and my scouts tell me they've set up tents, just as if they were on parade."

"An attack of the kind you propose is exactly what the Yankees are counting on," Beauregard said.

"What do you mean?" Bragg asked.

"Think about it, Braxton," Beauregard replied. "Why are they setting up tents? Why have they built no fortifications? Because they are hoping to draw us out in a bold and foolish attack.''

"Do you think boldness is inappropriate?" General Johnston asked.

"Not at all, General," Beauregard replied. "But I think boldness should be tempered with caution. I prefer a defensive offense.''

"You talk in riddles, sir," Bragg said, and the other generals laughed.

"Yes, General, perhaps you would share with us what you mean," Johnston said.

Beauregard stood up, brushed off the back of his trousers, and cleared his throat. "I think we should take up a position that would compel the enemy to develop his intentions to attack us. Then, when he is within striking distance of us, we should go on the offensive and crush him, cutting him off, if possible, from his base of operations at the river. If we could then force a surrender from such a large army, the North would have no choice but to sue for peace. We could win the entire war, right here, right now."

The others all began speaking at once, and Johnston had to hold up his hand to quiet them.

"Gentlemen, gentlemen, I appreciate your suggestions and ideas, but as I am in command here, the ultimate responsibility rests with me. General Beauregard, your contention that we could win the war right here is a good one. That is why we must not let the opportunity slip out of our grasp. But I believe General Bragg's suggestion offers us the greatest chance for success. I believe that it is imperative we strike now, before the enemy's rear gets up from Nashville. We have him divided, and we should keep him so, if we can."

Johnston's word was final, so there was no further argument on that subject. The discussion then turned to the plan of battle, and in this, Johnston decided to form the army into three parallel lines, the distance between the lines to be one thousand yards. Hardee's corps was to form the first line, Bragg's the second. The third would be composed of Polk on the left and Breckinridge on the right.

"As second in command, General Beauregard will coordinate your efforts. Gentlemen, please have your elements in position by seven o'clock Saturday morning. We shall begin the attack at eight.''

There was a buzz of excited conversation as, for a few moments, the generals discussed the orders with each other.

"And now, I am certain that you all have staff meetings to conduct, so I release you to return to your units," Johnston said by way of dismissal.

The assembled officers stood then and, as one, saluted. After that they trooped outside, clumped across the porch, then mounted their horses to return to their units. Beauregard stayed behind.

Johnston stood at the front door for a long time after the others left. He hung his head, as if praying, and during that time, Beauregard said nothing. The only sound in the room was the popping and snapping of the wood fire burning briskly in the fireplace.

"Excuse me, sir," Coates said quietly, and Burke stepped out of the way as the young private, carrying coffee, moved into the living room to give each of the generals a fresh cup.

"Thank you, soldier," General Beauregard said.

Coates left, and Burke felt that he should leave, too. After all, this was a private moment between the two top commanders in the field. Yet it was that very thing, the fact that he was an observer to such a private moment, that kept him glued to his position in the doorway. His presence was either not noticed or unobtrusive enough to cause no problem, for neither Johnston nor Beauregard indicated that he should leave.

The coffee was hot, and Johnston sucked it noisily through extended lips.

"Gus, I've drunk coffee around hundreds of fires on dozens of campaigns over the years, but I tell you now, tomorrow will be my last," Johnston finally said.

Beauregard looked up with a startled expression on his face. "Why, General, whatever do mean?"

"I fear I will not survive the battle which is coming."

General Beauregard tried to dismiss Johnston's statement with a laugh. "General, you've been in battle before. You know that every man, be he general or private, feels fear."

Johnston shook his head. "No, you don't understand. The funny thing is, I am not afraid. I am certain that I shall be killed, and with that certainty has come the biblical 'peace that surpasseth all understanding.' I can't explain it to you, Gus. It is something you must feel, though you can't feel it until you are facing the same situation.''

"But you can't know with a certainty," Beauregard argued. "The hour of his death is known to no man."

"Until it is upon you, Gus, then you know. Then you know," Johnston said again, quietly, as if talking to himself.

Beauregard made no further efforts to dissuade General Johnston. Instead he just put down his coffee and left quietly by the front door. Burke felt now that he, too, was somehow intruding upon a very private moment, so he turned and walked back through the kitchen, leaving by the back door.

General Albert Sidney Johnston was left alone with his thoughts.

"Watch your head, Cap'n, caisson comin' down!" a gruff voice shouted.

Dan was at Pittsburg Landing on the Tennessee River, where a riverboat was being offloaded. He looked up to see the caisson being swung off the steamer with a rope and tackle. He ducked, then watched as it was swung over to willing hands on shore.

Dan had just arrived at Pittsburg Landing, making the trip from Island Number Ten in two days. It was night, and though the early April air was cool, it was not brutally cold, a fair departure from the month of privation he had put up with at New Madrid.

"Lieutenant," Dan called to one of the officers supervising the unloading of the steamer.

"Yes, sir?"

"Where might I find General Grant?"

"Captain, his headquarters is up at Savannah," the lieutenant said. "But he's been spending every day down here, and far into the night as well." He pointed to the steamer that was being offloaded. "And since the boat is still here, like as not the general is here, too. You'll find him around here somewhere."

"Thanks," Dan replied, and he started picking his way

through the hustle and bustle of the troops to look for the short, bewhiskered commander.

Everywhere Dan looked there was activity, and the sight of so many men and so much matériel was a thrilling one. But—and this nagged at him a little—it was also a frightening sight, for he saw no signs of defense. Few of the men he saw were even carrying arms. Rifles were stacked. Even the cannons being unloaded had not yet been assembled, and Dan couldn't help but think what a fine target they would make should the Rebels decide to launch an attack.

Dan climbed up the steep riverbank and saw what appeared to be a thousand campfires scattered out through the fields and hills, stretching nearly as far as the eye could see. Now he breathed easier, for who would dare attack an army this large and this grand?

Then, not fifty feet in front of him, Dan saw General Grant. The general was sitting on a fallen tree trunk, listening to the reports of a couple of cavalry officers. His leg was stretched out in front of him, and a pair of crutches leaned against the log beside him. Dan started toward them.

"Well, Captain Morris," Grant said, smiling at his approach. "It is good to see you here."

"It is good to be here, General," Dan said, pleased that Grant had recognized him so quickly. He nodded toward the crutches. "Have you been wounded, General?"

"Nothing so glamorous as that," Grant replied. "My horse slipped in the mud and fell on my leg. It's painful, but the soft ground kept it from being any worse."

"We were very lucky the general wasn't hurt badly," one of the nearby officers said.

"Yes, well, enough of that," General Grant said, dismissing the subject. He looked to the two officers who were with him. "Gentlemen, I would like you to meet Captain Dan Morris. Regardless of what you might hear from General Pope or Commodore Foote, I want you to know that Colonel Bissel and this man are the true heroes of Island Number Ten."

"I'd hardly say that, sir," Dan said, laughing self-consciously under the unexpected praise.

"But I would say it," Grant replied. "I believe that the canal you dug is going to go down as one of the engineering feats of genius of this or any other war. Our great-grandchildren will tell of it.'' Grant chuckled. ''I just wish I had assigned you to General Buell.''

''General Buell?''

''Yes,'' Grant said. He sighed. ''It has taken his engineers twelve days to build just one bridge. Twelve days he's been sitting up there, ninety miles from this very spot, waiting to ford one river. God's whiskers, I never saw a slower or more cautious man in my life! He should have been here by now.''

''Are we badly exposed here, sir?'' Dan asked.

''Exposed? Of course we are exposed. But I doubt they will attack us. They will be spending all their time erecting defenses around Corinth, and while they are occupied doing that, we'll be growing stronger and stronger.''

''What is the size of the Confederate Army now?'' Dan asked.

''Who can say? We've had estimates of everything from twenty thousand to seventy thousand. These men have just returned from a scouting expedition and are in the process of giving me a report. This is Colonel Norton and Colonel Thomas. Why don't you remain and hear what they have to say?''

''Thank you, General,'' Dan replied.

The two officers Grant introduced were both younger than Dan, yet they were lieutenant colonels. They had obviously proven their worth in battles before now to have obtained so high a rank at such a young age.

''General,'' Colonel Norton said, ''I ranged nearly nine miles, and I encountered a pretty large body of cavalry. We skirmished somewhat, killed a few of them, and we lost two of our own. They broke off after about half an hour.''

''How large a body was it?'' Grant asked.

''I'd say battalion size,'' Colonel Norton said.

''And I'd agree, sir,'' Colonel Thomas put in. ''They had a battery of artillery with them.''

''Any infantry?''

''None that we could see.''

''Hmm,'' Grant mused. ''I'd say it was just a nuisance raid. More than likely they were going to unlimber the artillery pieces, throw a little iron our way just to keep us on our toes, then skedaddle on back to Corinth. Nevertheless, advise Generals Sherman and McClernand to be especially watchful.''

"Yes, sir," the two colonels said as one. They rendered a sharp salute before retiring. Grant returned the salute almost halfheartedly, as if bemused by the whole thing. After they left, he pointed to the tree trunk.

"Have a seat," he invited Dan. "Are you hungry? I have some hardtack and jerky here."

"No, sir," Dan said. "I had supper on the boat."

"You don't mind if I have a bite?" Grant asked. He opened his haversack. As he rummaged through it, Dan saw the unmistakable glint of a bottle of whiskey.

"Maybe you'd like a little drink instead?" Grant offered, making no effort to hide the bottle but handing it directly to Dan.

"Don't mind if I do," Dan replied. He uncapped the bottle, turned it up for a generous drink, then returned the bottle to Grant.

Grant held it up and examined the remaining liquid. "Not much sense in saving that," he said offhandedly, and he turned up the bottle, draining the rest in one long draft. When he finished he wiped his mouth with the back of his hand, then tossed aside the bottle. Dan heard it break with a tinny crash.

"I'm technically in command of Buell," Grant said, bringing up that general's name again. Dan could see from Grant's behavior that Buell was more or less steadily on his mind. "But until just a couple of weeks ago he was senior to me, and to tell the truth, I'm a little hesitant to make an issue of it. But here it is April already, and he was supposed to be here no later than the twenty-fifth of March. If he hasn't shown in two more days, I want you, personally, to go up there and prod that outfit he calls his engineers. I want you to get them across that damned river.''

"Yes, sir," Dan replied, wondering how he, a captain, would deal with the colonel who would be Buell's chief of engineers.

"You know what the problem is, don't you?" Grant asked.

"No, sir."

"Halleck is supposed to arrive next week to take overall command. I think Buell wants to wait for that moment, rather than put his army under my command. After all, I've still got a cloud over my name. Halleck even relieved me once, did you know that?'' Grant asked.

Dan did know of it, but he knew that Grant wanted to talk, needed someone to hear him out, so he said nothing.

''Halleck sits up there in his damned Federal Building in St. Louis, giving fancy dinner parties . . . entertaining politicians,'' Grant said derisively, and Dan blushed a little, wondering if Grant knew that he had been a guest at one of Halleck's celebrated parties.

''And if I don't tell him every time I blow my nose, Halleck gets all upset,'' Grant continued. ''Then, he got the idea that I left my command without proper authority and he decided to relieve me. So, he relieved me and appointed General Smith in my stead. But within a week Smith had everything so botched up that Halleck had no choice but to give me my old job back. Politics, Captain, politics. Lord, how I hate politics.''

''General, the steamer is ready to return to Savannah,'' someone said, coming upon the two men.

''Thank you,'' Grant replied. He stood up and reached for his crutches. When Dan handed them to him, Grant looked at him with a disarming smile. ''One of your duties, Captain, is not to pay too much attention to what I say at times like this. It's just like a safety valve on a steam engine. I need to let a little of it out every now and then.''

''I understand, General,'' Dan replied.

''Oh, I am sure you do, Captain, or I would have never said a word. Find yourself a billet down here somewhere, would you? I think it would be good for me to have someone from my staff stay here all the time.''

''Your staff, sir?''

''Yes, my staff. Did you think I had you brought over here because of your good looks? You are my liaison officer.''

''Yes, sir,'' Dan replied.

''By the way, didn't you spend some time with the Seventh Kansas? What do they call themselves? Jayhawkers?''

''Yes, sir,'' Dan said, curious as to why General Grant would bring that up.

''They are here,'' Grant said.

''Doc Jennison is here?''

"Yes," Grant said. He lifted one of his crutches and pointed. "They are bivouacked just on the other side of that little clump of trees. Most unmilitary group I believe I have ever seen. Let's just hope they can fight."

The boat captain blew his whistle.

"The navy seems anxious to get me back to Savannah," Grant said. "I guess I'd better go."

Dan watched Grant's swinging gait as he hobbled down to the boat.

After General Grant left, Dan took a trail through the trees to the site where the Seventh Kansas was encamped. He saw Collins relieving himself into the river.

"Didn't you men dig sinks for that?" Dan asked, disgusted at seeing someone use the river that was also providing drinking water for the entire army.

"Big as this river is, a little pee ain't goin' to hurt it none," Collins said, buttoning his trousers and then turning around. When he saw Dan he smiled, a wide, gap-toothed smile. "Well, lookie who is here! We thought you was dead."

"Is Colonel Jennison here?"

"He's over yonder, playin' cards with some of the other boys," Collins said with a nod of his head.

Dan walked farther into the camp. General Grant was right. Of all the campsites, this one was the most disorganized and unruly. Trash was strewn everywhere, there was no semblance of order in how the tents were pitched, there were no sentries posted, and there had been no attempt at entrenchments. Half a dozen campfires were burning, many with green or wet wood, which gave off a great deal of smoke.

"Shee-it! Where the hell did that ace come from!" someone said disgustedly, and several others laughed. Dan saw Jennison and four other men sitting around a log, playing cards.

"Hello, Colonel," Dan said.

Jennison looked up, then spat. "If'n you're lookin' to join back up with us, we don't want you," Jennison said.

"I'm on General Grant's staff."

"Hear that, boys? He's on *General Grant*'s staff," Jennison said. He twisted the words "General Grant." "We thought you was dead," he added.

"Yeah, we thought a Rebel cannonball landed slap on your ass," one of the others said, and they all laughed.

"I must say, I'm a little surprised to see you here," Dan said. "I would've thought you would be cashiered by now."

"What is that? Cashiered?"

"Kicked out of the army," Dan said. "General Halleck assured me that the Union could do without your kind."

"Yeah, well, see, here's the thing," Jennison said. "Me'n the boys here don't work for General Halleck and the Union Army. We work for General Lane and the Kansas Militia."

"But you are here," Dan said.

"Yeah, we're here. I reckon when push come to shove, the Federals needed a few of us Kansans to help 'em out."

"That's right. We're goin' to show all you regular army boys what fightin's really about," one of the others said.

"I'm sure it will be an eye-opener," Dan replied. He turned and started to walk away.

"Morris!" Jennison called.

Dan stopped, then looked back toward the little man in the high-top boots and the hat with the sweeping feather.

"I ain't forgettin' that you carried tales to General Halleck about me and my boys."

Dan fixed Jennison with a cold stare. "Do you want to do something about it?" he challenged.

"No," Jennison said calculatingly. "No, not now. But when the time is right, why, I reckon your hash will be settled."

As the Confederate Army maneuvered into position early the next morning, an abrupt April thunderstorm broke over the winding columns. The rain filled hat brims, flowed down the soldiers' backs, and drummed into puddles on the dirt trails. Wagon and artillery wheels cut through rain-soaked roads, turning them into muddy quagmires that caked up on the wheels and gathered in great mudballs on the shoes of the marching soldiers, making every inch of progress a most difficult procedure. The army moved, when it moved at all, in jerky, halting operations. Periodically they would stop for long periods of time while the men stood, made miserable by the falling rain. Then the army would lurch into movement that would inevitably cause the trailing columns to have to break into a difficult and exhausting trot just to keep up.

Scattered on both sides of the road during all this were the discarded items of soldiers on the march: overcoats, shovels, rain-soaked playing cards, letters, newspapers, and even Bibles.

Finally the army was called to a halt so that General Johnston's orders, which by now had been transcribed into a score or more copies, could be read to the various regiments. Burke stood in the rain with the others of the headquarters detachment, listening as the chief of staff shielded the orders from the rain by holding his hat over the piece of paper on which they were written.

" 'Soldiers of the Army of the Mississippi,' " the colonel read. Then, clearing his voice, he moved into the body of the orders:

> I have put into motion to offer battle to the invaders of your country. With the resolution and disciplined valor becoming men fighting, as you are, for all worth living or dying for, you can but march to a decisive victory over the agrarian mercenaries sent to subjugate and despoil you of your liberties, property, and honor. Remember the precious stake involved; remember the dependence of your mothers, your wives, your sisters, and your children on the result; remember the fair, broad, abounding land, the happy homes and the ties that would be desolated by your defeat.
>
> The eyes and hopes of eight millions of people rest upon you. You are expected to show yourselves worthy of your race and lineage, worthy of the women of the South, whose noble devotion in the war has never been exceeded in any time. With such incentives to brave deeds, and with the trust that God is with us, your generals will lead you confidently to the combat, assured of success.

The colonel looked up. "And it is signed by A. S. Johnston, General."

"Hip, hip!" someone shouted.

"Hoorah!" his call was answered.

"Hip, hip!"

"Hoorah!"

"Hip, hip!"

"Hoorah!"

Although it had been General Johnston's intention to have the men in position by seven and begin the attack by eight, eight o'clock came and passed with the Southern columns still bogged down in the stop-and-go marching that had thus far marked their progress on the muddy arteries that were the roads.

General Bragg, a West Point graduate and hero of the Mexican War, was beside himself with consternation. One of his divisions was lost somewhere in the rain on the jammed, muddy roads, and the lateness of his corps was causing the entire operation to dissolve. Beauregard was riding him mercilessly, and though Bragg had done everything within his power to keep to the schedule, he made no excuses to General Beauregard because he knew that the ultimate responsibility lay with the commander. And as Bragg must suffer the tirade from Beauregard, so too would Beauregard hear from Johnston, who, in turn, was ultimately responsible to the governors of Tennessee, Mississippi, and Alabama, as well as to Jefferson Davis and the Confederate Congress.

As the men began reaching their positions, the sun finally came out. By the time it made its first appearance, however, it was already high in the sky, for the eight o'clock deadline had long since passed. The men, fearful that the rain may have dampened the powder in their rifles, began testing the powder by snapping the triggers. As a result, all up and down the line their muskets popped and banged, well within earshot of the Federal outposts.

In addition, the untrained and untested men who made up the Confederate Army had their spirits so invigorated by the warming sun that, excited at the prospect of the battle and glory that lay before them, they began giving a series of Rebel yells. Some started shooting rabbits and doves to cook for their lunch, justifiable in their minds because most had eaten their three days of rations in the first day.

For two more, dragging hours Generals Johnston and

Beauregard stood by as Bragg continued to bring up his corps. By now the sun was straight overhead, but the rear division was still nowhere to be seen.

"General Bragg," General Johnston said, "we are waiting."

"Yes, sir. I'm sorry, sir."

"Where is your division?"

"I'm not certain, General," Bragg said. He pointed south. "It's back there, somewhere. The mud, the crowded roads . . ." He stopped in midsentence. Since the others had had to put up with the same conditions, the excuse sounded feeble, even to his own ears.

General Johnston took out his watch and looked at it.

"It is twelve-thirty," he said. He snapped the watch shut and put it back in his pocket. "This is perfectly puerile! This is not war!"

It took two more hours for Bragg's lost division to come up front, and two more hours beyond that for it to be put into position. By that time it was four-thirty in the afternoon and the shadows were growing longer.

Suddenly there was the unmistakable sound of a drummer giving the long roll. General Beauregard put his hand to his head in consternation. "Is there to be no respite from the bungling?"

Looking around, he saw Burke.

"Captain, would you please find the idiot who is beating on that drum and silence him?" he commanded.

"Yes, sir," Burke replied.

Once mounted, Burke rode down the line toward the sound of the beating drum. When he reached a point quite near it, he stopped and summoned a sergeant.

"Sergeant, I want you to find whoever is banging on that drum and have it stopped at once," he ordered.

The sergeant and several of the men around him laughed.

"What is so funny?" Burke asked, irritated at the unexpected response.

"Don't rightly know how I'm goin' to get that drum stopped, Cap'n," the sergeant replied. "Seein' as it's over in the Yankee camp."

"The Yankee camp?"

"Yes, sir. I can walk over there'n tell the little feller to stop, but like as not he won't pay no attention to me,'' the sergeant joked, and again the men laughed.

"Never mind, Sergeant," Burke said, laughing with him. He looked across the woods toward the sound of the drum. "I doubt he would even pay attention to General Beauregard. Very well, men, carry on as you were."

"Yes, sir," the sergeant said, still smiling at the joke.

Burke returned to General Beauregard to give him the news that they were listening to a Yankee drum.

"Well, that does it, then," Beauregard said. "If we can hear them, there's no doubt they have heard us."

General Johnston was speaking with General Polk. Polk had been Johnston's roommate at West Point but more recently had been ordained an Episcopal bishop; as a result, he was referred to as "the Bishop" fully as often as he was called General.

"General Johnston, we have lost all possibility of surprise," Beauregard said. "By now the Yankees will be entrenched to the eyes."

"So, what are you telling me, Gus?" Johnston asked.

"I'm suggesting that you might want to reconsider the attack order. Perhaps we would be better served by withdrawing to Corinth to strengthen our defenses and let the Yankees bring the fight to us."

"No, no, I strongly disagree," General Polk said. "Our troops are most eager for battle. Consider this, gentlemen. They left Corinth to fight, and if they don't fight, they will be as demoralized as if they had been whipped."

"I totally agree," General Bragg said. "We can't even consider withdrawal now."

"Funny you should say that, General Bragg, as it was your delay that has put us into this situation," Beauregard reminded him.

"I apologize for the disruption in plans my corps caused," Bragg said. "I make no excuses, but I do apologize."

General Breckinridge rode into the camp then and, when he dismounted, was surprised to learn that the impromptu war council he had happened upon was even contemplating withdrawal.

"What is your opinion, General?" Johnston asked Breckinridge after outlining the situation for him.

"Gentlemen, I say we attack. Speaking for myself, I would as soon be defeated as retire from the field without a fight."

"Well, that leaves us only Hardee to hear from," Beauregard said.

Breckinridge chuckled. "Hell, Gus, you know where Bill stands on this. He's already deployed, and anxious for battle. If he were here, he would vote to attack."

"Then it looks to me as if the vote is in," Johnston said. "And there's no doubt as to the way it has gone. The attack is still on."

"Now? With darkness nearly upon us?" Beauregard asked. "Do you intend to launch a night attack?"

"No, we would have no means of control during such an attack. We will go at first light, tomorrow," Johnston said. "Gentlemen, once all your troops are in position, put them at ease and have them sleep on their arms in line of battle. At least tomorrow we will have no unexpected delays in arrival."

"General, there is one more thing you should consider," Beauregard said, not yet ready to give up his argument.

"What is that?" Johnston asked.

"General Buell," Beauregard said. "He has, in all likelihood, joined with the others by now, and if so, that would bring the number of men arrayed against us to nearly seventy thousand or more."

"The attack order stands," Johnston replied.

"Very good, sir. I will see that everyone gets the word," Beauregard said. The decision having been made, Beauregard was, once more, the loyal subordinate.

Beauregard and the other generals left to attend to their various duties. Johnston watched them ride away, then he turned to Burke, who had listened with great interest to the entire discussion. Burke could see the look of determination in General Johnston's eyes.

"You were listening to our conversation?" Johnston asked Burke.

"Yes, General."

"You understand, don't you, Captain Phillips? We have no choice but to attack. We have given away too much ground as it is, and now the Yankees are on our very doorsteps. If we don't stop them here, they will occupy all of our cities in six months' time. General Beauregard is worried because their numbers may be seventy thousand? Hell, I would attack if they were a million.'' He was silent for a moment longer, then, inexplicably, he chuckled. ''But don't worry, my young friend. Ultimately, the numbers are unimportant. Like us, the Yankees are spread out between Lick Creek and Owl Creek, and they can present no greater front between those two creeks than we can. In fact, the more men they crowd in there, the worse we can make it for them.''

''I agree, sir,'' Burke said.

Johnston chuckled softly. ''Good. If I am questioned, I shall say that the liaison officer from General Price's army, an army that is trapped in Missouri, has concurred with my decision.''

''I'm sorry, General, I didn't mean to be presumptuous.''

Softening, Johnston put his hand on Burke's shoulder. ''I know you didn't, son, and I didn't mean to be sarcastic,'' he said. He was silent for a long moment. ''It's just that, after this battle, the country's mood is going to change. Never again will men go off to war with bands playing, flags waving, and women throwing flowers at marching troops. We are in for a day or two of bloodletting the likes of which this nation has never seen. It will change our way of looking at war forever.''

Johnston wandered off several steps, and Burke knew that he wanted to be by himself. Respecting the general's need for privacy, Burke pulled some cold jerky from his saddlebag, then, after accepting a cup of coffee from the general's orderly, walked over to an exposed root and sat down to have his supper.

Though the day had begun with rain, it was ending now with a clear, red sunset, shining through oaks that were green with new growth. The moon, in crescent, rose in a dark blue twilight, then, finally, the sky darkened and the stars came out.

Burke could hear faint bugle calls in the distance, and he looked toward the dark woods that separated the two armies. On the other side of the woods was the enemy. There, men dressed in blue were bedding down for one last night before the killing began.

Whippoorwills called from the woods, and as Burke

looked back toward his own side he could see the glow of campfires around which men in gray, sharing the same language, culture, religion, history, and in some cases family as those in blue, waited for the events of tomorrow.

"Tomorrow, boys, tomorrow," the veterans teased the recruits.

"What about tomorrow?" some of the green soldiers asked. "What will happen tomorrow?"

"Why, tomorrow, you'll see the elephant," a grizzled old sergeant said, and the other veterans laughed at the recruits' discomfort.

Laughing softly at the nervous antics of his men, Burke pulled some paper and a pencil from his haversack and began writing.

Near Corinth, Mississippi, April 4, 1862

Dear Miss Darrow,

I have only recently arrived here from New Madrid, Missouri, and from Island Number Ten, where we held the Yankees bottled up in the Mississippi until now. I left New Madrid with General McCown, but he took ill and lost the will to fight, or even to avoid capture. When last I saw him, he was sitting on a fallen tree in the Reelfoot Swamp, waiting for the Yankees to come get him.

I tried to get him to go on, but he refused to do so, though he did let me call for volunteers, which I did, and thus led more than one hundred men to this place.

I must tell you that very soon now, there will be a battle the likes of which has never been seen on this continent. The Confederate Army is bivouacked here under General Johnston, with 70 or 80 thousand soldiers. General Grant is nearby with 70 or 80 thousand Yankees, and General Buell is in the area with another 20 thousand soldiers, ready to join Grant. When the battle commences the rivers and streams of this place will run red with blood, for there will be killing on an unprecedented scale.

Miss Darrow, the exchange of letters over the last several months, though infrequent, has been very important to me. Pleasant thoughts of you have sus-

tained me through the difficult times, and for that I
am, truly, grateful.

> Your obedient servant,
> Burke Phillips
> Capt. CSA

Sixteen

From *Harper's Weekly;* April 5, 1862:

HUMORS OF THE DAY

"Why is a Rebel general like a drum?"
"I don't know."
"Do you give it up?"
"Yes."
"Because he is made to be beaten."

Dan put out his bedroll in the area that General William T. Sherman had chosen as his headquarters. It was chosen because it was on a small ridge, thus affording drainage from the frequent April rains. But Sherman's army was not the first to recognize the physical advantage of the lay of the land, for long ago a group of Methodists had realized it as well, building upon the ridge a crudely constructed, log church house, which they called "Shiloh Meeting Ground."

The men of Sherman's corps were spread out in both directions from Shiloh, not for tactical reasons, but for comfort, as they had selected the best places for water, as well as level ground for their tents. At breakfast the next morning, Dan commented on the lack of defensive positions to Colonel MacKenzie, Sherman's chief of staff, and to General Prentiss, whose brigade was bivouacked nearest Sherman's headquarters.

"Don't worry about it, Captain. We aren't here to fight a defensive battle," General Prentiss said, dismissing Dan's worry. "We're here to attack the Rebels at Corinth."

''Nevertheless, shouldn't we be prepared just in case the Rebels decide to surprise us?'' Dan asked.

''You think the Rebels might attack us?'' Colonel MacKenzie asked.

''I think there is that possibility, yes,'' Dan said.

''You want to tell that to Sherman?''

''I don't figure it's my place to tell him,'' Dan replied.

Both Prentiss and MacKenzie laughed. ''No, and you aren't going to find anyone else who thinks that, either,'' MacKenzie said. ''Not after yesterday.''

''Why? What happened yesterday?''

The commanding officer of the Fifty-third Ohio sent word to General Sherman that he believed a large force of Confederates was camping just on the other side of the woods. When General Sherman rode over to confront him, Colonel Peters went on and on about the buildup of forces. Finally, Sherman just jerked the reins to turn his horse back toward Shiloh. 'Take your damned regiment back to Ohio,' he told Colonel Peters. 'Beauregard is not such a fool as to leave his base of operations and attack us in ours. There is no enemy, but pickets and scouts, any nearer than Corinth.' ''

''Did Colonel Peters take his regiment back?'' Dan asked.

''No, he stayed,'' MacKenzie said. ''But he was damned humiliated.''

''By the way, where is the general this morning?'' Prentiss asked. ''I haven't seen him.''

''I saw him ride out before dawn,'' Dan said.

''He mentioned last night that he was going to visit all the positions. I didn't realize he was going to get such an early start,'' MacKenzie said.

''Well, you know our general,'' Prentiss teased. ''He is nothing if not a strong believer in the early bird.''

''Gentlemen, biscuits and coffee are ready,'' a private called. The mess orderly was standing by a big, blue steel coffeepot that sat on a grate over a fire. Dan, General Prentiss, and Colonel MacKenzie took over their collapsible tin cups to hold them out as the private served the dark, aromatic brew, then each of them took a biscuit.

A moment later, as they were eating their breakfast, the earth shook with the sound of distant thunder.

"Damn, that's all we need now. Another thunderstorm," MacKenzie said disgustedly. He slurped hot coffee through extended lips.

Immediately thereafter came the sound of whistling cannonballs. Tree limbs crashed to the ground as the heavy balls ripped through the timber. The balls were interspersed with shells that burst loudly, throwing out singing shards of shrapnel.

"The Rebs must've moved some guns up during the night," Prentiss said, sucking the last of the biscuit from his fingers. "I'm certain they don't have anything with that kind of range."

Suddenly General Sherman came back into the camp at a gallop. "The Rebels are coming! The Rebels are coming! Get to your posts, quickly!"

Almost immediately behind General Sherman a cannonball crashed heavily through the nearby trees.

The officers tossed away their remaining coffee, then hastened into activity.

Dan hurried over to the Seventh Kansas to transmit the alarm. When he arrived he found them all bunched together in a ravine. Jennison, their commanding officer, was lying facedown behind a tree.

"Colonel Jennison! Colonel Jennison! We're being attacked! What are you doing? You have to form your men for the defense!" Dan called.

Another barrage of incoming artillery smashed through the trees and exploded in rosy plumes of fire, smoke, and whistling death.

"This is no place for us!" Colonel Jennison said. "This is no way to fight . . . not against cannons! Why don't the Rebels come out and fight like men?"

"Colonel, you must form your men, sir! You must deploy in a skirmish line! Otherwise the Rebels can roll right over you!"

Jennison raised his head and looked around, his eyes glowing with a wild look. "Yes!" he said. "We need to deploy. But not here! Fall back, men!" he shouted, standing up and running toward the rear. "Fall back!"

"Jennison! You cowardly son of a bitch! Come back here!" Dan called after him.

When Jennison started to the rear, the other members of

the Seventh Kansas Volunteer Cavalry, men who until now had seen battle only when the odds were overwhelmingly in their favor, stood and ran, following the example of their leader.

Angry and disgusted with the action of men he had once ridden with, Dan returned to the Shiloh Meeting Ground. Here, the fighting was at its most intense, and Dan saw Sherman moving from one point to the other, issuing orders and inspiring the men to fight. He had already been hit twice, first in the hand and then again, a bare nick, in the shoulder. Sherman wrapped his wounded hand in a handkerchief and thrust it under his jacket, unconsciously assuming the pose, so characteristic of many military photographs, called *carte de visite*.

"My God, look at that!" MacKenzie said, and Dan looked in the direction the colonel pointed.

There, coming down a gentle slope just in front of them and already within easy musket range, was a huge body of Confederate soldiers. They were massed many lines deep, moving toward them like an ocean of gray, flowing down the hill, rolling over small shrubs and fence lines and crossing roads as if they were an unstoppable and mighty force of nature.

General Prentiss was shocked at the sight of so many, but he recovered quickly. "Attention, men!" he shouted to his brigade. "Ready, aim, fire!"

The muskets of Prentiss's brigade sounded as one, and Dan saw scores of the gray-clad warriors go down. Nevertheless, the Confederate Army continued to move forward.

Dan carried only a pistol as a weapon. He pulled it from his holster and began shooting back. Though he wasn't hit, bullets were whizzing around him like angry bees, and he could feel the shock waves of those that passed very close.

"Hurrah, boys!" Colonel MacKenzie shouted. "Here comes a battery up! We'll give 'em hell now!"

Dan answered MacKenzie's shout with a cheer, as did most of the men. But the cheers soon turned to exclamations of surprise and horror as they realized that the gun was not Union, but Confederate. Within seconds after it was in position, it opened up on Dan and the others with grape and canister. MacKenzie was one of the first to go down.

"Fall back! Fall back!" General Prentiss shouted.

Dan saw MacKenzie's horse running by, riderless, the stirrups flapping in the air. He looked in the direction from which the horse had come and saw the colonel lying on the ground, face up to the sky, eyes and mouth wide open.

"Colonel!" Dan shouted, running to the fallen officer. But as soon as he got there he knew that it was too late to help the colonel.

"Fall back, men!" Prentiss shouted again. "Captain Morris, assume command of the left flank!"

"Yes, sir!" Dan shouted. He ran at a crouch to the left flank, where the shot and shell had already decimated the ranks.

Slowly Prentiss's brigade retired from one defensible position after another until finally they reached a roadway they had already named Sunken Road. Here, nature provided what General Sherman had hesitated to dig: a fortified position.

"We'll hold at this road!" Prentiss shouted to his men. He stood behind them, himself exposed to fire, and shoved and cajoled them back into position on the parapet of the road. "Stand here and fight, men!"

Several of the officers, themselves as green and new to battle as many of the men they commanded, sought the cover of the embankment. They lay there, as low as they could press their bodies, covering their heads and their arms and hands. But a few of the officers joined Dan in helping to stop the general retreat. They forced the men back to the line to take up firing positions against the enemy. Finally the men heeded their officers' entreaties, and the Union retreat was checked at Sunken Road.

With the lines momentarily holding, General Sherman came running toward Dan, bent over in a crouch as bullets whizzed by.

"Captain Morris! Hurry back to Grant," Sherman ordered. "Tell him if he has any men to spare, I can use them. If not, I will do the best I can. We are holding them pretty well, just now. Pretty well; but it's hot as hell."

"Yes, sir!" Dan shouted back. Bending at the waist, as had Sherman, Dan ran down to the river, where he saw a small paddle wheel skiff, its steam just built up. Jumping into the boat, he shouted to the pilot.

"Take me to the Savannah landing as quickly as you can!"

"Yes, sir! Any place to get the hell out of here!" the pilot shouted happily. He opened the throttle to full, and the rapidly spinning paddle wheel kicked up a froth as the little boat, pushing out a large, rolling, V wake, beat its way upstream faster, even, than a horse could gallop.

General Grant, who had heard the opening barrage while having his breakfast in the Savannah mansion that was his headquarters, was already aboard the large steamer. Seeing Grant on board the steamer, Dan pointed to him and called out to the pilot.

"There is the general! Take me over there!" He had to shout to be heard above the clacking engine and slapping paddle wheel.

The pilot pushed the tiller handle hard to the left, and the little boat swung toward the steamer, causing a long, curving bow wake to roll ashore. He cut the engine and let the boat glide up to close the last few feet. Standing in the boat, and holding out his arms to maintain balance, Dan timed it just right, then jumped quickly from the little boat onto the deck of the large steamer.

"General!" Dan shouted, hurrying toward Grant.

"Have you come to tell me that the Rebels are attacking?" Grant asked.

"Yes, sir!"

Grant nodded. "I thought as much, by the sound of things. I've already sent two notes, one to General Buell canceling our meeting and ordering him to come as quickly as possible, and another to General Nelson instructing him to move his division to Pittsburg Landing, to the sound of battle. How involved is the attack?"

"Very involved, General. The attack is along the entire front," Dan replied. "General Sherman asks you to bring up anyone you can spare. He says he's holding them, but it's hot as hell."

The steamer pulled away from the dock then and started at full speed toward Pittsburg Landing. "General! General! Any orders, sir?" someone shouted from the bank, and looking ashore, Dan saw General Lew Wallace running hard to keep pace with the boat.

"Wallace! Get your troops under arms and have them ready to move at a moment's notice!" Grant called.

"I have already done so!" Wallace replied, cupping his hands around his mouth to be heard.

Grant nodded and held up his hand, then walked to the front, where he stood, feeling the bow spray as the boat beat its way rapidly downriver.

When the boat docked a short time later, Grant, whose horse was on the boat with him, was already mounted, his crutch stuck down into the saddle scabbard. The woods were alive with the sound of musketry and the thunder of cannon. Wounded men and deserters were in full flight from the woods, streaking toward the riverbank. Stopped from retreating any farther by the river, they could only join the men of the Seventh Kansas and their leader, Doc Jennison, who were by now huddling fearfully below the river's bluff.

Grant had no time for the stragglers, and he urged his horse up the bluff toward the sound of the guns. With a disdainful look and a contemptuous dare to anyone to attempt to stop him from doing so, Dan commandeered one of the stragglers' horses, then hurried after Grant.

When Grant reached the Sunken Road, Generals W. H. Wallace and Prentiss reported to him.

"Thank God, you are here, General!" Prentiss said.

A shell exploded nearby, and Grant's horse reared, causing Grant to have to cling on to keep from being thrown. He finally managed to get the horse settled down.

"I had to see for myself if this was a full-scale attack," Grant said.

"As you can see, General, it is," W. H. Wallace said excitedly.

"I'm bringing up Lew Wallace and Nelson," Grant said. "In the meantime, I want you to hold this road. Do you hear me? At all costs, you must hold this road! Now I am going to find Sherman."

"General, request permission to stay here and help hold the road," Dan shouted amid the crash and din of battle.

"Granted," Grant said. "God be with you, son."

Slapping his legs against the side of his horse, Grant rode

off at a gallop as bullets, cannonballs, and shells whizzed, crashed, and exploded all around him. Looking in the direction in which Grant was riding, Dan saw the Stars and Stripes, along with several regimental flags, fluttering in the morning breeze. It was a thrilling sight.

A bullet clipped a tree branch very near Dan, bringing his attention back to the job at hand.

"You'd better get down, Captain!" General W. H. Wallace shouted. "That's not raindrops hitting the trees!"

Laughing at Wallace's grim joke, Dan joined the other Union soldiers lying along the edge of the sunken road, firing at the men in gray. Great billowing clouds of gunsmoke floated across the field, burning the eyes and stinging the nostrils, and Dan could see by the powder-blackened faces of the soldiers that the fighting had been intense. Taking aim with his pistol, he joined in the fray.

Half a mile away, General Sherman saw Grant and hurried over to report to him.

"How are you doing, Sherman?" Grant asked.

"My God, Grant, it's like a slaughtering pen out there. Men are being butchered on both sides," Sherman said, pointing toward the attacking men in gray. "We are cutting them down like wheat, but still they are coming!"

"You are doing a fine job," Grant said. "Keep it up. Hold here, as long as you can."

"We may have a problem with ammunition. We are using it up awfully fast."

Grant shook his head. "You can relieve your mind of that worry," he said. "It's already on the way up."

"General, do you have any idea how many we are up against?" Sherman asked.

Grant shook his head. "It could be as much as one hundred thousand," he answered.

"One hundred thousand?" Sherman repeated.

"Maybe more."

A shell crashed behind them, and the men ducked as shrapnel whistled all around.

"Where the hell is Buell?" Sherman asked.

"That's what I'd like to know," Grant replied. "Where the hell is Buell?"

*   *   *

The church campground that had been Sherman's place of bivouack during the previous night belonged now, by right of possession, to the Confederates. General Beauregard, who was second in command to General Johnston, made the little log hut his personal headquarters. From it he issued orders and dispatched reinforcements where they were needed, thus affording General Johnston the freedom to move up and down the line of battle, giving encouragement to his men.

Burke was with Johnston, who was at the moment on the extreme right end of the battle line. To those who needed a calming influence, Johnston spoke quietly. "Easy men, make every shot count. Keep calm, don't let the Yankees get you riled."

To those he felt needed more spirit, he injected a note of ferocity to his words: "Men of Arkansas, you are skilled with the Arkansas toothpick. Today, let us use that skill with a nobler weapon, the bayonet. Use it for your country! Use it for your state! Use it for your fellow soldiers! Use it well!"

General Johnston, who was a handsome man, was well mounted on a large, beautiful horse, and his presence among the men, whether he was speaking to them or not, was all the inspiration they needed. His progress along the line could be followed easily through the rippling effect of hurrahs shouted by the soldiers.

"Hey! Lookie here!" a soldier shouted as they came across what had been a Yankee camp. "These damn Yankees left their food, still a-cookin'!"

"Yaahooo!" another shouted, and to Burke's surprise and frustration, nearly half of the army broke off its pursuit of the fleeing Union soldiers to sit down and eat the breakfast the Yankees had so recently abandoned.

"You men!" Burke shouted. "Leave that be! We've got the Yankees on the run! Let's finish the job, then you can come back to it!"

"Are you kiddin'? There won't be nothin' left," a corporal said, grabbing a couple of biscuits and a hunk of salt pork.

"Captain, leave the stragglers be!" General Johnston shouted. "We have more important things to do! We're losing cohesion here!"

Burke could see at once what Johnston was talking about. The underbrush, gullies, twisting roads, and pockets of stiff, Union resistance had disrupted the orderly progress of the attack. The three lines of battle, so carefully sketched out on the battle map, had become terribly disjointed. Divisions, brigades, and regiments became so intermingled that men found themselves fighting side by side with strangers and listing to commands given by officers they didn't know. Over it all was the cacophonous roar of battle: thundering cannon, booming muskets, shrieking shells, screams of rage, curses of defiance, fear, and pain, the whole enshrouded in a thick, opaque cloud of noxious gunsmoke.

Burke had fought at Bull Run and had participated in half a dozen skirmishes with Quantrill's raiders, but he knew that everything that had happened in this entire war up until now, even if all put together, would pale into insignificance when compared with what was going on here, around the Shiloh Meeting House.

"Captain Phillips. Get back to Beauregard as quickly as you can. Tell him I wish to reorganize into four sectors, Hardee and Polk on the left, Bragg and Breckinridge on the right!"

"Yes, sir," Burke replied. "Where will you be, General?"

"I? I will be here, right in front of this, this hornets' nest," Johnston said, referring to the ferocious fighting that was going on in front of them.

As Burke rode away he looked around to see Johnston heading toward a peach orchard that was occupied by several pieces of Confederate artillery. The trees were in full bloom, and each time one of the guns would fire, the concussion would cause the flower petals to come fluttering down in a bright pink blizzard.

Across the way from the peach orchard a little band of Yankees held on, stubbornly, to a piece of elevated ground. Twice they had repelled Confederate charges, and now the soldiers in gray were milling around, as if wondering what to do next.

"Come on, boys!" Johnston shouted. "We must dislodge them from that position! Take heart! I will lead you!"

Holding a tin coffee cup he had just liberated as if it were a saber, Johnston rode at a gallop toward the Yankee defenders. With a Rebel yell, the men in gray surged after him. This time the Yankees gave way, and the small hill was captured. Johnston came riding back, smiling broadly, his uniform torn, one boot sole shot away.

"They didn't trip us up that time," he said. "We carried the day, boys. We carried the day. Tonight, we will water our horses in the Tennessee."

Suddenly Johnston began reeling in his saddle.

"General, are you hurt?" someone asked.

"Yes, and I fear seriously," Johnston replied quietly. He put his hand to his forehead.

The governor of Tennessee, Isham Harris, had volunteered to serve as Johnston's aide. Now he moved quickly to help the general out of his saddle. Johnston, who had now grown very weak and pale, lay down under a tree.

"Where are you hurt?" the governor asked.

"I . . . I truly don't know," Johnston answered. "But I have suddenly become very . . . dizzy."

Harris started unbuttoning Johnston's clothes, looking for the wound. Then he found it, a small, clean hole just above the hollow of the knee. From that neat bullet hole, Johnston was pumping blood profusely, the result of a cut artery. Harris put his hand over the wound, trying to stop the flow, but he was unable to do so.

"General, you seem to be bleeding very badly, and I don't know how to stop it. Tell me what I should do!"

Johnston's eyelids fluttered, and he tried to talk, but he no longer had the strength to mouth the words.

"Brandy!" Harris said. "Perhaps a little brandy will help!"

Harris ran back to his horse and fished a bottle of brandy from his saddlebag. He knelt beside General Johnston and tried to pour some liquor into the wounded man's mouth, but the brandy just rolled right back out again, unswallowed.

"Try to take some down, General. Try to take some down," Harris pleaded.

At that moment Burke returned from his mission, and seeing Johnston on the ground, he hopped down quickly and hurried over to provide assistance.

"What's wrong?"

"The bleeding," Harris said helplessly. "I can't stop the bleeding."

"Did you apply a tourniquet?" Burke asked.

"A tourniquet?" Harris replied, obviously confused by the term. He shrugged. "I don't know what a tourniquet is."

Quickly Burke removed his scarf and wrapped it around the general's leg, just above the wound. Putting a stick in it, he twisted it down as tightly as he could get it, then he looked into Johnston's face.

"General Johnston! General Johnston! Do you know me, sir? Do you know me?"

When there was no answer, Burke lifted Johnston's eyelid with his thumb and looked into his eye, then leaned forward to listen to Johnston's chest. Finally, with a sigh, he took off the impromptu tourniquet and stood up.

"Is he . . . ?" Harris asked.

"Dead," Burke said, answering the unfinished question. "If only someone had put a tourniquet on him in time to stop the bleeding. The wound wasn't that serious. He needn't have died."

"Oh, my God! Then it's my fault!" Harris said, realizing what he had done. "I let him die! I didn't know."

Burke remounted. "General Beauregard must be told," he said.

"What are your orders, General?" Burke asked after informing Beauregard that Johnston was dead.

"I have two orders," Beauregard replied. "First, we will make no announcement that Johnston is dead. I fear such knowledge might dishearten the men. Second, we will continue our attacks against the Sunken Road. The Yankees are holding there, and we must dislodge them."

"General, we have already launched twelve separate attacks against that road, all without success," said a colonel with a smoke-blackened face. "And the toll has been terrible," he added. "Each time we make an attack we must climb over the bodies of the men who were killed in the previous attack."

"Then we will launch attack number thirteen," Beauregard insisted. "And this one will not fail. I have ordered artillery support."

Burke watched as the heavy guns were brought up from other places on the field. One by one the caissons were unlimbered, swung around, then anchored in place. The gun crews went about their business of loading the guns with powder, grape, and canister. Then, at nearly point-blank range, sixty-two guns opened up on the defenders in the sunken road. The Hornets' Nest, as both armies were now calling this place, was enveloped in one huge crashing explosion of grapeshot, shrapnel, shards of shattered rock, and splintered trees.

"General Prentiss!" Dan shouted. Generals Wallace and Hurlbut are falling back!"

The Union line was bending into a horseshoe shape.

"Captain," Prentiss replied, "get out of here! Get out before the flanks collapse and we are completely surrounded! Tell Sherman I will not abandon this position! Do you hear me, Captain? I will hold this position!"

Dan mounted a nearby horse and, leaning low over the animal's neck, galloped to the rear. Around him, the dead lay like fallen wheat. As he rode through, he saw Hurlbut's and Wallace's divisions giving way, so that, gradually, the opening ahead was getting smaller and smaller. Spurring his horse, he just barely managed to get through before the Union attackers linked up, completely surrounding Prentiss and his men.

Dan passed through hundreds of stragglers as he galloped to the rear. Finally locating Sherman, he dismounted and gave his report.

"God bless Prentiss," Sherman said. "His bravery has bought time for the rest of us. All right," he said, running his hand through his hair. "We won't let him down." He turned to one of his staff officers. "Major Royal, tell McClernand to rally his men. We are going to hold right here."

"Yes, sir," Major Royal said, and started toward his horse. Dan began to head toward his own horse just as a courier arrived with a message for Sherman.

"Where are you going, Captain Morris?" Sherman asked as he received the message.

"I'm returning to General Prentiss."

Sherman looked at the note, then shook his head. "There's nothing to go to, son," he said quietly. He sighed.

"Colonel Hurlbut has withdrawn, General Wallace is dead, and General Prentiss has surrendered his division."

"General, the Confederates have arrived in strength, sir. They are on the other side of Snake Creek," a staff officer reported.

"Let's get down to the bridge!" Sherman replied. "That's the center of our line there."

Dan went with Sherman down to the bridge, where he saw a long line of grim, determined soldiers lying on the ground with their rifles pointing toward the other side of the creek. Their faces were blackened with gunsmoke, and their eyes were set in the stare of men who had already seen enough death to last a lifetime. Between the line of soldiers and the creek, and up the bank on the other side, hundreds more lay dead or dying.

Although the soldiers were lying on the ground, most of the officers were standing, moving back and forth behind the line with a saber in one hand and a pistol in the other, speaking quietly and reassuringly to their men. Dan moved down to join them.

"You reckon they'll come again?" asked one of the privates in the line.

"They'll come," another answered. "And when they do, we'll kill another bunch of 'em."

"My God, we done kilt more people than they got in the whole state of Mississippi, ain't we? Where the hell they comin' from?"

"They comin' from all over."

"Get those guns up here!" an artillery officer shouted, and Dan saw two caissons being wheeled into position, then turned around.

"Put 'em right up on the line!"

"Captain, shot or shell?" one of the loaders asked, poised at the muzzle of the gun he was servicing.

"Grape, boys. We'll give 'em a double shot of grape!"

"A double shot of grape won't carry much beyond the other side of the creek."

The artillery officer looked across the creek grimly. "That's about right. That's where we'll do our killin'," he said.

"Listen! I can hear 'em comin'!"

Conversation along the line quieted, and Dan strained

with the others to hear the approaching Confederates. He could hear, first, the beating of their drums, then the jangle of their equipment, and finally the shouts of the officers.

"There they are!" someone called, and across the creek, just emerging from the woods, Dan saw them. They came out in one long line, but—and Dan could see this quite clearly—the line was noticeably thinner, and the men were moving much more slowly. Now they were progressing almost as if they were sleepwalking. There were no challenging Rebel yells, no cheers, no vitality in their movements. Scattered throughout the first rank were the drums, whose cadence not only kept the men marching as one, but relayed the officers' orders. The drummers were young, some as young as twelve and fourteen, but already their eyes were glazed over with the same hollow stare as those of their older comrades.

"Hold your fire, men!" Sherman shouted. "Hold your fire until you get the word!"

The steadily advancing Confederate line moved down to the creek, then into it. The backwater slough was knee deep with mud and stagnant, standing water, and it slowed the attackers' advance even more.

Sherman looked over at his artillery commanders, then brought down his hand.

"Fire!" the artillery commander shouted.

In one horrendous volley, more than sixty cannons fired, belching out flame, smoke, and whistling death.

The artillery barrage was followed almost immediately by a volley of deadly accurate rifle fire. Hundreds of attacking soldiers went down in the withering fire, and the attack was stopped in its tracks. The remaining Confederate soldiers turned and scrambled back out of the water, up the embankment, and into the wood line beyond.

"Reload!" the officers ordered, and all up and down the line those who had fired began packing down powder, wad, and ball as they readied themselves for another assault.

But the sun went down, and no follow-up attack came.

The deep-throated boom of heavy guns, and the accompanying harassing fire, continued even after nightfall. The boom of cannon intermixed with peals of thunder so that it grew difficult to tell one from the other. Long, jagged streaks of lightning split the sky, illuminating the battlefield in harsh white and stark black, disclosing thousands of bodies lying where they fell . . . dead and dying. It began to rain, and when it rained, the misery knew no bounds.

In the tent that had been pitched for General Grant's headquarters, a rain-soaked and breathless messenger arrived.

"What is it, son?" Grant asked, looking up at him.

The messenger handed him a note. Shifting his cigar from one side of his mouth to the other, Grant read the message, then smiled.

"What is it?" Sherman asked.

Grant handed the note to Sherman. "General Buell has arrived," he said. "The tide of battle has turned."

✯✯✯

Seventeen

Because of the ebb and flow of the battle, the dead and wounded were scattered over an area of ten square miles. The first day's fighting had left a total of nearly ten thousand, counting the casualties of both sides, and during the night the sounds of their moans and cries could be heard even above the thunderous drumming of the rain and the incessant boom of artillery. The sound of their cries was heart-rending even to the most hardened ears.

Captain Dan Morris collected half a dozen canteens and started out onto the battlefield. Fortunately the rain stopped shortly after Dan went out, but the night was still dark and overcast, without moon or stars to light the way. Because the night was so dark, many of the men who prowled the battleground were carrying lanterns to help them distinguish the wounded from the dead. As a result, the battlefield looked like a great meadow filled with giant fireflies, as the lanterns, carried knee high, bobbed about from point to point.

A breeze came up, carrying on its breath a damp chill. Dan pulled his coat about him and continued on his mission of mercy, picking his way across roads and fields, now littered with the residue of battle: weapons, equipment, and, among the discards, the dead and dying.

"Water," a weak voice called, and Dan halted. "I beg of you, sir, be you Union or Confederate, if you are a Christian man, you'll give me water."

"Yes," Dan said. "I have water." He moved quickly to the soldier, a young Union private wearing the insignia of the Fourteenth Illinois on his collar, and held a canteen to his lips. The boy began to drink deeply.

"No," Dan said, pulling back the canteen. "You mustn't drink too much. It isn't good for you."

"Hell, Cap'n, I'm dying anyway," the boy said. "I'd rather die with my thirst quenched."

Dan nodded, then gave him the canteen and let him drink his fill. Finally the boy gave it back to him, with his thanks.

"I'll tell a surgeon where you are," Dan said.

"Don't bother none, Cap'n," the boy said. "There's oth-ers out here needin' a drink, too. You carry the water to 'em, 'n when you come back this way, why, if I happen to still be alive, I might just want another drink, if you don't mind."

"I promise to do that," Dan said. He stood up, looked down at the wounded soldier for a moment, then went to the next one and gave him water as well. This man was a Confederate.

"I thank ye kindly, sir," the Confederate soldier said. He raised his hand, caked now with dried blood, and pointed. "They was a Yankee boy over there a-cryin' out for water, too. Ain't heard from 'im in some time. Been prayin' for 'im, though. You might check."

"Thanks," Dan said. He saw the Union boy the Con-federate was talking about, then squatted beside him. "You want some water, soldier?" Dan asked, holding out the canteen. Then he jerked it back when he saw the boy's face was covered with ants. They were crawling in and out of his nostrils, mouth, and open but unseeing eyes.

"How is he?" the Confederate called across the open space between them.

"He's dead," Dan said.

"He told me his mother lived in Columbus, Ohio. You'll tell his mother, won't you, Cap'n? You'll tell her that her boy died bravely?"

"Yes," Dan answered. "I'll tell her."

As Dan continued on his mission of taking water to the wounded soldiers, Confederate and Union alike, he often passed within speaking distance of others who were doing the same. Men in blue and men in gray, who had fought bitterly throughout the long day, were now cooperating on the battlefield.

"Here's one of your'n, Yank."

"Hey, Reb, you've got one over here."

"No need to go over there, Yank, them boys is all dead."

"Run out of water down there, Reb, but there's still quite a few of your'n needin' some."

It was in this way that Dan saw someone moving across the battlefield, carrying canteens, stopping here and there to give aid and solace. It was too dark to make out the features, but something about the figure arrested Dan's attention. He gasped and stared at the familiar way the man carried himself.

"Burke?" Dan called in a hesitant voice.

The man stopped, then turned toward Dan. "Dan? My God, Dan, is that you?"

"Burke!"

The two men moved toward each other, then embraced, there in the dark, in the middle of the wounded and dead, on a field of battle in which half a nation had tried desperately to kill the other half.

"What are you doing here?" Dan asked.

"What are *you* doing here?"

"General Halleck sent me down. I'm attached to General Grant's staff."

"I'm with General Johns—" Burke stopped. "That is, I *was* with General Johnston. He was killed today."

"Yes, I heard that rumor. General Halleck will be sorry to hear that. He told me that he and Johnston were the best of friends."

"When you get down to it, we are perfect examples that this war can put best friends on opposite sides."

"Yes, we are," Dan said. "Burke, I knew you were fighting for the South . . . and I knew that you had returned to Missouri from Virginia, but I thought you were with General Price. I never thought we would actually be fighting against each other."

"Water!" someone called. "Please, sir. Can I have some water?"

"Water!" another called.

Dan and Burke looked at each other for a long moment, then Burke nodded toward one of the voices. "These boys are suffering quite a bit," he said. "We'd better get back to doing what we were doing."

"Yes, I expect so," Dan answered. He nodded toward the first voice. "I'll get this one, you get the other."

"All right," Burke agreed. The two parted, but they hadn't gone more than half a dozen steps before Burke stopped and called back to Dan.

"Dan?"

"Yes?"

"Be careful. Don't go getting yourself killed."

"Same to you, Burke. God bless."

"God bless, my friend," Burke replied.

Because the Confederate Army had carried the battle on the first day of fighting, they were better organized in handling their casualties than the Union Army was. The Confederate lines had advanced nearly all the way to the river, so that much of the battlefield lay within their control that night. Therefore, even though thousands of dead and dying Confederate soldiers were still lying out in the dark, thousands more had been brought back to the rear area, where a hospital was functioning.

When Burke emptied all his canteens and returned to the rear, he saw the wounded who had made it back on their own or had been brought in, lying shoulder to shoulder, stretched out in row after row of a hundred or more men. Some lay stiff and quiet, but many were writhing in pain, moaning and groaning, occasionally screaming out a curse or a prayer, screaming it in such a way that one couldn't be sure which it was.

Everywhere there was blood, dirty bandages, and the smell of unwashed bodies, purged bowels, and emptied bladders. Volunteers were working feverishly and, in most cases, futilely, to alleviate some of the suffering of the soldiers.

"Cap'n Phillips? Cap'n Phillips, is that you?" a strained voice called.

Burke stopped. "Yes," he answered. "I'm Captain Phillips."

"Cap'n Phillips, it's me, Coates."

"Private Coates," Burke said, moving toward the wounded soldier. "How badly are you hurt?"

"I'm goin' to be all right, I reckon. But, Cap'n, would you see to Tim? He's been sufferin' somethin' fierce, though he's quiet now, and I'm worried about him."

"Of course I will," Burke replied. "Where is he?"

"He's over by the fence there," Coates said, raising himself with an effort and pointing to a prostrate figure. "Me'n him come in together. His pa has a farm next to our'n, back in Missouri."

"Oh, yes, I see him," Burke said. "I'll see how he is."

Burke picked his way through the men, passing those who lay dull eyed, with hands clutched to wounds, glued there now by coagulated blood, until he reached Tim. He recognized him at once as one of the men who had volunteered to come across the swamp with him from General McCowan's beleaguered force.

"How is he?" Coates called. "How is old Tim? Tell me, Cap'n. Me'n Tim, we're good friends. How is he?"

Burke shook his head. "I'm sorry, Coates," he said. "Tim is dead."

"Damn the Yankees!" Coates said. "Goddamn all the goddamned Yankees!"

Burke left the hospital area and walked back to the Shiloh campground, where General Beauregard had established his headquarters, sleeping tonight where Sherman had slept the night before. He saw the Union General Prentiss sitting at a field table, drinking coffee. General Prentiss, who had chin whiskers but a clean-shaven mouth, was wearing a look of exhaustion and concern. But even in defeat there was a defiance in his eyes.

"You were in command of the Union center today?" Burke asked. "At the Sunken Road?"

"I was," Prentiss replied.

Burke squinted his eyes as he studied Prentiss. "I know most of the Union generals from my own military service," he said. "But I don't believe I know you."

"I left the military after the Mexican War," Prentiss said. "I'm a merchant now. Or at least I was when this war started."

"That's not a Northern accent," Dan said.

"I live in Illinois now, but I'm from Virginia."

"Then you are a Southerner?"

"I'm an American!" Prentiss said resolutely.

"If you're a Virginian fighting for the Yankees, you're a goddamned traitor!" a nearby lieutenant said.

"No, Lieutenant. He is a man of conviction," Burke said resolutely. "And a brave officer. General, your performance today was nothing short of brilliant. I congratulate you, and I can only wish that you had been able to see it in your heart to join our cause. I salute you, sir.''

Burke snapped a sharp salute, and Prentiss, somewhat surprised by the action, put down his coffee cup and returned Burke's salute.

"I appreciate your sentiment, son," Prentiss said. "And I tell you now that though you boys may have carried the day today, it will be a different story tomorrow. General Buell is sure to come up during the night."

After that, Burke went over to pour himself a cup of coffee, then walked back to the edge of the clearing, looking in the direction of the river. The fighting wasn't over yet, he knew. There were still two armies out there, poised to settle the issue.

No, he decided, amending his thought. There weren't two armies out there. There were three: the blue, the gray, and the bloodied.

During the night General Buell finally arrived with his troops. He brought twenty thousand men with him, fresh and unscarred by the previous day's fighting. His arrival meant that General Grant now had even more available men than when the battle had begun. The Confederate Army, on the other hand, had suffered terrible casualties on the first day's fighting, including the loss of their commanding general. Even those who were left unscathed were exhausted from their efforts.

And the exhausted got very little sleep during the night.

Their lack of sleep came from the constant bombardment, kept up throughout the night, by the eleven-inch guns of the river gunboats. The soldiers upon whom the bombs fell were so in awe of the huge two-hundred-pound shells that they dubbed them "washpots" and "lampposts." They could follow the deadly path of the missiles by the sputtering red sparks emanating from the fuses as the shells described a high arc through the sky, screaming loudly as they slammed down to explode among the weary Confederate soldiers.

The bombardment continued all night long, without letup. Then, as the eastern sky grew gray, the measured thump of the naval barrage was joined by the sharper crack of field artillery and, finally, by a rapidly increasing rattle of musketry. The second day of fighting had begun, and it was the Union Army, thought to be defeated, that opened the ball.

Beauregard called his commanders together. "We must prepare to fight defensively today," he said.

"Defensively?" Bragg asked. "General, we have them on the run. It would take but a little more effort to push them right into the river. We were victorious yesterday."

"Yes, we were. But I fear another victory as costly as the one we had yesterday will be the death of us," Beauregard said. "Our casualties were very high, gentlemen. Have you looked at the battlefield? It is so strewn with bodies that you can walk from here to the river without your feet once touching the ground."

"There are as many Yankees out there as there are our boys. More, even," Bragg insisted.

"Perhaps so, but the Yankees can better afford to lose them. General Buell came up during the night," Beauregard said. "With at least twenty thousand fresh men."

The news disheartened the other generals.

"You are certain? It isn't just Grant bringing up his rear to make us think it's Buell?"

"No, it's Buell," Beauregard said. "One of our scouts recognized him."

"What about Generals Price and Van Horn?" Polk asked. "Any chance of their getting here in time?"

Beauregard shook his head. "As far as I know they are still somewhere in Missouri or Arkansas. And even if they were in Memphis, it would take half a day to load onto trains, then another half day to get here."

"That is if the Yankees haven't already destroyed the track somewhere between here and Memphis," someone added.

"All right, General, I agree with you. With Buell up, we could not make another attack," Breckinridge said. "So, what are your orders?"

"Bring up the artillery and put them in line with the infantry. We'll hold this ridge for as long as we can," Beauregard said.

"Then?"

"At some point today the situation will be reversed. The Union troops will go on the attack." Beauregard's black eyes glistened, and he held up his finger. "But let them! We can't dislodge them, but neither can they dislodge us. Today it will be we who have the strengthened positions. Let the Yankees bleed, as we did yesterday. We will inflict so many casualties on them that the Northern newspapers will be bordered in black. And when the Yankees withdraw to lick their wounds, we will return to Corinth."

Beauregard's withdrawal to fortified positions was much more smoothly executed than had been the attack the day before. As Polk, Hardee, and Bragg pulled back their corps and consolidated the lines, they took the time to load their wagons with battlefield plunder . . . artillery and rifles, powder and ammunition, food, clothes, blankets, ponchos, tentage, livestock, and several regimental and U.S. flags.

Breckinridge, with his cannons brought up on line with his infantrymen, formed a defensive wall along the ridge just south of Shiloh Chapel. He maintained a steady barrage of fire as the remainder of the army repositioned itself, thus keeping the Union Army away and allowing it to be a well-executed maneuver.

Several times during the day it rained, sometimes in drizzles, other times in thunderous downpours that soaked the men to the bone. After a day of meeting repeated Union attacks and inflicting upon them, as Beauregard had promised, even more terrible casualties than had been the case the previous day, the Confederates bivouacked that night in virtually the same place they had been two nights earlier.

During the night the rains came down heavier than ever, and once again the roads were turned into streams. By the time Beauregard began withdrawing his army to Corinth just before daybreak the next morning, the roads were such quagmires that he had no choice but to abandon some of his larger guns. He spiked the cannons, then tumbled them off their caissons before continuing his withdrawal.

By midmorning of the third day, the wind changed to come out of the north, and whereas there had been times in the previous few days where the men had suffered bitterly from the heat, now it was unseasonably cold. The rain turned to sleet, and the men, many of whom had discarded

their coats in the heat of the previous few days, shivered
and suffered in silence.

As the Confederate Army marched back toward Corinth,
Beauregard rode up and down the line of soldiers, encour-
aging them, buoying their spirits by extolling the fact that
they had "whipped the Yankees the previous day," and
promising to "make the Yankees pay up, interest and all.
. . . The day of our glory is near, boys!" he told them.
"And you brave lads brought it about!"

As Beauregard rode up and down the long gray column,
his whereabouts could be marked by the cheers he received
from the men, who affectionately called him "the little
black Frenchman."

"Gen'rul," a bearded colonel said, approaching Beauregard. The colonel, Burke knew, was Nathan Bedford Forrest, an uneducated but wealthy Mississippi planter. "The
Yankees is done sent a brigade to chase us down."

"Only a brigade?" Beauregard said. He pondered the
situation for a moment. "No doubt he wants to make a
show, just to let us know that he is driving us from the
field. They won't be much more than a nuisance to us."

"Gen'rul, if'n you'd approve it, I could take my men
back down to Fallen Timbers and meet 'em."

"And do what, Colonel?"

"Fight 'em," Forrest said matter-of-factly.

"Didn't you say they were coming in brigade strength?"

"Yes, sir."

Beauregard shook his head. "You don't have more than
a couple hundred men. It would be suicide to try to stop
them with one battalion. Better to avoid them."

"I'd like to give it a try, nevertheless. You say they are
a-fixin' to nuisance us; why not let me an' my boys hole
up back there a ways, and nuisance them some?"

"General, an ambuscade could slow them up," Burke
suggested. "Not only would it prevent them from inflicting
any damage upon our repositioning column, it would also
prevent them from finding out just exactly what our
strength is, and what we are doing. And, properly deployed,
a battalion could accomplish that task."

"All right, Forrest, go ahead," Beauregard said.

Forrest spat out a wad of tobacco, then grinned broadly.
"Thankee, Gen'rul."

"General Beauregard, request permission to accompany Colonel Forrest," Burke said. He looked quickly toward Forrest. "That is, with your permission, Colonel."

"You willin' to fight, boy?" Forrest asked.

"Yes, sir."

Forrest pulled out a plug of tobacco, then cut off a piece and put it in his mouth. He chewed for a moment, and when some brown spittle ran down his chin, he wiped it off with the back of the hand that still held the knife.

"I mean my kind of fightin', boy," Forrest said. "It ain't always purty."

"I have been with Quantrill," Burke said. "He doesn't always fight pretty, either."

"That a fact? Quantrill, huh?" Forrest said. He expectorated, then again wiped his chin. "All right, boy, reckon you'll do. Come along. There's always room for someone who's willin' to fight."

Burke looked back toward Beauregard, and the general nodded his head in assent.

Burke rode back with Colonel Forrest to a place called Fallen Timbers. This was a half-mile-wide boggy depression. At the other side of the depression there was a hill where anyone approaching could be seen in silhouette. It was the perfect spot for observation, and Burke looked around as Colonel Forrest began positioning his men.

Forrest might have no formal military training, Burke thought. But he knew instinctively the best way to set up an ambuscade.

"Here they come!" someone said, and at Forrest's orders the men all took cover and waited.

The Union brigade moved forward in textbook attack formation, the skirmish lines proceeding at intervals of two hundred yards. The Yankee soldiers were well drilled and maintained a disciplined advance. It was awe-inspiring, and Burke couldn't help but notice the contrast when he looked at the men around him. These were the undisciplined soldiers of the most unprofessional and unmilitary commander in the entire Confederate Army.

As the Federal soldiers entered the area of fallen trees, however, their precise military formations came apart. They had to abandon their alignment in order to pick their way around stumps, over fallen logs, and through quagmire holes.

Suddenly, from beside him, Forrest jumped up and ran to leap into his saddle.

"Charge, charge!" Forrest shouted, and he began to gallop down the hill toward the advancing Federals. Some, but not all, of Forrest's troops followed after him.

The advancing Federal troops were shocked at the sight of the charging Confederate cavalry. Thinking they were here only to maintain contact with an army they thought was defeated and fleeing, many panicked, turned, and ran. Those who stayed were cut down by blasts from shotguns and pistols. Finally, they too turned to run.

"Let's go, boys! Fight 'em! Kill 'em!" Forrest shouted, leading the charge.

Most of Forrest's men didn't listen to him, however. Seeing the initial advance of the Union soldiers checked, they halted their own charge, some to take prisoners, others to gather up the weapons that had just fallen into their hands. Forrest, either unaware or uncaring, continued his own charge, a single Confederate soldier now surrounded by angry Federals.

Seeing that the Rebel commander had overrun his own troops, the Union soldiers attempted to regroup.

"The son of a bitch is alone!" one of the Union soldiers shouted. "Kill the bastard! Shoot 'im out of the saddle!"

Several men in blue moved toward Forrest, attempting to follow the orders, but Forrest's horse was rearing and kicking, and Forrest, holding on with his knees, was cursing, slashing with his sword in one hand and firing pointblank into the attackers' faces with the pistol in his other hand.

One man in blue managed to stick the barrel of his rifle right into Forrest's side, then pull the trigger. The impact of the blast caused Forrest to stand in his stirrups, but he wasn't unhorsed. Instead he jerked his horse around, reached down and grabbed the soldier by the collar, and with sheer strength picked him up, threw him across the rump of his horse, and using him as a shield against other Yankee bullets, galloped back toward his own lines. Halfway back, he threw off the stunned and terrified soldier, then rode back up to the ridge, where he was applauded by his men.

"Are you badly hurt, Colonel?" Burke asked.

"Damned if I know," Forrest said. He put his hand down to cover the wound, then drew it back to look at the blood. "Got a bullet in me, but it didn't seem to hit any of my vitals." He laughed. "So, tell me, Captain. Did you ever see Quantrill do it that way?"

Burke shook his head. "I've never seen anyone do it that way," he said. "I've only read about it."

"Who?" one of Forrest's men wanted to know. "Who'd you read about goin' right into the enemy like our colonel done?"

"Samson, slaying the Philistines with the jawbone of an ass," Burke replied.

"Samson? Hell, that lily-livered bastard ain't got nothin' on Nathan Bedford Forrest," one of Forrest's men said, and the others, laughing, agreed.

* * *

Eighteen

From *Harper's Weekly,* Domestic Intelligence; April 19, 1862:

THE BATTLE OF PITTSBURG

A terrible battle has taken place in the Southwest. A dispatch dated Pittsburg, via Fort Henry, April 9, 3:20 A.M. says:

One of the greatest and bloodiest battles of modern days has just closed, resulting in the complete rout of the enemy, who attacked at daybreak Sunday morning.

The battle lasted without intermission during the entire day and was again renewed on Monday morning and continued undecided until four o'clock in the afternoon, when the enemy commenced their retreat and are still flying toward Corinth, pursued by a large force of our cavalry.

The slaughter on both sides is immense. We have lost in killed and wounded and missing from 18,000 to 20,000: that of the enemy is estimated at from 35,000 to 40,000.

The statement of the loss is probably exaggerated. On Sunday the advantage seems to have been undetermined: but on that evening General Buell arrived with fresh troops and attacked the enemy at daybreak on Monday 7th. The battle raged fiercely all day. The dispatch above quoted thus describes the victory:

About three o'clock in the afternoon General Grant rode to the left, where the fresh regiments had been

ordered and, finding the Rebels wavering, sent a
portion of his bodyguard to the head of each of five
regiments, then ordered a charge across the field,
himself leading, as he brandished his sword and
waved them on to the crowning victory, while
cannonballs were falling like hail around him.

The men followed with a shout that sounded even
above the roar and din of the artillery, and the Rebels
fled in disarray, as from a destroying avalanche, and
never made another stand.

General Buell followed the retreating Rebels,
driving them in splendid style, and by half-past five
o'clock the whole Rebel army was in full retreat to
Corinth, with our cavalry in hot pursuit, with what
further result is not known, the cavalry not having
returned up to this hour.

We have taken a large amount of their artillery,
and also a number of prisoners. We lost a number of
our forces (prisoners) yesterday, among whom is
General Prentiss. The number of our force taken has
not been ascertained yet. It is reported at several
hundred. General Prentiss was also reported as being
wounded. Among the killed on the Rebel side was
their General in Chief, Albert Sidney Johnston, who
was struck by a cannonball on the afternoon of
Sunday. Of this there is no doubt, as the report is
corroborated by several Rebel officers taken today.

In his St. Louis office, General Halleck tossed aside the
paper with a snort of disgust. "If we could fight the battles
as brilliantly as the reporters describe them, we could bring
this war to a successful conclusion within a week. General
Buell arriving in the nick of time to play the hero? Where
the hell was the damned fool? If he had been there a week
earlier, we wouldn't have lost half as many men as we
did."

"Perhaps so, General, but we are fortunate that he arrived when he did," Dan said. "Another day like the first
and we would have been forced to surrender the biggest
portion of our army."

"I wonder, if Johnston had not been killed, would the
Rebels have been able to consolidate their advantage and

push on to victory before Buell arrived?'' General Halleck
mused. "He was, after all, their brightest commander.
Beauregard is but a pale imitation of Albert Sidney Johnston.''

"I'm sure there will be scholars who will debate that
very question for many years," Dan said. "But the truth
is, the Rebels were too exhausted and their ranks too decimated to go any farther." He recalled the futile Rebel advance across Snake Creek, against Sherman's massed
cannon.

"The fact that the people can read about our victory,
even in reporters' hyperbole, makes our appalling losses
somewhat easier to accept."

"If the people actually believe what they read," Dan
said.

Halleck looked at Dan. "You don't think we had a great
victory?"

"No, sir. I believe our losses were every bit as great as
the losses suffered by the Rebels, perhaps greater. It was
only the arrival of fresh troops on the evening of the first
day that kept us from being swept from the field. And now
that it is all said and done, both armies are back exactly
where they started."

"Yes," Halleck said. "Well, in a sense, that's exactly
where you are about to be."

"I beg your pardon, General?"

"I'm sending you back to the western part of the state."

"General, you know that I serve at your discretion, and
will go without argument where you send me. But I would
rather not serve with the Seventh Kansas again. I watched
too many brave men fight and die that first day, while the
cowardly Mr. Jennison and his band of Jayhawkers hid
themselves on the bank of the Tennessee."

"It wasn't just the Seventh Kansas who ran," Halleck
said. "A lot of men broke on that first day. But fortunately
a lot of them, including the Seventh Kansas, managed to
find their courage on the second day."

"Maybe so, sir, but not until the tide of battle had
changed in our favor."

"Oh, I have something for you," General Halleck said.
He reached into one of the cubbyholes of his desk and

pulled out a set of shoulder straps, then without ceremony
handed them to Dan.

"You have been promoted."

"Thank you, sir!" Dan said happily.

Dan took the shoulder straps and looked at them for a
moment, then, with an expression of confusion on his face,
he handed them back. "I think you've made a mistake,
General. These are the insignia for lieutenant colonel."

Halleck glanced at them for just a moment, then handed
them back. "No," he said. "There is no mistake. We've
skipped you over the rank of major. You don't mind, do
you?"

Dan's mouth spread into a large smile. "Mind? No, sir,
of course I don't mind. But I must say this is a most pleasant surprise."

"Well, you can thank General Grant for your promotion," Halleck said. "You seem to have made quite an
impression on him down at New Madrid. And you can
thank General Sherman for your new assignment."

"My assignment with Jennison, you mean? Well, at least
my rank will be equal to his."

Halleck shook his head. "You won't be with Jennison.
General Sherman wants you assigned to General Thomas
Ewing Jr. He wants to keep you in the family."

"Family?"

"Ewing is Sherman's brother-in-law. And according to
Sherman, you are a man who knows his way, equally,
around a battlefield or a headquarters."

"I am flattered that General Sherman thinks so highly of
me."

"He does indeed. And he wants his brother-in-law to
have the advantage of your counsel. Ewing has a very tough
job. He is in command of the District of the Border. Sherman thinks your being there will make it easier for him."

"Of course I'll be glad to do whatever I can," Dan said.
He smiled again. "Especially since I won't be with Jennison."

"I thought you might see it that way," Halleck said.

"What is General Ewing's mission?"

"His mission is to hunt down and eliminate, by whatever
method it takes, Quantrill and his guerrillas. Quantrill

thinks he owns that part of the state, and if you read the local newspapers, they agree with him.''

The shock waves of the explosion moved across the field and hit Burke, making his stomach shake. The blasts were set off by long fuses but timed to go together, starting as flashes of white-hot flame, then erupting black smoke from the points where the charges were laid. The underpinnings of the trestle were carried away by the torpedoes, but the superstructure remained intact for several more seconds, stretching across the Blue River with no visible means of support, as if defying the laws of gravity. Then, slowly, the tracks began to sag and the ties started snapping, popping with a series of loud reports like pistol shots, until finally, with a resounding crash and a splash of water, the whole bridge collapsed into the river.

"Now," Quantrill said. "That'll keep the Yankees from bringin' in any fresh troops by train. You did a good job, Burke." He laughed. "Did you learn how to do that while you were down in Mississippi, fighting with the regulars?"

"More or less," Burke agreed.

"Well, speaking for myself, I'm just glad that General Price and General Beauregard and all those fine, fancy generals let you go so you would come back to us. Right, boys?"

"Right!" said Jesse James, answering for the others and smiling at Burke. Of all Quantrill's riders, Jesse seemed the most genuinely glad to see Burke return to them.

"Let's go, men," Quantrill ordered. "We've some business to take care of."

With the bridge down behind them, Quantrill led his band of raiders toward the little town of Olathe, where his scouts had located a wagon train of Union supplies.

Cresting a hill, Quantrill held up his hand, ordering a halt. The band of sixty or so men stopped as Quantrill pulled a telescope from his saddlebag, then examined the supply train.

"Looks like they are guarded by a couple of companies of infantry," Quantrill said. "And I see one . . . wait, two, no, three. I see three cannons." He handed the telescope to Burke. "Burke, you're my military expert. What kind of cannons are those?"

Burke looked through the glass. The three guns were howitzer six-pounders. Though too small to be of much effect in a major battle, they were good for duty such as this, for they were relatively light and easily drawn. But the artillery pieces were on the other side of the wagons, not out where they could be quickly brought into play. Also, the muskets of the men were in stacks, scattered about the camp, while the men themselves were engaged in such various pursuits as cooking their supper, playing cards, reading, and writing letters. A group of half a dozen or more were taking a bath in the Blue River. The officers, or at least the only officers Burke saw, were sitting at a table in front of a tent, being waited on by enlisted orderlies.

Burke snapped the glass shut and handed it back to Quantrill.

"What do you think?" Quantrill asked.

"I think those boys believe the war is taking place down in Tennessee or Mississippi, or out in Virginia," Burke said.

Quantrill laughed. "They sure as hell aren't looking for us, are they?" he asked.

"It wouldn't take much of a demonstration for us to capture the lot of them."

Quantrill raised his eyebrows. "Capture them?" he said. He snorted. "Now, what the hell would we do with them if we captured them? We wouldn't have any place to keep them, and no one to turn them over to." He pulled his pistol and spun the cylinder, examining his loads, then reholstered it. "No, sir," he added. "Those boys down there have only two choices. They can fight, or they can run."

Before Burke could answer, Quantrill stood in his stirrups and let out a bloodcurdling yell. The yell was picked up by the others in the band, then Quantrill started down the hill, leading them at a gallop toward the shocked and terrified Union soldiers.

The raiders started firing long before they were in range. This was their way, for even before the bullets could be effective, the sound of firing guns, in conjunction with the raiders' hideous shrieks of challenge, had a terrifying, almost stupefying effect on their hapless victims.

It was no different this time. Many, if not most, of the soldiers were unarmed and considered themselves too far away from the rifle stacks to get to their weapons. They started running.

"No, men, no!" Burke heard one of the officers shouting. "To arms! To arms!"

Both of the officers were wearing their pistols, and they drew them and stood fast, returning fire. And, by their example, some of the soldiers called upon enough courage to run not away from their weapons, but toward them.

One of the weapons a few of the men ran toward was one of the artillery pieces.

"Jesse! Frank!" Burke shouted. "Don't let them get to those guns! If they load it with grape, they can take down a quarter of us!"

Burke pointed to the cannons, then broke away from the rest of the pack, riding toward the guns. Jesse and Frank rode with him.

Jesse James, though the youngest of any of the raiders, was also the most daring, as he had proved on many previous occasions. He showed it again this time, for in order to ride to the guns he took the shortest distance, which meant that he had to ride right through the middle of a group of Union soldiers who were armed and who were mounting a spirited defense.

Jesse was a deadly accurate shot, however, and he had six charges in each of the four pistols he was carrying, whereas the defenders were limited to one round per rifle before a painstaking reloading process.

Three of the defending infantrymen shot at Jesse as he approached, but they were so badly frightened, and so awed by the blazing pistols of the man riding toward them, that their shots went wild. On the other hand, nearly every one of Jesse's bullets found its mark, and by the time he rode through he had already shot down four of them. The other Union soldiers, rather than take the time to reload their discharged muskets, threw down the heavy rifles and started running.

Jesse was the first to reach the three cannons, and with a whoop of victory he leaped from his saddle and ran over to claim one. Burke, and Jesse's brother, Frank, were right behind him. Quantrill and the other raiders had taken a somewhat different path here, and though they were now closing with the Union defenders, they were at the opposite end of the supply train from Burke, Frank, and Jesse.

"Hey, Burke! Come show me how you load this here thing!" Jesse shouted.

Burke swung down from the saddle, then opened the ammunition box on the caisson. Several linen bags of powder were already prepared, as well as a rack of solid, six-pound balls. He saw no grape or canister. That was proof, Burke thought, that a cavalry attack on the wagon train was the last thing on the Union commander's mind.

"Get the gun turned around and lined up," Burke ordered. Excited at the prospect, Jesse and Frank wheeled the gun around. Burke poked the powder bag down into the gun, then put in the ball. After that he stuck a wire down through the touchhole to puncture the bag, then he lit a slow-burning fuse. Squatting behind the gun, he lined it up on a wagon at the far end of the train, around which nearly a dozen Union soldiers were putting up a spirited defense. "Stand clear," he ordered.

"Let me do it, Burke!" Jesse asked.

Burke handed Jesse the fuse and pointed to the touchhole. "Right there," he said.

Jesse touched off the gun, and it roared and belched flame and smoke as it leaped back several feet. Burke watched the black cannonball fly across the open area, then crash into the side of the farthermost wagon, breaking it up into splinters.

"Yahoo!" Jesse yelled excitedly.

The defenders around the wagon were so shocked and frightened at the prospect of one of their own guns being turned against them that, to a man, they threw down their weapons and ran.

Some of Quantrill's raiders, particularly the one the others called Bloody Bill Anderson, chased after them, one by one, shooting down those they were able to catch. The whole affair was over in no more than a couple of minutes, and by the time the sound of the last shot was echoing back to them, and the gunsmoke was drifting away, the area had taken on the look of a small battlefield.

At least fifteen to twenty dead Union soldiers were lying around. Two raiders had also been killed. There was absolute silence for a moment, then Quantrill shouted to the others.

"All right, boys! The train is ours for the taking! Have what you will!"

With shouts of triumph and excitement, the men leaped from their horses and ran to the wagons, then started going through the bounty. Burke watched as first one and then the other would whoop out loud, then hold up his "treasure" for the others to see. Sometimes it would be something as valuable as a slab of bacon or a barrel of flour. Other times it was as ludicrous and as useless to men on the move as a mantel clock.

"Jesse, you'd better get over there and get in on that before it's all gone," Burke suggested.

Jesse was studying the gun with great interest. "Ahh," he said, dismissing the others with an impatient wave of his hand. "Let 'em have it. It's all worthless junk anyway. The chief makes everyone put all the food into the pot, so I'll eat. And nothing else over there interests me." He continued to study the cannon as he spoke. It was clear to Burke that the looting the others were enjoying was of no interest to him.

"Say, Burke, when did you learn how to shoot off one of these things? While you was in the army?"

"Yes," Burke answered.

Jesse ran his hand caressingly along the smooth barrel of the gun. "Whooeee, now," he said. "Wouldn't it be somethin' to be in the regular army and be shootin' off one of these things regular? Did they use lots of 'em down at that battle you was just in?"

"Constantly," Burke said. "It was like rolling thunder that never grew quiet."

"Oh, now, what I wouldn't have given to be there," Jesse said. He picked up one of the solid iron shots. "These here things explode?"

"No. That's solid shot."

"You mean just like a big bullet? It doesn't blow up or anything?" He pointed to the wagon. "Then how did it come to completely destroy that wagon?"

"Because of its weight," Burke answered. "It creates a tremendous amount of destructive force from a combination of mass and velocity."

Jesse got around behind the gun and squatted, sighting

over the barrel. ''Wish I was shootin' one of these things off regular,'' he said.

''You'd be good at it,'' Burke said.

''You think so?''

''I *know* so. I've seen the way you handle guns. Big guns, little guns, it doesn't make any difference. You are a natural.''

''Burke, do you ever get to wishin' sometimes that we wasn't doin' all this?'' Jesse asked. He took in the pandemonium with a wave of his hand.

''You mean the war?''

''Well, not just the war. I mean, it's not like we was fightin' a real war, like the kind they have over in Europe.''

Burke thought of Shiloh, the strategy of maneuver, the courage of the men under fire, the sheer drama of thousands upon thousands of men met upon the field in classic battle. Then he looked at the wild men of Quantrill's ''army,'' many so young they weren't much more than boys, most little removed from highwaymen.

''Yes,'' Burke answered quietly. ''I know what you mean.''

''Sometimes I think I'd like to leave this raidin' stuff and go join up with General Price, or General Van Dorn, or someplace where there's real fightin' goin' on.''

''Why don't you?''

''I don't know,'' Jesse replied. ''I guess it's because, when you come right down to it, I'm fightin' here on the border because I hate the Kansas bastards who started it all. Oh, I know these aren't exactly the same people who burned our family's house and barn, and then burned out our neighbors. But, like as not, they are neighbors of the ones who did do it. For me, that's made the fightin' personal.''

''Personal,'' Burke said.

''Yeah. If I was down in Kentucky, or Alabama, or out in Virginia or some such place, why, I wouldn't know the people I was killin'. And if I didn't know 'em, I couldn't hate 'em. Seems to me like it wouldn't be Christian, somehow, to start in a-killin' people you don't hate.''

''Yes,'' Burke agreed. ''You are right. It doesn't seem right to kill people you don't hate.''

★★★

Nineteen

Dan was in the Boatman Hotel in Kansas City, reading the *Kansas City Commercial Journal,* when he heard a familiar voice. Looking across the lobby, he saw Doc Jennison engaged in conversation with half a dozen other officers whom Dan did not know.

"I tell you, if'n Grant had a-listened to me, the war would be over by now," Jennison was saying.

"How so, Colonel?" one of the other officers asked.

" 'Cause if'n he'da let me'n my Kansas boys circle around behind Beauregard like I wanted to, we coulda squashed ol' Beauregard between us like a bug. Think of it! Grant'n his boys on one side o' Beauregard, me'n the Seventh Kansas on the other side."

"What a brilliant strategy!" a young lieutenant said enthusiastically.

"It is!" Jennison insisted. "But I couldn't get Grant to go along with it."

"But why would he refuse to accept a plan of such obvious merit?"

"Don't ask me," Jennison replied. "You tell me why. If truth be told, I'm thinkin' Sherman just didn't want to share none of the glory with the Seventh Kansas."

"Yes, I'm sure that was it, Jennison," Dan suddenly said, interjecting himself into the conversation. "Of course, it might also have been difficult for him to hear your plan since you and the other 'brave' soldiers of Seventh Kansas were cowering below the river bluff." He twisted the word "brave," making it slide out in a sarcastic sneer.

"Sir, just what are you intimating?" the young lieutenant asked, springing quickly to Jennison's defense.

"Intimating? Why, if you think I'm just intimating, Lieutenant, I'm obviously not making myself clear. So, listen to me carefully, for I'm saying it right out. Jennison and the Seventh Kansas disgraced themselves at Pittsburg Landing."

"You are mistaken, sir. Colonel Jennison was a hero in the battle of Pittsburg Landing. And the Seventh Kansas was mentioned in the dispatches. What is the source of your spurious and insulting information?"

"My source, Lieutenant? *I* am my source. I was there, and I watched the Seventh Kansas, and this cowardly son of a bitch, run, while good men were dying."

"I see you have been promoted," Jennison said. "But the fact that we are equal in rank does not mean you can—"

"Equal?" Dan said. "There is nothing equal about it, Jennison. My commission is in the regular army. And in my book, the lowest-ranking private in the regular army is worth more than every Seventh Kansas officer combined."

"Sir, *I* am an officer in the Seventh Kansas," the young lieutenant said. "And I take issue to your remarks, for you are casting dispersions at me."

"Were you at Pittsburg Landing?" Dan asked.

"No, sir. I only joined the regiment a couple of weeks ago."

"Then this has nothing to do with you."

"It has everything to do with me, Colonel. You have impugned the honor of my unit." The young officer turned to Jennison. "Colonel, request permission to defend our good name, sir, upon the field of honor. I would like to challenge this impudent oaf to a duel!"

"Thank you, Lieutenant, but that won't be necessary," Jennison said. He smiled, an evil smile. "I will deal with Colonel Morris in my own time."

"At your convenience, Jennison," Dan said. "Now, if you will excuse me?"

As Dan turned to leave he saw a carriage pull to a stop at the curb in front of the hotel. A woman stepped out of the carriage, and when she did so, Dan recognized her as Catherine Darrow.

Smiling, Dan went outside quickly to meet her. "Miss Darrow!" he greeted her.

Looking up at him, Catherine smiled warmly. "Why, I thought we had moved beyond that," she said. "When last we met, you called me Catherine."

"Yes, and I would willingly do so now, if I could be certain it wouldn't be too forward. I mean, it has been some time since we have seen each other. May I ask what you are doing in Kansas City?"

"Oh, just some business to take care of. I thought I would take a room for the night, then return to Independence tomorrow."

"Does that mean you will be in town for dinner?"

"Yes."

"I would be most honored, Catherine, if you would dine with me tonight."

"I would be delighted."

"Wonderful. Suppose we meet at the restaurant next door, at six?" Dan suggested. "That is, unless you have in mind another place you would rather meet?"

"No, no, the restaurant next door would be fine. Six o'clock it is," Catherine said.

Dan gave Catherine a half bow, then left. Catherine went into the hotel to secure a room. Exactly one hour later there was a knock on the door of her room.

When Catherine opened the door there were two middle-aged women standing in the hall. One was short and stout, with dark hair turning to gray. The other was tall and thin, and her ash brown hair cloaked the hawklike features of her face in tight ringlets.

"Miss Darrow," the tall woman said, "I am Edna Ashley, and this is Sally York. We represent the Ladies Education Society. I understand that you teach school in Independence; is that right?"

"Yes, I'm a schoolteacher," Catherine said with a puzzled look on her face. "Is there something I can do for you?"

"I wonder if we could come in and discuss your curriculum with you? In this time of war and strife, it is imperative that the children have a strong moral code to follow . . . a code that is a part of the school curriculum."

"Yes, of course. I would be glad to talk about it," Catherine answered. "Come in and have some tea with me."

"You are so kind," Edna said.

Catherine stepped back to let her two visitors into the room, then leaned out to look up and down the hall just before she closed the door.

Once inside Catherine's room, the three women smiled at each other, then embraced in warm friendship. The formal exchange outside Catherine's door had been for the benefit of anyone who might overhear. In fact, the women weren't strangers at all, but old friends of long standing. And they weren't there to discuss the school curriculum. Like Catherine, they were members of the Missouri Emancipation Society.

Missouri, though technically loyal to the Union, was still a slave state, and thus the emancipation society, and the Underground Railroad, were still in operation. Edna and Sally, like Catherine, were conductors on the railroad.

"You have some passengers for us?" Edna asked.

"Yes," Catherine answered. "At my house in Independence there are four men, three women, and two children."

"My, you have quite a few this trip."

"One of the children is quite ill," Catherine said. "She is from the southeastern part of the state, in the swamplands, and she has the ague. Thelma is looking after her now, but we are nearly out of quinine."

"We'll send some back with you," Edna promised.

"And you will be prepared to take them on into Kansas as soon as we bring them to you?" Catherine asked.

"Yes, as soon as we get them. Everything is ready."

"Good. If all goes well, you may look for them tomorrow night," Catherine promised.

Catherine and Dan sat at a table in the farthest corner of the restaurant, a single candle lighting the distance between them.

"It was an excellent dinner, Dan," Catherine said.

"I'm glad you enjoyed it."

"I did, though I must confess that it makes me feel guilty, having stuffed myself when I know that there are so many who are suffering from this war."

Dan smiled and reached across the table to put his hand over Catherine's. "Catherine, you can't take everyone's suffering onto yourself," he said.

Catherine's first reaction had been to pull her hand back

from his, but she found the sensation quite pleasant, so she made no effort to pull away.

"I know I cannot," she said. "But under such conditions as we are facing today, I do think about the trials and travails others are going through while I am safe here. Just as I thought about you when you were down in Mississippi."

"I am pleased that you thought of me."

"Was it terrible?" Catherine asked.

The smile left Dan's face. "Yes," he said. "It was terrible."

"I received a letter from Burke. He was there, also."

"Yes, I know," Dan said. "I saw him there."

"You *saw* him?" Catherine raised her hand to her mouth. "Oh, Dan, you weren't . . . you weren't actually trying to kill each other, were you?"

"No, we didn't have to. There was enough killing taking place without our meager contribution."

"I read about it in the papers, of course. So many young men, on both sides, killed and maimed," Catherine said. "But such numbers! One can't actually comprehend what it must have been like."

"Perhaps this will help you visualize it," Dan said. "There were more men killed in the two days of that one battle than have been killed in all the wars and Indian battles this country has fought in the eighty-seven years of its existence."

Catherine shuddered, then put her other hand over the top of Dan's hand. "How awful it must've been for those of you who were there."

Suddenly Dan smiled, and the melancholy mood was gone.

"Have I gone crazy?" he asked. "I must have. Otherwise I wouldn't be speaking of such things when I am dining with a beautiful woman. That, no doubt, shows how far removed from civilized society I have become."

A man approached their table.

"Thank you, we don't need anything," Dan said, dismissing him with a wave of his hand.

"Beggin' your pardon, sir, but I ain't the waiter, I work in the livery," the man said. He looked at Catherine. "Would you be Miz Darrow?"

"Yes."

"I've got a message for you from your nigger."

Catherine flinched visibly. "I don't like that word," she said.

"Yes'm, sorry. I mean your colored man. He wants to speak to you, says it's very important." The man scoffed. "I told 'im there ain't nothing a nig—that is, a colored man can say to a white woman that's important enough to call her away from her dinner. But he give me a quarter to come fetch you."

"Where is he?"

"He's in the alley, behind the hotel."

"Please tell him I will be there directly," Catherine said.

"Yes, ma'am," the messenger said.

After the man left, Catherine smiled across the table at Dan. "Thank you for a wonderful evening," she said. She pushed herself away from the table and, quickly, Dan was around to help her stand.

"Must it end now?"

"I'm afraid so. Willie never sends for me unless it is very important. I had better go see what he wants."

"Please let me go with you," Dan said. "The alley is no place for a lady."

"Thank you for your concern, but I will be safe with Willie."

"Nevertheless, I would feel better if—"

"It's all right, really," Catherine said. Then, by explanation, she added, "Sometimes Willie is very shy. If you are with me, he may not even tell me what is wrong. I appreciate what you are trying to do, but honestly, it will be all right."

"Very well," Dan said. "But, please remember, I am in the hotel if you need me. I'm in room two twelve, on the second floor."

"I, too, am on the second floor," Catherine said. "Why, we are practically neighbors."

Excusing herself, Catherine left the restaurant, then walked along the side of the building to the alley behind. Willie was waiting for her.

"I'm sorry I had to send someone to disturb your dinner, Miss Catherine," Willie said.

"That's quite all right, Willie," Catherine replied. "What is it? What's wrong?"

"There is no quinine to be had anywhere," Willie said.

"No quinine? But that's impossible! Where would it all be?"

"The army's got it all. A lot of the soldiers caught the ague while they were down south, so the army confiscated every bit of quinine there is."

"Oh, Willie, we must have some. I'm afraid that child will die without it."

"I was thinking maybe you could . . ." Willie stopped. "Never mind, I've really got no business making such a suggestion."

"What suggestion? Willie, I'm open to anything. We have to have some quinine, you know that."

"I was thinking about the man you were having dinner with. He's a high-ranking officer, isn't he? Maybe he could get us some quinine. That is, unless you don't want to ask him. I'm sorry. Just forget that I brought it up."

"No, no," Catherine said, holding up her hand to stop him. "It is a good idea. It's a very good idea, and I'm ashamed I didn't think of it in the first place. It's just that, if I ask for it, he's going to get suspicious and start asking questions. And we can't afford to have too many questions asked."

"You're right. Never mind."

"No," Catherine said, again waving her hand. She took a deep breath, held it, then let it out. "We have to have it. Otherwise the child may die. All right, I'll ask him, then deal with the questions."

"Yes, ma'am, whatever you think best," Willie said.

"You didn't arouse any suspicions trying to locate the quinine, did you?"

"No, ma'am, I was very careful."

Catherine reached out to put her hand on his. "Please continue to be careful," she said. "I don't know what I would do without you and Thelma."

When Catherine went to Dan's room later that night, the door was standing slightly ajar. Pushing it open quietly, she saw Dan standing at the window, looking out onto the street. As his back was to the door, she was reasonably certain that he was unaware of her entrance.

Catherine cleared her throat quietly, and Dan turned.

"Catherine!" he said, obviously surprised to see her standing in his room.

"I was going to knock," Catherine said, waving toward the door. "But it was standing open, so I just came in."

"Both of us seem to have a habit of leaving the door unlocked," Dan teased.

For a moment Catherine was confused, then she realized that he was referring to the time he had barged in on her bath. She blushed. "Oh," she said. "What a terrible moment that was for me."

"Please forgive me. It was inappropriate for me to have brought that up, even by reference. I'm sorry if I have caused you any discomfort."

"No, it's all right," Catherine said. She smiled. "And if one can set aside the embarrassment, there really is some comic aspect to it."

"At any rate, I'm glad you came in," Dan said. He stepped over to the table and lit the kerosene lamp, then turned it up so that the bubble of light encompassed the entire room.

"I see you have a view of the street," Catherine said. "I'm afraid my room offers no lovelier a view than the roof of the restaurant next door."

"The view in my room has suddenly become much lovelier," Dan said.

"I beg your pardon?" Then, realizing that he was referring to her, she blushed a second time. "Now you have embarrassed me again."

"Yes, but I make no apologies this time," Dan said. "You are a beautiful woman."

"I'm flattered that you think so."

"Catherine, do you remember what happened before? When we were together in St. Louis?"

"Nothing happened," Catherine replied.

"Oh, but something *did* happen," Dan said. He reached over and took her hands into his. "I fell in love with you. Do you not remember my telling you that?"

"Yes, I remember," Catherine said.

"And, remembering that, you came into my room anyway? You've taken quite a risk, you know. Last time we were together I was able to stop myself. I don't know if I can again."

"I . . . I'm not all that sure I would try to stop you," Catherine heard herself saying.

The quinine. She was there for the quinine. Yet in all honesty, securing the medication seemed the most remote thought in her mind at that moment.

"Do you mean that?"

"I . . . I don't know what I mean. I'm afraid you've got me all in a titter right now." She laughed nervously. "I'm acting like a schoolgirl. If you think of me at all, you must think me a very flighty young woman."

"*If* I think about you?" Dan replied. "Catherine, don't you realize that you have been uppermost in my thoughts ever since we were together in St. Louis? I thought of you during the long, hard hours of work, digging the canal around New Madrid. I thought of you on the night before battle, and I thought of you when I learned that I would be returning to this part of the state."

"I'm very flattered," Catherine said, not knowing how else to respond.

"But, I must know. Am I alone in feeling this way? Have you thought of me?"

"You are not alone," Catherine said. "I've thought of you as well."

Dan put his arms around her and pulled her to him, pressing his lips against hers. A tide of exciting sensations swept over Catherine, leaving her bewildered and somewhat frightened. He had kissed her before, and she had experienced the same quick flash of heat. But the other time had been spontaneous and unexpected. This time she was entering into it without pretense.

Catherine surrendered easily to his kiss, and when he grew more bold, she didn't resist. His lips traveled from her mouth down her throat to the top button of her gown. She allowed him to do with her as he wished. She was totally submissive to his will, bending to his bidding like a slender reed in a strong spring breeze.

Dan's fingers opened the buttons that fastened her dress and then unlaced her camisole. Her small but well-formed breasts shone like golden globes in the spill of lamplight, and he couldn't keep himself from moving his hand across her skin, cupping her breast, tenderly stroking the nipple with his thumb.

Suddenly he realized what he was doing. He had been carried this far by his own passion and by a desire stronger than any emotion he'd ever before experienced. If he was going to stop, he would have to stop now. With every ounce of willpower in his body, he pulled his fingers away and with trembling hands started to close her camisole.

"No, Dan, please, do not stop," Catherine said in a breathy voice. She put her hand up to his fingers. "I want to. Don't you understand? I want to!"

Inflamed by desire and emboldened by her invitation, Dan began undressing, even as Catherine slipped out of her own clothes. A few moments later they were both nude, and Dan led her over to the bed.

"Catherine," he whispered huskily, "are you sure?"

"If you try to get away from me now, I will chase after you," Catherine said through clenched teeth.

Dan moved his body over hers and began to enter her. He felt her wince and he stopped, but she put her arms on her shoulders and pulled him to her.

"No, it's all right," she said firmly.

As Dan continued, he abandoned all thought of right and wrong, all thought of what might lie in the future. He knew only the pleasure of the moment and knew that she was feeling the same thing, for she rose up against him, giving him all that was hers to give.

"Oh, Dan!" she whispered in a sharp, rising voice. "Oh, Dan, it's . . . it's wonderful!" she gasped.

Then it started for Dan, a tiny, tingling sensation that began deep inside him and pinwheeled out, spinning faster and faster until every part of his body was caught up in a whirlpool of pleasure.

Dan had touched the deepest, innermost part of Catherine. Now she felt as he felt, thought as he thought, and for an instant they were one. For several long moments they lay side by side without touching and without speaking, until, gradually, they began to be aware of sounds from outside themselves.

A horse clopped down the street.

Some men passed by on the board sidewalk below, laughing and talking loudly.

From somewhere they could hear the sound of a piano.

A baby cried.

"Are you all right?" Dan asked.

Catherine turned her head on the pillow to look at Dan, and she smiled. "Yes, I'm fine," she answered.

"Catherine, will you marry me?"

"I don't want you to feel that you must marry me," Catherine said. "Even if I become, uh, well, even if you *think* you should marry me, I wouldn't want you to feel obligated."

"I don't want to marry you because of any sense of obligation," Dan said. "I want to marry you because I love you."

"Please, Dan, don't ask me that. I can't marry you."

"Why not?"

"Because I have other . . . obligations."

"Burke? Is it Burke? I didn't even think about him."

"No, it isn't Burke," Catherine said. "Although I think he would be terribly hurt if you and I were married. And I don't think you would want that, would you?"

"I don't want to hurt Burke, no. But I do want to marry you."

"Dan . . ."

Dan raised his hand and put his fingers to her lips. "Hush," he said. "You don't have to answer now. I don't even want an answer now. But I do want you to think about it. And I do want you to believe that I love you. You do believe that, don't you?"

"Yes," Catherine said, nodding her head slightly. "Yes, I believe that."

"Then, think about that, and that only. I withdraw my question, for now. I'll ask it again, when I think the time is right."

"Thank you, Dan," Catherine said. "Thank you for not making me choose now."

"Someday, Catherine. Someday I will make you choose."

Suddenly Catherine remembered why she had come to his room in the first place, and she felt a strong sense of guilt over the fact that the thought had just now come to her. She cleared her throat.

"Dan?"

"Yes?"

"Can you get me some quinine?"

Dan looked at her in surprise. "Quinine?"

"Yes. Quinine, like the kind they use to treat the ague."

"I suppose I could, but why would you need quinine? Ague is not common in these parts."

"Perhaps not," Catherine said. "But I have a friend who is suffering from the malady."

"Oh, my God, it's Burke, isn't it? He was down in southeast Missouri, in the swampland. Has he contracted the disease?"

"It isn't Burke."

"Another Rebel soldier?"

"Why do you think that?"

"It has to be a Rebel, for I know that our army has an adequate supply for its own."

"Suppose it is for a Rebel soldier. Wouldn't it be an act of Christian kindness to supply the medication if you could do so?"

"If he would surrender himself, I would see to it that he got adequate care. But I'm an officer in the Army of the United States, Catherine. It wouldn't be proper for me to provide aid and comfort to the enemy."

"Then you needn't worry, for it isn't a Rebel soldier," Catherine told him.

"If not a Rebel, then who?"

Catherine shook her head. "Please don't make me say, Dan. If you are a man of compassion, and I know that you are, you will give me the medicine without asking all these questions."

"Catherine, you aren't being fair," Dan replied. "I explained my situation to you. I have certain obligations. I can get the quinine for you, but I need to know why you must have it."

Catherine sighed. "All right, I suppose you do have the right to know. One of my passengers is ill. A child. I need the quinine desperately."

"One of your passengers? What do you mean, one of your passengers?" Dan asked, puzzled by her strange answer.

"I am a conductor."

"A conductor?"

"Dan, are you completely unaware of the Underground Railroad?"

Dan gasped. "The Underground Railroad? My God, Catherine, don't tell me you are involved with that bunch of radicals?"

"I am."

"But I don't understand. How can you be involved? You own slaves."

Catherine shook her head. "No, I do not," she replied. "Willie and Thelma are free, and have been free for some time. They merely pose as slaves, in order to help me."

"You are crazy, all of you," Dan said. "Besides, I didn't even know that the Underground Railroad was still in operation. I thought it ended when the war began."

"Oh, no," Catherine replied. "As a matter of fact, the Underground Railroad operates now at a much grander scale than it ever did before the war." She smiled again. "My house is one of the depots, and I am a conductor."

"Catherine, you must give that up!" Dan insisted. "You must give it up at once! Don't you understand? Missouri is still a slave state! You are violating not only the law of the Rebels, but the laws of the state and federal governments as well. You could go to prison . . . or worse!"

"I cannot . . . I will not give it up," Catherine said. "Don't you understand, Dan? This is as important and meaningful for me as what you do is for you."

"But it is dangerous," Dan said.

"And what you do is not dangerous?"

"Of course what I do is dangerous, but . . ."

"But what? But you are a man, and therefore it doesn't matter?"

"I don't mean it that way."

"Then how do you mean it?"

"I just mean that I don't like to think of you being engaged in so dangerous a pursuit."

"Nevertheless, I am engaged. I have been, and I shall continue to be," Catherine said. "And now, that brings me back to the question at hand. Will you help me get some quinine? Because if I don't get any, I'm afraid the child will die."

"Of course I'll help," Dan said. "What kind of person would not help a child?"

Smiling, Catherine put her fingers on Dan's cheek. "Thank you," she said. "I knew I could count on you."

"But Catherine, please, be very careful."

"I always have been," Catherine said easily.

✫ ✫ ✫

Twenty

From *Harper's Weekly,* Domestic Intelligence; October 11, 1862:

A PROCLAMATION
BY THE PRESIDENT OF THE UNITED STATES OF AMERICA

Whereas, It has become necessary to call into service, not only volunteers, but also portions of the militia of the States by draft, in order to suppress the insurrection existing in the United States, and disloyal persons are not adequately restrained by the ordinary process of law from hindering this measure, and from giving aid and comfort in various ways to the insurrection. Now, therefore, be it ordered, that during the existing insurrection, and as a necessary measure for suppressing the same, all rebels and insurgents, their aiders and abettors within the United States, and all persons discouraging volunteer enlistments, resisting militia drafts, or guilty of any disloyal practice affording aid and comfort to the rebels against the authority of the United States, shall be subject to martial law, and liable to trial and punishment by courts-martial or military commission.

Second: That the writ of habeas corpus is suspended in respect to all persons arrested, or who are now, or hereafter during the rebellion shall be, imprisoned in any fort, camp, arsenal, military prisons, or other place of confinement, by any military authority, or by the sentence of any court-martial or military commission.

In witness whereof, I have hereunto set my hand and caused the seal of the United States to be affixed.

Done at the City of Washington, this Twenty-fourth day of September, in the year of our Lord 1862, and of the Independence of the United States the eighty-seventh.

ABRAHAM LINCOLN

Near Helena, Arkansas, October 22, 1862
Dear Catherine,

It has been some time since I wrote, but you will understand, I am sure, that the conditions of my service now are such that private communication has become very difficult. I am not a member of a regular army brigade such as I was when I was assigned to General Johnston's staff this spring, and therefore the posting, or the receiving of mail, is quite infrequent.

I must confess that I miss the order and structure of a regular army unit. I am, after all, a graduate of the Military Academy and had chosen the army as my profession until the war changed all my plans. Now, not only my method of service has changed, even the flag I serve, has changed.

I am currently a member of Quantrill's guerrillas. I am sure you have heard of us, for we have caused the Yankees no end of difficulty in the last two years. We are now in Arkansas, where Quantrill plans to spend the winter, as he believes that foraging will be easier here, both for man and horse.

The size of our band varies from as little as eighty to as many as three hundred men as our "volunteers" come and go according to their personal whims and dictates. There are some among us, however, who are constant members, and, though their ways may be untrained, they are, I believe, in fighting spirit, boldness, and skills, the equal of any officer's staff in any brigade in either army.

I would like to, by way of this letter, introduce you to a few of them.

First there is the leader of our group, His name is William Clarke Quantrill, though the men call him "Charley" or "Chief." Quantrill is about five feet nine inches tall, and slender of build. His complexion is pale, even after days in the sun. His eyes are light blue and rather heavy-lidded. He is an excellent marksman, and I have seen him make some amazing shots, even while riding at the gallop.

Second in command is Bill Anderson, sometimes called Bloody Bill. Bloody Bill is quick-tempered and deadly, but he is a person who can be depended upon in a fight. I have staked my life on him several times, and he has always come through.

George Todd is third in command. The relationship between Todd and Quantrill is somewhat strange, for he and Quantrill hate each other, and have even come close to fighting a duel. Nevertheless, Todd is a good soldier who has, thus far, obeyed every command Quantrill has given him. In fact, to see how well coordinated are their efforts in battle, one would never realize the bad blood that exists between them.

Cole and Jim Younger, one of the many sets of brothers who ride with the group, are unimaginative, but good, dependable men, and I would be honored to have them serve in any command of mine. Cole and Jim are the first cousins of the James brothers, Frank and Jesse.

Frank James read Shakespeare once, several years ago, and committed it to memory. The rest of us suffer because of it, for he often shows off by breaking out into some long soliloquy which he intones with all the proper inflection of voice.

But of them all, Jesse James is, by far, the most interesting. Jesse is little more than a boy. He is fair featured, with the kind of smooth, pink-skinned complexion that many a lovely young woman would envy. He has soft, clear blue eyes and a habit of blinking them frequently, thus giving him the illusion of a shy, young maiden.

Jesse is moved easily to tears at the death of a friend, horse, or dog. But that is the most deceptive part of his character, for Jesse can kill a man as easily as swatting a fly. When he is angry, or acting out of hate (and he truly hates the Yankees), he is as frightening to behold as anyone in the band . . . anyone, including Todd, Bloody Bill Anderson, or Quantrill himself.

You may ask where I fit into this band of ferocious men? I am, officially, an observer and liaison officer between Quantrill's guerrilla band and General Price's regulars. As such, I consider myself apart from the others, though I am certain that if ever captured by the Yankees, I would, no doubt, be tried and hanged as readily as any of those I have just described to you.

I have been told that Dan Morris has returned to the Kansas City area and is now assigned to General Ewing's staff in pursuit of Quantrill. I hope that is not true, for if it is, it has finally set two dear friends against each other.

General Ewing's mission enjoys the validity of a national commission, and he is sanctioned by recognized governmental authority to commit atrocities that are as great as, or greater than, any that have ever been committed by Quantrill, or Shelby, or Marmaduke, or any other Confederate guerrilla leader. That he conducts himself in such a sanctimonious manner just makes him a hypocrite more to be despised than admired.

Catherine, as I am certain you must understand, my status as a member of Quantrill's guerrilla band makes it somewhat difficult for me to be seen in public. Therefore I have restrained from calling on you, even when I found myself in your vicinity. But, if ever the opportunity presents itself, I would like, very much, to come see you.

> Your obedient servant,
> Burke Phillips
> Capt. CSA

Catherine read the letter, then looked up at the very pretty young woman who had, but a few moments earlier, delivered it to her.

"Thank you for bringing the letter to me, Miss . . ." She let the sentence hang, hoping the young woman would provide the name.

"Smith," the woman said. "My name is Josephine Smith." She smiled. "But please, call me Josephine."

"Yes, well, as I said, Josephine, I thank you for the letter."

Josephine cleared her throat. "If you will notice the date, it was mailed last October. That was almost six months ago."

"Yes," Catherine replied. "I did notice that."

"I hope you understand, Miss Darrow, that I have not been holding the letter this long. It was only recently brought to me, by my brother."

"Is your brother with Captain Phillips?" Catherine asked.

"Yes."

"How is he?" Catherine asked. She held up the letter. "I mean, as you pointed out, this letter is six months old."

"He is well," Josephine said.

"Do you know where he is?"

"No, I'm sorry, I don't. But I know that he is well."

"That is good to hear," Catherine said. She smiled again. "If I wanted to get a letter back to him, would I be able to do so, through you?"

"Yes," Josephine said. "Sometimes a rider comes to the house to bring mail from my brother, and to pick up mail. If you would give me a letter, I would see that it got back to him."

"Thank you. I have nothing now, but I may at some point in the near future."

"Miss Darrow—"

"Please," Catherine interrupted. "If I am going to call you Josephine, couldn't you call me Catherine? You sound as if you are one of my students."

Josephine smiled. "Oh, no. None of my schoolteachers were as nice as you are."

"How kind of you to say so. Now, you were going to ask a question?"

"Yes. Some of the ladies in the area are holding a quilting bee on Saturday night. We would be very honored if you would attend."

"Oh, I thank you for the invitation, Josephine, but I don't want to intrude. I would be the stranger there, I fear."

"No, you wouldn't," Josephine insisted. "I know that some of your friends will be there. Marcie Caulder is one."

"Marcie?"

"Yes. You remember her, don't you?"

"Of course I do. Her husband and child were killed by Jayhawkers, and her farm burned. I remember that only too vividly. But I haven't seen Marcie in quite some time now. How is she doing?"

"She is doing very well, thank you. And I know she would like to see you. There will be other friends of yours there as well. Won't you please come?"

Josephine thought for a moment. Perhaps such an innocent social occasion with some of the other women of the county would be good for her. She smiled, then nodded.

"All right, I'll come," she said. "Where is this quilting bee?"

"It's at the Maury farm," Josephine said. "Do you know where that is?"

"Yes, it's about three miles east of town. I know the place."

"That's where it will be," Josephine said. She stood up to leave. "Then I shall see you Saturday night?"

"I'm looking forward to it," Catherine said.

Promising to take care of it, a young boy took charge of Catherine's horse and buggy when she arrived at the Maury farm Saturday night. Having seen Catherine arrive, Josephine came out of the house to welcome her as she stepped down from the buggy.

"Oh, I'm so glad you could come," Josephine said. "I was beginning to wonder if you would."

"Isn't anyone else here?" Catherine asked. "I see no conveyances."

"Yes, there are several here already, but we thought it best to keep the horses and wagons out of sight. We don't want to arouse anyone's curiosity."

"Yes, I suppose that is a good idea," Catherine agreed. Catherine started up the brick walk toward the house.

"No, it's this way," Josephine said, starting toward the barn.

Catherine looked over in surprise. "My goodness, a quilting bee is being held in a barn?"

"Well, as I explained, there are several people here," Josephine said. "And there is much more room in the barn."

"All right, the barn it is."

Catherine followed the pretty young woman to the barn. Then, when she stepped inside, she gasped in surprise.

This was no mere quilting bee. It was a full-blown party, complete with musicians, food, ribbons, banners, and flags! And the flags, Catherine noticed, were Confederate flags. The men—and there were several men at the party—were all wearing Confederate uniforms. Some of the soldiers were in full regalia, others wore little more than a rakish hat and colorful sash.

One of the men in full uniform started toward her, and when she saw that it was Burke Phillips, Catherine had to admit she wasn't all that surprised.

"Hello, Catherine," Burke said, smiling at her and touching his fingertips to the brim of his hat.

"Burke Phillips. My, but it has been a long time since I've seen you. Did you set this up?" Catherine asked.

"The meeting with you? Yes, I did set it up," Burke admitted. "But I didn't organize the dance." He took in the gaily decorated barn with a sweep of his hand. "The dance was all Josephine Anderson's idea."

"Anderson?"

Josephine smiled, then apologized. "My true name is Josephine Anderson, not Josephine Smith. I'm sorry if I was dishonest with you before, but one can't be too careful during these times."

"I suppose that is true," Catherine agreed. "Anderson? Are you—"

"Bill Anderson is my brother," Josephine interrupted, answering the question before it was asked.

"Then you are wise to be cautious," Catherine said.

"Choose your partners for the Missouri stomp!" the band leader shouted. "The dancin's about to begin!"

"Will you do me the honor?" Burke asked, offering Catherine his arm.

Catherine smiled. "It would be my pleasure," she answered.

The music began then, with the fiddles loud and clear, the guitars carrying the rhythm, the accordion providing the counterpoint, and the dobro singing over everything. The band leader clapped his hands and stomped his feet and danced around on the platform in time to the music, bowing and whirling as if he had a girl and were on the floor himself. The dancers stepped and swirled, a kaleidoscope of color and movement.

Around the dance floor stood those who were without partners, looking on wistfully. Over at the punch bowl table, several soldiers started adding their own ingredients, and though many drank from the punch bowl, the contents of the bowl never seemed to diminish. A couple of young men got into an argument over the favors of one of the young women, but the ruckus was quickly and quietly settled so that nothing disturbed the party.

At a break in the music, Burke took Catherine around the party, introducing her to various members of the raiders. She was surprised at how small Quantrill was, though there was a man named "Little Archie Clement" who was even smaller. Bill Anderson took off his hat and made a sweeping bow when he was introduced. George Todd nodded but said nothing. Frank James kissed her fingers, and the Younger brothers shook her hand awkwardly.

"Where is your friend?" Catherine asked Burke. "The young one you wrote about."

"Jesse?"

"Yes."

"He's over there." Burke pointed to an area over at the side of the barn where several children were sitting in a hayrick, watching the dance.

"Where? I see no one."

"He is there," Burke said. "On the end. The one wearing the hat."

"Burke, you must be joking with me," Catherine said. "He is just a boy."

"That's right. Come meet him."

When Jesse James saw Burke and Catherine coming toward him, he slid down from the hayrick, then smiled shyly at them as they approached. He rubbed his hand on his pants leg, then stuck it out toward her. He was, Catherine noticed, about two inches shorter than she was.

"You must be Miss Darrow," he said in a soft-spoken voice. "Burke has talked a lot about you."

"And you are Jesse James?"

"Yes'm," Jesse said. He smiled again. "But lots of my friends call me Dingus. You can, too, if you want to."

"Oh, if you don't mind, I think I would prefer to call you Jesse," Catherine said. "It is a much more dignified name. It has character, don't you think?"

"Don't know," Jesse answered. "Don't know as I ever thought about it before."

"Jesse, Jesse, you promised we'd play mumblety-peg," a young boy called.

Jesse blushed. "Darn fool kids," he said. "Tell 'em somethin' an' they never let you alone. I reckon I'd better go do what I said I'd do."

"It was nice meeting you, Jesse," Catherine said.

"You too," Jesse mumbled, then he moved toward the group of young boys, all of whom were waiting to play. It was obvious that the game of mumblety-peg held much more attraction for Jesse James than the dance.

"Could I get you a plate?" Burke asked. "The ladies fried chicken for the party."

"I feel guilty eating the ladies' food," Catherine said. "I didn't bring anything."

Burke laughed. "That's all right, neither did they," he said. "We brought the chicken."

A few minutes later Burke and Catherine had staked out a place in a distant part of the barn and they sat on the wooden floor, balancing their plates on their laps as they ate and talked.

"Have you seen Dan?" Burke asked.

"Yes," Catherine answered.

"How is he doing?"

"He is healthy," Catherine said. "He is concerned about you."

"I saw him at Shiloh."

"Yes, he said as much."

"No," Burke said, shaking his head. "I'm not talking about the meeting we had during the night. I'm talking about the next day. I had a dead bead on a Yankee officer whose back was to me. I nearly squeezed the trigger, then I stopped. Something told me to wait just a second longer.

Then, when the Yankee turned I saw that it was Dan and I lowered my gun.''

"He didn't see you?"

"No. I was behind a tree. If I had not waited that extra second . . .'' Burke let the sentence hang.

Catherine reached over and put her hand on his. "I am so glad you were able to stop in time," she said. "I am glad for both of you."

"How did it ever get to this point, Catherine? How is it that men who bear no malice toward each other, men who are closer than brothers, can find themselves in a situation where one might kill the other?"

"Great and learned men were unable to prevent the war," Catherine said. "So who are we to answer such a question?"

"We are the ones who pay for the follies of these 'great and learned' men," Burke said.

Suddenly there was a commotion at the front door. "Yankees are comin'! Yankees are comin'!" someone shouted.

"How far?" Quantrill called back.

"Five minutes away. Maybe ten. They're comin' in battalion strength."

"Let's fight 'em!" somone shouted, and his challenge was answered by several assenting voices.

"Not here! We won't put the ladies in danger," Quantrill said. He smiled. "But we'll hit 'em before they get back to town, you can count on that!"

"Yahoo!"

"Let's go, men! The horses are out back!"

There was a flurry of activity as the men started through the back door. Several lingered behind to kiss and embrace their wives and sweethearts.

"Burke, please be careful," Catherine said.

Burke had started toward the door, then, as if emboldened by Catherine's words, he turned and came back to her. Before she could react, he put his arms around her. He pulled her close, then pressed his lips against hers. She felt his tongue, first brushing across her lips, then forcing her lips open and thrusting inside.

Catherine had been so surprised when Burke first grabbed her that she didn't struggle against it. Now all struggle was impossible as the pleasurable sensations overwhelmed her.

No, she thought. This is impossible! I am in love with Dan, Burke's best friend! How is it that I am letting this happen? How is it that I am enjoying it so?

Finally Burke broke off the kiss and withdrew his hand, leaving Catherine standing there as limp as a rag doll.

"Just so that you know," Burke said with a crooked smile. "I haven't surrendered to Dan, neither on the battlefield nor with you."

"Burke, I . . ."

Burke put his fingertips on her lips to quiet her. "No," he said. "Say nothing now. This is neither the time nor the place."

"All right," Catherine said, more confused now than she had been at any time since she'd met Burke and Dan.

"May I have this?" Burke asked, reaching for a yellow ribbon in her hair. He untied the ribbon, and when he did so, a long tress of Catherine's hair fell softly by her face. Smiling at her, Burke tied the ribbon in the second buttonhole of his jacket. "Now," he said, "every time I look down, I'll think of you."

"Captain Phillips! We must go now!" Quantrill shouted.

By now Burke was one of the last men left. He started toward the back door, stopped halfway there to blow Catherine a kiss, then was gone. A moment later Catherine heard the thunder of hoofbeats as the men rode away.

"Ladies, we must act quickly!" Josephine shouted, and the women began scurrying about the barn, erasing any signs of a party. The punch bowl was dumped onto the ground outside. Two women grabbed the tablecloth and picked it up with the food inside, then started into the house with it. Other women jerked down the ribbons and flags, and in less than a minute there was no sign that the barn had ever been anything but a barn.

"Inside!" someone else called, and as they left the barn, all the lanterns were extinguished so that by the time Catherine stepped onto the front porch, the barn was a dark, empty building with no function other than that for which it had been built.

Once inside, Catherine saw that preparations had already been made for just such an occurrence. Two quilts were laid out, with chairs placed strategically around them for the "quilting" to take place. The tablecloth containing the food from the barn was spread out on the hutch. Someone sat at the piano and began playing, while half a dozen others gathered around to sing.

Outside, they heard the beating hooves of approaching horses, then the squeak of saddle leather and the jangle of dangling equipment.

"Battalion!" a muffled voice called.

The supplemental commands came back:

"Troop!"

"Halt!"

A horse whinnied.

There were loud voices, then heavy footfalls on the steps and the front porch. Someone knocked, hard, on the door, and Mrs. Maury got up to answer it. Looking toward the door, Catherine saw three Union officers. One was a brigadier general.

"Yes, gentlemen? Is there something I can do for you?"

"Where are they?" the general asked.

"I beg your pardon?" Mrs. Maury replied. "Where are who?"

"You know who I'm talking about. Quantrill. This is the Maury farm, isn't it?"

"Yes," Mrs. Maury said. "I'm Mrs. Maury."

"Well, I have very good information that there is a party here tonight for Quantrill and his band of brigands and cutthroats."

Mrs. Maury smiled, then stepped away from the door. "Well, I don't know anything about that, but there is a party here tonight," she said. "A quilting party. Would you like to come in and have a look around?"

General Ewing pushed his way in even before Mrs. Maury had stepped completely aside. He made a careful perusal of the room, looking at the ladies who were in position around the two quilts or over by the piano.

"As you can clearly see, General, neither Colonel Quantrill nor any of his men are here."

"Colonel Quantrill?" Ewing said, twisting his mouth. "Don't dignify that scoundrel with a military title."

There were more footfalls on the front porch.

"General, you want to come out here to the barn and have a look around?" another officer called.

"Did you find something?"

"I think so," the officer answered. "The lanterns are all warm, as if they had just been extinguished. And just outside the back door of the barn it stinks to high heaven where someone dumped some liquor."

Ewing chuckled. "Must've galled that bunch of no-accounts to see good liquor poured out on the ground."

"Yes, sir, I reckon it did."

"Bring the wagons up," Ewing said. "And put the women in them."

"I beg your pardon?" Mrs. Maury asked, shocked by the statement.

"You're under arrest, Mrs. Maury. All of you," Ewing added, looking at the others. "You are all under arrest."

"On what charge?"

"Don't you ever read the papers?" Ewing asked. "I don't need a charge. The writ of habeas corpus has been suspended for the duration of the war. You are the wives, sweethearts, family, and friends of known guerrilla raiders, operating in this area. That's all I need." Ewing turned to one of the officers standing nearby. "Take 'em out, Captain Foster, and put them in the wagon. Set a guard over them, make certain none of them gets away."

"Yes, sir," Captain Foster replied.

"Now, Mrs. Maury, is there anyone else in the house?"

"I've already told you, there are no men here," Mrs. Maury answered.

"I'm not talking about that," Ewing said with a dismissive wave of his hand. "I mean is there anyone else, any old people, young children, or invalids who might be upstairs or in some other room?"

"No."

"You are positive about that?"

"Yes, I'm positive," Mrs. Maury answered resolutely. "Unlike the Yankee women you are used to dealing with, sir, I do not lie."

"Good," Ewing said. "Very good." He turned to Captain Foster. "As soon as you have all the women out of here, burn the place."

"What?" Mrs. Maury shouted. "General, you can't be serious!"

"Burn the house, the barn, and all the outbuildings, including the grain bins."

"No! My God, no! You can't do this!" Mrs. Maury screamed.

"Get them out of here," Ewing said, paying no attention to Mrs. Maury's pitiful entreaties.

As Catherine rode into town with the rest of the women, she twisted around in the wagon and looked back toward the farm she had just left. The sky above the house and barn was orange and filled with glowing sparks that climbed the heat wave high into the sky, to join there with the cold blue stars. She could hear the terrible snapping and cracking of burning wood, even from this far away, and she could smell and see the thick black smoke.

In the front of the wagon Mrs. Maury was sobbing uncontrollably at the thought of her home being so callously destroyed.

"Yankees," Josephine said bitterly, under her breath. "They will rue this day, you mark my words. My brother will not let this go unavenged."

Twenty-one

Advertisement from *Harper's Weekly;* August 1, 1863:

THE SECRET ARMOR, OR
BULLETPROOF VEST

Is light, comfortable, and a sure protection against bullets, bayonets, and sabers. Price for Officer's style, $8; Private's, $6.

Money must accompany the order; also the Express charge, and the measure around breast and waist. Sold by MERWIN & BRAY, 292 Broadway, N.Y.; Wm. Read & Son, Boston, Mass.; and H. P. Hoadley, Wholesale and General Agent, New Haven, Conn.

P.S.—Reduction to the trade. Agents wanted.

From the same issue:

THE FALL OF VICKSBURG
"THE NEGOTIATIONS FOR SURRENDER"
(HEADQUARTERS MAJOR GENERAL MCPHERSON, JULY 3, 1863.)

The eyes of the gallant men in the rifle pits in front of the Division of General A. J. Smith have been gladdened by the long-expected flag of truce that is, we hope, to close this eventful siege.

The Confederate officers General Bowen and Colonel Montgomery were received by the "officer of the day" for the Division, Captain Joseph H. Green, of the Twenty-third Wisconsin Regiment, and by him conducted to the headquarters of General Burbridge, Captain Green having first taken the precaution to blindfold the officers. At the quarters of General Burbridge, the General, who has been quite ill for some days, received them, with an apology for his inability to rise from his couch. The handkerchiefs were soon removed, and the message of which they were bearers was sent to General Grant, who returned word that he would meet General Pemberton at three o'clock in the afternoon, when the officers took their departure, blindfolded as before, walking out to the lines.

At three o'clock in the afternoon the meeting of Generals Grant and Pemberton took place near the Rebel work Fort Hill.

After a conference of some two hours, in the most quiet and courteous manner, the two officers parted with a handshake that seemed most friendly.

Quietly seated upon the grassy slope near the Rebel works, one could only look with the greatest interest upon the scene.

Meantime a conference was being had nearby by Generals McPherson and Smith, and General Bowen and Colonel Montgomery, the officers of the Generals' staffs being en group.

At ten o'clock the next morning, it being July 4th, the Confederate Army under Lieutenant General Pemberton marched out of their works and stacked arms and colors.

So close were our saps to the Rebel works that in many instances the arms were stacked in our trenches. While the arms were being stacked, General Grant, with his staff, rode past to enter the city; while upon the parapet of Fort Hill stood Pemberton, Hebert, Taylor, and other officers. It is, of course, impossible to illustrate more than a small portion of the act of surrender, as each regiment stacked arms in front of the position they had held so gallantly during the siege, the works extending for nearly nine miles.

From *Harper's Weekly;* August 8, 1863:

The Fight at Gettysburg
Longstreet's Grand Attack upon Our Left Center

After much solicitation from his subordinates, General Lee permitted General Longstreet to send his grand division on a charge upon the cemetery. The Federal soldiers were on the alert. They were hid behind their embankments, some kneeling, and some flat on the ground. The Confederate artillery opened. It was as fierce a cannonade as the one the day before, but instead of being spread all over the line, every shell was thrown at the cemetery. Experienced soldiers soon divined what was coming, and in every portion of the Federal line the cannon were directed toward the valley in front of the cemetery. All were ready. Amidst the furious fire from the Confederate cannon scarcely a Federal shot was heard. The artillerists, implements in hand, crouched in the little ditches dug behind their cannon. With arms loaded, the infantry awaited the charge. It soon came. From the woods of short, scrubby timber and the rocks near the seminary there rose a yell. It was a long, loud, unremitting, hideous screech from thousands of voices. At the yell the Federal cannon opened. Soon the enemy's columns emerged from the woods. They came on a rush down the hill, waving their arms and still screeching. They climbed the fences and rushed along, each one bent upon getting first into the cemetery. The cannon roared, and grape and cannister and spherical case fell thick among them. Still they rushed onward, hundreds falling out of the line. They came within musketshot of the Federal troops. Then the small arms began to rattle. The Confederates approached the outer line of works. They were laboring up the hill. As they mounted the low bank in front of the rifle pits, the Federal soldiers retreated out of the ditch behind, turning and firing as they went along. It was a hand-to-hand conflict. Every man fought by himself and for himself.

Myriads of the enemy pushed forward down the hill, across into the works, and up to the cemetery. All were shouting, and screaming, and swearing, clasping their arms and firing their pieces. The enemy's shells flew over the field upon the Federal artillerists on the hills above. These, almost disregarding the storm that raged around them, directed all their fire upon the surging columns of the enemy's charge. Every available cannon on the Cemetery Hill, and to the right and left, threw its shells and shot into the valley. The fight was terrible; but despite every effort the enemy pushed up the hill and across the second line of works. The fire became hotter. The fight swayed back and forth. One moment the enemy would be at the railings of the cemetery; then a rush from the Federal side would drive them down into the valley. Then, with one of their horrid screeches, they would fiercely run up the hill again into the cemetery; then a rush from the Federal side would drive them down into the valley. Then, with another of their yells, they would again storm up the hill, where they would have a fierce battle among the tombstones. It was the hardest fight of the day, and hundreds were slain there. Reckless daring, however, will not always succeed. Several attempts were made to take the place, but they were not successful; and late in the afternoon, leaving thousands of dead and wounded behind them, the enemy's forces slowly retreated upon their own hill and into their woods again.

It was the middle of the night when the wagons transporting Catherine Darrow and the other women of the "quilting bee" arrived in Kansas City. They were taken there by the soldiers who had raided the Maury farm. The little column halted in front of a liquor store, an old, leaning, dilapidated three-story building, the brick walls of which glowed orange in the reflected light of half a dozen flickering, smoking torches.

"All right, this is it," Captain Foster called to his prisoners. "Everyone out."

Exhausted, confused, and frightened, the women started climbing down from the wagons, not helped, but watched over by the armed soldiers, who now formed a double line from the wagons to the building.

"Quickly, quickly!" Captain Foster shouted. "We haven't got all night."

"Captain, we are moving as quickly as we can," Catherine said. "We've been through a lot tonight, and we're exhausted." She looked at a couple of the older women who would not have been able to respond at all had not some of the younger women helped them. "And some of the older ladies aren't very strong," she added.

"Ladies?" the captain replied with a smirk. "I don't see any ladies here. All I see is Rebel trash."

"Please, sir, I want to go home," said one of the older and more confused women.

"Home?" the captain replied. He pointed to the old building. "From now on, this *is* your home."

"You can't be serious," Catherine gasped when she looked at the old building. It was leaning so badly that there were actually timbers in place to hold it up. "You're putting us in a liquor store?"

"Upstairs," Captain Foster said.

"But look at that building. It's about to fall down."

"Miss, have you been elected the spokeswoman for this group?" Captain Foster asked.

"No."

"Then if you don't mind, I've heard about all from you I'm going to. Now, either go through that side door there, and climb up those stairs, or I'll have one of my men carry you." Captain Foster turned toward the others. "And that goes for all of you! Go with the sergeant who is holding the lantern. He will lead the way."

"You women follow me," the sergeant called, holding up the lantern. He spat a stream of tobacco onto the wooden porch, barely missing the skirt of one of the women, who with a little shout of alarm jerked her skirt back out of the way. The sergeant chuckled at her discomfort, then went through a door that opened onto the stairs leading up to the second floor.

The second floor of the building was poorly lighted by two more dimly glowing, smoking lanterns that hung suspended from posts on the second floor. In the faint light Catherine studied the place of their confinement. Their makeshift prison was a large open room, interspersed by several four-by-four timbers that, while obviously not a part of the original construction, had been called into service to help support the ceiling. It was from a couple of these posts that the additional lanterns were hanging.

"Here you are. Make yourself comfortable," the sergeant said, taking in the room with a sweep of his hand.

"Why have you brought us here?" Josephine asked.

"It's General Ewing's new strategy," the sergeant replied. "If we can't get the bushwhackers themselves, we'll get their whores." The sergeant spat another stream of tobacco, this time on the floor, then he smiled, showing stained and crooked teeth. "That means you," he said. "You're Rebel whores."

"But how are we supposed to stay here? You've made no provisions for us. There are no rooms, no furniture, there aren't even any beds," someone asked.

"Beds? Whores don't need no beds," the sergeant answered. " 'Cept when they're whorin'," he added with a laugh. "And I can tell you right now, you ain't goin' to be doin' no whorin' here. That is, 'lessen some of you wants to get on *my* good side, if you know what I mean." He laughed again.

"You are a disgusting man," Josephine said.

"Oh?" the sergeant mocked. "Does that mean you don't love me?"

"I hate you!" Josephine said.

"Well, now, ain't that just too bad? You Rebel whores want a bed? Go down there and get yourselves a blanket and make your bed on the floor. One blanket," he emphasized, holding up his finger. "We'll prob'ly be bringin' in some of your 'sisters' pretty soon, an' we don't want you people of the 'gentler sex' fightin' over blankets."

Captain Foster came upstairs at that moment. "What's keeping you, Sergeant?" he asked.

"Sorry, Cap'n, I was just gettin' 'em settled in up here."

"Captain, I protest," Catherine said. "These accommodations are totally inadequate. One blanket to be used for a bed? That's inhumane."

"There's no doubt many a soldier tonight who would be glad to have your one blanket," Captain Foster said. "And at least you have a roof over your head, which is more than I can say for the boys in the field.''

"What about, uh, our, uh, needs of nature?'' a woman asked, embarrassed at having to form the question.

There's a couple of chamber pots over there,'' Captain Foster answered, pointing toward them.

"But they're out in the *open*,'' Josephine protested. "Surely you don't expect us to use those.''

Captain Foster stroked his chin for a moment, then looked over toward the sergeant. "Sergeant, get a couple of extra blankets and rig up a privacy screen,'' he ordered.

"Since when do whores need privacy screens?'' the sergeant asked.

"Just do what I said, Sergeant.''

"Yes, sir,'' the sergeant answered, duly chastised.

"Have you ever heard of habeas corpus, Captain Foster? It means that you have no right to hold us, unless you charge us with a specific crime,'' Catherine said. "And since we have committed no crime, there can be no charges, hence, you cannot hold us.''

"Habeas corpus, huh?'' Captain Foster replied, smiling condescendingly at Catherine. "Well, I'm impressed that you even know about it. Perhaps you also know that President Lincoln suspended habeas corpus nearly a year ago. And that means General Ewing can keep you women prisoners for as long as he wishes, until the end of the war, if he wants to.''

"You don't think our men are just going to let us stay here, do you?'' Josephine asked angrily. "They'll come get us out!''

Captain Foster smiled. "Well, now, that's exactly what we're wanting them to do. Because when they come to get you, we'll get them.'' He touched the brim of his hat in a casual salute. "Oh, I wouldn't get any ideas about escaping if I were you. I'll have guards posted around the place twenty-four hours a day, with orders to shoot to kill, if they have to.''

Captain Foster and the sergeant left, and Catherine heard them slip a heavy bar lock across the door before they tramped back down the stairs.

"What do we do now?'' someone asked.

"I don't know about the rest of you,'' another answered,

"but I'm going to get myself a blanket and make myself as comfortable as possible. I am exhausted."

"Good idea. I'm going to do the same."

Catherine joined the queue with the other ladies at the pile of blankets, then, with blanket in hand, she found a spot near a window. As she spread the blanket on the floor she peered out through the window and saw several armed soldiers standing sentry duty in the dark street below. Captain Foster had not been bluffing.

What an unexpected turn this day had taken, she thought. She had awakened that morning on clean sheets in her own bed, a free woman. Tonight she was going to sleep with one soiled blanket on a filthy floor in a falling-down building, a prisoner of the Union Army.

It was in the small hours of the morning, and Lieutenant Colonel Dan Morris was practically asleep in his saddle as he led his weary battalion back into Kansas City. Two weeks earlier Dan had left Kansas City with 270 men, on the trail of a bushwhacker named Freeman, who, if not as well-known or as flamboyant as Quantrill, was nevertheless just as deadly.

When Dan located Freeman's camp a skirmish broke out, in which thirty bushwhackers and eight of Dan's men were killed. Freeman and his men managed to break out of the trap Dan had set for them, and a running gun battle followed. That resulted in the deaths of four more bushwhackers and two more of Dan's men. During the night a severe thunderstorm, complete with high winds, broke over them, and the bushwhacker Freeman, using the storm to cover his movement, was able to slip away. As the rain obliterated his tracks, Freeman's getaway was total.

Dan then led his men back to the camp, where he expected Freeman would show up. When Freeman didn't return, Dan burned the Rebel stores of corn, flour, and grain and confiscated their stash of arms and ammunition. For the next week he continued to search for the Rebel leader, but without success. Finally, running low on supplies and with no new leads, he was forced to return to Kansas City.

Dan halted his men at General Ewing's camp just on the outside edge of town. After dismissing his command, he was met by Lieutenant Marcus Pond, who was serving as officer of the day.

"How went the search for Freeman, sir?" Pond asked.

Dan shook his head. "Not the way I wanted it to. We found Freeman's camp, had a small skirmish, and killed thirty or so. But Freeman and the main party got away."

"Shall I awaken General Ewing?"

"No, no," Dan said. He stretched and yawned. "If I had better news to share, I'd be glad to wake him. As it is, I'll just give him my report in the morning."

"Very well, sir," Lieutenant Pond replied.

"Here is a list of our casualties," Dan said, pulling a piece of paper from his pocket. "I'll just leave it on the desk, if you'll be so kind as to give it to the adjutant in the morning."

"Yes, sir."

Dan went into the headquarters tent to lay the casualty report on the desk when he saw, lighted by a kerosene lantern, two issues of *Harper's Weekly.*

"Still getting issues of *Harper's Weekly* mailed to you, I see," he commented.

"Yes, sir, my father sends them to me on a regular basis. I know it sounds silly, but it makes me feel like I'm home."

"I understand. And besides, the *Journal of Civilization,* as they call themselves, makes interesting reading."

"I really enjoy the 'Humors of the Day,' " Lieutenant Pond said. "Listen to this one." Clearing his throat, he began to read: "Two Scotsmen, observing a pretty girl in a milliner's shop, one of them proposed to go in and buy a watch ribbon in order to get a nearer view of her. 'Hoot, mon,' said his friend, 'there's nae occasion to waste the money. Let us go in and see if she can give us two sixpence for a shilling.' " Pond laughed. "That's a good one, isn't it?"

Dan laughed as well. "They say the Scots are a thrifty race," he said, picking up the paper. "I see they have an account of the surrender at Vicksburg."

"Yes, sir, and the other issue carries the story of our great victory at Gettysburg. What a bloody show Gettysburg must have been. They say twice as many were killed there as fell at Shiloh."

Dan shook his head. "Surely the South will not be able

to sustain such losses much longer. The Union forces are achieving success everywhere.''

"Including here, sir," Lieutenant Pond said.

"Here?"

"In your absence, General Ewing struck quite a blow against Quantrill's Raiders," Pond said.

"We've captured Quantrill?" Dan's eyes lit up with excitement.

"No, but we have imprisoned all of the guerrilla women."

"The guerrilla women? Who are the guerrilla women?"

Pond told of the raid on the Maury farm. "The Rebel women were giving a party for Quantrill and all of his men," he said. "It was a regular cotillion, can you imagine that? Anyway, we got word of it, and General Ewing mounted a battalion to surprise the bushwhackers. But someone alerted them, and they got away before General Ewing could get to them. So, in retaliation, the general burned the house, the barn, the granary, and all the outbuildings, then he arrested all the women."

"You mean the women of Maury farm?"

Pond shook his head. "No, sir, I mean *all* the women who were there," he said. "There were twenty-seven of them. We're holding them prisoners down at the old liquor store building right now."

"The liquor store building? Isn't that the building the engineers said was unfit to be confiscated as a barracks?"

"Maybe it isn't good enough for a barracks, but it will work just fine as a prison."

"Maybe so," Dan said. He stretched and yawned again. "I'm tired, Lieutenant, and I'm going to bed. Please tell the adjutant that I will give my report to General Ewing in the morning."

"Yes, sir," Lieutenant Pond said, saluting.

Pond remained standing until Dan left, then he picked up the paper and began reading again. From outside, as Dan walked toward his own tent, he could hear Lieutenant Pond chuckling over another of the jokes in "Humor of the Day."

The women prisoners were provided a rather tasteless mush for breakfast. Many of them complained loudly about the fare, but Catherine, realizing that complaining would probably get her nowhere, ate her breakfast without comment.

"How can you eat that?" Josephine asked. "This stuff is awful. We feed our coloreds better than this."

"What choice do we have?" Catherine replied. "I certainly don't plan to let the Yankees starve me to death."

Josephine thought for a moment, then nodded. "You're right," she said. "The damned Yankees would probably like nothing better than to see us starve." Making a face, she shoved a spoonful of the mush into her mouth, chewed a couple of times, then shuddered. "Delicious," she said.

Catherine laughed. "I'm glad to see you've kept your sense of humor."

At the end of the room, a Union soldier came through the door.

"Miss Darrow? Is there a Catherine Darrow in here?" the soldier called.

"I'm Catherine Darrow."

"You come with me."

"What do you want with me?"

"I'm just a private. They don't tell me those things," the soldier said. "All I was told was to come get you."

"I have no intention of going with you until I know what this is about," Catherine insisted.

"Look, miss, you can come one of two ways," the soldier said. "You can either come peaceable, walkin' out of here on your own power. Or I'm going to carry you out. Now, which will it be?"

"You wouldn't dare do such a thing."

"Would you care to try the experiment?"

"Go with him, Catherine, please," Josephine urged. "He looks just crazy enough to do what he says."

Catherine remained where she was for a moment longer, staring defiantly at the soldier; then, when she saw him make a menacing move toward her, she held up her hand.

"All right, I'll go," she said. She turned to Josephine, and the two women embraced. "Maybe this is good. Maybe I can find out a little bit about what is going on," she suggested.

With Catherine walking in front, the private took her down the stairs. A buckboard was parked in front of the building, and the private indicated that she should get in.

The same sergeant who had escorted them up the stairs on the previous night was now sitting on the seat, holding the reins to the team.

"I don't know who you know, lady, but the colonel hisself wants to see you," the sergeant said as they drove away.

"You would be surprised who I know, Sergeant," Catherine said, hoping to put the sergeant on the defensive.

A flash of lightning split the sky, followed by a peal of thunder. The sergeant looked up at a heavy black cloud rolling in from the west. "You're lucky," he said.

"Why is that?"

"It's about to rain. The ones back there in that buildin' are goin' to get just as wet as if they was standin' outside in the street. But you'll be nice an' dry in the colonel's quarters."

In fact, Catherine was wet before they even reached the colonel's quarters because the rain started falling in large, heavy drops, hurtling down from the sky with all the fury of a waterfall.

A captain, carrying an umbrella, hurried out to meet the buckboard when it arrived. He opened the umbrella and held it over Catherine in an attempt to protect her from the rain.

The solicitous captain was none other than Captain Foster. There was, however, a drastic change in his demeanor from the night before.

"Miss Darrow, you should've spoken up last night," Captain Foster chastised gently. "I would've never put you in with all those other women, if I had known who you are."

"And just who do you think I am?" Catherine asked, confused by the sergeant's sudden change toward her.

"Why, you're a friend of General Halleck's," Captain Foster said. "And a friend of Colonel Morris. He told us how you've been helping us by undertaking secret operations for the Union. Please forgive me, I was only doing my duty."

"Is Colonel Morris here?"

"Yes, ma'am. I'm taking you right to him," Captain Foster said. He raised the flap of a tent, then stepped back to allow Catherine to go in first. Inside the tent, she could hear the rain drumming hard against the canvas. Captain Foster stepped in behind her.

"That will be all, Captain Foster," Dan said.

"Yes, sir. I was just trying to explain to her that I wouldn't have done anything if she had only spoken up. I didn't know that—"

"I said, that will be all, Captain," Dan said again, his words more clipped than before.

"Yes, sir," Captain Foster replied, saluting. Dan returned the salute, then Captain Foster stepped back out into the rain.

"Catherine, I'm sorry about all this," Dan said. "My God, what you must've gone through."

"Dan, is this what the Union Army is doing? Are they making war on innocent women now?"

Dan pointed in the general direction of the building where the women were being held. "Catherine, be fair. Those women aren't all that innocent," he said. "Don't you understand? We have been so close so many times, only to have Quantrill slip through our fingers. And almost always it is because he knows where we are, what we are doing, and what our plans are. And how do you think he gets such information? He gets it from these women," Dan added, answering his own question.

"They can't all be guilty. Look at me. I was caught up with them, yet I haven't provided the bushwhackers with any information."

"But we don't know that, do we?"

Catherine blinked in surprise. "What . . . what do you mean?"

"You have been corresponding with Burke, haven't you? And while I'm certain you would never pupsely tell him anything, it is entirely possible that you may have inadvertently provided him with useful information."

"I'm sorry you have so little faith in my loyalty."

"Catherine, I don't have the slightest doubt as to your loyalty. That's why I went out on a limb to get you freed," Dan said. "I told the general that you'd been gathering information for me."

"Why did you tell him that? You know it isn't true."

"It was the only way I could explain to the general why you were there with the other women."

"But you didn't have to lie about why I was there, Dan. I wasn't there for any nefarious reason. I was there because I had been invited to a quilting bee."

"A quilting bee? For heaven's sake, Catherine, this is me you're talking to. I'm on your side, remember?"

"Are you?" Catherine shook her head. "I don't know that I want to be on the side of someone who could countenance such treatment of women as I have seen over the last eighteen hours."

"Why were you at the Maury farm that night, Catherine?"

"I told you. I was invited to a quilting bee."

"Stop that!" Dan snapped. "I won't be lied to, do you hear me? You went there to meet him, didn't you?"

"Him?"

"Burke. You went there to meet Burke."

There was a long beat of silence before Catherine spoke again, this time very quietly. "So that is what this is all about. You are jealous of him, aren't you?"

"Do I have a reason to be?"

"Dan, he is your friend, too. And he was your friend long before he was mine," Catherine replied, not directly answering his question. "If Burke was there—and I'm not saying that he was—do you think I could tell you? I can no more help you destroy him than I could help him destroy you."

Dan sighed, then ran his hand through his hair. He nodded at her. "Of course you are right," he finally admitted. "I won't ask any more questions. I'm just glad that I found out where you were, so I could get you out."

"I'm glad you understand. Now, what about the other women who are there? Is there anything you can do for them?"

Dan shook his head. "I'm sorry, there is nothing I can do. They are General Ewing's responsibility."

Suddenly there were several shouts and calls of alarm from outside. Whatever it was, it had the men so agitated that their raised voices could be heard even over the deafening timpani of the rain on the tent.

"What is it?" Catherine asked. "What's going on?"

"I don't know," Dan answered. He started toward the

tent opening, but before he got there Captain Foster stepped inside. Foster's face was ashen.

"Colonel," Foster said, "the building—" He stopped in midsentence, though his hands continued to gesture in the direction of the town.

"Well, what is it? Speak up, man, I can't read your hands!"

"The building, the one with the women," Foster said.

"What about it?"

"The rain," Captain Foster said. "The rain must've caused it. The building collapsed, sir."

"Collapsed?"

"It just fell in, right on top of the women. The whole thing just came tumbling down."

"My God!" Catherine said. "The women? What about the women?"

"We don't know about all of them," Foster said. "But it looks bad, very bad. They're trying to dig them out now."

"Any fatalities that we know of?" Dan asked.

Captain Foster nodded. "Five, so far," he answered.

"Marcie Caulder and Josephine Anderson," Catherine said. "Do you know anything about them?"

Captain Foster looked directly at her. "I'm sorry, Miss Darrow," he said. "They are two we do know about. I'm afraid that both of them are dead."

* * *

Twenty-two

Quantrill, using the butt of his pistol as a hammer, tacked one of the posters containing Ewing's General Order Number Ten to the wall of the little cabin on Blackwater Creek, where his group was bivouacked. After it was posted, he turned around to look at his men, and he pointed to the poster.

"There it is," he said with a snarl. "There is the proof that the Yankee bastards we are fighting against are nothing but hypocrites. They raise hell about our outlaw ways, but have we ever harmed any of their women or children?"

"No!" the men shouted.

"Did we ever round up all their women and put them in a deathtrap building, then collapse it on them?"

"No!"

"Well, by God, the Yankees did!" Quantrill shouted. He pointed to Bloody Bill Anderson, who was still grieving over the loss of his sister. "Ask Bill how he feels about the Yankees right now."

"I'll tell you how I feel," Anderson shouted back. "I feel like riding into Kansas City now and killing every-one!"

"We can't kill ever'one in Kansas City, Bill," Cole Younger said. "Some of us got kinfolk there. Not ever'one in Kansas City is a damn Yankee."

"No," Quantrill agreed. He smiled. "But everyone in Lawrence is."

"Where is Lawrence?"

"It's in Kansas, about forty miles on the other side of the border. It's got a nice, fat bank, several rich stores, and it is all Yankee. And get this," he added. "Lawrence is also the home of Jim Lane."

"Hell!" Anderson shouted. "Let's do it!"

With Anderson's enthusiastic support, the others cheered loudly. Smiling, Quantrill turned and aimed his pistol at the poster. He pulled the trigger, and a small black hole appeared in the zero of the number ten.

"Yahoo!" Jesse James shouted, and he shot at the poster as well. That opened up a fusillade of shooting, and for the next few minutes it sounded as if a battle were under way as the raiders, whooping and hollering, banged away at the poster, which was by now nothing but a ragged and un-readable piece of paper.

The long line of horsemen, riding in columns of four, snaked its way across the Kansas plains under a star-filled but moonless night sky. Burke was riding near the head of the column, and occasionally he would turn to look at the column following along behind him. What he saw looked like a monstrous snake, creeping down upon its prey.

Burke had no idea whether Catherine Darrow was dead or alive. He knew only that she had been captured with the rest of the women that night at the Maury farm. The raiders hadn't actually run away that night. They had merely moved into ambush positions, intending to attack the Union soldiers as they returned to Kansas City. They had no idea that the soldiers would be putting the women in wagons and taking them back into town, and when they discovered that, they canceled their attack for fear that some of the women might be hurt.

In retrospect, Burke was absolutely certain that they should have attacked. Maybe some of the women would've been hurt, maybe even killed. The only difference between that and what actually happened was that the women wound up getting hurt anyway, and not one Yankee was held accountable.

It was just before dawn when Quantrill held up his hand, stopping the long column on the top of a hill, about a quarter of a mile out of town. They sat quietly for a moment, studying their objective. Here and there, in the little town before them, golden patches of light shone from the dark houses, indicating those who were early risers. The smell of frying bacon drifted up the hill, toward the men.

Some roosters crowed.

They could hear the high-pitched yap of a dog.

A door slammed, and they saw a man walking toward the outhouse, carrying a newspaper with him.

A mule brayed.

"I don't know, chief," someone said.

"You don't know what?" Quantrill replied without looking back. He had not taken his eyes off the town from the moment they had arrived.

"We been on the trail for two days now. Could be someone seen us, and sent word back to these folks that we're comin'. They could be a-waitin' for us."

"Does it look like they're waiting for us?" Quantrill asked.

"No, but if it was a trap, if they was plannin' an ambush, they wouldn't be dumb enough to let us see 'em."

"Well, you can do as you please," Quantrill said. "I am going into Lawrence."

He then drew one of the four revolvers he carried in his belt, spurred his horse into a gallop, and started down the hill. "Charge!" he shouted at the top of his voice.

Quantrill's abrupt move galvanized the others into action, and as one, the entire column, even the rider who had urged caution, thundered down the hill and onto the main street of Lawrence.

"Kill! Kill!" Quantrill was shouting as the horses

pounded into town. "Lawrence must be cleansed, and the only way to cleanse it is to kill! Kill!"

At the house nearest the extreme edge of the town, Pastor Snyder had just put his three-legged milking stool down alongside his cow. He slid the bucket into place, then grabbed the cow's teats and started to milk. Startled by the sudden appearance of a column of men, he looked up. But even before his mind could formulate a question as to what this was, a bullet crashed into his brain and he fell dead.

The raiders thundered on into Lawrence, firing their guns and screeching the word "Osceola!" which they had adopted as their own peculiar battle cry. More than a dozen men of the town, wondering what was going on, stepped into the front doors of their homes to look outside. When they did so they were shot down, not by one bullet, but by fifteen or twenty bullets.

A detachment of twenty-two Union soldiers, recruits awaiting orders to join the army in the east, had pitched their tents in the street, right in the middle of town. They had never been any closer to the war than the thrilling stories they read in the newspapers, and, drowsily, they were just beginning to crawl out of their tents when Quantrill and his men arrived.

Totally unsuspecting of any enemy activity this far away from the center of the war, they watched the galloping riders with excitement, thinking it was a detachment of their own cavalry.

"Soldiers! Kill them! Kill them!"

Several of the riders broke free of the column, then started toward the just wakened soldiers. When they realized that the wild-eyed riders coming toward them had hostile intent, the young recruits, some of them still dressed in the long johns they had slept in, turned and tried to run. Some were clubbed down, some were killed by saber thrusts, some were shot, and others were trampled under the pounding hooves of the horses. Only five recruits from the entire bunch managed to get away.

When they reached the front of the Lawrence Hotel, which was the most imposing building in town, Quantrill held up his hand, signaling a halt.

"All right, men, you know what you have to do. Your first order is to find Jim Lane. Find him and bring him to me. But I want him alive, do you hear me? We're going to take that son of a bitch back to Missouri for a public execution. Captain Phillips, you come with me," he ordered, and dismounted. He and Burke together headed for the hotel restaurant.

"What is this?" a frightened, well-dressed man asked, running to the front door as Quantrill and his officers, including Burke, came in. "What's going on?"

"Are you in charge here?"

"Yes. I am the concierge," the man answered, pulling himself up proudly.

Quantrill sniggered, then looked over at Burke. "He is the concierge," he said, pointing to the civilian with his thumb.

"Who are you?" the concierge blustered.

"I am Colonel Quantrill of the Confederate Army," Quantrill said. "This is one of my officers, Captain Burke Phillips."

The concierge gasped and turned pale. "My God! Quantrill!"

"It looks like he's heard of us," Quantrill said to Burke. Then, to the concierge, he said, "I want you to bring breakfast to us."

"Ye . . . yes, sir," the concierge stammered. "What do you want?"

"Eggs, pancakes, bacon, sausage, ham, whatever you have, we want the best and we want plenty of it!" Quantrill ordered with an impatient wave of his hand.

"What about our men?" Burke asked.

"Oh, I'm sure the hotel hasn't enough to feed them all," Quantrill replied. "Bill," he called back through the door.

"Yes, Charley?" Anderson said. He had dismounted and was standing on the wooden porch in front of the hotel.

"Tell the men that they are on their own for breakfast. Get it from the citizens of town. If anyone refuses, kill them. Then I want you to bring in everything of value: money, jewels, anything we can carry with us. Bring it all to me. After we've cleaned everyone out, burn the town."

"Colonel Quantrill, is it really necessary to burn the town?" Burke asked.

"Yes. From now on, whenever someone says the name 'Quantrill,' I want them to say it with fear."

"You don't think the people are just going to stand around and let you burn their town, do you?"

"Good point," Quantrill said. He walked back outside to Anderson, who had remounted. Anderson leaned down from his saddle to talk to Quantrill. Burke couldn't hear the conversation.

"I told Bill about your concern. He's going to take care of it."

By the time Quantrill and Burke reached a table in the dining room, waiters were already beginning to bring out the breakfast. Two large platters, one containing fried eggs and bacon and another filled with steaming biscuits, were put in the center of the table. Quantrill filled his plate, then offered the platter to Burke.

"I really should be outside with the others," Burke said.

Quantrill shook his head. "This is our war, not yours."

"What do you mean, your war, not mine?"

"You are a regular officer. This is guerrilla fighting. I figure to keep you out of it. It's better for you that way."

"Keep me out of it? How do you plan to do that? Hell, you've already introduced me to the concierge. He knows my name. When the report of this gets out, no one is going to think of me as a regular anymore."

Quantrill smiled. "You won't have a problem," he said.

"What do you mean, I won't have a problem? I told you, the concierge knows my name! Up until now, I've managed to keep my name out of the papers. That's not possible now."

"I told you, you won't have a problem."

Outside, the early morning street still echoed with the sound of gunshots, and Burke could hear, in addition to curses of anger from the men, the screams and cries of women and children.

"The men aren't harming the women, are they?" Burke asked.

Quantrill shook his head. A yellow stream of egg yolk ran down his chin. "I gave them strict orders," he said. "Not one hair on one woman's head is to be harmed. You don't have to worry any about that. Unlike the Yankee sons of bitches, we aren't heathens."

"Nevertheless, I should be out there keeping an eye on things for you," Burke said, getting up from the table.

"No, they don't need you out there. Bill Anderson is handling things. You stay in here with me," Quantrill said. "I told them to bring the treasure of the town in here, and I need someone I can trust standing guard for me."

Burke hesitated for a moment, then, with a nod, he sat back down.

"Have some more bacon," Quantrill offered.

"Thank you, but I'm stuffed," Burke said. "I can't eat another bite."

Quantrill laughed. "I'm full, too," he said. "But it's not that often we get to eat like this, so I figure I'd better take advantage of it while I can." He opened a biscuit and covered it with a generous portion of butter and honey.

Half an hour later the first of the town's booty began coming in. There were money boxes, jewelry cases, watches, and rings. Quantrill, who had finally finished eating, now cleaned off the table by the simple expedient of pushing everything—dishes, uneaten food, and half-full coffee cups—onto the floor.

"The concierge isn't going to like that," Burke said. He looked around. "I wonder where he is, anyway? I haven't seen him in a while."

"We've been fed, we don't need him anymore," Quantrill answered. "Besides, I told you, you don't need to be worrying about him. He isn't a problem."

"I guess not, or he would've already been in here, raising hell about the mess," Burke agreed. He nodded toward the growing pile of treasure. "Looks like we're getting quite a haul."

"Yeah, let's just take a look at the 'tax' we collected," Quantrill said with a mocking laugh. And, using the table as a desk, he began to take inventory of the spoils.

"Look at it, Burke!" he said. He scooped his hands through the pile of small jewelry and gold coins, then lifted them, palms up, to let the gold, sparkling in the morning light spill through his fingers like water. "Did I tell you this was a good idea? Some of you didn't believe me."

Anderson came into the restaurant then. There was blood on his shirt and face, and he smelled of smoke. His eyes blazed wildly.

"We just got word that some Federal troops are on the way here," he said.

"All right, get Lane and let's go."

"The son of a bitch got away from us," Anderson said. "He's not in his house! He's nowhere to be found!"

Quantrill stood up so quickly that the chair turned over behind him. "Dammit, Bill! Seems to me like I gave you an easy enough job. All in the hell you had to do was find one old man and bring him to me."

"Yeah, well, he's a cagey bastard. He changed the nameplate on the outside of his house so we couldn't find it right away. And by the time we did find it, he was gone. I'm not magic, Charley! I can't make someone appear out of thin air."

Quantrill looked at his watch for a moment, then snapped it shut. "All right, it's half-past eight. We've been here long enough, especially if troops are coming. Pull all the men back in. That is, if it's not too big of a job for you to handle," he added sarcastically. "Then have the boys load up as much food as they can, and let's get out of here. The soldiers will be coming soon."

"Why are we running? Hell, Charley, we've got nearly four hundred men here now. That's the biggest our outfit's ever been. Why don't we just wait for the soldiers and ambush them?" Anderson suggested.

"Why would we want to do a damn fool thing like that? We've done what we set out to do," Quantrill answered. "We should leave while we are ahead."

"Colonel, I agree with Bill," Burke said. "If we could defeat a regular Union army unit here, in Kansas, it would legitimize our raid."

"Legitimize? I don't want to be legitimized. Don't you understand yet, Burke? If we are legitimate, we have to follow all the rules of war. And if we were following the rules of war, we wouldn't get to keep any of this." Quantrill pointed to the table.

"Then think of the trouble we could cause for the Yankees by defeating some of their regulars. It would force them to move some of the war into Kansas, and they would have to bring in fresh troops from Missouri and Arkansas to handle it. That would relieve some of the pressure on General Price and General Van Dorn."

"Yeah, well, Price and Van Dorn have their war to fight," Quantrill said as he started stuffing money into his pockets, ''and I have mine. Now, pick up the rest of this, and let's get out of here.''

Without waiting for them to follow him, Quantrill swaggered across the floor, then out the door. Burke and Bill Anderson were left standing in the restaurant.

''I've had about all I can stomach of Mr. Quantrill,'' Anderson said as he started scooping money and jewelry into a big cloth bag he took from his belt. ''I'm thinkin' about pullin' out an' startin' my own company.'' He held up the bag he had just filled. ''And this is enough to get me started. Why don't you come with me, Burke? As my second in command?''

''I have to think about it,'' Burke said. He started looking around the hotel.

''What are you looking for?''

''The concierge.''

''The what?''

''The hotel manager,'' Burke said. ''I don't know where he got off to.''

''Hell, he didn't get off to nowhere,'' Anderson replied. ''He's lyin' out there in the street with the others.''

''The others?''

''While you an' Charley was in here, me an' the rest of the boys was carryin' out Charley's orders.''

''What were his orders?'' Burke asked. He was beginning to have a queasy feeling in the pit of his stomach.

''We was told to kill every man big enough to carry a gun, and by God, that's just what we done,'' Anderson said easily.

''You did what?''

Anderson chuckled. ''Charley said you wouldn't approve. That's why he had you stay inside with him whilst we was carryin' out his orders.''

Burke moved quickly through the front door, then he stopped and, made dizzy with what he was seeing, put his hand on the porch pillar for a moment to support himself. The street was filled with smoke and flying ash, because more than three-fourths of the buildings, both commercial and private, were burning fiercely. Scores of bodies lay sprawled in the street, most of them shot more than once.

Burke left the front porch and walked into the street among the dead. He had seen the dead after Shiloh, and he thought the experience had inured him. But the men at Shiloh had been soldiers, and they had died soldiers' deaths in a battle that pitted armed men against armed men.

The dead here had not been killed in battle. They had been murdered. Among the victims were boys, some as young as nine or ten, and the old, one or two of whom Burke was sure were eighty or more.

And, standing in the street, crying bitter tears over their loved ones, were the women of the town. By Quantrill's orders they had not been physically injured. Burke knew, however, that the pain inflicted upon these women's souls would never diminish.

Burke saw the concierge, and he went over to look down upon the man who, but a short time ago, had served him his breakfast.

"What did I tell you, Captain?" Quantrill asked. He was already mounted, and he rode over by Burke. "I told you you didn't have a problem with this Yankee knowing your name."

"No, I guess not," Burke replied quietly. He could feel the heart-chilling loathing in the stares of the women nearby. His soul detached itself from his body and moved over to be at one with these grieving and accusing women. Burke wanted to tell them that he was sorry, that he hadn't known about this, and that he didn't approve. He wanted to tell them that he was innocent and didn't deserve their hate.

But he couldn't tell them, because he knew it would be a lie. He had been with Quantrill for three years now, and he knew well what kind of man Quantrill was. What did he expect would happen when four hundred armed men descended on a defenseless town?

In the final analysis, there was no one in town who grieved more, nor was there anyone in town who was more condemning, than Burke. The only difference was that the object of Burke's condemnation was himself.

"You going with us, Captain?" Quantrill asked.

By then Burke realized that he was the only one not yet mounted.

"Or do you want to hang around here and let these 'ladies' tear you apart?" Anderson asked, smiling, as he brought Burke's horse to him.

"If my staying here and allowing them to do that would be the propitiation of all the South's sins, I would gladly do so," Burke said. He sighed, then took his reins from Anderson and mounted. "But I know that it would not."

"Let's go," Quantrill said, and the four hundred men left town the same way they had entered it—at a gallop.

Burke stopped when they reached the top of a hill about a mile out of town and looked back toward the town. The smoke from over one hundred burning buildings gathered into one huge column of black to boil and surge into the sky. Even from here Burke could hear the wailing sobs of the grieving wives, mothers, and daughters of the slain.

Jesse James came over beside him. "You goin' to stay here all day?" he asked.

"Can you hear it, Jesse?" Burke asked.

Jesse looked confused. "Can I hear what?"

"The sounds from the town."

Jesse shook his head. "It's too far away. You can't hear anything from out here."

"Maybe that's why I can hear it."

Jesse laughed. "You ain't makin' no sense, Burke," he said.

But Burke was making plenty of sense to himself. He knew that the reason he could hear the wailing sobs of the town was because he'd left his soul there.

★ ★ ★

Twenty-three

Near Fayette, Missouri, October 4th, 1864

Dear Catherine,

I am no longer with Quantrill. He and Bill Anderson had a parting of the ways and Anderson formed his own company. Along with Jesse and Frank James, the Younger brothers, and Archie Clement, I have chosen to ride with Anderson. I believe that was the final step in my descent into hell.

No longer am I the soldier who, guided by honor, chose between loyalty to the Nation I once swore to defend, and to the State which nurtured me. I am not worthy to have the word "honor" uttered in the same breath, nor inscribed on the same page, as my name.

I am not entirely certain of how, or even when, this happened to me. I know only this. The man with whom you so generously shared your box lunch at that social, oh so long ago, no longer exists.

I told you how, at Shiloh, Dan and I met on the ground hallowed by the blood of so many brave young men. Dan and I met there as friends, equals, and soldiers. But we must never meet again, for I am no longer worthy of his respect, let alone his friendship. If we meet again, I must kill him . . . or he must kill me.

How easily comes the thought of killing someone who was once my friend. That is because in my present incarnation I can kill without remorse or compunction.

Let me tell you a story to illustrate this point, though I am sure you have read about it in your newspapers.

On the evening of the 26th ultimate, Anderson and a group of 30 of his men rode into Centralia, Missouri. When they reached the depot they found a barrel of whiskey and a crate of boots. Thinking it would be great sport to do so, they poured whiskey into the boots, then made several of the townspeople drink. Of course, they weren't going to let all that whiskey go to waste, so they drank quite a bit of it themselves, then they looted the town and set the depot on fire.

A train arrived at about that time, and though the engineer wanted to continue on, he was forced to stop because flaming railroad ties had been laid across the track. Anderson and the others boarded the train and ordered all the passengers off. Twenty-five of the passengers were unarmed but uniformed Union soldiers, who were going home on furlough. They were wearing the same uniform I once wore. They were privates, just like the ones I used to command. They were patriots who were serving their country with dignity and honor. Anderson had them stripped naked, publicly humiliated, then murdered, as they stood shivering on the depot platform.

I was not in Centralia, but I must say in all candidness that even if I had been there, I could have done nothing to prevent what happened.

I am ashamed to say that I did take part in what happened next. A detail of 135 soldiers came after Anderson. Because only 30 had taken part in the Centralia raid, the Union commander must've felt secure in his numbers. What he didn't realize was that we had over 300 men waiting for them. When they came over the rise and saw what they had ridden into, their commander made a foolish and fatal decision. He ordered his men to dismount and form a skirmish line, to fight on foot. The Yankees were outnumbered nearly three to one, and their weapons were single-shot muskets, whereas we were armed with revolvers and repeating carbines.

There was no contest. Within minutes, we had killed every one of them. But slaughtering them wasn't enough for some of the more debased of our men. Many of the Bushwhackers went crazy, scalp-

ing and mutilating the bodies of those brave, but fool-
ishly led soldiers. The sight of human vultures
moving from one body to another to visit their fiend-
ish atrocities upon them sickened me . . . but I made
no effort to stop them.

I don't know why I am confessing this to you,
Catherine. Certainly it is not for absolution, because
it is far too late for the redemption of my soul.

Yours in shame,
Burke Phillips

Dan Morris looked through a pair of binoculars at the approaching horsemen. He counted forty, and though he may
have missed a few, he knew that he couldn't have missed
many. Behind him were one hundred and ten men, not
green recruits but seasoned cavalrymen. Some had fought
at Wilson's Creek, some at Shiloh, some at Antietam, and
a few at Gettysburg. They were tough, skilled veterans
whose primary purpose was to extract revenge from the
ones who had massacred and mutilated the men of the
Thirty-ninth Missouri.

Dan put away the glasses, then rode back down the hill
to where Captain Harris was waiting.

"Did you see them, Colonel?" Harris asked.

"Yes. It's Bloody Bill Anderson, there is no doubt about
it."

Captain Harris turned in his saddle and held up his right
arm, fist clenched. That was the signal to the others that
Anderson had been spotted, and so well disciplined were
these soldiers that instead of breaking out into a cheer, as
the more inexperienced would do, a cheer that Anderson
might have heard, these soldiers just nodded and stared
ahead with grim determination. Hunting down and killing
Bloody Bill Anderson was no game to them; it was deadly
serious business. They had faced men like Beauregard,
Polk, Longstreet, Jackson, and Lee: the best the Confederacy had to offer. They weren't about to be intimidated
by a guerrilla chieftain, no matter how infamous he might
be.

"What are your orders, sir?" Captain Harris asked.

"We'll form up just below the crest of the hill in two
equal skirmish lines," Dan said. "I'll lead the first line,

you take the second. Leave the carbines in the scabbard. We'll use pistols only.''

''Yes, sir,'' Harris replied.

''Get the men in position,'' Dan ordered.

Captain Harris's quietly given orders were picked up and transmitted down the line by the sergeants and corporals until, a moment later, they were formed in columns of twos.

''By the right, face!''

The two columns turned to the right.

''First rank, forward,'' Dan said, and when the line moved forward, he positioned himself in front. Captain Harris took up his position in front of the second rank.

''Draw pistols.''

As one, the men drew their pistols, then held them, barrels pointing up, elbows bent at a ninety-degree angle.

''Forward at a walk.''

Slowly the two lines advanced up the hill to just below its crest, and there, Dan halted them.

The men waited in silence, listening to the clopping, creaking, jangling sounds of the approaching riders.

''Hey, Bill,'' Dan heard one of the Rebels say, his voice sounding curiously close in the still, cool October air, ''they got'ny whiskey in Richmond? We ain't had no whiskey since . . . when's the last time we had any whiskey, Frank?''

''Centralia. We had whiskey in Centralia.''

''Well, yeah, hell, but that don't count. Little Archie give half of it away to the townfolks.''

There was more casual conversation from the guerrillas, graphic indication that they had no idea anyone was waiting in ambush for them.

Dan waited a few moments longer, until he was sure they must be very near the top of the hill, just on the other side. Then he raised his pistol over his head.

''Now!'' he shouted, spurring his horse forward. He was followed immediately by the two lines of riders who made up his detachment.

The Union soldiers broke over the crest, then rolled down the other side in a full-blown charge against the approaching and unsuspecting Rebels.

''What the hell?'' Archie Clement shouted, seeing two

long lines of well-disciplined soldiers coming toward them. "Where'd them Yankees come from?"

Bloody Bill Anderson didn't give it a second thought. Pulling his pistol, he stood in his stirrups, then looked back over his shoulder.

"Charge!" he yelled at the top of his voice as he spurred his horse forward.

"Bill, no! We can't charge in column, we'll be flanked!" Burke shouted.

Anderson paid no attention to Burke's warning. He had called for a charge, and he was leading the way. Neither did any of the other raiders hold back. They had been a party to Anderson's charges before, and those charges had always produced victory.

Burke went along as well, but he tried to salvage the situation as best he could. "Form a skirmish line!" he shouted desperately. "Form a—"

Burke felt a sharp pain in his side, then a numbing blow to his shoulder. That was followed by a bang on the head, then nothing. . . .

"They got 'im! They killed Bloody Bill Anderson!" a rider said, galloping through the streets of Independence. "Turn out! Turn out! Anderson! Bloody Bill Anderson and his gang is all lyin' dead at the depot! Turn out and have a look!"

Catherine was just leaving the school building as the rider, a young boy of about fifteen and a former student of hers, rode by.

"Glen!" Catherine called. "Glen, wait!"

Glen pulled up, then turned his horse and trotted back toward Catherine. He took off his hat. "Afternoon, Miss Darrow," he said.

"What were you shouting, just now?"

"I'm tellin' folks about Bloody Bill Anderson," Glen said. "He got hisself kilt today. Him and near 'bout his whole gang got wiped out. The army's got all their bodies lyin' out on the platform down at the depot."

Catherine clutched at the neck of her dress. "Here?" she asked. "They brought the bodies here?"

"Yes, ma'am," Glen said. "The army put 'em out down there, and is askin' the townfolk to come identify 'em. They ain't no doubt about Anderson, they's done been half a dozen or so identified him. It's the other ones they're wantin' identified.'' Glen put his hat back on. "Ma'am, I got to get on with my business. The sheriff give me a dollar to get folks to go down there an' have a look. You ought to go down there, too, Miss Darrow. It's quite a sight to see.''

Glen turned his horse then and spurred it into a gallop.

"Turn out! Turn out! Anderson! Bloody Bill Anderson and his gang, lyin' dead at the depot! Go have a look!''

The last thing Catherine wanted to do was go down to the depot to look at dead men. But she had to know if Burke was among them.

Glen had done his job well. More than half the town had turned out, and quite a crowd was gathered around the depot platform. They were talking quietly, as if they were in a funeral parlor, and in a way they were. Two or three of the women were sobbing quietly. The fact that so few were reacting in such a way was testimony to the thoroughness with which the Union Army had carried out General Ewing's orders to expel all known female relatives and associates of the guerrillas.

Most of the attention seemed to be around one man who was lying a little apart from the others.

"That's him all right," a man was saying. "That's Bloody Bill Anderson.''

Holding a handkerchief to her nose and mouth, Catherine stepped up to have a look at Anderson's body. He was lying on his back with his arms folded across his stomach. His right hand was clutching a revolver. A second revolver was in his right holster, butt forward. His hat, with its brim pinned up and decorated by a large, gold-cloth star, lay on his thigh. His vest was pulled back to show his embroidered shirt. His mouth was clamped in a death clench, one eye had drifted slightly open, and his long black hair was fanned out around him.

"We 'bout got 'em all identified now," someone said. " 'Cept that one down at the end.''

"Ain't he that feller used to work at the livery stable?''

Burke had worked at a livery stable, Catherine recalled. Gasping, she moved down the line toward the man in question. She stopped a few feet away and looked at the body, one foot turned out unnaturally. Steeling herself, she stepped up for a close look.

It wasn't Burke.

"Is this all of 'em?" someone asked.

"It is, 'less someone crawled off into the grass and died," another answered.

Catherine turned away from the depot and started walking back down the street toward her house. She had ambivalent feelings about what she had just gone through. She was glad Burke was not lying down there on the depot platform, but she worried that he might be back on the battlefield, perhaps still alive, slowly dying under a bush somewhere. If that were the case, he would be better off lying at the railroad station.

When Catherine reached her house she saw a cavalry horse tied up out front. Dan Morris was sitting on the top step of her front porch, waiting for her, and he stood as she started up the walk.

"Have you been down to the depot?" Dan asked.

"Yes."

"Figured you probably had. I wanted to save you from having to go through all that. Burke wasn't one of them."

Catherine nodded. "Yes, I saw that."

"You know, don't you, that it's only a matter of time until he is lying out there like those men?"

"I know," Catherine said.

"Whatever is his fate, Catherine, he brought it on himself. And though I pray it won't be me, if I ever come face-to-face with him, I won't hesitate to do my duty."

"I understand," Catherine said. "You must do what you must do."

"Surely the war cannot last much longer," Dan said. "The South is being defeated at every turn; they are running out of money, matériel, and men. All they are doing now is holding on until after the election, hoping McClellan defeats Lincoln, and they'll get a better peace settlement from him."

"Will they?"

Dan shook his head. "No. In the first place, McClellan won't be elected. And even if he is, he won't give the South what they want, which is recognition."

"So many have suffered for so long," Catherine said. "God grant that it end soon."

"Well, I must be going now," Dan said, starting down the steps. He stopped on the bottom step and looked back up at her. "Catherine, are you still involved in your, uh, Railroad activity?"

"Yes."

"Why do you continue to take the risk? Lincoln freed the slaves."

Catherine shook her head. "No, he didn't. A bitter irony of the Emancipation Proclamation is that it only freed the slaves in the rebellious states. Officially, Missouri remained loyal, so the slaves in this state have not been freed."

"Half of Missouri is loyal, half is disloyal. Maybe they should free half the slaves," Dan suggested with a chuckle.

"Dan, it's no laughing matter to the poor people who are caught up in this."

"No, I suppose not," Dan said. "And I won't tell you to stop. But I will tell you to be careful."

"You be careful as well," Catherine said. She watched as Dan walked back out to his horse, mounted, then gave her a half wave before he rode off. She had just turned to go up the steps and into her house when she heard a hissing noise.

"Psssst!"

Curious, she stopped and looked around.

"Pssst! Miss Darrow!" The voice, a harsh whisper, was coming from behind the shrubbery of winged euonymus.

"Who is it?" Catherine called, looking toward the red bush. "Who is there?"

"Is there anyone lookin'?" the voice whispered.

"Who is it? Show yourself."

"Don't want to get caught." This time the words were spoken in a normal but quiet voice. There was a rustle in the crimson leaves, then someone stepped out. Catherine looked closely, then she gasped.

"You're Jesse James, aren't you?" she asked. "I met you at the party at the Maury farm."

"Yes'm. I'm Jesse James. You might remember, I was Burke's friend."

"Was?" Catherine said with a catch in her throat. "Oh, do you mean he's . . ."

"He's here, ma'am. With me," Jesse said. "I thought it best to lie low 'til that Yankee left."

"Where is he?"

"Here, behind the bushes," Jesse said. "He's hurt pretty bad. I didn't know where else to take him."

Looking around to make certain no one was watching, Catherine stepped into the fire-red leaves, then looked behind them. There, sitting on the ground and leaning back against the latticework around the bottom of the porch, was an ashen-faced Burke. A bloody bandage was around his head, there was a mass of coagulated blood on his shoulder, and he was holding his hand over his side. Blood had spilled through his fingers and dried on his hands and on the skirt of his jacket.

Burke tried to smile. "Hello, Catherine," he said.

"Burke, my God! You're wounded!"

"Am I?" Burke asked. He pulled his hand away and looked at it. "So that's where all this blood came from," he said, trying to make a joke of the situation.

"Miss Darrow, I have to go now," Jesse James said.

"What? No, you can't just leave him here like this."

"Can't take him with me," Jesse said. "This is the only place I could think of. My brother and my cousins wanted me to just finish 'im off, but me an' him been friends a long time now. I couldn't do that."

"But what am I to do with him?"

"That's up to you, Miss Darrow. He ain't in my hands no more. You can take care of him, or you can take him to a Yankee doctor," Jesse said. "Only thing is, if you take him to a Yankee doctor, they'll get him fixed up, then they'll hang 'im."

"No, you were right to bring him here. I'll take care of him. How long have you . . ." Catherine turned, then stopped in midsentence. She didn't finish the question, because there was no longer anyone to hear it. Jesse James was gone.

The candles cast a soft, wavering light on the brick walls of the cellar beneath Catherine's house. Burke was lying on a hard canvas cot, naked except for a towel that lay across his groin. There was a small black hole in his shoulder and another in his side. All of the dried blood had been washed away, and now, as Catherine stood by, watching anxiously, Thelma began digging for the bullet in his thigh. The one from his shoulder was already sitting in the bottom of a shallow pan of water, from which rose tiny bubbles of red spiraling up to the water's surface.

"Here it is," Thelma said after a few more moments of digging. She dropped this bullet into the pan with the other one. "It didn't hit anything vital," she added.

"Thank God," Catherine said. She leaned over and looked into Burke's face. His eyes were closed.

"He passed out a while ago," Thelma noted.

"Pain?"

Thelma shook her head. "No, I don't think so. I think he is just weak from losing so much blood. He's bled an awful lot."

Thelma washed her hands, then looked down at Burke. This was the same "hospital" area she had been using for the past five years to treat the "passengers" of Catherine's Underground Railroad. Now she was treating someone who belonged to a band of men who had, over the years, been the very people her patients had been running from.

"Will he be all right, Thelma?"

"I wish I could answer that question for you, Miss Catherine," she said. "It's a funny thing, losing so much blood. Sometimes a body just bounces back, real quick. And sometimes it don't seem to ever get over it. Especially if a lot of blood has been lost." Thelma shook her head. "And this poor soul has lost lots of blood."

"Is there anything you can do for him?"

"The best thing we can do for him now, I guess, is just watch him for a while. Miss Catherine, this man is a bush-whacker, isn't he?"

"Yes," Catherine said, nodding.

"If the Yankee soldiers caught him down here, you would be sent away, wouldn't you?"

Again Catherine nodded. "I'm afraid so," she said.

"Then, if you don't mind my askin', what are you doing putting yourself in danger because of a no-'count man like this?"

"You don't understand, Thelma. He's not like that."

"He isn't? Didn't he just get himself shot for ridin' with Bloody Bill Anderson?"

"Yes, but he isn't like the rest of them, I know he isn't. At heart, he is a good man."

"He is also nearly a dead man," Thelma said bluntly.

It was several hours later, early in the morning, when Thelma came into Catherine's bedroom to wake her.

"What is it?" Catherine asked, sitting up.

"Your friend is dying."

"Is he still conscious?" Catherine asked, reaching for her robe.

"Yes, ma'am, but just barely," Thelma said. "If you want to say good-bye to him, I reckon you'd better get down there and do it now."

Following Thelma, who was carrying a kerosene lantern, Catherine hurried down the stairs, then down into the cellar. She saw Burke lying very still on the cot, his face a grayish blue. She went over to him and took his hand. He opened his eyes and looked at her.

"Thank God, he's still alive," Catherine said. "Burke? Burke, can you hear me?"

Burke moved his lips, and Catherine bent down to listen to him.

"I should have died . . . in the field," he whispered. "Not right to come here like this. Not right to put you in danger."

"You let me worry about that," Catherine said. She looked at Thelma. "Isn't there anything you can do?"

"There's something I could try," Thelma said. "I read about it once, in a book your papa had. I don't know if it will help, though. Nobody knows why, but according to the book, sometimes it works, while other times it just makes things worse, so most doctors never use it."

"Oh, please, try it!" Catherine begged. "Whatever it is, try it."

"It is very dangerous."

"Maybe so, but what other choice is there?"

"None," Thelma agreed, then she called out to her husband. "Willie, bring another cot over here and put it down next to this one."

"What are you going to do?" Catherine asked.

"When someone loses a lot of blood, you can put some back by taking it from another person. It is called a 'blood transfusion,' and several have been performed in Europe, and one or two in America. In some cases transfusions have restored the near dead to life. But, as I said, they don't always work. In many cases, shortly after the new blood is put in, the patient suffers a seizure of some sort, then dies almost immediately. No one knows why this is.''

"Where will you get the blood?" Catherine asked.

"We will get it from Willie," Thelma offered. She looked up and smiled. "I hope this fine Southern gentleman appreciates the irony of having a colored man's blood in his veins. Especially if he survives."

"Is there any danger for Willie?"

Thelma shook her head. "No, there is never any danger to the blood donor. All the danger seems to be to the person getting the blood."

Willie came back with the cot at that moment, and Thelma directed that he put it alongside Burke, then lie on it. After that she pulled up Willie's sleeve, then took his dark black arm and put it alongside Willie's pale white arm.

"I need something to tie their arms together," Thelma said.

Catherine located a couple of pieces of twine, while Thelma took a long goose quill, stripped the feathers, then blew through it to make certain it was clear on the inside.

"We need a tube to transfer the blood," she explained, holding up the quill. "And this will work."

After the two arms were tied together, Thelma made an incision in each arm, then inserted the denuded quill. She began pushing down on Willie's arm. Catherine saw the dark red blood come up through the quill, then flow into Burke's arm. Thelma "pumped" the blood for several moments, then she pulled out the quill and untied the cord.

After she was finished, Willie sat up, bending his arm and holding a small bandage over the wound.

"What now?" Catherine asked.

"Now, we wait," Thelma answered. "And pray."

★★★

Twenty-four

Burke opened his eyes.

"Mama, the white man be awake now," a child's voice said.

Turning his head, Burke saw a young black boy of no more than six or seven standing by the cot, looking directly at him.

"Hello," Burke said.

The boy turned and ran away, and Burke raised up onto his elbows to look around. He didn't know where he was, how long he had been here, or even how he'd gotten here.

Then he remembered the fight, how Anderson had charged a battle line in column. They had been flanked and gunned down, Anderson being one of the first to fall.

Burke remembered being hit, then nothing after that until, later, he seemed to recall being put on a horse and led by Jesse James. That was twice now that Jesse James had taken a personal interest in bringing him to safety.

"Miss Thelma, Miss Thelma, the white man be awake," Burke heard a woman's voice call.

A moment later Burke saw a black woman he recognized. "I know you," he said.

"Do you? Well, that's a good sign," Thelma said. "Although the pistol ball only creased your head, you sustained quite a blow. I was afraid it might have left you insensible."

"Wait a minute," Burke said, confused by Thelma's speech. "Maybe I don't know you."

"Oh, yes suh, Mista Burke, yo' knows me all right. I be Miz Catherine's colored girl, Thelma," Thelma said, affecting a strong accent.

"Now I am confused," Burke said.

Thelma laughed. "Don't be," she said. "Sometimes we 'colored folk' have to talk the way white folks expect us to talk. It's a matter of survival."

"I think I see," Burke said. He looked around. "Thelma, would you mind telling me where I am?"

"You are in Miss Catherine's Underground Railroad depot," Thelma said.

Burke sat up quickly, and when he did, his head began to spin. He put his hand to his head for a moment, then looked out into the dark shadows of the cellar. He saw the same boy he had seen when first he'd awakened. He also saw a little girl and an adult man and woman, all black.

"Underground Railroad?" Burke said. "You mean, smuggling slaves?"

"Yes, sir, that's what I mean."

"Where is this depot?"

"It's in the cellar of Miss Catherine's house," Thelma replied.

"Catherine Darrow smuggling slaves?" Burke chuckled. "And all this time I thought I was the only one taking risks." He looked down at his side and saw a small bandage. When he touched it, he felt how sore and tender he was there, but obviously he was on the mend. He looked back up at Thelma. "You did this, didn't you? I remember."

"Yes."

"You have my thanks, Thelma," Burke said. "But I sure never would've thought I would find myself in the same boat as fugitive slaves."

"Why not?" Thelma asked. "You're just like they are."

Burke chuckled. "I guess maybe you are right at that," he said. "They're fugitives, and I'm a fugitive."

Now it was Thelma's time to laugh. "Oh, you're more like them than just being a fugitive," she said. "You are one of us now. *Really* one of us."

Burke was confused. "What do you mean, *really* one of you?"

Before Thelma could answer, Catherine arrived. She came over to the cot to look at him. "How are you feeling?"

"Fine," Burke said. "I feel fine."

"We've been awfully worried about you," Catherine said. "You've been in and out of it for the last two weeks. We didn't know if you were going to live or die."

"Two weeks? I've been here two weeks?"

"Two weeks and three days, to be exact. Do you remember none of it?"

"I don't know," Burke replied. "I think I do, but it's all sort of dim, like a hard-to-remember dream." He looked at Thelma. "I do remember you working on me," he said. He looked over at the black family. "And I remember when you arrived and . . . there was another group before them, wasn't there?"

"Yes."

"And I seem to remember . . ." Suddenly Burke stopped in midsentence and looked directly at Willie. "My God! I know what Thelma is talking about now. I have your blood in me!"

"Yes," Thelma said.

Burke shook his head. "I've never heard of such a thing, putting one person's blood in another person. And a colored person's blood!"

"A colored man's blood is red, just like yours," Thelma said.

"Why did you do it?"

"She had to do it, Burke," Catherine said. "You had lost so much blood you would have died if she hadn't."

"But to put one person's blood in another person? I didn't even know such a thing was possible."

"It isn't, always," Thelma explained. "Sometimes it saves the patient, sometimes it kills the patient. This time it saved you."

Burke held up his arm and looked at it. "I'll be damned," he said.

"Your skin's not going to turn black," Thelma said, laughing at him.

"How do you know?" Burke asked. "Has anyone ever put a colored man's blood in a white man before?"

"As a matter of fact, I don't know if that's ever been done or not. Maybe you have a point, Mr. Burke. It could be that you're going to turn black after all."

Burke got a strange look on his face, and he held out his

hands and looked at them for a long moment. Then, suddenly and inexplicably, he began to laugh.

"What is it?" Catherine asked. "What do you find so funny?"

"I was just thinking, it might not be such a bad thing if I did turn black. I could sure fool the Yankees."

Burke laughed again, and this time everyone, including the children, laughed with him.

"Are you hungry?" Catherine asked.

"I'm so hungry I could eat a mule," Burke replied.

"Funny you should say that," Willie said. "I guess you are already starting to turn."

"What do you mean?"

"Didn't you know? Mule is colored folks' favorite food."

"What?" Burke gasped. "No, that's just an expression, I didn't mean . . ." Suddenly he realized that Willie was joking with him, and again they all laughed.

Over the next few days Burke learned the names and a little history of the fugitive family. The father was named Amos, the mother was Sarah. The young boy was Deon, and the girl was Millie. The man who owned them had sold Sarah and Deon, breaking up the family. Amos explained that he couldn't stand the thought of having his family separated, so in the middle of the night, before Sarah and Deon were to be taken, they ran away. A few "depots" later they were here, at their last stop before going into Kansas.

"A man has to do what a man has to do," Burke said, surprising himself by siding with Amos.

A few days later Willie came down the steps quickly. "Bushwhackers!" he hissed. "There's bushwhackers upstairs!"

"Lawd, save us!" Sarah whimpered.

"It's all right," Burke said, quickly holding out his hand to calm them. "I'm sure it's some of my friends, coming for me."

Happy over his impending "rescue," Burke started upstairs to go with them. Then he looked over at the black family with whom he had shared living quarters for the last few weeks. They were gathered together, the mother and daughter shaking, the little boy's eyes wide in fear, the father's face set in an expression of grim determination to fight and, if need be, die for his family.

"Look," Burke said, "you don't have to be afraid. It's me they've come for."

The fugitive family said nothing. Burke hesitated, then sighed. Although he believed that going upstairs to join the bushwhackers offered no danger to the runaways, it was obvious that they didn't share his opinion. And because he knew the volatility of some of his former companions—had indeed been unable to prevent some of their past excesses—he had to admit to himself that there was a chance he might expose his fellow refugees. Nodding, he held out his hand as if to tell them not to worry, then he went back to his cot and waited quietly until the guerrillas were gone.

Sometime later a group of Jayhawkers arrived to see if any passengers needed safe escort into Kansas. This was what Amos and his family had been waiting for, but because their going with the Jayhawkers might expose Burke, Amos told Willie to say that no one was here. Burke could not believe that Amos and his family gave up their own chance for freedom just to protect him. Their sacrifice touched him more deeply than anything ever had before.

A few days after that Willie was able to arrange for transportation for the black family, and Burke sat on his cot in the middle of the night, watching as, by candlelight, Amos and Sarah packed their meager belongings.

First Deon and then Millie came over to the cot to tell him good-bye. After that, Amos and Sarah came over.

"Mister Burke, you 'bout all healed up now," Amos said. "But you needs to be careful an' don' go gettin' yourself shot no more."

"I'm going to try to take your advice, Amos," Burke replied.

"God go with you, Mister Burke," Sarah said. "I hopes you gets away, too."

"Thank you," Burke said. He looked at the family who had become his unlikely friends. "God go with you as well," he said. "And keep you safe."

"Come on," Willie called to them. "The wagon is ready. We need to leave now, in order to be across the border before first light."

Burke walked over to the bottom of the stairs with them,

then watched them climb the steps and hide themselves in the large wagon crates. Then the cellar door was closed, and Burke found himself all alone for the first time since coming to this place.

It was a cold day in early December when Dan knocked on Catherine's door. In Dan's jacket pocket was a set of orders assigning him, once again, to General Grant's staff. But this time he would be serving in the East, where Grant and Sherman had Lee reeling. The war was almost over, and Dan was going to have the honor and privilege of being in on the final curtain.

Catherine opened the door, then smiled. A gust of cold wind blew her hair out of place, and she brushed back a fallen tendril.

"Won't you come in and have some coffee?" she invited him. "It's much too cold to be standing outside like this."

"Thank you," Dan said, scraping his boots on the mat before going inside.

"What brings you out on a cold day like this?" Catherine asked, pouring his coffee. She put it on the kitchen table, indicating that he should take a seat.

"You," Dan said simply.

"Me?" Catherine smiled. "My, you can turn a girl's head with such talk."

"Catherine, I've come to ask you to marry me."

"What?" Catherine asked, looking up in surprise. "You can't be serious."

"Why not? It shouldn't come as that much of a surprise to you. For some time now you've known how I feel about you."

"I know, but there has been the war, and my work, and yours. Things have conspired to keep us apart. I wasn't sure you still felt the same way."

"I told you I was in love with you then," Dan said. "And I am still in love with you. And now, with the war nearly over, I no longer see any obstacle in our way. I want you to marry me, and I want you to come east with me."

Catherine blinked. "Go east with you? When?"

"In two weeks." Dan took out his orders to show her and smiled broadly. "Catherine, General Grant himself has sent for me. I'm to join him for the final battle."

"And you're pleased by that?"

"Yes, why shouldn't I be?"

"For one thing, there is still fighting going on back there. I know you say the war is nearly over, but people are still being killed, and if you go where the fighting is, you could be one of them."

"I am a career officer, Catherine. Being able to be with General Grant at the end is the greatest honor that could come to me. No, the second greatest honor. The first would be for you to tell me that you would be my wife. So, what is your answer?"

"Yes, Catherine, what is your answer?" Burke asked, suddenly appearing in the door that led from the kitchen to the cellar.

"Burke! My God! What are you doing here? I thought you were dead!" Dan gasped.

"I know you would prefer that," Burke said. "It would make things very easy for you, wouldn't it?"

Recovering quickly from his shock, Dan pulled his pistol and pointed it at the gaunt young man standing in the doorway.

"Are you going to shoot me, Dan?"

"I'm sorry about this," Dan said. "But you are now my prisoner!"

"Dan, no! You can't!" Catherine cried. "I have given him sanctuary here!"

"There is no sanctuary for his kind," Dan growled. Waving his gun toward the front of the house, he continued, "Let's go. I'm sure they've got a place for you down at the jail."

Dan waited in the front of the jail until the sheriff returned from the cells at the rear.

"Never thought we'd see this one," the sheriff said as he hung the keys on a hook. He turned toward Dan and rubbed his hands together in glee. "He rode with Quantrill and Anderson, and with Russell Hinds before that. Yes, sir, I'm goin' to take personal pleasure in pullin' the lever to hang this bushwhacking son of a bitch!"

"He's not your prisoner," Dan said. "I've just brought him here for safekeeping."

"The hell he ain't my prisoner. He's a bushwhacker, and

the government has said that Missouri can take control of all bushwhackers.''

"He's not like the other bushwhackers," Dan said. "He's a member of the regular Confederate Army. He was just riding with the bushwhackers.''

The sheriff laughed. "You're funnin' with me, ain't you, Colonel? Puttin' a mule in a horse harness don't make him a horse.'' He pointed toward the cells in back. "He's a bushwhacker, by God, and he's goin' to die like one. Hanging by the neck till he's dead, dead, dead!''

"I know he was once your friend," General Ewing told Dan as he puffed on the cigar he was lighting. "But I don't believe even you are prepared to defend what this man has done.''

"I make no effort to excuse him, General," Dan said. "If he is to hang, so be it. But I think he should be hanged by a military court, not a state court.''

"Look at it this way, Dan. The military has run things in Missouri for almost five years. Isn't it about time we turned things back over to the state?''

"I guess if you put it that way, General, there's not much I can argue about.''

"I tried to get the army to take jurisdiction over him," Dan told Catherine that afternoon. "But the general is adamant about it. He wants the state to hang Burke.''

"To hang Burke, not to try him," Catherine said.

"Well, to try him, of course.''

Catherine nodded. "And then hang him," she said. "Even you said it, Dan. You know it will just be a show trial.''

"And you know that Burke is guilty," Dan replied. "He told you as much in the letters he wrote.''

"It was the war. You and he were great friends before the war. Do you actually think that the Burke you once knew could do all this, unless something changed him . . . something beyond him?''

"A lot of men fought in this war," Dan said. "We didn't all become like Burke.''

"So what are you telling me? That there are degrees of killing? Because if you are, I fail to make the distinction, and I doubt that the families of the boys who lie dead on the battlefield can make the distinction, either.''

"What is it you want from me?"

"You asked me to marry you, and go east with you. All right, I will go. I'll do anything you want. But please, help Burke.''

"Do you love him that much?" Dan asked.

"Please, you must help him.''

"All right," Dan said with a resigned sigh. "I'll do what I can.''

Several hundred people were gathered around the gallows now. There were men in sheepskin coats and long dusters, women with shawls wrapped around them to keep out the cold wind. Even children threaded in and out of the crowd, chasing one another around the square, for despite Catherine's protest, the school board had dismissed school for the hanging. A few enterprising vendors passed through the crowd, selling lemonade, beer, pretzels, popcorn, and sweet rolls. In one corner of the yard a black-frocked preacher stood on an overturned box, taking advantage of the situation to deliver a fiery sermon. The man was of average height and build, with a full head of thick black hair. Standing on the box, he jabbed his finger repeatedly toward the gallows as he harangued the crowd.

"In a few moments a poor lost soul is going to be hurtled to eternity . . . sent to meet his Maker with blood on his hands and sin in his heart.''

He waggled his finger at the crowd. "And hear this now! That sinner is going to be cast into hell because not once, not one time, did he repent of his sins.

"It's too late for him, brothers'n sisters. He is doomed to the fiery furnace of hell! Doomed to writhe in agony forever!''

Some of those who were close enough to hear the preacher shivered involuntarily at his powerful imagery and looked toward the gallows. One or two of them touched their necks fearfully, and a few souls, perhaps weak on willpower, sneaked a drink from the bottle.

"It's too late for him, but it's not too late for you! Repent! Repent now, I say, for the wages of sin is death and eternal damnation.''

The preacher's voice carried well and was certainly heard by the man for whom the sermon was being preached, for once or twice someone in the crowd would see Burke's face at the window of his cell, looking out almost as if disinterested in what was going on. A couple of young boys approached the cell and tried to peer in through the window, but a woman called out to them and they returned to the crowd.

Inside the jail, Dan and Catherine arrived for one final visit. Though the jailer didn't realize it, Dan had managed to get a key to Burke's cell, and while there, he slipped it through the bars to Burke.

"What is this?" Burke asked.

"What does it look like? It's the key to your cell," Dan answered.

Burke looked at the key, then at Dan. He shook his head. "I can't believe you are doing this for me."

"I'm not doing it for you," Dan said. "I'm doing it for the Burke who was once my friend."

Burke nodded. "All right," he said. "I'll accept that."

"Burke, there is one condition to this."

"What's that?"

"When you get out of here, get out of my sight. I never want to see you again."

"Easy enough to do. I'll go to Texas. That's a big state," Burke said. "I think I would like to go back down there."

Dan held up his hand. "Don't tell me where you are going. Not only do I never want to see you again, I don't even want know where you are."

"Sounds fair enough."

"Now, be ready," Dan said as he and Catherine backed away from Burke's cell.

A few moments later Catherine, as if overcome with emotion, began to cry uncontrollably.

"Control yourself, woman," Dan said harshly. "Jailer, have you any water?"

"Yes, sir," the jailer answered. "I'll get some right away."

When the jailer went to the back of the building to respond to the request for water, Dan signaled for Burke to get out of his cell. He watched as Burke unlocked the cell, then slipped through the back door of the jail. Not until then did Dan sound the alarm.

"Jailer! Jailer! Your prisoner is escaping!" Dan shouted.

The jailer rushed to the rifle rack, but the weapons were locked up and the key ring had disappeared . . . having been pushed off into the trash can while the jailer was getting water. Outside the jail, a horse could be heard galloping down the alley.

"Hurry! I can hear him getting away! Never mind the rifle, man, get outside and see which way he is going!" Dan demanded in an authoritative voice.

"Yes, sir!" the jailer replied. Running to the door, the jailer saw the galloping horse, which by now was at the far end of the alley. The jailer ran back inside.

"Did you see him?" Dan asked.

"He went north!"

"Well, don't just stand here, man, go tell the sheriff! Get a posse together! Go after him!"

"Don't you think—" The jailer stopped. He had already made one mistake in front of this high-ranking officer. He didn't want to make another.

"What is it, man, what is it? Speak up!" Dan demanded. He knew that he was making the jailer nervous, and that was by design. The longer he could keep the jailer confused, the better Burke's chances of getting away.

"Maybe I'd better give the alarm."

"I think that's a good idea," Dan said. "There are enough people in town for the hanging, surely we can put together a posse."

"Yes," the jailer said. "A posse." He ran out front then and, standing on the porch, began to shout.

"Jail break! Jail break! The prisoner got away! I need a posse!"

As if a smoking bomb had been dropped in their midst, the crowd around the gallows scattered. Several men ran for their horses, and a moment later a dozen or more were outside the sheriff's office. Dan was mounted as well, and prepared to lead them, when the sheriff arrived.

"I'll lead the posse if you don't mind, Colonel," the sheriff said.

"All right," Dan replied. "I just hope you are better at

leading a posse than you are at keeping a prisoner once you have him.''

"Let's go!" the sheriff yelled, and, whooping and hollering, two dozen men rode north out of town. When they reached the outskirts of town, however, the only rider they saw was a lone black man. It was Willie Crawford who had galloped down the alley, leading the posse astray.

Willie threw up his hands when the posse reached him. "Lawd, what fo' you chasin' me?" he asked in his thickest dialect, rolling his eyes in exaggerated fear. "This heah colored man ain't done nothin' to get the law down on me!"

As the frustrated posse returned empty-handed to the sheriff's office, a wagon rolled slowly through the streets of town, pulled by a team of mules. Sitting stoically on the driver's seat of the wagon was Thelma Crawford. The wagon was piled high with old clothes, and a sign on the side of the wagon read "Clothes donated for the relief of the needy.''

Lying quietly underneath a pile of clothes, Burke Phillips peered cautiously out at the street, silently bidding Independence, Missouri, good-bye for one last time. It was a final bit of irony, he thought, that he was being helped to escape via the same Underground Railroad that had once been the target of his pro-slavery activities.

"All right," Catherine said to Dan after all the excitement was over.

"All right what?"

"I am ready now. I told you I would marry you."

Dan shook his head. "No," he said. "This isn't how I wanted it. I mean, if you really love Burke, I don't want you to marry me as a reward for saving his life."

"Dan, I don't love Burke," Catherine said. "I don't want to see him hang, but I don't love him, and I never have." Then, unexpectedly, she put her arms around his neck and smiled up at him. "*You* are the one I love, Daniel Morris. You are the only one I have ever loved."

They kissed.

Epilogue

From *Harper's Weekly;* June 10, 1865:

PRESIDENT JOHNSON'S AMNESTY PROCLAMATION

On the 29th of May President Johnson issued a proclamation granting amnesty to all persons who have directly or indirectly taken part in the rebellion, with the restoration of all rights of property excecpt as to slaves, and except in cases where legal proceedings have been instituted for the confiscation of property, on condition of their taking an oath to defend the Constitution of the United States and the Union of the States, and to obey all laws and proclamations which have been made during the rebellion with reference to the emancipation of slaves. There are excluded from pardon, except on special application to the President, the following classes of persons: Those who have, in order to aid the rebellion, left judicial positions or seats in Congress, or who have resigned commissions in the army or navy, or absented themselves from the country; thsoe who were educated at West Point or in the United States Naval Academy; those who have engaged in any way in torturing our prisoners; those who have engaged in the destruction of our commerce, or who have made raids from Canada into the United States, all persons in military, naval, or civil confinement as prisoners of war; all persons who have voluntarily participated in the rebellion, and the estimated value of whose taxable property is over twenty thousand dollars; all who have taken and

violated the previous amnesty oath; and all officers
of the Confederate service above the rank of colonel
in the army or lieutenant in the navy.

The Grand Review at Washington

In the Spring of 1861 there was raised a cry of
alarm: ''The Capital is in danger!'' and thousands of
young men from the store, from the work-shop, and
from the farm rushed with muskets in their hands to
the rescue. We remember the sense of security which
was felt when it was known that the gallant Seventh
had bivouacked in the streets of Washington. Others
came, a long train of armed men from every hamlet
in the loyal States, and from the streets of that capital
these men, and others who have joined their ranks,
have for years been marching and fighting until they
have reached the victorious end . . . until they have
swept from the field all those who once menaced the
safety of the Government, conquering most of them
in battle, and dismissing the rest to their homes as
paroled prisoners. What a record of heroism is
compressed within the limits of those years! Too
toilsome has the strife been and far too severe for
grand military displays during the war. Little
attention could be given to dramatic proprieties on
the march, or on the battlefield . . . the only idea of
the march was to find the enemy; the only idea of
the battle to get the advantage of him, and capture or
drive him from the field.

It was fitting therefore that when the work had all
been done, our soldiers who have borne the burden,
should, as they returned bringing Peace back with
them as a gift to the people, receive in turn some
token of the popular appreciation of their services.

It was no ordinary pageant that turned all the
people's eyes and so many of their steps toward
Washington on the 23rd and 24th of May. It would
never recur of seeing two hundred thousand soldiers
passing in review. It was no mere idle curiosity, but
a deep, glorious, solemn sentiment. This sentiment

was one of pride mingled with infinite pathos ... pride in the youthful strength of a republic tried and found steadfast ... pathos from the remembrance of countless heroes who have received their crowns, not from mortal hands, nor upon mortal brows, who died many of them while the strife seemed yet uncertain.

Only the soldier can appreciate the full meaning of this grand march through Washington. He has been the actor all along while we have been but spectators, even as here. Some of these soldiers have marched from Washington, and have returned by a circuitous route through the bloody campaigns of Chattanooga, Atlanta, and the wearisome marches through Georgia and North Carolina.

For two days the glorious parade continued, starting each day at 9 o'clock A.M., passing around the Capitol to Pennsylvania Avenue, and up the avenue to the Aqueduct Bridge, and thence back to camp.

On the north end of the Capitol the scholars of the intermediate and grammar schools took their places, the boys on the hill and the girls on the Capitol steps. The girls were dressed in white; the boys wore white pants and blue jackets. As the veterans passed by, these children greeted the column with songs, and, as they were a numerous choir, the effect was very beautiful. The children also displayed a large number of banners. On the northwest corner of the Capitol was the following very appropriate motto: "The only national debt we can never pay is the debt we owe to the victorious Union soldiers."

**They were soldiers young and brave in a war
that would change America forever.**

Some came from the gray cliffs of West Point. Some came
from the bloody caldron of the Civil War. By train and
steamship they traveled West to fight against an enemy
battling for a way of life. They were the men of the U.S.
Seventh Cavalry, whose name would echo in history.

Joe Murchison was a young officer who learned that no
amount of training could prepare him for life and death on
the frontier. Rising through the ranks, he fought toe-to-toe
with an enemy who sometimes was not what he seemed.
And above him loomed the dashing figure of George
Custer, the man who would lead Joe and the Seventh
Cavalry to glory and tragedy.

YESTERDAY'S REVEILLE

Robert Vaughan

**"[Vaughan] brings to life the personal side of
the story."**

—*Publishers Weekly*